Book 1:
Call of the Danna

THE KINGBLADE CHRONICLES

Saga 1:
Tarnadins of the Elder Forest

Book 1:
Call of the Danna

by Jarrett Skaddisson

Printed in the United States of America
First Printing, 2015
ISBN 978-0-9963792-0-5
Published by Siloa Press
Printed by IngramSpark
Ingram Content Group, Inc.
1 Ingram Blvd.
La Vergne, TN 37086
www.IngramSpark.com

This Work Is Dedicated
to the
True Tarnadin

ACKNOWLEDGEMENTS

Here I wish to heartily thank those who have helped bring this book
from my head to your hands with their various skills and talents: Max
Garrison for editing and consulting, Ferdinand D. Ladera for cover art,
Blaine Morehead for font and cover design, Cornelia Yoder for maps,
Dawn Allman for text layout and design, Shang Tea for countless cups
of refreshing and inspirational tea, my wife and all my family
and friends for inspiration and encouragement.

Table of Contents

Appendices

Maps

Preface

all of the Danna is the story of an adventure, an adventure which has had a considerable impact on the one who was obliged to write it down. Such is the case with all decent adventures: namely, that they do not leave one unchanged. And, in this case, I have most certainly been changed for the better, having seen our own world more clearly by looking closely at the world of Orona. By probing the Deep Lore of Orona, I have, I think, gained a better understanding of the Deep Lore of our own world. And this, I believe, is the great beauty of fantasy. Fantasy is a mirror, and the more accurately it reflects the truly fantastic nature of our world, the better a mirror it is. And, as everyone knows, one of the best ways to see oneself is to look in a mirror.

Now, it is one thing to sit around and talk about adventuring, as folk do on occasion at the Ploughman's Shanty in the village of Siloa, where this story begins. It is quite another thing to set out upon an adventure and to see and do things which one has never seen or done before. But we needn't travel to the other side of the world, nor even to the next town, to have such experiences. We need only awaken each day, as I have tried to do, seeking to live as if life really means something in the end, not simply because it will make us feel better if that is the case but because it is actually true. Life *does* matter, and life most certainly *is* an adventure, whether we wish it to be or not. Yet, in the end, it falls to us to decide what sort of adventure it will be. We cannot, of course, choose what lot or time we are given, but we can choose how we will wield them—for good or for ill. And that choice will make all the difference.

With this volume, the tales of the Kingblade Chronicles begin, and I anticipate there will be many more to come. At the very least, I would hope that Aradis and Girion will be able to finish their business in the Elder Forest, although quite a few adventures beyond that have already presented themselves to me, and I would be sorry indeed to see them untold.

I must say with complete candor that I have immensely enjoyed writing this story. Now it is my sincere hope that readers will find as much pleasure in the reading of the tale as I have found in the telling of it.

Sincerely Yours,
Jarrett J. Skaddisson

The Way of the Tarnadin is a road of woes,
A path that is harrowed by grievous foes;
E'er it is troubled by darkest night,
Yet he who would tread it must put fear to flight.

For the Tarnadin's task is clear and plain:
He must battle darkness for others' gain.
Indeed, for himself he must have no regard,
But passing through fire, he will emerge uncharred.
He takes up the cause of those who are weak,
Though he himself be the meekest of the meek.

When the powers of shadow upon flesh bear down,
And the cries of all mortals in anguish are drowned,
The Tarnadin stands in their stead to fight
As a bearer of hope, a bearer of light.

When the strength of the strong has at last come to naught,
It is clear that a Tarnadin must then be sought.
Indeed, all are in need of the Tarnadin.

The Way of the Tarnadin from mercy proceeds,
Then on through shadow and flame it leads,
Yet Death's Blade will be shattered and night be no more;
And the Tarnadin will stand in glory e'ermore.

Orona

Murnia
Tassaru
Estereth
Jassuna
The Bushbelt
The Eldritch Isles
Byram
Quarana
Fenrost
75°N
60°N
45°N
30°N
15°N
0°
15°S
30°S
45°S
60°S
75°S
180°W
150°W
120°W
90°W
60°W
30°W
0°
30°E
60°E
90°E
120°E
150°E
180°E

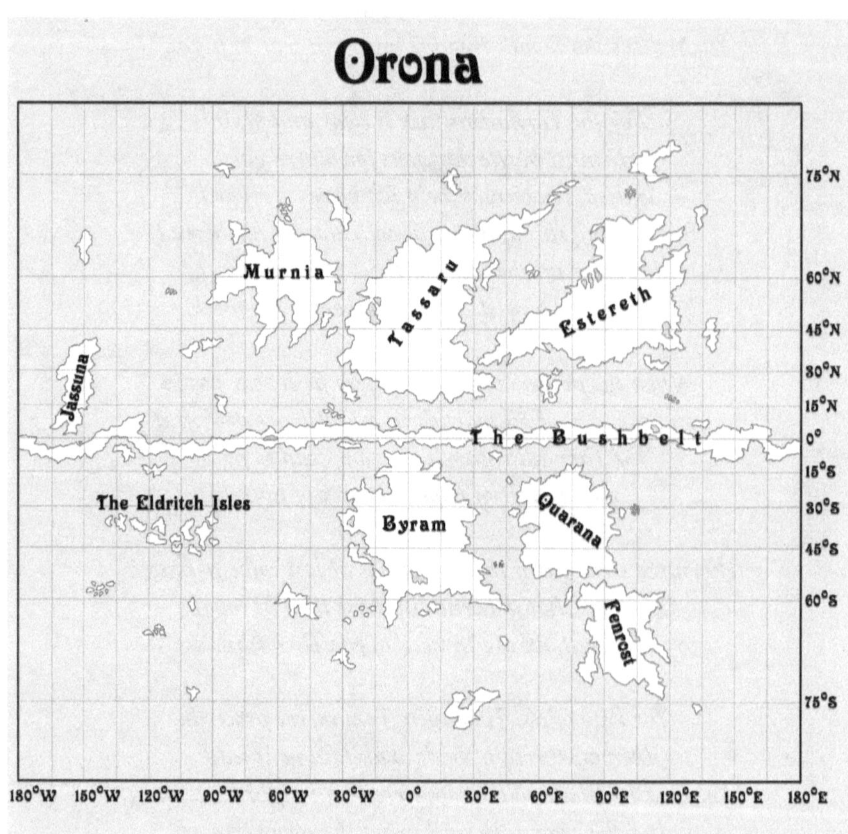

CHAPTER ONE

The Coming of the Khasidim

It was just as a late afternoon in the bright month of Elaya ought to be in the village of Siloa: clear, gentle and full of the promise of summer close at hand. A soft breeze blew across the Plains of Agleri, which lay east of the hamlet, and the melodious chatter of an assortment of woodland birds could be heard in the trees of Rimwold Forest to the west. Out on the plains, the farmers were nearing the end of their labor for the day and were preparing to make their way to the Ploughman's Shanty, the local tavern, for many a hearty mug of ale, some warm food by the hearth, and, undoubtedly, several hours of light-hearted conversation. In the forest, the woodsmen would also soon finish their work and join them in town. Indeed, all the hardy folk of Siloa and their families would shortly share food and fellowship, rejoicing in the triumph of spring over another harsh winter and delighting in the work of their hands and the simple life which they led. There was certainly a marvelous tranquility to be found in Siloa; a hard life it was, to be sure, but there was little in the wide world of Orona that could rival the satisfaction of such an unpretentious people on such a fine spring evening as this. A remarkable peace and contentment rested upon that little village, but none of that precious peace or contentment found its way into the heart or mind of Aradis Kingblade that day.

"Aradis!" Girion called out from a ways across the field in which Aradis was drearily heaving a scythe through the standing grain. "If you keep working that hard, dear friend, I'll be surprised if you have any strength left to make it back into Siloa! You've hardly stopped swinging that scythe since sunrise."

Aradis, tall and fair in complexion, somewhat slender, with insistent green eyes, a handsome countenance and a short beard and mustache, had indeed been at his work since the stroke of dawn. Now his rough farmer's garments, consisting of a coarse white shirt, russet breeches and tall brown leather boots, were soaked in sweat, and his shoulder-length blond hair lay wet across his neck.

Girion, similarly attired, brown-eyed, well-built and also rather tall, with dark, thick, curly hair on his head and stubble on his chin and cheeks, ran toward him, as Aradis replied, "Well, there's good winter wheat to be harvested, isn't there, Girion? And I am getting paid to work, am I not?"

"Indeed you are," Girion laughed, as he came up beside him. "And you've undoubtedly been working harder than anyone else in all Siloa today or in this whole blessed land of Velaris, for that matter, and I simply think it's time you be done with it for the day. Let's go down to the Ploughman's Shanty and have a nice talk with the other lads, and you can take your mind off of everything. I know you, Aradis. All day you've been out here in the golden grain, just you and your thoughts. And you've only become more miserable as the day's gone on. Do I speak true?"

Aradis sighed and leaned wearily on the scythe he had been wielding. "Naturally I've just been thinking about everything. And, of course, it doesn't help to dwell on it all day; I know that full well. Yet my labor gives me some consolation, for as it is said: a tired body softens a troubled mind."

"So it does," Girion agreed. "Now weren't you about to put that in the barn?" he asked, nodding toward the scythe Aradis was using to prop himself up.

Aradis looked at his friend with affectionate exasperation. "I suppose if I don't go stow this scythe and follow you down to the Shanty, you won't leave off until I do, eh?"

"Quite correct," Girion said, smiling.

"Very well," Aradis laughed quietly. "I will not trouble you to trouble me," he said, also smiling a little, and trudged off to the barn to put the scythe away, knowing it would be less than a dozen hours before he would be back to pick it up again.

When he emerged, Girion was waiting for him, and the two of them turned and headed west for the two-mile walk into town through the sprawling farmland.

For some time they merely walked side by side along the worn dirt path that ran through the grainfields, neither of them speaking. But, at length, Aradis said quietly, "Girion, I can't thank you enough for what you're doing for my family."

Girion responded, "There is really no need to thank me, Aradis. My mother and father are only too glad to pay you for the outstanding labor you've provided us this spring harvest. And you know it will ultimately serve your family better, if you allow your brother to mind the forge while you work out in the fields, so that he also can learn smith's work."

Then, glancing at Aradis' rather pensive expression, he exhorted, "Now listen to me, my friend. You've really got to quit being so glum all the time. You cannot continue to imagine that things will only get worse; you're already down enough as it is. Take heart! Hard times are the lot of most men; few are they who never have periods of want and trouble, but know too that these times of dearth and scarcity will come to an end."

"In any case, we can hope that will be so," Aradis sighed, looking back over his shoulder at the golden plains to the east.

Girion continued, "You remember, I am quite certain, that my family also came upon hard times when my father could no longer fare profitably as a cooper in Aragest, and so we came to Siloa, thinking to make a better lot for ourselves in a farm village of Velaris than in that den of unrest from whence we had come. In truth, my whole family was in a bad way at that time in every regard. Yet, when we arrived, you were a friend to me from the first, and I have not forgotten it, even though six years ago that was. Indeed, we were still quite young then; I was but fourteen and you thirteen. Yes, my father, my mother, and I had truly left everything we knew, all that anchored us, but when we found ourselves here in far-flung Siloa, you and your family showed us great kindness and honor. Now it is only right that the kin of Girion Ringmark should give aid to the kin of Aradis Kingblade."

"I suppose it is even as you say, Girion," Aradis conceded. "Things will get better. My father will recover. He must! And I will get enough together to be able to support a wife and start a family. Someday anyway. The Danna is good to us after all. He knows our troubles, and he will see to it that we are taken care of." Then he added, "At least, so you tell me, and so my father tells me."

"Yes," Girion replied, "The Danna sees the troubles of all the Barada, the mortal kin of this world, and he cares for them. And he will take care of you and your family."

"Well, even if he doesn't," Aradis returned, "I will. Mark that. As long as my father remains ailing day and night, confined mostly to bed, I must see to it that my family is fed. And I will do whatever it takes to make that happen," he finished confidently.

"I know you will," Girion affirmed.

Just then the lads climbed over a little hillock. The sun had begun to set, and the spring sky was now ablaze with warm streaks of glorious orange and red. Down below them, at the base of a very gentle hill, lay the village of Siloa, a collection of around seventy thatched, single-story, timber-frame buildings, a mixture of houses, sheds and tradesmen's shops, most of which doubled as dwellings. Smoke poured out of the stone chimneys and drifted lazily over the little settlement before dissipating above the dark pines of Rimwold Forest. Three wide streets ran north and south between the rows of buildings. At the middle street's north end, on its west side, was the Ploughman's Shanty, and already various folk could be seen meandering in that general direction. This was quite customary in Siloa on any day of the week as evening approached.

Girion clapped Aradis on the back and said, "I'm going to head on down to the Ploughman's Shanty and chat with the fellows there a while. I suppose I'll see you in half an hour or so?"

"Aye," Aradis replied. "First I've got to go by the forge and see how Teric is doing." He looked down at the village, and a moment later he mumbled, "At least it looks like he hasn't burned the place down."

"Don't be silly. Teric knows what he's doing for the most part. But, of course, he isn't a master blacksmith if that's what you're expecting of him."

"No, he certainly isn't. And I only expect that he do his part. But Teric is lazy."

"Compared to you, Aradis, anyone is lazy!" Girion remarked, setting off down the hill. "See you at the Shanty!" he called, as he waved.

Aradis lingered there for a while watching Girion go on down the hill. It was somewhat restorative for him to stand in that spot and look out over the forest and the town, to look up at the magnificent sunset and remember the days when life was simpler for him and his family, for there had been many joyous memories in lovely Siloa in times past, times not that long ago. And so, for perhaps ten minutes, he stood there immersing himself in a past that had slipped away. But then his mind churned like a dark sea and the present came back to the surface like a terrible monster. Then, deep in his gut he felt a dreadful anxiety, an almost tangible disquiet surging up, and there was naught he could do to quell it. For he knew he must go home and face the reality of his broken situation, that of a lot he utterly despised: one of impoverishment, frustration and a very real possibility of the death of his father. And so, heavy of heart, he marched off down the hill toward town and his father's forge.

Aradis really did not want to go by the forge, but knew he must. For it was, in his estimation, an absolute certainty that Teric had done something amiss, either from negligence or ignorance, and Aradis would probably have to rectify whatever errors his feckless brother had made. Yet the last thing he wanted was to get into another dispute with him. They had quarreled frequently of late, primarily because Aradis wanted desperately for Teric to be more responsible and hardworking than he was. "He is seventeen, after all, and needs to take life more seriously," Aradis thought to himself, "especially in this time of need when money is not to be had."

Indeed, the Kingblade family had to beg food off of neighbors more often than not, which flew directly in the face of everything Aradis believed about self-sufficiency. And so he had taken it upon himself to reform Teric on a daily basis, with the ultimate aim of making things easier for his father. But both of the lads were rather hot-tempered, though Aradis had the greater heat, and so their quarrels could be quite grievous. And this, rather than helping matters, only upset his father all the more. Aradis could not bear to see his father be so dismayed again in his condition, so he resolved to do his best to rein in his ire if it began to show itself toward his brother.

The central street that ran through Siloa was filled with its denizens, who were driving wagons to their sheds, pulling carts into alleyways or stopping by shops of the tradesmen before they ambled down to the tavern or retired to spend the evening with their families. Aradis entered this main street, known as Lampler's Lane, through an alleyway between the houses of Faenard the tailor and Faenard's cousin, Gandrian the tanner, and then turned south toward the forge, which lay on the west side of the street on the southern edge of Siloa, fourth from the end. The Kingblade home was right next to it, just to the south.

Without knocking, Aradis simply flung open the door and walked inside the dimly lit forge. The window on the back was left open just a little to let in some light, and various tools and implements were strewn about on the earthen floor. The fire was still blazing, and Teric was busy shaping a piece of glowing metal on the anvil.

"Hullo, Aradis," Teric grunted, as he swung the hammer. Teric was of similar build to Aradis, but with shorter, darker hair and keen green eyes.

"How goes it, Teric?" Aradis inquired, with as much jollity as he could muster (which was not a great deal). "How many of Harwin's tools did you get repaired today?"

Teric knew what was coming, so he swung the hammer a few more times before replying. "Some," he finally answered. "And I know I should have finished all of them . . ."

Aradis cut him off, snapping, "Of course you should have and then some! What have you been doing all day? Gone off to meet up with your dear Rayela in the forest while I've been out breaking my back on the Ringmark farm?" He firmly regretted saying this even as the words left his mouth, for he could already sense his temper welling up, yet he felt helpless to do anything about it.

Teric thrust the molten metal he had been working on into a nearby wooden tub filled with water, and steam hissed up to the timbered ceiling of the forge. In great indignation, Teric flung the hammer to the floor and retorted, "I suppose if I had myself put together as well as you do, Aradis, I would have gotten all the work at the forge done and still had a full day to go out and work on the wheat harvest! And then I would have—"

Aradis interjected angrily, "I've never claimed to be perfect, but money is scarce for us, and we need to get as much of it as we can as fast as we can! No money means no food, Teric! You know full well we lost nearly everything we had to those swine from the Sardolia last autumn, out collecting taxes for the Ruphani, our so dearly beloved ruler." This description of Velaris' potentate could hardly have been infused with greater sarcasm. Aradis continued his tirade, "And it just won't work for you to continue disregarding life and labor, as if the heavens would dump gerrin after gerrin into our laps free of charge. Money must be worked for, you lousy laggard! Everyone in our family seems to understand that but you! And what makes it even worse is that you know how hard Father worked to gain back what we lost just to make it through the winter, and that's no doubt why he's in such a terrible state as he is now!"

"Must you constantly pretend as if I don't know what's going on with my own family?" Teric lashed back.

"Why should I not?" Aradis raged. "Where were you this winter when Father became sick? Did you come out with me to chop wood in that terrible blizzard or go hunting about in the forest when our food ran out? No! As I recall, you stayed at the house with our mother and Mellora and feigned illness to get out of having to raise a finger and help for a change."

"But I really was sick!" Teric protested fiercely.

"Certainly you were! Sick in the head. Our father needs us, Teric, and if I had my way you'd be out working in the fields, and I would be manning the forge. But I'm doing this for *him* because *he* thought you needed to learn the trade. By the time I was your age, I could have run my own forge, but you—you were never around when Father tried to show you how to wield the hammer and tongs. You were always off in the forest and out in the fields and doing whatever you jolly well pleased. If I behaved like that, I'd hate to think what would happen to this family. I don't know if Mother and Mellora could make it alone, but both of them are doing more than you've ever done, what with Mellora working as a milkmaid five miles down the road and Mother selling whatever articles of wool she can make a byrna or three grandigs on. At the very least, just help us out until Father recovers or we get enough money to be stable again. Then you can go back to your old ways. Maybe you can just wander off in the forest with those half-wit friends of yours, and then none of you will ever have to work again, and none of us will ever have to see your miserable, lazy self again."

Teric was nearly boiling over, and he shouted back, "Maybe I just want to enjoy life while it lasts before we die like everybody else in this horrible little village, hated by all the other Barada, drained to the last tarion, scrounging just to stay alive! Maybe I don't want to spend all my days working myself into the ground and doing what I'm supposed to do for nothing in return!"

"Nothing in return?" Aradis spat. "The love of your own family and the preservation of your own honor isn't enough for you? What ambition could you possibly have? Are you going to set out on some grand adventure and through the gifts of conquest and fortune become Teric the Magnificent, renowned throughout Orona?"

"Who knows what I might be if I were rid of you and your nagging arrogance! You always have thought too small, Aradis. You studied to become a skilled blacksmith—for what? To take care of your wife and children that you don't have? You haven't even caught the eye of a girl in Siloa because you're shoved so deep in your work and your responsibility and your blasted honor to notice anyone but yourself! Even if you had enough money to get married and support a family, you'd spend so much time working that you'd forget that you were married and that your wife had borne you children. Personally, though, if I were a marriageable young lady, I wouldn't give you the time of day. You're too much of a cocky jackass," Teric finished scathingly.

Aradis could bear his wrath no longer, and he swung his fist at Teric, his heart pounding. Dodging the blow, Teric leapt aside and shoved Aradis into the wall. Metal tools from a nearby high shelf clanged to the floor, and Aradis bore full upon his younger brother. Just then, as they grappled furiously, hissing and spitting, the door to the forge swung open and in stepped Darion Kingblade, their father.

"Stop this madness immediately! Let him go, Aradis! Enough of this, Teric!" he ordered his sons, and then began coughing, struggling to breathe.

Aradis thrust Teric from him and then turned to his father, panting like an enraged animal. "Only for your sake will I let this scoundrel leave this forge without further injury," he said darkly. "If you had heard some of the things he said, you would not have ordered me to let him go."

"Do you really think it does any good for you two to quarrel as you do?" Darion asked, catching his breath and looking back and forth between his sons. "If we're going to get through all this, we're not going to do it by shoving each other around the forge like drunken barbarians. Now surely there cannot be such malice between you two that you cannot look upon each other and forgive whatever spiteful things may have been said in moments of heat."

Teric glared at his brother, his eyes still burning with anger. Aradis stared back, equally livid, and then turned to his father. "Let me put it this way, Father. I count that accursed captain of the Sardolia, who scorned our very lives, dearer than your son Teric."

"That's another thing," Teric growled. "Where do you come off acting like you're such a hero for trying to fix a mess *you're* responsible for? If you hadn't shouted rude insults like a regular ruffian and thrown that bag of money right in Fragezi's face, it's almost certain he wouldn't have set our family's taxes so high. I'm surprised he didn't kill you right on the spot for something like that, as high up as he is in the government. It should send a pretty clear signal that serious lines have been crossed if the highest military official in this entire barolla—the whole district of Feldryn, for crying out loud—has to make a personal visit to Siloa just to collect some taxes! Did it ever occur to you that things might just have been all right if *certain* people were able to keep themselves under control in the presence of—"

Aradis took a step toward Teric and angrily interrupted, "Well, I wasn't about to stand there like the rest of the cowards in this town and just let that scurrilous knave have his say and mock us Menfolk so openly! I noticed you didn't say a single thing that day, O bold and noble Teric!"

"Of course not! I'm not an idiot like you, Aradis!" Teric flashed, as he got right in his brother's face.

"You're just as much of a coward as that vermin Fragezi!" Aradis seethed.

"Stop it now!" Darion shouted, and the lads, breathing heavily and narrowly having avoided yet another fierce tussle, slowly turned to face him.

Darion tried to speak, but then coughed and wheezed some more. Aradis and Teric stood there respectfully, waiting for what he had to say. Finally, when Darion could manage it, he said calmly, "You cannot mean that, Aradis, and you must never say such things. Whatever else he may be, Teric is your brother, and I will not have you speak of him in that manner."

"Then tell him to no longer act and speak as a fool and a traitor to everything we hold dear," Aradis countered.

"Aradis, you must not—" Darion began, but then started coughing uncontrollably again.

Aradis knew that if he did not depart in haste, he would end up attacking Teric again, so he shoved past his father and out the forge door, calling to him as he left, "You can listen to Teric's false account of the quarrel now, and I will give you the true one later. I'm going down to the Ploughman's Shanty to see Girion."

He heard Teric shouting through the walls, "Now who's going off to gallivant about with his friends and leave his sick father alone for the night?"

It took every last bit of Aradis' strength to not turn around, charge back into the forge, and give Teric the beating of his life. But he steeled his resolve and marched on north up the street.

When he had gone about halfway through town, he saw his sister, Mellora, walking southward toward him, just now returning from the dairy farm up to the north where she worked as a milkmaid. She was a beautiful girl, fourteen years in age, with long, wavy blonde hair and eyes of a winsome blue. She was walking along barefoot, clad in a simple brown skirt and a white tunic, looking as merry as she could be. Of their family, Mellora was always the happiest, and even during the past winter when things had been especially hard, she would speak often of hope and of things getting better by and by. This had been of great comfort to Aradis during that time.

As Mellora approached, she remarked, "You look as if your day has not gone well at all, Aradis."

"Ha!" he laughed in reply. "It's showing then, is it, Mellora? Well, my day was actually going quite nicely until I got back to the forge and found that Teric had gotten hardly a thing done since daybreak."

"You didn't fight with him again, did you?" she asked concernedly, as she came up to him.

Aradis looked down at her, ashamed. He put his hand on her shoulder and said, "I didn't say anything that didn't absolutely need to be said."

"How is Father?" she anxiously inquired.

Now Aradis was even more ashamed. "He came into the forge while we were fighting and I—well, I thought it would be better to leave before I did something I really regretted."

"What did you say to Teric?" Mellora pressed, looking into Aradis' shifting eyes.

He hesitated, then replied, "Teric said some horrible things about our family and said he felt like everything he did for our sake amounted to nothing."

"Surely not!" Mellora exclaimed. "That might have been only how you took what he said, not how he meant it."

"Whatever the case," Aradis returned, "I could not listen to that rubbish and keep my head, so we fought again."

"Well, let us thank the Danna that our father showed up," Mellora sighed.

"I suppose," Aradis said, then patted his sister on the back and started walking on down the street, calling out over his shoulder, "I'm going down to the Shanty to see Girion for a bit. Say hello to Mother for me, and I'll see you at home."

"Aradis!" Mellora called after him. Aradis stopped and turned to look at her. "You really must stop fighting with Teric, if only for Father's sake. It's only tearing the family apart."

"There'll be no more fighting, Mellora. I promise," Aradis assured her, as he continued on down the street.

As Aradis kept walking toward the Ploughman's Shanty, he looked up at the sky and noticed that the dimness of twilight had fallen. The sky was calm, inexpressibly calm, over the plains, and to the west, only a faint glimmer of sunlight remained beyond the hills of Rimwold Forest. For a moment, Aradis thought he saw a streak of bluish white light pass quickly over the forest to the west, perhaps a shooting star or something like that.

On the western horizon, the silver sliver of the waxing crescent moon, Eoreth, had now taken the place of golden Marda, the sun.

As Aradis came up to the heavy wooden door of the Ploughman's Shanty, he thought of how grateful he was for having run into Mellora, for already his anger was somewhat assuaged, and perhaps after an hour or so of some genuinely jovial conversation with his friends, he would be able to go back home and make things up with Teric. And so, thus heartened, he pulled open the oaken door and entered the bustling tavern.

The Ploughman's Shanty was a humble, but inviting, alehouse that contained three and a dozen large oak tables, a clean floor of wooden planks and a great stone hearth with a roaring fire on the south wall. There were a few windows on every wall except the west wall where the counter was, for behind the counter were a few storage rooms and behind them a hallway connecting a half dozen rooms that were available for travelers to spend the night. The hallway was accessed by a creaky old door at the southern end of the west wall in the corner of the tavern proper. Orinn Berthaway, the proprietor of the place, a sturdy man with a thick brown beard and a perennially amused expression, stood leaning against the counter, talking to one of the farmers who came in daily for a drink and a chat. Blazing lanterns sat on all of the tables, but even so, the tavern was fairly dark, though still welcoming. About forty people, both Manfellows and Maenas (that is, male and female Menfolk) were seated in various places around the room chatting away or roaming from table to table, catching snatches of all the latest gossip. Villagers would be trickling steadily in and out of the place for another hour or so.

Aradis looked over to the right and saw that Girion was seated with three of their friends at their customary table against the north wall. Girion looked up from his conversation and nodded at Aradis, who then came over and sat on the bench beside him with his back to the wall.

"That's exactly what I heard too," their friend Corim Timberfall was saying. Corim was about Teric's age, had a full head of unkempt blond hair and was thoroughly enamored with the sound of his own voice. "There was more trouble than they could handle up in Aragest. Well, you would know that better than anyone, Girion. Your family had to leave because of it."

"Yes, people already didn't think much of Menfolk in the capital when I was there," Girion agreed, "and that was more than half a decade ago."

"Well, it's much worse elsewhere," Corim continued. "Neldon Broadbuckle told me that up in north Velaris, in Falzari or some such barolla up on Cape Loresso—or was it Passera—well anyway, the authorities arrested some Menfolk on false charges and had them executed the same day without a trial."

"If I were you, I wouldn't believe everything you hear from Neldon Broadbuckle," their less loquacious friend Tallis Pestleman piped in. "Or anything, for that matter. Unless it's about food or sleep, things which dear Neldon knows quite intimately. I'm actually surprised you need to be reminded of how unreliable Neldon is, Corim, since you've known him for years. But still, I've heard too much about other Narthanna, other Kindreds, treating Menfolk poorly to not believe there's some genuine hatred out there for our kind. For example, just take that run of uppity Elven tax collectors who came by here last fall and milked the whole village for every tarion they could get."

"Until the Siloa cow ran dry," their witty companion Darmon Barnwain chimed in. "It's not so enjoyable to go around guzzling up Menfolk monies when you know you're going to get an earful from the likes of Aradis Kingblade."

"Let's not bring that up right now, Darmon," Aradis moaned, as he exasperatedly rubbed his eyes.

"Why not?" Corim exclaimed. "That's something you ought to be proud of, Aradis, telling those Elven louts off when no one else would. Though of course, it didn't turn out so well after you'd mouthed off to three separate tax collectors, and Captain Fragezi of the Sardolia was sent to personally take care of the so-called insurrection in Siloa."

"Exactly," mumbled Aradis.

"But that was really something, you know," Tallis remarked, "chucking your family's taxes right at his noggin. That took a lot of courage."

"Or stupidity," Aradis muttered, wishing now that he had just gone for a quiet walk instead of coming down to the Shanty. That was just like his friends, talking about things they knew annoyed him.

"Lucky for you, Fragezi's son Carello calmed him down, or you'd probably be dead, eh?" Darmon laughed.

"Can we just talk about something else?" Aradis asked, highly aggravated now.

"Like what we're all going to do to Fragezi when he returns this spring?" Darmon offered.

"Oh, I do hope he comes back soon," Corim started up again. "I'll tax his ugly face till he's sorrier than a Yeti in the heat of the Bushbelt."

"How are you going to manage that, Corim?" the ever jocular Darmon teased. "You couldn't win a fight with a bunny rabbit. Besides, you don't really think trouncing one of this entire barolla's most highly regarded military officials would go unnoticed, do you? The whole thing is already bad enough as it is."

"Would you like to see me beat a bunny rabbit?" Corim queried, annoyed. "Go out and catch one, Darmon, and I'll show you a thing or two."

"Catch your own rabbit!" Darmon pertly retorted. "I've got better things to do."

"Of course you do," Corim said, rolling his eyes. "But as I was saying a minute ago, things are getting bad for us Menfolk. And our friends are few and far between among the other Kindreds. Think about it—when's the last time you heard about a Dwarf, a Gnome, an Elf, or what have you, standing up for the Menfolk? Hasn't happened in our lifetime. And the Druids are the worst of the lot. They'd like to see us all dead, I'm sure— every last one of us."

"The Druids were by far the worst in Aragest," Girion noted. "Downright nasty to us and all the other Menfolk in our quarter of the city."

"Well, let's all be grateful to the Danna that few of the other Narthanna ever come through Siloa," Corim exulted, raising his mug of ale. "Keeps us out of trouble, it does."

"I'll drink to that," Tallis said, gulping down a large swig of his own ale.

"You'll drink to anything, Tallis," Darmon chuckled.

The friends continued chattering away while Aradis sat in silence, still plagued by his own mournful thoughts, absentmindedly itching his beard, as he often did when greatly troubled by something. This had not gone unnoticed by Girion, who leaned over to Aradis and asked quietly, "How's your father?"

Aradis said nothing for a moment, and then whispered back, "Not well, as usual. I went back by the forge to check on things and I—well, I'll tell you about it later. I'm going to go up and get myself some ale."

Girion clapped Aradis on the back as the latter got up and then engaged again in the others' banter. Meanwhile, Aradis walked up to the north side of the counter, the short side, and motioned to the bartender, Orinn, who was pouring out drinks for others a ways down. Just then, Aradis noted a stranger in a dark brown traveler's cloak. His hood was pulled over his head in such a manner that his face could not be seen, and he was leaning against the counter not many feet down from Aradis, facing the west wall.

Wayfarers were not terribly uncommon at the Ploughman's Shanty, for often people traveling north or south in this part of Velaris would take the byway that skirted along the edge of Rimwold Forest and thus would pass through Siloa. Aradis surmised that this stranger was most likely a Manfellow (as hardly any other sort of Barada would routinely be found in a wholly Mannish tavern). Under normal circumstances, he would have at least greeted the fellow, but in such a depressed condition as he now found himself, he could not even muster the cordiality to offer a polite "Hullo."

As Aradis stood there, he thought again of how miserably he had erred in quarreling with his brother and how utterly angry and ashamed he was that his father had walked in on him and Teric, two grown men, wrestling like stupid children.

Just then, Orinn came up with a mug of ale and plopped it in front of Aradis, who tossed him a copper gerrin, which Orinn deftly inserted into his apron as he walked off to tend to other customers. Aradis took a long gulp of the ale, and as he did so, the stranger in the cloak abruptly said in a low, imperial voice, "I would hope for much better than rage and brawling from a son of Darion Kingblade."

To say that Aradis was taken aback by this would be a terrible understatement. Dumfounded, he held the ale in his mouth, set his mug on the counter, slowly swallowed, and, shocked beyond belief, said, "Excuse me?"

The man did not turn to look at him. He simply said, directly and with such authority in his voice that one dare not question him, "Aradis, I need to speak to you outside." Then he turned and walked over to the door and went out into the night.

Aradis had never been so stupefied in all his life. He could hardly have spoken if he had tried with all of his might, so struck was he by the absolute insanity of what had just happened. All his thoughts about Siloa, his family, his friends, the troubles of Velaris and all else besides, were strangely expelled from his mind. He could not think, he could not speak and, yet, he could not stay. It was as if all his powers of volition had been annihilated by the sheer bizarreness of that brief encounter, and he had no choice but to obey the man's request. It certainly would not do to let him slip away never to be seen again.

If Aradis could not get some answers about who the man was or how he had known his name and even seemed to be reading his very thoughts, he would be driven out of his mind. Already he was reaching desperately for some sort of mundane explanation, such as that the man was an old friend of his father's and had spoken with him before coming down to the tavern. But when would he have done that? Although it was possible, it wasn't very plausible, as there wouldn't have been much time. And why would he be so secretive? Had the man already been standing at the counter when Aradis first entered? He could not remember. And the more he tried, the less sure he was about everything. And so, he reluctantly turned and headed for the door. Just then, Girion raised his head and noticed that his friend was leaving. Aradis motioned with his hand that everything was all right. Then he opened the door and stepped out into the darkened street.

As soon as he was outside, he looked around in all directions for the stranger and saw him a ways south up the street. The man was looking at Aradis, and as soon as he saw that Aradis had spotted him, he disappeared into an alleyway that led west toward the edge of town. At this point, Aradis was concerned that perhaps the man meant to draw him out and then do him some ill, such as robbing or even killing him, but even this possibility did not faze his curiosity. "I must find out who this man is," he thought to himself, "or I shall wonder about this for the rest of my days." So he put his hand on the dagger he always carried at his side, went up the street and turned into the shadowy alleyway.

Once there, he passed through it and continued out of town, across a field and then on to the slope that rose west of town up toward the meadow at the edge of Rimwold Forest, a place that had been dubbed Midsummer Meadow by the people of Siloa, for several festivals were held there at the height of summer. He could see the man nearly at the top of the slope, his form barely outlined in the pale moonlight. Aradis began hiking up the hill after him, and when the stranger disappeared from sight over the crest, he climbed all the faster.

When he reached the top, he saw the man once more, this time on the far side of the meadow, now at the very edge of the forest. Once more, as soon as the man knew Aradis had seen him, he passed into the shadows of the enormous pines of Rimwold Forest.

At this juncture, Aradis knew that if he really were in his right mind, he should have turned around. It is, of course, ill-advised for anyone, no matter how clever or strong he may think himself to be, to wander off into the forest in the dark of night at the invitation of a complete stranger, but Aradis could not shake the maddening thought that if he did not discover the truth about this man, he should regret it until his dying day. His heart pounded in his chest, so loudly that it nearly drowned out the soft humming of insects in the moonlit meadow, but he had made up his mind. He would simply have to trust that everything would be all right, and if it were not, he would do his best to make it out of this alive. And this, he thought, was not unmanageable, for it could not be said that he was shabby with a blade. Thus, he held his dagger tighter still, ran across the meadow and ducked into the cover of the forest.

He peered into the shadows, using the weird patches of moonlight that lay upon the forest floor to aid his vision, but he did not see the stranger anywhere. Cautiously, he pressed farther in, and when he was perhaps two hundred feet deep into the forest, he came to a clearing that he knew quite well. There he saw the man standing on the far side, facing him dead on. Aradis gripped the dagger as tightly as he could, ready for almost anything. Still, he was terrified to his very marrow.

The stranger then cast the hood from his face and thus was revealed a somber visage of olive complexion. He was a Manfellow, sure enough, just as Aradis had suspected. His head was crowned with dark, curly hair and adorned with an elegant mustache and beard. In the darkness of the forest glade, it seemed almost as if the man's eyes reflected the dim blue sheen of the moonlight.

"You needn't fear me, Aradis," the man said in a deep voice. "I have not come here to harm you, but to bring you a message, a message which will ultimately be for your benefit and the benefit of many."

"How do you know my name? And how do you know my father?" Aradis stammered. The man stared back at him, now silent as the trees which stood around them. "Who are you?" Aradis demanded, his voice rising.

"I am Nagello, one of the Khasidim," the man replied. "And I have come to you with a message of great urgency."

Aradis now released his hold on the dagger. He was utterly flabbergasted. "A message? From whom? Who are the Khasidim?"

"The Khasidim are of the Hadathi; they are the Messengers of the Danna."

Aradis was more flabbergasted still. He cried out, stumbling repeatedly over his own words, "It cannot be! The Hadathi are—well, they're from the Haedra! Yes, the place of the Immaterial, and you're—you're one of them? How can this be? One of the Hadathi, beings of the invisible world, more powerful than the greatest of the Barada? And you have spoken with the Danna himself? Can it really be so? But I thought the Danna was—well, I always thought he was more the sort of being who wouldn't—well, that he wouldn't—are you really one of the Hadathi?"

At that very moment, Nagello burst into a blaze of blue light, and his aspect was transfigured. He still had the form of a man, though he was naked now, save for a dazzling garment around his loins, and he radiated an unspeakably fierce light, a deep blue flame. His form was regal in every regard; it was the very pinnacle of human perfection in body. From a purely material perspective, it might have been described as translucent in that it was not fully physical, but in another strange sense, it was densely immaterial, more substantial than any physical object could ever be. And now Nagello's eyes burned brighter than the summer sun at midday. Aradis only looked upon him for a moment before he collapsed to the ground and blackness overtook him.

CHAPTER TWO

Farewell to Siloa

hat seemed like a moment later, but in actuality may have been much, much longer, Aradis was abruptly awakened as a strong hand took his own hand and pulled him to his feet. The lad glanced up to see who had roused him.

It was Nagello, who had resumed the guise of a mere man, a humble traveler. Aradis looked around and saw that he was still in the clearing in Rimwold Forest, and it was still night. Gasping in amazement, he rubbed his eyes vigorously to assure himself of his surroundings.

Waiting until Aradis had recovered from his daze, Nagello quietly addressed him. "What you have seen was shown you that you might know with certainty that I am indeed a Messenger of the Danna," he said. "For you will have to do many hard things in the days to come, and you will need to clearly remember this night to be strong enough to do them."

The image of Nagello's unveiled splendor still burned vividly in Aradis' mind. "Please sir," Aradis exclaimed, panting, "tell me—are all of the Hadathi as terrifying as you in their true forms?"

"To the Barada, yes," the Khasidim returned. "And some to an even greater degree than I. All Hadathi are exceedingly powerful but not all are frightening to mortals for the same reason. For there are Hadathi who are uncorrupted, and they are terrifying to the impure on account of their great purity. Such am I. But there are also Hadathi who are defiled and depraved, and it is their great malice and atrocity that strike fear into the hearts of the Barada."

"You have shown me beyond all doubt that the existence of the Haedra is not to be doubted, and that it is to be held in great esteem," Aradis stammered, shaking a little. "But may I beg your pardon, sir? For I must ask—how am I to know that you are not among the wicked Hadathi and that you do not mean to deceive me or do me great harm?"

"Fear not to ask such a thing, son of Darion," Nagello replied. "In truth, it is a necessary inquiry. For there are, as I said, sinister Hadathi, and these may feign good intent and, yet, lead the Barada into darkness. Yet the hallowed and the profane may be differentiated in three main respects. First, the acts and speech of the Eladar, that is, the uncorrupted Hadathi, always lead to the increase of true light in Orona. This is not so with the Kalathar, the Hadathi who have become wayward. Secondly, the Kalathar speak messages and perform deeds which are contrary to the behests of the Danna. Such is never the case with the Eladar. And finally, the proclamations of the Eladar all come to pass, while those of the Kalathar do not. Thus, regard me as a vile imposter and pernicious deceiver, if all that I am about to tell you does not take place exactly as I foretold that it would. But if all things do happen according to my word, then know that I am who I claim to be."

"If this is so," Aradis wondered, "how am I to know I have not gone amiss in my own understanding of the Danna and his directives? For this very night, I have found my images of the Danna and the Haedra badly disturbed. Indeed, I had thought the Haedra to be a comforting place where the Danna drifts about in a happy country called Erdion. But seeing you as you really are annihilated all such convictions. Now I don't know what to think about all this."

Nagello explained, "The correct apprehension of such things was given long ago, and all falsehoods have come afterward. And there is a testimony of it which is known as the Elyrion. But it is not yet time for you to know all such things as have been revealed there. Indeed, only what is requisite shall be given you now."

"As for the Haedra," the Khasidim went on, "it is neither comforting nor troubling in and of itself; it is what it is, just like Orona. But the things which take place there are sometimes of great consolation and are other times violently unsettling. But, most importantly, it must be pointed out that the Danna does not 'drift', as you say, Aradis, like some untethered mist. Neither is he a sedentary being. All this you ought to have known if you had heeded the instruction of your father."

"Yes, I suppose my father did explain that to me," Aradis admitted, looking down sheepishly at the forest floor.

"Your father taught you other things as well," the Hadathi asserted. "He taught you the name of the Danna—his personal name." He looked hard at Aradis. Then he quietly asked, "And what is that name?"

Aradis thought for a moment, then tentatively replied, "Telyon. But we usually just refer to him as the Danna."

"As do many," Nagello remarked. "And the Danna he is, though many have strayed from a proper understanding of that designation. But his name is Telyon. He is the True King of both Kazamar, the Material, and the Haedra, the Immaterial. He reigns from the great hall of Rastobeth atop glorious Mount Azaru in the bright city of Everhold in Erdion, which is a happy country indeed—the happiest, in fact. And he is fully aware of all that comes to pass in Orona, which is the reason I knew of your quarrel with Teric, even of the guilt you felt for being caught in the act of fighting with him as your father entered the forge."

At this point Aradis no longer found it quite so arresting that Nagello knew such things as these. Why should he not know them if he really were one of the Hadathi, the mighty creatures of the Haedra? But still, he was greatly ashamed of what he had done that evening.

"You know my father then?" Aradis inquired abruptly.

"Aye, I know him," Nagello answered. "And that is why I said I hoped for better from a son of his. But you are not yet what you ought to be, and you will not become thus until the Danna should bring it about in his own manner and at his own time. For still there is much you do not know about the world that you will learn in the days ahead. But mark this well, son of Darion: do not forget that it was Telyon who sought you out, not the other way around, and it is he who will bring these matters concerning you to completion. And it is by his hand that the name of Kingblade shall be called blessed, as it was long ago."

Nagello's words were quite cryptic now, as Aradis might expect from one of the Hadathi, but he pressed him, "Long ago? How long ago? When my father was young? Sir, I have no doubt you know my father, but does my father know you?"

"Ask him yourself before you leave," Nagello replied curtly.

"Before I leave? What are you talking about?" Aradis asked, astounded.

"The message I came to bring you is that you must leave Siloa immediately, this very night."

Everything in Aradis' mind rejected this notion wholeheartedly. "No! You cannot ask that of me! No, you do not understand! I cannot simply leave Siloa in the middle of the night, no matter what it is that—"

"You would gainsay Telyon?" Nagello asked, raising an eyebrow.

"Well, Telyon surely knows that I am needed here and that I can't just go traipsing off into the blue one night," Aradis explained.

"Telyon knows a great deal more than you give him credit for, Aradis Kingblade. And it would be exceedingly foolish on your part to think you know better than he what you ought to do with your life."

"But see here!" Aradis protested even more adamantly. "I can't just march off and leave my family and do whatever it is that you're going to try to convince me to do!"

"Aradis," Nagello said firmly, "Telyon has commanded that you leave Siloa this very night. And if he has thus commanded, there can be no greater path of wisdom than to obey. Do you really imagine that he can be fully aware of every word that passed between you and your brother, every aching cry of your father, the resilient spirit of your sister and the admirable dedication of your mother and still be utterly oblivious to what is best for you and your family? Is Telyon some dolt who will be told what is best for all concerned by the likes of Aradis Kingblade?"

Nagello's voice now resonated deeply as he continued, "Were you there when Telyon came forth from Innamaras, the Timeless Vaults, and opened the Doors of the Hours at Osora, the Last Mountain, when the world began? Were you present at the forging of the Kalarna, the Jewels of Time? Was it you who uttered the first of the Kesina, the proclamation which brought all of the Haedra into being? Do you really suppose you have greater knowledge and wisdom than Telyon? Tell me, if you can, what lies on the far side of Rimura, the Sea of the Heavens, where even the Hadathi cannot go. Do all the winds of Orona heed your call, and can you guide the path of Marda, the sun, and Eoreth, the moon? Have you passed into the heart of Orona through the flaming forges of Tynaegryn, the Fire-Realm? Have you journeyed to the deepest vales of Solansu, the Realm of the Sea-Lords? Is your advice to be weighed more heavily than the king over both Kazamar, the Material, and the Haedra, the Immaterial? Can you command all of existence by the mere power of your word? If not, then I suggest you do as Telyon commands."

There was nothing Aradis could possibly have said to counter this without sounding like an utter fool, and he recognized that ultimately he would have to do whatever it was that Telyon mandated. So he sighed grimly, much humbled, "With such words I cannot dispute. Very well, then. What is my task?"

Nagello replied, his voice hushed and fiercely articulate, "Now listen carefully, Aradis. You must not forget a single thing I say to you. You are to leave Siloa this very night and go to the port of Tarwyn. There you will purchase passage to the Fontskals in the Indurian Deeps, specifically to the island of Stragmore. There is a town there named Dankdocks, and in that town there is a place not far from the shore called the Draughtfish Inn. There you will inquire after a man named Felding Starwash, who is well known by all the people in that town. He will provide you with passage to the great Neathmarda of Byram, to the port of Gorondil, and from there you will go to the great city of Anganor, the capital of the Kingdom of Argonis, which lies in the region known as the Elder Forest."

Aradis was becoming greatly aggravated. "I don't really know where any of those places are except for Tarwyn," he protested, "mostly because it's in Velaris and rather an important city, though still several hundred miles from here. But Byram—that's thousands of miles away, isn't it? Am I really to travel so far across the world? But I can't possibly remember all of these names you're telling me."

"You will remember them," Nagello assured, and then continued, "Now upon your arrival in Anganor, you must seek audience with the king of Argonis, Thornoak by name. He is one of the Ingans."

"And who exactly are the Ingans?" Aradis inquired.

"You would know them as the Treefolk, for that is how they are oft referred to in your tongue, especially by those who do not regularly associate with them; however, the Ingans themselves do not much care for the term 'Treefolk'. Nevertheless, the name is somewhat apt, for they do look rather like trees with faces and arms and legs, although they are not much taller than Menfolk. Yet trees they are not, for they are Barada, just like Menfolk, Elves, Dwarves, Gnomes and all the rest of the Narthanna. Now, as I was saying, when you reach Anganor, you must seek audience with King Thornoak. That task alone will be no simple matter, though once you have spoken with him, he will be able to help you accomplish your ultimate business there."

"And what is that?" asked Aradis, who was growing more bewildered every moment.

"You must heal the hurts of that land and reunite its people, who have succumbed to bitterness, strife and fear to such a degree that the kingdom is on the verge of collapse. Once you have done this, you must commence a far more difficult task. You must destroy the Witch Ravinia the Heartless who has taken up residence in Blackbough Woods, a dark and wild region several hundred miles to the west of there. And in so doing, you will rescue the Kingdom of Argonis and its people from an even greater peril than their own dissension: that of the Fell Alliance, the union which Ravinia has formed among all the wicked Barada of the Elder Forest."

Aradis' evening had already become more outlandish than he could ever have imagined, but this was too much. "Who does Telyon think I am, and why in all Orona has he decided I should go do this thing?" he blurted out. "I've heard of Witches, I suppose, but I did not know they really existed. But from everything I've heard about them, it sounds as if they are unspeakably powerful. What qualifications have I for saving a kingdom and defeating a Witch?"

"None whatsoever," Nagello responded bluntly. "You are not being sent because there is something remarkable about you, Aradis Kingblade. Rather, it is because Telyon desires to extend Keshara unto you, that you may join the ranks of the Staffborn. And Keshara is a great treasure indeed, one that the mercy of Telyon alone can provide in full. In short, lad, the true purpose of my coming is to proclaim that the Call of the Danna has been issued unto you."

"The Call of the Danna?" Aradis asked, uncertain of whether that was something he really wished to receive or not.

"Yes, it is the greatest call that any Barada could ever receive. It is a greater call even than that which you are being given in the quest in the Elder Forest. It must be understood that your business in Argonis is *a* call of the Danna, but not *the Call*. Yet in that quest, you are being offered a magnificent opportunity, Aradis. Know this, and know it truly—Telyon will use you to destroy the Witch and save Argonis if you will let him. But a greater glory than this is the Keshara of which I spoke, the Keshara which is the inheritance of the Staffborn."

"Keshara? The Staffborn?" Aradis repeated these words which had only served to increase his mystification. "You may as well be speaking in another tongue, for I know nothing of these things. Tell me plainly, what does the Danna mean to do with me?"

Nagello looked sternly into Aradis' eyes, then said slowly, "He means to kill you, Aradis, in order that you may live."

Extreme exasperation now gave way to complete stupefaction. Aradis' jaw dropped open in disbelief, as he exclaimed, "So I am to be sent halfway across the world to be murdered?"

"I am not speaking of the sort of death you are thinking of, Aradis. Death to you means only such things as slaughter by the sword or succumbing to disease or falling to the relentless decay of old age. I am not speaking of the death of your body, which is what you imagine. But you are not yet ready to see what I am speaking of. That time will come though, sooner than you expect. Yes, your eyes will see as they have never seen before. But now you must go to your home, for your father has something to give you. Immediately after you have received it from him, you will go east across the plains to Tarwyn."

"So I am to leave my father in his weak and sickened condition?"

"Whether you go or stay, your father's health rests in the Danna's providence, not your own."

Aradis could see the sense in this, but it still deeply troubled him. "I will be able to say farewell to my family before I leave then?" he queried.

"Only to your father," Nagello said, as he started off through the forest back toward the meadow and motioned for Aradis to follow him.

Indignant, Aradis exclaimed, "Can I not kiss my sister Mellora and my mother Eribeth goodbye?"

"If you awaken them, their sorrow at your departure will only be made that much worse. If you trust Telyon as I hope you will, you will let them sleep, and he will comfort them in the morning when they learn you are gone."

"What of my brother? Am I not allowed to mend my quarrel with him and apologize for the things I said in foolish anger?"

Nagello replied, "Not at this time, for you made the choice to act as you did when you were in the forge a few hours ago, and now you must live with the bitter fruit of your deeds."

Aradis sighed heavily, greatly grieved at what was soon to befall him, for he knew he must leave that very night as Nagello had said. And he had not the presence of mind to even think about this task he had been given to accomplish in the Elder Forest. It was too foreign, too fantastic to even contemplate. He would simply have to go step by step, if he were going to do it at all.

Soon they reached the edge of the meadow and stood still in the soft moonlight. Nagello then turned to address the lad once more. "Now, Aradis," he said, "it is imperative that you recognize that what you are being asked to do is absolutely impossible, as the Barada might reckon it. That needs to be made perfectly clear. I do not wish for any false hopes to present themselves to you."

Aradis' heart sank, his mind staggered, and he felt a cold despair rising within him, but he was so struck by this revelation that he remained mute.

Then Nagello's voice rose like fiery dawn over the plains, "But do not be afraid of what is to come, for what is impossible for the Barada can yet be accomplished. That which you have been commissioned to do can indeed be brought to completion. The Call of the Danna will not be without effect. Yet, it will not find its fulfillment in Aradis Kingblade, but in Telyon himself, who shall stand behind you and before you and beside you when you go into the dark places of Orona. And make no mistake; your path will be dark and terrible. Before all comes to an end in fury and fire, shadows will pursue you and blackness will hem you in. Night will bear down upon you, and you will nearly succumb unto the weeping of death itself. But there will always be a way, a way of hope, a way of escape, and this will be the doing of the Danna. In all things you must pursue him and the road he has laid before you. But imagine not for one moment that you will succeed by your own power or your own strength. The tasks you have been given are grave indeed, and they are far beyond the ability of even the mighty among the Barada to accomplish. You are small in strength; help must come from beyond you, for it will by no means come from within you. And yet in all this, do not think that the might of Telyon absolves you of the responsibility to act. Act you must, or you will indeed fail. But you must act in the strength you are given. And hope will be poured out from on high as a light unto you."

Aradis inhaled deeply, his very soul sapped and his body on the verge of collapse from the gravity of what Nagello had just told him. Then, looking up at the darkened firmament, sparkling with the silver gleam of the moon and stars, he thought of Erdion, the land where the Danna dwelt, and he thought of the hope which would cascade from that high realm upon him when things were blackest and despair had nearly crushed him. He had a small taste of that remarkable hope and comfort even now. Now, looking back at Nagello, he expelled his breath and awaited the last words of the Khasidim.

Nagello then laid his hand upon Aradis' shoulder. "Now, take this," he said, as he handed the lad an object about half the size of his palm that appeared to be some sort of medallion or amulet. The medallion looked to be the right half of a splendid emerald leaf edged by finely wrought silver; it seemed as if the other half had been unevenly sundered from it, and so the piece which Aradis held looked decidedly incomplete. The medallion shard was attached to a thin silver chain, so that it could be worn as a necklace.

"What's this?" Aradis asked.

"You will not need this for some time, but it will have a tremendous role to play in your quest before all is said and done. There will come a time when you will require this medallion to win the aid of those who doubt you, even after someone they respect has spoken highly of you. It will be a great sign unto them. Do not worry about when to reveal it, for it shall be made manifest at the proper time."

"More riddles?" Aradis asked, as he hung the medallion around his neck and tucked the emerald leaf shard into his tunic.

"They are mysteries now," Nagello concurred, "but they will soon be unveiled." Then he handed Aradis a heavy leather pouch.

"And what am I to do with this?" Aradis inquired.

"Purchase passage for two from Tarwyn to Dankdocks."

"For two? Will I not be alone? Who is going with me?" the lad asked, as he attached the money pouch to his belt.

"Your friend Girion Ringmark," Nagello replied, smiling.

"But how in the name of all that is sane and decent am I going to convince Girion to go with me on this mad venture?" asked Aradis, who was dumbfounded and delighted all at once.

"You will not need to," Nagello assured him. "Now, make haste! Return to your home, get that which is needed from your father and naught else, for all your needs of food and supplies will be taken care of. Then hurry to Girion's house, and he will be waiting for you there. After that, immediately set out eastward, and you will have covered many miles by dawn."

"Your travel this night is much needed," the Khasidim went on, "for you must reach Tarwyn ere the fourth Passing of Marda from that which has just transpired, the fourth twilight from this moment. And mark this well, Aradis Kingblade: whatever may befall you, you must not turn around, not for any reason. I say unto you, as surely as Telyon dwells in Rastobeth, all shall go ill and come to ruin if you should come back to Siloa before your quest is ended. And you must on no account stop at the house of anyone until you have reached the town of Hardonac, a little more than thirty miles to the east of here. You cannot delay; you must journey straight on until dawn, for there is a need of haste of which you yet know not."

"But what is—" Aradis stammered, but Nagello instantly cut him off. "There is no time to lose! Your lingering doubts will be quelled later, not now!"

Now Aradis turned to go, realizing he could receive no further consolation from the Khasidim. Suddenly, he felt Nagello's firm grasp upon his shoulder. He turned to look back into the Hadathi's face and saw his eyes flickering with the glories of Erdion.

"Remember all that I have said to you," Nagello charged the young Siloan. "And do not fail to follow even the least of the instructions I have given you from Telyon. Now go!" he finished abruptly.

Aradis took this command quite seriously and begun running full bore across the flowering meadow. When he was a ways out, he turned back and looked at Nagello, who stood half under the shadow of the trees. Nagello raised his hand in farewell, and Aradis hurried on. When he had gone a little farther, he looked back again and saw that the Khasidim had disappeared. Whether he had gone back into the forest or returned to the Haedra, invisible now to mortal eyes, Aradis knew not. His mind was reeling, as he raced over the crest of the hill and saw the little village of Siloa in the valley below. Thin trails of smoke rose from the chimneys, the lights of hearthfires had died down in nearly every home, and even the windows of the Ploughman's Shanty were dim. Not a soul could be seen in the streets, and all was hushed. Aradis hurried down the hill and through the alley that ran along the north side of his house. Around front, he quietly opened the door and went inside.

His father was sitting in a crude chair by the hearth, stroking his brown beard and staring at the dying embers in the fireplace. "Aradis," he coughed softly, as he looked up, "I'm glad you're home. I thought you might have spent the night at Girion's. It's nearly midnight now."

Aradis realized that a great deal of time must have passed since he fainted from seeing Nagello's true form, but he could only think of one thing to say to his father. "Have you ever been given a message directly from the Danna?" he asked.

Darion began to answer, but stopped short, his mouth still open, and his countenance suddenly grew very strange indeed. For a moment, Aradis thought he had gone into a trance, but Darion then muttered slowly, as if he were talking to himself, "Is this the night he spoke of, then?"

"Father, do you know a Hadathi named Nagello?" Aradis asked, looking straight at him.

Darion glanced up to meet his son's gaze, smiling, and said, "Yes, I know him, and I see you now know him too. Come, I have something to give you."

Aradis could contain his bewilderment no longer. "My mortal mind!" he uttered incredulously, once more completely stunned. "What is all this about? Why did you never tell me of these things? How can it be that you are giving me something just as Nagello said you would? How much of this world have I been ignorant of my whole life? What is going to happen to us—to me, to you, to our whole family?"

Darion ignored his son's barrage, grabbed a crowbar from a pile of assorted tools near the hearth and then walked over to a particular floorboard in the middle of the room. As Aradis watched, his father, with some effort, pried up the board as quietly as he could, so as to not waken the others slumbering behind the closed door to the Kingblades' sleeping quarters. To Aradis' astonishment, Darion reached into the dark hole beneath the board and drew out a sword with a rather unremarkable black metal sheath. Then, he pushed the board back down and handed the blade in its sheath to Aradis.

"This is Brightbeam," he said solemnly, "a blade I bore for some time. Now you must bear it. At last, all the time I spent teaching you the way of the blade out in the forest when you were a child will be put to good use. For surely I did not endow such knowledge and skill unto you purely for your own enjoyment. Though there is no need for swords in Siloa, there will come a time in the near future when you will be glad that Brightbeam is your companion."

Looking the scabbard up and down, Aradis declared, "I do remember well how you took me many an evening up into the woods to show me how to wield a sword properly, but I never imagined—well, I never imagined that you were preparing me for a time such as this. So you knew all along; every time we went out for swordplay, you knew this day would come."

"Yes, son, I did," Darion returned gently.

"Why didn't you tell me?"

"Wisdom would have been thwarted if I had. Either you would not have believed me, as often you have been prone to doubt things I have told you, especially about the Deep Lore of Orona, things about Telyon and the Hadathi and the Forgotten Days, or else it would have gone to your head, for it is a heavy burden for a lad to know that he will someday be summoned to accomplish a great task by the Danna himself."

"I suppose you're right," Aradis said thoughtfully. "Father, how did you come by this sword?" he asked, as he quietly drew the blade out a few inches and looked upon it.

Darion chuckled softly and then coughed, "That's a long tale indeed, my boy, and one neither you nor I have time for this night. I will tell you that story upon your return."

"How do you know I'll be coming back?" Aradis pressed. "Nagello told me Telyon intended to kill me."

"Of course he does," Darion replied matter-of-factly. "No better fate could befall you. But as for how I know you'll be returning: long ago an old Yeti by the name of Tuldrak began telling me a story that, unfortunately, he was unable to finish. And yet Nagello promised me by the power of the Danna that my firstborn son would tell me the end of that very important story. And you, my lad, are my firstborn son. When you return, I fully expect I will hear the end. So we shall each tell each other our stories when we meet again, for I have a story to tell you as well."

Aradis was desperate for answers. "Story? What story? Father, there is so much I do not understand. Can this really be happening to me—to us? What do you know about all this? Please help me! Am I losing my mind?"

"Don't worry; you're quite sane," Darion said, smiling. " But your mind certainly is being opened tonight, so it may feel like you're losing what you have. Trust me; this change is for the best. Now you must go without delay, just as Nagello said."

"How did you know Nagello told me to leave immediately?" Aradis returned.

"He told me," Darion answered drily, blinking.

"When? Tonight?"

"No. A long time ago," Darion said, his voice trailing off, lost in the memory.

"Tell me what happened to you," Aradis demanded. "Did Nagello send you halfway across the world too? Tell me about this sword."

"There's no time now, Aradis," Darion insisted. "You must go now. Do not linger here."

Aradis cast his arms about his father, whispering, "I love you, Father. And I don't want to leave. But I know I must. Yet I don't know if I'll ever come back alive," he said, as tears began to form in his eyes. "And I want so much for you to get better and for everything to be all right and for us to have enough money. For me to stop fighting with Teric and for Mother and Mellora to be provided for."

"The eyes of the Danna will ever be upon us, Aradis, and they also will be upon you. You will come back alive. Have no doubts about that. The story must be finished. Thus it was foretold, and thus shall it be," Darion consoled his son, as he held him tightly.

Aradis was greatly comforted in this, but still as mystified as ever. "I love you, Father," he breathed again, releasing him from the embrace. Quickly, he went over to the door, knowing that he would not leave, if he did not force himself to do so.

"I know," Darion said affectionately.

Aradis looked longingly at the door to the sleeping chambers. He so wished to say farewell to his mother, his dear sister Mellora and even lazy, bad-tempered Teric, but he remembered what Nagello had told him.

Darion saw his glance and said, "It will be much better if you don't waken them. If you do, you will not be able to leave, and their hearts will be more broken than they would be if they simply awoke in the morning to find you gone."

"That's what Nagello said too," Aradis sighed.

"And you would do well to trust him," Darion affirmed. "Incidentally, where are you going?" he added.

"To Byram, to the Elder Forest, to defeat a Witch named Ravinia and rescue a kingdom called Argonis," Aradis replied, somewhat startled that he had just said this, as if it were something he were really going to go and do.

"Ah, good then," Darion said. "You will learn much, I expect, and come back a better man. Now you must go, but we will have much to talk about upon your return, both for your part and mine."

Darion then practically pushed Aradis out the door, saying, "Goodbye, son. I love you very much, and Telyon will be with you."

"You too, Father," Aradis returned softly, as Darion closed the door, and Aradis was left alone in the night once more.

The lad knew it was best not to linger, so he left the silent, starlit central street of Siloa and headed through an alleyway that led toward the east edge of town and thus in the direction of the Ringmark farm. It was, in fact, the very same alleyway between Gandrian's house and Faenard's tailor shop that he had taken around sunset. Then he climbed up out of the shallow valley in which Siloa lay and hastened down the path that led through the fields of standing grain.

In a short while, he reached the Ringmarks' farmhouse, and sure enough, Girion was standing outside waiting for him, leaning on a walking staff. He was dressed in the same outfit he had been wearing earlier: a white shirt with blue stitching, a leather jerkin and girdle, dark brown breeches and tall black leather boots. Aradis ran up to him, panting, "How can this be?"

"What? That I'm waiting for you?" Girion grinned. "Nagello said that you'd be surprised, even though he would have told you about this ahead of time."

"You met Nagello too?" Aradis asked, shocked for not the first time that night.

"Just a while ago," Girion replied. "He told me about everything, and I prepared to leave shortly thereafter."

"It sounds as if we have a great deal to talk about," Aradis laughed, still amazed by it all.

"Indeed we do," Girion concurred. "But let us talk as we go along the road. There is a long journey ahead of us tonight."

"And for some time to come," Aradis added, as the two of them set out upon their eastward journey across the Plains of Agleri.

Up above, the stars shone with a cool, pale light, and the fields of golden grain were all tinged with the magical blue hue of starlight and moonlight mingled together. By the edge of the pine woods, the village of Siloa slept peacefully under the blanket of night. And, in the west, a blue streak of light, just like a shooting star, rose up from Rimwold Forest and vaulted high into the heavens, where it disappeared from sight.

CHAPTER THREE

The Snare of the Sardolia

eaving the Ringmark farm behind, the two companions climbed over the hillock to the southeast and came down upon the path to Hardonac, another farm village which lay some thirty miles to the east. Aradis had been there once, nearly ten years ago now, and he remembered it being much like Siloa, only bigger. As reluctant as he was to leave so much he held dear behind, he was at the same time filled with anticipation and excitement at the prospect of seeing that great, wide and magnificent world, the whole of Orona, which lay beyond his own world of wheat fields and pine forests, thatched cottages and the fires of his father's forge—a world which was already unimaginably large.

Aradis had fully expected that once he began walking with Girion, they would have so much to converse about that they would not grow quiet until dawn or even after, but, strangely enough, neither he nor the cooper's son had the urge to speak of the things which had befallen them. This was partially because they had not fully grasped it themselves, needing time and thought to do so, and partially because the night itself seemed to be demanding quietude. The breeze only whispered as it rustled the prairie grasses, and even the smaller birds and beasts of the plains seemed loath to break the silence. In fact, only a half-hearted chorus of crickets could be heard presenting their droning tune as an offering to the night's solemnity.

However, when they had covered nearly a mile from Girion's home, Aradis spoke up. "Girion, what did Nagello reveal to you?" he asked. "Where and when did he appear to you? Did he tell you that he is one of the Hadathi?"

"He did indeed," Girion replied. He strode on for a few moments, thinking, and then remarked, "If I'm going to explain all of this properly, I suppose I should start at the point when you left the tavern."

"Very well, then," Aradis said.

Girion then began to recount his evening. "I didn't stay at the Ploughman's Shanty much longer after you left because Corim started trying to convince Tallis and me to set him up with Harlia Harrowdell again."

Aradis chuckled at this remark. "Oh, I'm sure his newest plan was the most refined, eh?"

"His plan was, to put it quite frankly, idiotic, even for his usual fare. But he was really quite set on us helping him. I wanted no part of any of it though, so I just told him I had to talk to my parents before they went off to bed, and I suggested he see if Neldon would go in on the scheme with him. Well, as soon as I finished my ale, I stopped by Lerrin Stockwright's place to give him back those maps I borrowed a couple weeks ago and then headed home."

"As it turned out, my mother and father were already retired for the night, and I planned to soon join them. Yet, as I lay down to slumber, there came a fierce rapping at the door, and we all sprang awake to see who it might be. My father opened the door, and there stood a Manfellow all wrapped up in a brown cloak. When my father asked him his business and his title, he said he was but a traveler named Nagello in need of a morsel of food for his journey. My mother went to fetch him aught and, meanwhile, he spoke to us. Oddly enough, he knew my name and the names of my parents. Indeed, as soon as my mother offered to bring him refreshment, he said, 'That's very kind of you, Anella.' To this my father said, 'How do you know her name?' And to this Nagello replied, 'Is it so strange to you that I should know the names of those to whom I am sent, Dugamar Ringmark?'"

Aradis looked at his companion and shook his head in amazement. "I imagine all your faces looked just like mine when Nagello called me by name in the Shanty," he laughed.

"It was no small shock to us, to say the least!" the cooper's son affirmed. "But before we even had time to recover from it, he went on to say that if I would have it, there was a great task being offered to me by the Danna, but I would have to depart shortly after midnight to partake of it. For some reason, at that juncture, he made a point of clarifying that the Danna of whom we spoke was one and the same as he who was called Telyon by the Menfolk of old. He then explained that my role in this quest, which Telyon was extending unto me, would be to accompany you on a great journey and aid you in any way I could in the mission which had been appointed to you. We wondered greatly at this, as you might expect, yet my father strangely did not deride him but, rather, inquired how we might know the veracity of his message."

"And what did Nagello say to that?" Aradis inquired.

Girion answered, "He bade us bring him a pitcher of water, and this my father did. Then he bade us drink of the vessel that we might know most assuredly that it was naught but water. With this request all three of us complied, for my mother had then returned. Instructing us to stand back, he poured the water upon the floor so that it formed a shining pool. As he stepped into the pool, it sprang ablaze, and bright flames roared up to the ceiling. We cried out and fell to the ground in dismay, for there he stood, wreathed in terrible fire. Yet several moments later, Nagello strode forth from the flames, not the least bit singed. The fire vanished, and he handed my father the pitcher, which was again filled with water. Then he told us that the acts which he had just performed were a sign from the Danna, given to us that we might know he spoke truly. As you can imagine, we were all faint and badly shaken, but Nagello bid us be strengthened and then once more offered me the opportunity to go on this journey."

"He gave you a choice in the matter?" Aradis laughed. "For my part, there was no such courtesy!"

"Of course not," Girion returned, "for if Nagello had left it up to you, you never would have left Siloa."

"In that you speak the truth," Aradis sighed. "But what did Nagello share with you of our journey and its purpose? Did he tell you how grave our task is really to be?"

"Yes, he told me I would have to put up with you the entire time," Girion jested.

"No doubt it will be the other way round!" Aradis objected good-naturedly.

Girion continued his teasing, "Well, I was a bit concerned when he told me that he entrusted you with the fare for the ship we'll be taking out of Tarwyn. You didn't lose that, like that handkerchief I gave you the other day, did you? Now if I were in charge of—"

"No, I didn't lose it. It's right here," Aradis said, patting his right hip. "As for your handkerchief, I think I lent it to Neldon."

"It's definitely gone then," Girion lamented.

"But Girion, in all sincerity, what did Nagello tell you of our mission?" Aradis inquired again.

"He said that I would be accompanying you to Byram, to the Elder Forest, the eastern reach of the Five Fabled Lands of that great Neathmarda which lies across the Indurian Deeps. In that place, we are to fulfill two great tasks, the first being the uniting of the Kingdom of Argonis, which has become sundered and its people contentious through sorrow and malice, and the second being the defeat of the dreaded Witch Ravinia the Heartless, whose sole thought now is to destroy that kingdom and its leader, King Thornoak. He instructed us to seek Thornoak's aid when we reach Anganor, the chief city of Argonis, but warned that we would only come to stand before him through much toil and hardship. Oh yes, and he mentioned the name of one Felding Starwash, a ship captain who would take us to Byram. He said that we should look for him at a place called the Draughtfish Inn in the town of Dankdocks in the Fontskals and that all the locals would know him."

"All these things he told me also," Aradis remarked. "Did he say anything else?"

Girion expounded, "Nagello assured me that all our needs would be taken care of and that our path would be laid before us. He said that we would be protected in various ways from the many forces which will stand opposed to us. And this protection and all these provisions he called 'the Waybread of Erdion.' Apparently we are to have more than our share of it!" Girion laughed.

"No doubt," Aradis agreed glumly. "From what Nagello said, it sounds as if we are to have a most unpleasant time in the days ahead. We shall badly need this waybread stuff at some point, I suppose."

They walked on several steps more before Aradis inquired, "Did he inform you of the time by which we must reach Tarwyn?"

"Ere twilight on the fourth day," Girion confirmed. "And he enjoined us not to stop at any house whatsoever until we had come to Hardonac, for there would be a cause for great haste of which we are now unaware. Indeed, he said that we must not cease our journey until dawn. And he forbade us from turning back for any reason once we had left Siloa, at least until our task was ended."

Aradis replied, "He related all this to me as well, and I thought it strange indeed, for he also warned that if we did turn back, much woe would come of it. But how did he convince you to leave in such haste and without preparation or proper farewell?" he pressed, still amazed that Girion was really going on this adventure with him.

"I had time for suitable goodbyes," Girion replied, "for Nagello left shortly after delivering his message and its particulars, and I sat for nearly an hour with my parents discussing all these things before we said our farewells and they went back to bed, or at least lay down anyway. I doubt they're asleep even now. Nagello told me I would need to pack nothing, yet he advised me to carry a staff for protection and for walking great distances. And so, having naught else to do, I went outside and awaited your arrival." Then, noticing Aradis' morose countenance, he remarked, "Your departure was rather more rushed, I would guess."

"Much more so," Aradis ruefully affirmed. "I was only able to speak with my father before my departure. And do you know what, Girion? I learned that my father had met Nagello before, a long time ago, and apparently Nagello told him then that he would be coming back some day to send his firstborn son on some sort of mad adventure. My father didn't exactly say that outright, but I gathered as much from his remarks."

"Really?" Girion returned inquisitively, and Aradis knew that his friend's brilliant mind was already generating a myriad of conjectures about what sort of interactions his father and Nagello may have had. "Well, this certainly qualifies as a mad adventure!"

"Indeed it does," Aradis agreed, as he looked eastward across the plains toward the peaceful horizon.

But though it was quite calm in the east, all was no longer still in the north. Across the open plains, there came a sound of many distant hooves galloping at great speed. The lads instinctively turned to search for its source, but their view was largely inhibited by a rather wide hill known as Dorman's Down, at the southern base of which lay the road to Hardonac.

"What do you think all that is?" Aradis asked his friend, knowing he would not have to explain what he was referring to, for they had both stopped dead the moment they heard the hooves.

"As surely as the siradel sings in the summer, I don't know," Girion responded, puzzled. (The brightly plumed siradels indeed sang every summer, as they wove their nests in the boughs of Rimwold Forest.) "But, in this hinterland of Velaris, there is no cause for persons of peaceful intent to be riding in a great company in the middle of the night," he reasoned. "Rather, an errand of evil or mischief is almost certainly afoot."

"Judging from the sound, I'd say the riders are still a little ways off, and they're coming from somewhere almost directly northeast of here," Aradis said. "Up that way, the nearest town of a decent size is Dallyn, of course, but I'd wager there aren't enough horses in that whole place to make that much racket."

"Perhaps it's a group of bandits from deep Rimwold or something like that," Girion stated quizzically. "They have been known to foray into Agleri on occasion. The only other thing I can think of that would warrant such a large number of Barada on horseback would be a dispatch of the Sardolia, though it would be nothing short of bizarre for the constabulary from Tellig, which is a good twenty leagues or more from here, to be roaming about so far afield at such an hour as this. Unless—"

"Oh, that's all we need is those filthbags!" Aradis fumed. "Well, regardless of who these riders are, I would certainly prefer they don't see us traveling out here in the middle of the night. It will probably only lead to trouble."

"You're quite correct in that regard," Girion concurred.

"Then let's find a place to lay in hiding until they pass," Aradis called, running south and a little eastward into a field of tall winter wheat awaiting the spring harvest.

The two companions raced some distance into the field and then flung themselves down upon the ground. There they waited, crouched, fearing what business so many riders had abroad in the dark of night. Breathing heavily, they saw each other's eyes flit back and forth in the dim moonlight. All the while, the sound of raging hooves drew closer and closer.

They had lain there a short time indeed when the company on horseback came into sight, riding directly around the eastern foot of Dorman's Down. These riders had not been taking the road that ran down to Hardonac, but rather riding brazenly through the fields of the Menfolk to the northeast, wantonly trampling down their grain harvest. Aradis guessed there may have been fifty of them in all. A few of them bore torches, in the light of which it could be seen that they were Plains-Elves, Elves of the far eastern grasslands of Quarana, the Neathmarda on which Velaris was situated. In many respects, they were exactly like Menfolk, only perhaps slightly taller and having pointed ears and keener senses in general; their hair was also finer. But these Elves wore the unmistakable garb of the Sardolia, much to the Siloans' chagrin. The Sardolia was stationed in the capitals of all the barolli, the districts of Velaris, and its agents were charged with acting as a standing army, collectors of revenue and keepers of the peace. But more often than not, they simply acted as harriers of the Menfolk.

These Elves were clad in light armor, leather jerkins and the like, upon the breasts of which were emblazoned in a field of dark blue the axe and the scythe of the Ruphani, the ruler of the kingdom of Velaris. The axe was for the woodlands of Rimwold Forest in the west and the scythe for the Plains of Agleri in the east, while the field of blue stood for the Brines of Ferassi, that great sea which lay eastward of Quarana, on the border of which lay Aragest in northeastern Velaris. The brown-cloaked riders were all outfitted with their customary armaments: Elven longswords and shorter curved blades called jenassi, which were the traditional weapons of the Gnomish tribes who had dwelt in the region of Agleri several centuries ago.

Now, to the great dismay of the two hidden travelers, the leader of the company called out a halt, and the riders came to a standstill only several tens of yards north of where they lay hidden.

"Now, let us be reminded once more of our course once we reach Siloa," the leader called out, as he turned to the riders behind him.

Aradis clenched his fists in rage—that voice he had not forgotten. It was the haughty, calloused voice of that selfsame captain who had come to Siloa last fall and plunged his family into veritable ruin. Girion recognized it too, and though a measure of hardship had been brought upon his family by the excessive taxation, it was nowhere near the degree that afflicted the Kingblades. Regardless, he knew that Aradis would be more inflamed than he. So, laying his hand upon Aradis' arm, he whispered, "Don't do anything foolish."

Aradis hissed back, "Gladly would I embrace folly if it meant striking down the very one who brought my family to so much misery! Curse that vile Elf Fragezi! How dare he show his face this close to Siloa!"

Meanwhile, the Plains-Elf had gone on with his announcement, "Of course, all the people there will be asleep; they will not be expecting us. But when they hear us coming, some of them will undoubtedly be aroused, so we must do what is necessary to achieve our objective before they have a chance to ready themselves for aught done in defense. We will seize several of the weaker folk instantly as hostages, for that will greatly dampen the petty farmers' instincts to do something rash. Several of you will stand ready with torches to set the town ablaze if there is any trouble. Upon my word, do not delay to kill the hostages or light up their ramshackle homes if I so direct you."

"But Captain Fragezi," one of the Elves farther back called out, "do you really think that if word of this reaches the surrounding villages that the Sardolia will not be brought into disrepute throughout all Velaris? For it may be told that we were the instigators of the violence and bloodshed."

Aradis was nearly beside himself. From where he lay in the tall, dark wheat, he seethed like a great cauldron ready to boil over. Were he able, he would have charged into the midst of these brigands and slaughtered every last one of them singlehandedly. Girion was rather cold than hot, listening grimly to all the heartless cruelty that was about to be unleashed on the softly slumbering folk of Siloa. Hatred of Menfolk had long been simmering in Velaris, but now it was about to erupt in a gross display of Elven treachery and contempt.

Fragezi responded pedantically, "We've already been through all this. Do not concern yourself with such things, Sandesso, for there will either be none of Siloa left alive to tell of this night, or the only ones who will be able to verify the tale will be Menfolk, and it is widely known that Menfolk have traitorous, war-mongering tongues. Aye, if perchance the village is utterly destroyed this night, other folk may even rejoice that Siloa is no more, for what use has Velaris for the children of Men?" Then he laughed wickedly, and there was a derisive snickering also among the rest of the company. "But if we can manage it," Fragezi went on, "it would likely serve the Ruphani better if we cowed them into submission and received agreement from them to pay the increase in their taxes. For even a Manfellow is of more use alive than dead if he can fatten the treasury of Aragest!" Again, there was unwholesome guffawing among the Elves. And again, Aradis felt his blood blazing like his father's furnace.

Fragezi explained further, "You must all understand that the goal of this venture is to make an example of Siloa to all the Menfolk, for in so doing, we shall achieve greater control over them. Bearing this in mind, our first order is to seize the hostages, and those of you I have charged with this, make it your aim to choose for the greater part pretty young girls, fair Maenas, for they shall be pleasing to both us and the Ruphani. Oh yes, the Ruphani will be very pleased indeed." Once more, there was dark laughter among the Plains-Elves.

Aradis, gritting his teeth, whispered, "Mellora! They will surely take Mellora!"

Fragezi continued, "And while that is being tended to, those of you charged with torches must get into position. The people of Siloa will gather in the street, and there I will make the demands of a tax increase. If the people comply, we will ride off with our hostages, and they are to be made servants of the Ruphani. In this we shall justify ourselves, saying that the hostages are taken in place of the tax money which they will most assuredly be unable to pay. And what father or brother will fail to work all the more to win back his daughter or sister? And verily, if word spreads of this, it shall rather benefit us, for it will strike fear of the Sardolia into the hearts of Men. But concern yourselves not with the rest of Velaris, for to them this deed will seem right and just. We shall all be held guiltless, I tell you. As I have been saying, the taxes must be paid, and if the money is not to be had, then the families of those negligent louts must pay in service. Are not taxes the law of the land? And is not failure to pay them ultimately an act of defiance against the Ruphani?"

"Aye, Captain Fragezi," a chorus of voices emphatically replied.

The Plains-Elf went on, "But as I said before, any fool who acts in force against us is to be killed on the spot, and I will warn the people that if any seek to resist us, the hostages will pay with their lives, and the town shall be turned to ashes. If that miserable blacksmith's son is about, you can be sure he will give us trouble, for thrice he insulted our tax collectors last autumn. And when I myself came to Siloa that same season, having been informed of his impudence, he spoke many rash words even to me, Fragezi, a captain of the Sardolia! It was only the counsel of my son Carello that stayed my sword from lopping off his head then and there. However, the course of sparing him proved to be fortunate, for at that time it would not have been expedient to ignite a rebellion in this part of Velaris, and rebellion would most certainly have come then at the hands of those bloodthirsty mongrels. No, the time was not ripe, as much else was troubling the Ruphani in that period. But now, let them rebel if they will. Truly, enough Velarisians have naught but contempt for the Menfolk that perhaps we shall be able to crush their contumacy once and for all. But keep an eye out for that lad, and mark me well: if he should attempt aught tonight, he will sorely regret it, for Carello is not with me now to arrest my blade."

It took every fiber of Aradis' being to not leap up and run in a blind rage to slay Fragezi. But Girion's grip upon his arm was firm, and Aradis knew any rash action such as this would now only lead to their demise.

Fragezi then turned to two Plains-Elves near the front of the company and said, "Now, Hilleggo and Dasari, you two are to ride back eastward until you encounter the other dispatch of the Sardolia. Relay to them the details of the plan, and if we have not returned to this very spot within the span of half an hour, by all means send the other company on to join us."

Fragezi now turned to face forward again, and his mount reared up in the moonlight. His voice full of malice and ill intent, he cried out, "Now, let us ride swiftly on, for Siloa is near, and let us do what we have come to do. And when we have done it, we shall come back eastward with our fair captives, and make our way northeast to Tellig. After that, we shall send our prisoners on to Aragest. And woe to all whom we find in our path!" With this parting statement, he sped off westward down the road, and the company followed swiftly behind him, save Hilleggo and Dasari, who rode off in the opposite direction. And before long, the thundering hooves passed off into the night.

As soon as the riders were out of earshot, Aradis exploded to Girion, still crouched down among the tall wheat. "Why has such great evil come upon us?" he sputtered. "Why have we in all Orona been chosen to endure such misery? For surely Nagello knew these evil Plains-Elves were on their way to Siloa when he told us not to turn back for any reason. Why has the Danna cursed us like this? Has he sided with those filth of the Sardolia? For he has certainly not sided with us. How can we leave our families to this terrible fate? Of course we cannot outrun riders on horseback, but surely we can do something to help them!"

Girion now laid his hand on Aradis' shoulder and said, "Aradis, you know as well as I do that we must not turn back to Siloa. For if we do, great evil shall come to pass, even as Nagello said it would. Will you so soon forsake your intent to fulfill the task that has been imparted to you? If you cannot endure this task now, how shall you endure it when you must face Ravinia herself? Let us take what we have been given and be on our way. For it was a great mercy granted to us that we were not seen by the Sardolia."

"A mercy indeed!" Aradis returned angrily. "I would rather they had seen us, for then my sword would have cut short the laughter of that villain Fragezi!" Breathing heavily, he continued, "And you, Girion—how could you be so heartless as to turn your back on your family and all your friends and let us be content to simply go on as if nothing had happened?"

"This has nothing to do with my heart, Aradis," Girion said. "We cannot act on the basis of our hearts, as it were. We must act on the basis of what we know. And Nagello told us that if we returned to Siloa, naught but evil would come of it. And, in saying this, he was presenting to us the very words of the Danna."

"Naught but evil shall come of it if we do not go back!" Aradis retorted. "And if the Danna has no more pity on us than to let us suffer in this way, then I would just as soon not go running halfway across the world for him," he finished bitterly.

Girion's voice grew quite stern and emphatic now. "Aradis, you must not say such foolish things. I, too, am terrified of what will befall the people of Siloa tonight. Do not think that I care nothing for our people. Even now my heart breaks for them. But I also know that if the Danna has specially appointed you and me to do his bidding in Orona, and he has sent us a personal messenger to inform us of what we must do and what we must not do, then there would be no greater fools than Aradis Kingblade and Girion Ringmark if we should turn back. And Nagello said also that we must not quit our journey until dawn. I don't know how we shall even reach Tarwyn in time as it is. So, now we must still the voices of our hearts, for the Danna surely knows better than us what the right road is. Come, let us hurry far away from this place before we too are caught in the snare of the Sardolia."

"Too much is asked of us," Aradis fiercely lamented, and he felt his rage burning on his flushed face. "To leave Siloa to its fate, I must slay my own heart."

"So be it," Girion replied, "for there is really nothing we can do for our kin until we get to someplace like Hardonac where we can report the misdeed. You know as well as I that we have been instructed not to stop at any house until we come to that place."

"Aye," Aradis acknowledged resentfully. "And I curse Nagello and the Danna nearly as much as Fragezi for what ill fortune has befallen us."

Girion shook his head and sighed, "Well, be angry then, and call curses upon those who cannot be cursed, but let us not linger here any longer. There is a company of riders just to the east of us, which will arrive at any moment."

Just then, to the east, they heard the sound of dreadful galloping down the road, and Girion shot up, saying, "Quickly, south through the field! We shall gain the road later, once we have passed east of the riders!" Then he ran directly southward at breakneck speed.

But Aradis had not followed Girion. He was, in fact, running in the opposite direction, and before Girion realized it, Aradis had gone all the way back to the road.

"Has your reason been slain along with your heart?" Girion shouted at him across the field.

But it was too late. The riders had come into sight, and although they had not seen Aradis yet, night as it was, they would at any moment distinguish his outline upon the barren country lane. Drawing his sword, Aradis stood ready to slay as many of these riders as he could. It would not be an exaggeration to say that he would rather go down in a fountain of vengeance and blood at that moment than follow the course that had been imparted to him by the Khasidim. Thus, Girion did all he knew to do at that point. He raced back toward Aradis and grabbed his arm to pull him into cover in the field.

"Get off into the field, you idiot!" Girion demanded.

"I would rather die!" Aradis exclaimed, struggling in return.

"You may get your wish!" Girion snapped at him, immediately after hearing a shout from one of the approaching Plains-Elves.

Suddenly, the extremity of their own helplessness and utter inability to rescue the people of Siloa struck Aradis as bluntly as could be, and he realized how grave their own immediate peril really was. Recognizing then what a very foolish thing he had done, he needed no urging from Girion to run south into the wheat field.

The presence of anyone out on the road at night was enough to warrant the Sardolia's attention, especially so with anyone seen fleeing, but even more so when this particular dispatch of the Sardolia was in the midst of carrying out a murderous plot to potentially decimate an entire village of Menfolk. "After those two!" shouted a Plains-Elf angrily, and six riders swerved southward into the field where Aradis and Girion were running.

Now, this particular field had been traversed before by both of the lads, for it lay less than two miles from the Ringmark farm, and although Aradis had just been released from a madness, as it were, he was now able to think quite clearly, and he remembered that a rather short wooden fence lay on the far side of the field, separating the wheat fields of Yerrig Clayspin (in which they had lain when they overheard Fragezi's plan) from those of Pordis Steedback to the south. As the grain was ready for harvest, it was quite high and might well conceal the fence; perhaps the riders would not see the fence in the dark, and their mounts would founder upon it. It was a very small hope, but a hope nonetheless. As he raced alongside Girion, he panted, "Maybe the fence will give them some trouble!"

"I doubt it!" Girion replied, as they hurtled toward it.

The riders were closing in now, and the two fugitives vaulted mightily over the split-rail fence and then veered ever so slightly eastward. Not long afterward, the riders reached the same barrier and their mounts easily cleared it.

Aradis' small hope had been extinguished, and now there were no further saving graces which could aid them against their pursuers. When the Plains-Elves reached them, as they most assuredly would in short order, that would simply be the end of it. But still they ran on; if they must flee without hope, they thought, that would be better than to do nothing at all.

But a grace unforeseen came to them, for the blast of a great horn, dark and high and terrible, piercing the night, came from the north, yet the sound seemed to have come from beyond where the company was stationed on the track to Siloa. It had come from the far side of Dorman's Down, in fact. Moments later, there was the tumultuous blowing of a whole arsenal of horns of varying pitches, and there was yet another pounding of hooves as a group of riders on horseback poured over the wide hill just to the north of the road.

Now, few things indeed would have been sufficient to draw the attention of those six Plains-Elves away from their quarry, but when shouts of alarm and the drawing of blades was heard in the company with which they had come, they turned about and saw that a group of riders, composed of at least one hundred and fifty Barada, had appeared out of the north and was galloping madly down to assault their unit. The fifty or so Elves of the Sardolia were completely caught off guard by this unanticipated force; they were instantaneously thrown into a panic. With a shout of "It's an ambush! Fly! Fly to the east!" from their leader, they sped off down the road in the direction he had ordered, galloping in wild disarray behind him. Aradis and Girion only saw all of this over their shoulders, but not for one instant did they slow down, for they could ill afford even one spare moment for the sake of mere curiosity.

The Siloans' pursuers drew their mounts up and one of them called, "Ho! What's this? We're under attack! But no one knew of our coming! How can this be? Zaladro, you keep on after those two in the field, and we'll go back to help the company. It's probably easiest for you to just kill them, seeing as you'll be taking care of both of them by yourself. Of course, perhaps it would be better to take them for questioning, as they may have been part of this whole surprise attack; their role may have been to draw as many of us away from the company as they could. Ah, I suppose you should just kill them and be done with it. Now do not fail, Zaladro. Surely those two must die this night. Now the rest of us—to the Sardolia!" he shouted, as he turned his steed around and raced back toward the road. Meanwhile, the mysterious riders from the north were still blowing their horns incessantly, as they turned to pursue the fleeing Sardolia eastward down the road.

Now, one rider pursuing them instead of six was an arrangement much more in the fugitives' favor, but still Aradis and Girion bounded madly through the wheat. Thankfully, the time bought for them by the horn blasts, the bewildering appearance of the company out of the north, and the announcing of the Plains-Elf's instructions had given them enough of a lead that they were now climbing a gentle hill. When they reached the top and went down the other side, they would be out of sight from their lone pursuer. Now they both knew they could not ultimately outrun him, so Girion breathlessly proposed, "When we get over the hill, let's run straight east, then lie down and hide in the wheat, and if he finds us, then we fight; if not, we lie hidden until he is gone, and then we go on our way."

In reply, Aradis gasped, "That's better than racing on till he rides us down!"

And so, when they reached the top of the hill, they raced down the other side until their heads were out of sight and then went as far east as they thought time would allow before Zaladro gained the hilltop. Then they threw themselves down in the wheat, facing the direction from which he would come. Aradis laid his hand on Brightbeam's hilt just in case they were found, and Girion tightly clenched his staff.

They were there only a few moments before Zaladro appeared at the top of the hill, riding at full speed. Now he reared his mount up and halted at the crest. While the sounds of frenetic pursuit and the continuous racket of hunters' horns came from the chase on the road, his Elven eyes cast about for any clue as to where his prey had gone. Suddenly, there was a rustling in the grass off to the south, as a deer rose from the grain and bounded off to the west.

"Aha!" Zaladro laughed. "Even the animals have turned against you Menfolk vermin!" he spat, as he rode over to investigate where he thought they lay hidden.

"Now let's go back over the hill before he turns around!" Aradis whispered. "And when we're out of sight, we run like mad and don't stop until we get to Hardonac!"

The lads moved as quietly as they could, crouching down all the while, and as the top of the hill was not far off, they quickly disappeared over the other side, once again out of the Plains-Elf's sight. Having accomplished this maneuver, they took a few deep breaths to calm themselves.

Then they ran straight eastward harder and faster than they had ever run in their lives. If Zaladro had seen them again, they would have been forced to fight him, and he, being a trained warrior of the Sardolia and having the decisive advantage of being on horseback, would almost certainly have subdued and slain them. But the deer which he had so mockingly assumed had betrayed them had, in fact, saved them from his grasp.

They had run perhaps a quarter of a mile east when they turned to the southeast, so as to distance themselves from the road. When they had achieved this goal, they turned straight east again and ran on. A few minutes later, they heard the thundering of hooves off to the north, moving from west to east, and then galloping farther away into the north. They were uncertain as to which group of riders they were hearing, but their hearts rested easier when the beating of hooves became indiscernible.

The two Siloans could hardly think or feel now, as all of their energy, all of their strength, even their very lives, were poured into racing across the Plains of Agleri, fleeing death, which they had so narrowly evaded. For a full hour they ran and ran and ran, until their hearts were weak and their bodies screamed at them, and then they ran some more, for there was nothing to ensure that Zaladro would not find their trail and yet pursue them. Now they knew what Nagello meant when he had warned of a need of haste of which they were yet unaware. Indeed, haste such as this had never befallen either of them. Though there were many lingering fears and sorrows and questions that nagged at them about what had become of their beloved village of Siloa and their families, and about the mysterious militia which had appeared at Dorman's Down, the sheer terror that drove them on through the night largely numbed all those feelings and thoughts. Through these dark hours, they felt almost as if their bodies were carrying them, running on their own without consent of their wills, and their spirits were being borne along in a drunken stupor, barely clinging to their mortal vessels.

And so the night wore on, but, ultimately, the limitations of their flesh would not let them maintain such a great speed, and so they slowed, but yet always ran, never walked. Only once did they stop to relieve themselves, and they did not speak, for they were still numb and had no strength for words. Across the dark plains they went, under moonlight and starlight through golden grain, and the land became smoother as they drew farther away from Rimwold, a change in topography of substantial relief to them, for it made their flight easier.

Several hours before dawn, they had slowed considerably, so that it could not be properly said they were really running any longer. And finally, still with no words passing between them, they mutually agreed to simply walk and not even feign that they were running. Wearily they trudged eastward, and though they were worn far past their limits, they knew they must continue. It could not be assumed, even now, that the Sardolia had given up on finding them or what had even become of the Elven riders. But they did feel safe enough to begin conversing with one another. So, at last, in those few hours before the advent of bright Marda, the sun, they shared their minds and spoke of their own reflections on all that had befallen them. This was much needed for both of them, as many ponderous things had come upon them, such things as would be terrible indeed to bear alone. For Erdion, the Land Beyond the Stars, had intruded quite forcefully into their lives and had launched them on an unthinkable journey, a journey which had already cut their hearts to the core. Not only were they compelled to leave their loved ones behind, they had to press on with the knowledge that cruel Barada planned to enslave or slaughter them. Verily, before even an hour had passed upon their journey, they themselves had to flee for their very lives.

As they talked, they turned back north toward the road, and the sun rose and the prairie was set ablaze with crimson and gold fire. The dawn of Agleri was a glorious sight to behold, and it brought new hope and strength to the two travelers. A cool spring breeze had begun to blow, and the stalks of wheat nodded sleepily as dawn came upon them. This was a sunrise they would not soon forget.

"The Song of Marda," Aradis sighed wistfully. "I don't think it's ever been so beautiful to me as it is this morning."

"A long, terrible, black night is behind us now," Girion breathed. "Yet Marda sings most when night reigns most bitterly."

A particularly effulgent sunray seemed to ratify Girion's statement, as it shot across the waving grasses of Agleri.

Seeing this, the two friends smiled at each other, treasuring the small solace that could be afforded them at that moment. Death had sought them earnestly that night, but now they stood safely at dawn's doorstep.

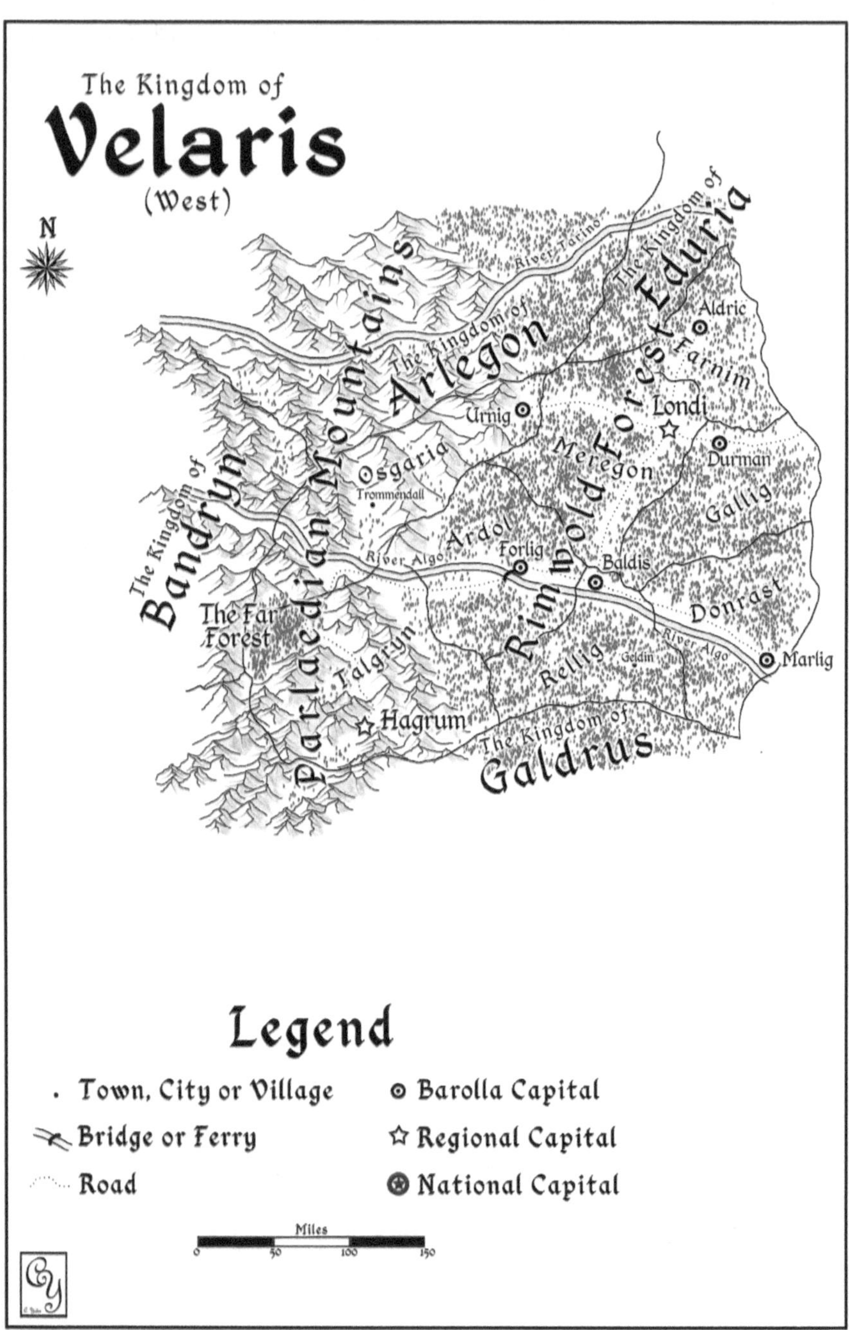

The Kingdom of
Velaris
(West)
N
Bandryn Mountains
The Kingdom of Bandryn
The Far Forest
Parlaedian Mountains
The Kingdom of Arlegon
River Torino
The Kingdom of Eduria
Aldric
Farnim
Urnig
Londi
Durman
Osgaria
Trommendall
Meregon
Gallig
Ardol
Forlig
River Algo
Rimbold Forest
Baldis
Donrast
Talgryn
Rellig
Geldin
River Algo
Marlig
Hagrum
The Kingdom of
Galdrus
Legend
Town, City or Village
Bridge or Ferry
Road
Barolla Capital
Regional Capital
National Capital
Miles
0   50   100   150

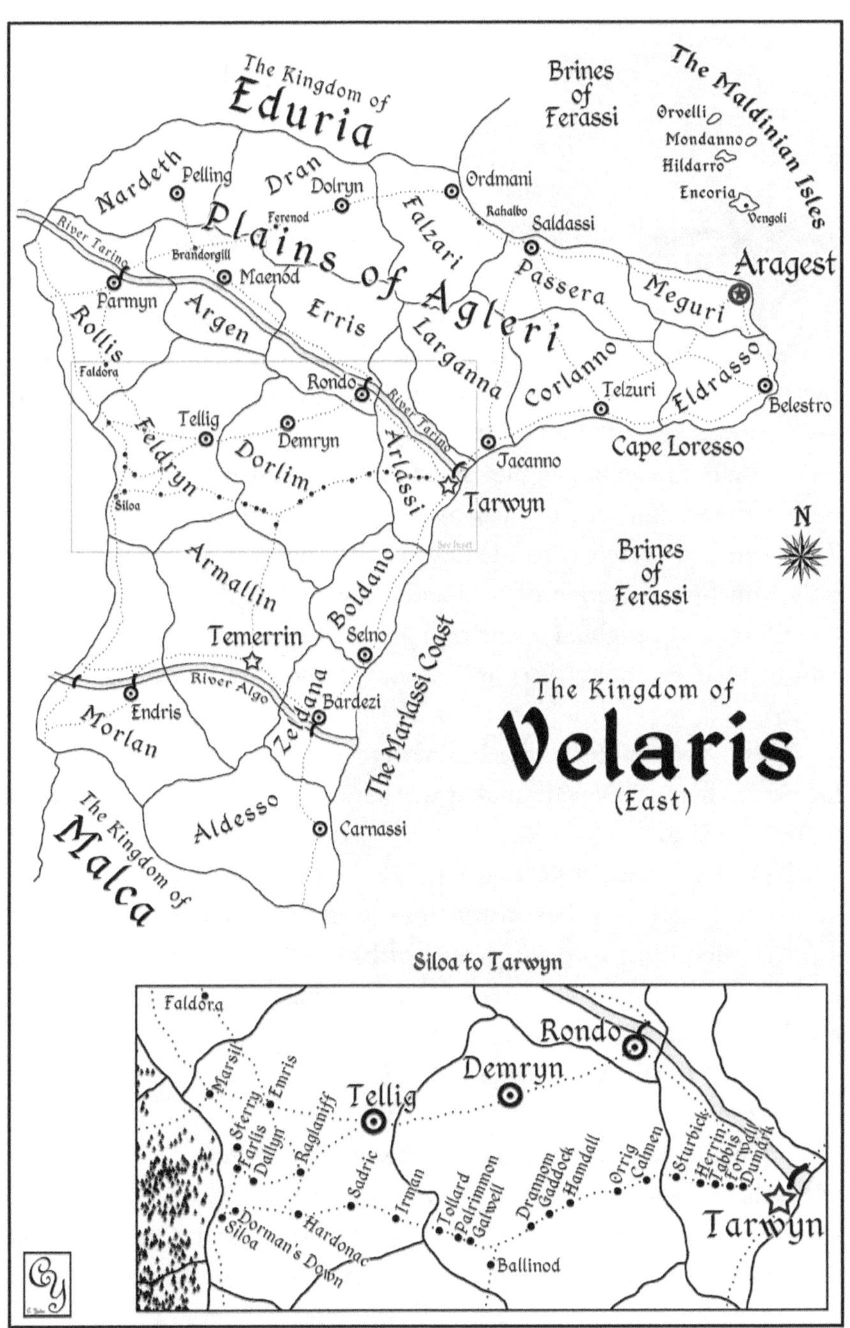

The Kingdom of
Eduria
Brines
of
Ferassi
The Maldinian Isles
Orvelli
Mondanno
Hildarro
Encoria
Vengoli
Nardeth
Pelling
Dran
Dolryn
Ordmani
Aragest
River Tarino
Ferenod
Falzari
Rahalbo
Saldassi
Brandorgill
Plains of Agleri
Passera
Meguri
Parmyn
Maenod
Rollis
Argen
Erris
Larganna
Corlanno
Eldrasso
Faldora
Rondo
River Tarino
Telzuri
Belestro
Tellig
Dorlim
Demryn
Arlassi
Jacanno
Cape Loresso
Feldryn
Siloa
Tarwyn
See Inset
Brines
of
Ferassi
N
Armallin
Boldano
Selno
Temerrin
The Marlassi Coast
The Kingdom of
Velaris
(East)
River Algo
Bardezi
Endris
Zeldana
Morlan
Aldesso
Carnassi
The Kingdom of
Malca
Siloa to Tarwyn
Faldora
Rondo
Marsil
Emris
Demryn
Sterry
Raglaniff
Tellig
Fartis
Dallyn
Sturbick
Hertin
Sadric
Orrig
Labbis
Irman
Drannom
Calmen
Forwall
Dumark
Tollard
Gaddock
Palrimmon
Hamdall
Galwell
Dorman's Down
Hardonac
Tarwyn
Siloa
Ballinod

The Waybread of Erdion

ow the Siloans climbed a gentle bank and upon coming to the top, they saw the road to Hardonac lying about a half mile away. It was rather easy to pick out because a row of stout trees lined each side of the road for about two miles along this section. However, the lads both remembered that the trees stopped several miles short of Hardonac, so they knew they still had some distance to go before they could get some proper rest.

But the woeful state of their bodies could not be ignored any longer. They were desperately exhausted as they had never been before and terribly faint from privation of food and water, and so they collapsed upon the hilltop and delighted in the cool ground beneath their backs, as they rubbed their throbbing legs and massaged their tormented knees and ankles.

After a few minutes of this business, they sat up and Aradis turned to look at his friend. "Do you think it was a mistake for us to leave Siloa last night?" he asked.

"Not in the least," Girion replied. "I think it would have been most unwise to ignore Nagello's instructions to depart immediately. Without a doubt, submitting to the mandates of Erdion was the proper course to pursue. But that certainly doesn't lessen the pain of possibly losing our families and our homes. Not one bit."

"No, it doesn't," Aradis echoed. "I just wonder if they're alive or dead, captive or free."

"I don't suppose we shall discover that until we return, and who knows when that will be," Girion muttered. "But all the same, whether they are living or slain, we must commit their fates to the Danna's keeping. Had we stayed, we would have been apportioned the same lot as them but that was evidently not to be our destiny. To be perfectly honest, I think things would have gone worse if you had been in Siloa when the Sardolia arrived, if in fact they did. For you would certainly have tried to resist them and that would have prompted them to kill the hostages and you as well."

"You don't think anyone in our village fought back?" Aradis queried.

"Aradis, we don't even know for certain whether the Sardolia reached Siloa or what happened if they did go there," Girion returned. "I'm rather inclined to believe they did not, for once the second dispatch fled from the militia that came over Dorman's Down, we heard another group fleeing eastward, and I think we have good reason to believe that was the dispatch led by Fragezi. Indeed, what other mounted Barada would have been coming from the west? But if what we heard were Fragezi's unit, then I think Siloa lay safe last night, for there was simply not enough time for the Elves to have carried out their plot there."

"Then again, you always err in favor of optimism," Aradis muttered. "If that were Fragezi and his company, they had hostages in tow, no doubt."

"Perhaps, but I strongly advise you not to brood on the matter, for, in so doing, you shall only bring more misery on yourself, and if your family is in captivity, you accomplish naught for their cause merely by worrying about it."

"Keep your counsel, Girion, and I will keep mine," Aradis rejoined. "If I wish to worry, then worry I shall. And I am exceedingly worried that my sister has been kidnapped by Fragezi and his deplorable cohorts. Although, for the time being, I will consider my family to be alive, for that will help me, I think, to press on. And if it is not so, then later my heart shall be more fiercely rent asunder, but for now, I will be consoled."

Girion was looking intently at Aradis when he noticed the silver chain around his neck. "What is that?" he asked, nodding at it. In truth, he had an ulterior motive for inquiring about it, for he wished to divert Aradis' thoughts from his fretful ruminations about his family and Siloa.

"Oh, this?" Aradis mumbled, as he fingered the chain and drew out the medallion. "Nagello gave me this and told me that it would somehow—what did he say again? That it would be a sign to those who doubted our mission or something of that sort."

"Curious," Girion said, as he held the half-leaf medallion and carefully examined it.

"Do you have any inkling as to what it might be?" Aradis inquired.

"Just a medallion, I guess," Girion replied. "It's like nothing I've seen before. But half of it seems to be missing."

"That's what I thought too," Aradis said.

Girion, still looking at his companion, noticed that the scabbard and sword at his left side were ones he had never seen him bear before. "The sword and sheath," Girion indicated, nodding at them. "Also gifts from Nagello?"

"No, from my father," Aradis explained. "The blade is named Brightbeam. There's apparently a story of some significance that goes with it, and my father said he would tell it to me upon my return."

"I see," Girion returned, looking the blade up and down once more. Then, glancing up at his friend, he asked, "Say, did Nagello tell you how much money he gave us for the voyage to the Elder Forest?"

"No, he didn't," Aradis replied, as he began unfastening the money pouch from his belt. "I suppose we should count it, eh? I would hate to arrive at Tarwyn only to discover that we've been had for fools, having insufficient funds to purchase passage to our destination."

"I very seriously doubt Nagello would have failed to give us the proper sum," Girion remarked, somewhat annoyed at Aradis for his continued skepticism.

Aradis drew open the pouch and dumped its contents on the ground, and both of the lads' jaws dropped open as several dozen shiny silver coins spilled onto the dewy earth.

"Aradis, these are all skrannas!" Girion exclaimed, as he began sorting them out into stacks of four.

"I don't believe I've ever seen more than two skrannas at a time in my entire life," Aradis excitedly declared, marveling at the wealth which lay before them. "Since these are all skrannas, that would mean we've got the equivalent of several taldryns here, right? How many skrannas are equal to a taldryn again?"

"Eight," Girion returned. Then, having just finished totaling the coins, he announced, "Thirty-two skrannas. That's half the worth of an orgella! Unbelievable. We've been given a fortune, Aradis."

Aradis now looked back to the west and murmured, "If I had known we had so much money in that pouch, I would certainly have given some of it to our families before we departed."

Girion shook his head exasperatedly, replying, "That would have been extremely unwise, as I don't believe we have a single coin to spare. All of these skrannas will have to go toward purchasing berthing and rations aboard a ship to Byram. Do you really think Nagello would have told us to use this money for our voyage to the Elder Forest if he did not intend for us to employ it for that express purpose?"

It was now Aradis' turn to shake his head, as he began collecting the skrannas and putting them back in the leather pouch. "You've really given full assent and credence to everything Nagello said, haven't you?"

"Of course," Girion returned, blinking. "It's not as if he didn't give us some very good reasons to believe that he was one of the Hadathi and that he was, in fact, a representative of Telyon."

"Telyon this, Telyon that," Aradis sassed. "As near as I can figure it, the only halfway decent thing Telyon's done for us so far is help us escape from the Sardolia. Come to think of it, he probably had nothing to do with that. That deer likely just happened to be in the right place at the right time—for our purposes, that is."

"You're so sour, Aradis, that you'd put Galliga Greyloam's pickled radishes to shame," Girion yawned, as he lay back upon the grass and looked up at the sky. He was weary enough as it was without having to constantly argue with Aradis.

"Oh, not now, you lazy loafer!" Aradis chided, as he tossed a handful of dew-covered grass at his companion's face. "It's still some miles to Hardonac, and we've got to keep on moving to have any chance of reaching Tarwyn in time, right? Isn't that what you yourself said, Mister Broadbuckle?" Aradis teased, rising to his feet.

"I will most heartily devour my own words," Girion complied, as he too wearily stood up.

In the meantime, the Song of Marda had gone on, and now the plains were illuminated by the pure golden sunshine of that joyous period right after dawn.

"Do you really think it's safe for us to get back on the road yet?" Aradis asked, as his eyes scanned the wide trail, which led to the town of Hardonac.

Girion ran his hand through his curly black hair, as he often did when thinking hard, and responded, "If the Sardolia's goal is to return to Tellig as quickly as possible, as it most assuredly is, regardless of what happened to the second company, then Fragezi and friends will likely be riding back the way they came, as it would be more direct; I doubt they'll be coming through Hardonac. So I would say we should be able to return to the road without greatly endangering ourselves."

"All right then," said Aradis, as he marched off toward the tree-lined track.

When they reached the road and continued on eastward, they almost felt as if they had come out of the wild and were now back in civilization. And, in a peculiar way, they actually felt safer traveling on the wide lane to Hardonac than traversing open country.

They continued for ten minutes or so until they heard the neighing of a horse behind them. Alarmed, they turned about and there, in the distance but coming toward them, was a farm wagon driven by a Manfellow, pulled by two sturdy horses. Quietly, Girion advised, "Don't act like we have anything to be concerned about. Just keep walking, as if we are simply on our way to Hardonac."

"We are on our way to Hardonac," Aradis remarked drily.

Girion laughed, "But we are not *simply* on our way to Hardonac. I just don't want any trouble, you know. But that fellow shouldn't do us any ill. It's not as if he's an agent of the Sardolia, eh?"

They walked on and, before long, the wagon overtook them. The Manfellow driving it brought the horses to a standstill and called out a cheery, "Hullo and bright Marda to ya!" to the two Siloans.

He looked a very amiable sort of fellow, much like the majority of the folk of Siloa (barring a few curmudgeons like Marnis Applecot and Bernalla Elmensill). He had a brown, grizzled beard and somewhat shaggy hair, cheerful green eyes and looked to be middle-aged. He was dressed as are nearly all the men of Agleri, in farmer's garb of tunic, boots and breeches, all in variations of brown.

"Bright Marda!" Aradis and Girion replied, though not quite as perkily as the wagon driver.

The man looked them up and down and then remarked, "You two remind me of a pair of horses I had once, the day I drove them all the way from Brandorgill to Ferenod without a single rest, which is quite a long way, mind you. Those poor creatures were so wasted by the end of the day, they were just as likely to fall asleep standing on their heads as they were lying down in a pile of straw."

"I take it we look much the worse for the wear, then?" Girion replied, leaning on his staff.

"Well, if not worse for the wear, then worn to your worst!" the driver chuckled. "I'd wager you've been traveling quite far with no pause, eh? Now, I mean no offense but the tired look of you fellows doesn't come with the ordinary fatigue of a journey. I'll tell you what—if you'd rather walk on, go right ahead, but my wagon and I wouldn't mind a bit having the company if you're going on to Hardonac and points east."

"As a matter of fact," Aradis spoke up cautiously, "we are going to Hardonac . . . and points east."

"Hop up here then!" the man sang out heartily, banging the seat of his wagon. "You can help yourself to some breakfast in the back too if you like," he said, motioning to piles of various vegetables in the wagon bed, which were accompanied by a great many bulging burlap sacks and several wooden trunks.

Aradis and Girion looked at each other, then back at the smiling Manfellow. Having no misgivings about one who seemed to be merely a common farmer, they climbed aboard the wagon and sat beside him. He curtly called out "Hup!" and slapped the reins, and the horses began to trot forward again.

"Here, have a drink, lads," the driver offered, as he handed them a skin filled with cool water; of this gift they eagerly partook. They were severely dehydrated from having journeyed all night with no reprieve, and the pure liquid trickling down their dry throats was to them even as an elixir of life. When they had sated their thirst, they reached into the back of the wagon and procured some of the savory greens that were strewn about there. The lads began to consume these and felt significantly revived after doing so.

"I'm Harlin Halehand, by the way," the man said, as the wagon rolled merrily on down the road, "from the town of Faldora up north a piece; although this morning I've just come from Raglaniff. I'm a healer by trade; that's why I'm gallivanting about so far from home. Got a summons to go east and south to Temerrin and to be quick about it, so I left Faldora yesterday morning. By tonight, I hope to strike Ballinod, which would put me in Temerrin the following night. But you all aren't likely going as far as Temerrin, eh?"

"Farther, actually," Girion replied. Aradis would have answered, but he only had a vague idea of where Temerrin actually was, so he was uncertain if they were going past it or not. "But not in the same direction," Girion added. "I suppose you'll be turning south at some point to get to Ballinod, but we're going nearly straight east."

"I see," Harlin said, nodding. "Then you'll be wanting me to drop you off in Palrimmon or Galwell. Galwell's a bit farther along, and I know a family there that'll keep you quite well for the night—for free, I might add—and send you on your way."

"Really?" Aradis inquired. "If that were so, we should thank both you and them tremendously!"

"Who wouldn't after some of Hirana's cooking?" Harlin chortled. "She's the lady of the house; a regular queen she is, with hospitality to die for. And Andurad her husband is a right fine fellow. Wonderful children they've got too."

Looking about at the splendid prairie landscape in the light of early morning, Girion prompted Harlin, "Why were your services needed all the way in Temerrin? That seems a terribly long journey, even for a healer."

"Oh," Harlin mumbled. "Well, ah, the one who took ill is the Regent there, and he had asked for me to come in particular. And when a Regent says for a body to do something, well, you know, it's best not to keep him waiting too long."

"You were personally summoned by a Regent?" Aradis exclaimed. "Why that's practically like being summoned by the Ruphani!"

"Well, not quite!" Harlin laughed. "It's not really as big as all that. It's just he's heard about my work, I suppose, and wants to see what all I can do for him."

"Modest to a fault you are," Girion genially remarked. "That is quite an honor to be trusted enough by a Regent for him to place his health in your hands. Do you travel often then?"

"More often than not," Harlin replied. "I've got a network of stables available to me across this region of Velaris, so I can switch out my horses and cover more ground in a day. If it's a summons for an urgent job like this one, I can make a hundred or more miles a day that way, if need be, though I must start the day well before sunrise and finish several hours after sunset. You see, I used to go around on horseback and just put pouches of herbs slung on each side of the saddle, but as I've gotten more skill as a healer, I've unfortunately been needing more equipment instead of less. It seems to me it should be the opposite, but so it goes. Anyway, the past few years I've been taking a wagon, so I can carry all my equipment, potions, herbs, powders and whatnot. And I load up a lot of my own food for my journeys. That's what all those vegetables in the back are," he said, motioning to the little heaps of greens in the wagon bed. "But enough about me. I don't believe I've gotten your names," the healer remarked.

"Aradis Kingblade," Aradis offered.

"And Girion Ringmark," Girion added.

"Fine to make your acquaintance," Harlin returned, smiling. "And where are you headed?"

"To Tarwyn," Aradis replied. "And we've got to try to get there by nightfall two days after tomorrow."

"Then it's a very good thing you've come aboard my wagon," Harlin noted. "For it is highly doubtful you could make that journey on foot in time. Tarwyn is nearly two hundred miles east of here, and even if I drop you off at Galwell tonight, you'll have to march long and hard every day to make it. What's the rush, then? Have you got to catch a ship?"

"Aye," Girion confirmed. "To the Fontskals and thence to Byram."

"That's a far journey indeed for a few Menfolk of Agleri. And, if you don't mind my asking, what is your business in Byram?"

"We're seeking our fortunes there," Aradis hastily answered, uncertain of what Girion would say if he hesitated. He was afraid Girion might admit they had been sent there by the Danna, and this might well result in them walking the rest of the way to Hardonac if Harlin didn't fancy carting around a pair of apparent loons.

After Aradis' response, Harlin chuckled a little and then said, "Well, there's probably no better time for you two to be doing that sort of thing, being young and all. Go see the breadth of Orona while you can, I suppose, for sooner or later your bodies will give out, and you'll need people like me to fix you up. And where are you from then?"

"Siloa," Girion replied. "Do you know it?"

"Aye," Harlin answered. "It lies back west down this same road. Quite a small place on the edge of Rimwold, as I recall. I've been through there twice—no thrice—but that was years ago. I remember thinking to myself that it was a very peaceful place with the best sort of Menfolk, kind and sincere."

Aradis had a good feeling about Harlin; he himself seemed kind and sincere, and Aradis felt they could trust him. And so he mumbled, "It may not be so peaceful after last night."

"How's that?" Harlin asked, his eyebrows raised.

Girion bit his lip and then elucidated, "Harlin, we traveled from there through the night, as I'm sure you may have guessed, and, on the road, we encountered a unit of the Sardolia. Now I love Velaris as much as the next fellow, but Captain Fragezi of the Sardolia, who is the chief officer in Tellig, is a black-hearted Barada to the core, for we overheard him giving instructions to kidnap innocents of the town in the middle of the night if its people would not comply with increased taxes, and we—"

"Why that band of scum!" Harlin interjected. "I know the Sardolia's been up to no good, and we Menfolk have much to fear from its agents. And you needn't hold your tongue regarding the Ruphani when you're around me either. Why that pompous, indolent, conniving, Man-hating miser has been stirring up trouble for years and would have all the Menfolk of Velaris groveling in the dirt if he had his way! It wouldn't surprise me one bit to learn that he had a hand in this plot you're telling me about. Tell me more, so that when we get to Hardonac, we can ensure that all Velaris is privy to this treachery! I must know though—why did you come east instead of going back west to your kin?"

"The Sardolia saw us on the road, and we had to flee for our lives," Aradis explained. "Also, it would have been impossible for us to reach Siloa before they did, so we felt we could do more good by bringing word of all this to Hardonac."

"You made a wise choice," Harlin concurred. "And fortunate it was that I came upon you. Now I would hear the full extent of those marauders' mischief."

And so Aradis and Girion together explained all that they had witnessed the previous night regarding the incident with the Sardolia. Harlin was especially intrigued by the unexpected appearance of the other force which had come against the second unit of the Sardolia, but he was just as baffled as they were about it and could not guess who composed it or from whence it had come.

When he had heard all, he said, "We shall come to Hardonac in a short while. I know a man there by the name of Redic Twineweft. He has quite a few contacts in surrounding villages, and he can get the true story out about this faster, I think, than the Ruphani can spread a false account to cover his part in all this. This could become a scandal throughout all Velaris, my friends, and I hope it does. Redic will also best know what to do in order to rescue any of your fellows or kin who may have been taken captive. He's a good man, Redic. You can tell him your story when we get to town, and although I've got to be on my way as soon as possible after I've switched out my horses, you two can decide if you want to continue on with me or return to Siloa. Redic can help you with travel arrangements if you'd like to go back."

"We can't go back to Siloa," Aradis said morosely. "We have to go on to Byram, at least for now."

"So be it then," Harlin replied. "But sure as the Brines reek of salt and foam, there's more to your story than simply seeking your fortunes in another Neathmarda. For surely you would have to be attending to more serious business than that to abandon your families to the villainous designs of the Sardolia."

"There is indeed more to our story," Girion said guardedly, "and we may yet speak of it before we part."

"No need for it now though," Harlin remarked. "We'll arrive at Hardonac soon enough and when we do, I'll purchase you both some victuals and supplies at the Redhouse, the inn there, which is right next to Redic's place. We'll have a little chat with Mister Twineweft, and after we've taken care of things at the stables, you two can lie down in the back of my wagon and rest as long as you need to as we make our way eastward."

"You're very kind, Harlin," Girion gushed. "We can't thank you enough."

"Don't be silly," the healer laughed. "You boys have had a rough night, and you've got a far journey ahead, and, to be quite honest, it's the least I can do."

As they went on, the three Menfolk spoke more of happenings in Velaris and their families and the malevolent machinations of the Ruphani until the wooden dwellings of Hardonac came into sight, welcoming them from across the plains. Before long, they had reached the heart of town, which was rather reminiscent of Siloa, only there were several buildings with two stories and probably twice as many buildings altogether. The Redhouse was indeed red (it was one of the buildings with two stories), and it lay in the very center of town on the south side of the road by a sort of market where local farmers had raised stalls and were selling their produce.

Harlin told the Siloans to wait by the wagon while he hopped out and went into the Redhouse. In the meantime, Aradis and Girion climbed out of the wagon, leaned against it and watched the people of Hardonac going about their business in the marketplace. It certainly reminded them of Siloa, but it was unquestionably more hectic, as there were a great many more people going here and there. A few minutes later, Harlin emerged from the inn with two packs of supplies, which he flung in the back of the wagon, as he explained they were for the lads' journey.

"How much do we owe you for all this?" Girion asked, reaching for his coin pouch and then realizing that he had not brought it. Clearing his throat, he caught Aradis' attention and nodded toward the pouch, which Nagello had given him.

"Keep your coins, lads," Harlin said, when he saw Aradis starting to open the pouch. "You'll certainly need them if you're going all the way to Byram. I'm going to see Redic now to bring him out here to talk to you," he called, as he went over to a timbered house just to the east of the Redhouse. He knocked on the door, which opened a few moments later to reveal a balding, somewhat stout man with strong arms and a thick brown beard. After a short conversation, Harlin and the man returned to the wagon.

"This is Redic Twineweft, a very good friend of mine," Harlin announced, "and these fine lads," he continued, motioning to the Siloans, "are Aradis Kingblade and Girion Ringmark of the town of Siloa."

"Bright Marda and happy to meet you," Redic said in a low, robust voice. "Harlin tells me you've got some news that I would be interested in."

"That we do," Girion agreed.

And so they summarily told Redic the gist of what they had told Harlin about their encounter with the Sardolia the night before. When they had finished, Harlin turned to Redic and said, "Spread the word about this as quickly as you can, my friend, for the Ruphani will certainly try to hide the truth from Velaris. Now these lads must be in Tarwyn in just a few days and haven't time to rescue their own people, whatever has befallen them. So please do what you can to help the poor people of Siloa, and I will speak with you again about this matter when I return from Temerrin. I was called up to heal the Regent there, so, unfortunate as it is, we've got to be along to the stables immediately, as I must reach Ballinod tonight."

"I understand, Harlin," Redic said, as he heartily shook the healer's hand. "I'll do what I can." Then he turned to Aradis and Girion and shook their hands also as he said, "Be sure that the truth about this will be known from the Brines to the Far Forest if I have anything to do with it. And whatever people of yours are captive or in distress, I will do everything in my power to rescue them. And may the Danna hasten your horses!" And with that, the three travelers climbed into the wagon, and once again they were off as Redic waved farewell to them.

The stables were on the east end of town. When they reached them, Harlin once more left the wagon and went into the old wooden livery. Before long, two men emerged from a side door, leading two fine workhorses. Expert as they were, it took them a short time indeed, especially with the healer's help, to exchange Harlin's wearied horses for these fresh ones. Harlin thanked the men as they returned to the stables, and, climbing up into the wagon again, he bade Aradis and Girion lie down in the back. This they did after they had arranged several soft sacks to make a suitable place of repose.

"Help yourself to whatever food you find back there," Harlin said, as the wagon rolled down the road. "But I'd say you lads need sleep more than anything else."

That they did, and before long, even though the back of a wagon was certainly not the most comfortable place to sleep, Aradis and Girion fell into a dreary slumber of sheer exhaustion.

Throughout the day, they stirred only a few times, usually when Harlin stopped at a town to acquire fresh horses, which happened thrice after Hardonac as Aradis recalled. The landscape changed little as they drew eastward; in the region of Agleri there was little of note. There were only farm towns, golden fields and rolling prairies, with the occasional stand of trees as a windbreak. Aradis had never in his life been this far from home, and had he not been so utterly drained of strength and vigor, he would have watched intently as the miles rolled by. Girion had a great love of geography and maps and such, and he certainly would also have loved taking in every moment of this journey, but he too could do little but sprawl wearily upon the sacks of herbs and doze fitfully throughout the day. Harlin would inform them of their progress when they fleetingly awakened, but said little else. He mentioned the towns at which they had briefly halted: Sadric, Irman and Tollard. And every time they were roused, even a little, he encouraged them to eat a bit. But of their journey to Byram he inquired not.

And so it came about that, as the sun was setting and the Plains of Agleri were again made red and aurous by Marda's fire, they were passing the town of Palrimmon of which Harlin had spoken. And perhaps half an hour later, they came to the little village of Galwell where they were to part ways from Harlin. Well-kept farm cottages lined the lane, which ran through town, and all the windows were lit by the merry flames of hearthfires. They passed through the village and then the healer steered the wagon down a little lane and up to a farmyard that lay just north of the road beyond the eastern edge of the town.

"All right, lads," he said, as he leapt to the ground. "Here's where we say farewell. I hope the best for you and am sorry indeed about what happened to your village. Know that dear Redic will do all he can to make things right for Siloa, and know that I wish greatly that you find what you're looking for in Byram, whatever it may be. I would have liked to have spoken with you more about it, but sleep was what you needed most."

As he was saying this, Aradis and Girion grabbed the packs Harlin had gotten them and climbed out of the wagon.

"You cannot possibly know how much we appreciate all you've done for us, Mister Halehand," Girion said, enthusiastically clasping the healer's hand. "Had it not been for you, we would likely be only a meager distance past Hardonac now, and we would have as of yet had no rest. And these supplies—thank you for them also. And for having us speak to Redic. And for bringing us to a place where we might spend the night at no cost. Your kindness is overwhelming."

The healer merely smiled and replied, "I too have tasted of the Waybread of Erdion and would gladly share it with others."

"What did you say?" Aradis asked, startled.

"I said that I have oft partaken of the Waybread of Erdion, and it is my pleasure to share it with you. You know—the Waybread of Erdion—the good and timely provision of Telyon."

Aradis felt his heart stir at these words, especially because Harlin had unexpectedly called the Danna by his venerable, ancient name, and he quietly said, "Good sir, I thought you might think us fools if we told you the real reason for our going to Byram, but what you just said has convinced me otherwise. The truth is that one of the Hadathi came to us and commanded us in the name of Telyon to go to Byram and free the Elder Forest from a powerful Witch named Ravinia."

Now Harlin was somewhat taken aback, and Aradis felt somewhat sheepish for having blurted out everything all at once. But the healer grew more somber than surprised in a few moments and said, "Well now. Indeed, I did not expect it to be anything such as that, but make no mistake—I believe you, lad. I really do. And I don't know you from anyone, but I know Telyon well, and this situation has his mark all over it."

Both of the lads were struck by the singular oddity of this remark. How could Harlin claim to know Telyon well? Was Telyon even the sort of being who could be known, in the customary sense, by the Hadathi, much less the Barada?

The healer continued, "Two untried, unassuming lads—and no offense do I mean by that, dear friends—are exactly the sort of persons Telyon would send to do something of that nature. It's simply his style, if you know what I mean. Oh, I definitely believe you, and I am all the more glad I happened upon you on the road."

"As are we," Girion remarked.

Harlin continued, "There are, of course, many, if not most, who would think your mind already harvested if you told them the truth, but there are others like myself who understand there is more to Orona than sand and sea, forests and fields, mountains and men. And who am I to tell Telyon he cannot do such things? He has done them before; can he not do them again?"

Then the healer sighed and said, "In truth, I would learn much more from you of all this, but you must be off to bed, and I must be on my way to Ballinod. One last thing I must ask you: will you be going back to Siloa?"

"We dearly hope so," Aradis replied solemnly.

"Thayah," returned Harlin, as he walked across the yard and knocked on the farmhouse door. (Thayah was an old Mannish word meaning "may it so be.") There was a stirring in the house, and the voices of excited children were roused. The door swung open and a middle-aged man, a farmer of Agleri through and through, stepped out.

"Why, if it isn't Harlin Halehand!" he exclaimed, as he embraced his old friend. "How have you been, my dear fellow! And have I the pleasure of affording you lodging for the night?"

"I have been better than ever, Andurad," Harlin returned jovially, "but, unfortunately, I must be on to Ballinod for the evening. But I would ask for lodging for two good friends of mine," he continued, waving his arm toward the Siloans. "These are Aradis Kingblade and Girion Ringmark, travelers from over by Rimwold on their way to the Brines. If you might, treat them as you would me and hasten them on their journey."

Andurad turned to the Siloans and laughed, "All right then, if Harlin commends you lads to me, I must surely quarter you as he asks. Come inside, my friends. My lovely wife Hirana has yet some stew on the fire, and I'll have my little ones Fayna and Caldric prepare mats for you to sleep upon."

"Thank you, dear Andurad," Harlin said, grasping his friend's hand. "And now I must be on my way. I promise I will stop in and see you when

I return from Temerrin. The Regent's taken ill, and I've been called to fix him up."

"Now as for you, Aradis and Girion," the healer went on, turning to the two Siloans, "may your journey be blessed from Erdion, and when you return, as I'm certain you will, leave word with Andurad or Redic or both so that I may know how you fare, for I will not forget our meeting, and someday I may come through Siloa and see you. Now farewell," he finished, as he shook their hands once more and went back to his wagon and climbed aboard. The three at the door waved to him as the wagon drove back onto the road, and, before long, the kind healer Harlin Halehand had disappeared off into the shadows of the tree-lined lane that led back to the main east road.

"Well, come inside, good friends!" Andurad said, as he ushered them into his home. Aradis and Girion walked into the homely farm cottage, which boasted a roaring fire and a broad oaken table with several crude chairs. As they entered, they were boisterously greeted by a pretty little girl who was likely not yet ten and a cheerful little boy who looked to be about six. "Was that Mister Halehand, Daddy?" the boy exclaimed, jumping up and down.

"Yes, Caldric," he replied.

"And are these Mister Halehand's friends?" the girl asked.

"They are, dear Fayna," Andurad answered, as he patted her on the head. "And they're our friends too. Now run along to the loft and get them some mats to sleep on and bring them down here so they can lie by the fire tonight."

"Yes, Daddy," the two children happily sang, as they scampered up a narrow ladder and through a small opening in the ceiling.

Now a comely woman emerged from a trapdoor in the floor that evidently led to a root cellar or something of that sort. "Well, Andurad, who are these folk?" she asked, dusting off her apron.

"Friends of Harlin Halehand: Aradis and Girion by name," her husband replied. "He was here only moments ago but had to go all the way to Ballinod tonight, yet he urged me to take these lads in for the night and do whatever I can to aid them on their journey."

"Very pleased to meet you. I'm Hirana Torfield," the woman said, as she gently shook Aradis' and then Girion's hand. "Are you hungry, then?"

"Yes, ma'am," Girion said, nodding.

"Very well then, we've got some warm cullet stew on the fire and freshly baked rye bread. Please sit, and Andurad and I will bring you supper." Cullet was a tasty root cultivated throughout Velaris, but especially in Agleri, much used in the cuisine of that region. Right now, little sounded better to the worn Siloans than a bowl of cullet stew and some fresh bread.

It was not long before Aradis and Girion were sitting at the oaken table eating their cullet stew and munching on loaves of rye bread, washing it all down with creamy cow's milk and profusely thanking the Torfields for their hospitality. The children had come down from the loft, laid two woven sleeping mats near the hearth and were now eagerly conversing with Aradis and Girion about their journey. Andurad and Hirana tried to dissuade the little boy and girl from this, but Aradis and Girion didn't mind. It was a merry evening, and the Torfields' company brought solace to the two over their grief from leaving Siloa, though they did not speak of what had befallen them the previous night to their hospitable hosts.

Perhaps an hour later, Andurad said, "We could talk much longer, I imagine, but I know you lads must be exhausted, and you've got a fair way to go tomorrow. So, whenever you will, you may lie by the fire to keep warm, and I will rouse you some time before dawn. I've got a friend with a few good horses, and I'll go over to his place tonight to see if I can convince him to let us use two of his mounts. He's quite a generous fellow, and he'll likely agree to ride with you and I tomorrow at least to Drannom, which is about eight leagues east of here. You can walk on from there. Since you told me you must arrive at Tarwyn three days from now, I've been thinking on the matter, and I'm afraid if you don't gain some extra distance on horseback, you may not make it in time."

"Will not that journey consume much of your day?" Girion asked.

"Only the morning," the farmer answered. "If I'm back here by noon or thereabouts, I'll still be able to get all my work done for the day. But don't worry about it on my account. If you know Harlin like I do, you'd do anything for him or any friend of his. He's a right fine fellow."

"That's exactly what he said about you!" Aradis laughed.

Andurad smiled and said, "That doesn't surprise me. But now, it would probably be best if all of us went to bed soon."

Standing up, Aradis and Girion thanked him, and Fayna and Caldric came and hugged them, as did Hirana. They lay down by the fire, as the children went up to their beds in the loft, and Andurad and his wife sat at the table quietly talking. And there by the crackling light of the hearth flames, the companions soon fell asleep.

It was only a few hours before they were awakened by Andurad. Quietly, they collected their effects and followed him out into the farmyard. There were two horses there, and another man sat astride one of them. Andurad introduced him as Belwin Reinstay and said that Girion would ride the steed, Handuran, with Belwin. Aradis would sit behind Andurad on the stallion, Felduras. Neither Girion nor Aradis were expert horsemen, but they both had spent a modicum of time on horseback, so they were not wholly unaccustomed to this sort of travel. And so, several hours before sunrise, they set out again on the east road, their pace that of a rather brisk trot.

At length morning came, and it was glorious again on the prairie, and the tender zephyrs of the glad month of Elaya soothed their journey. Still, they rode on for about an hour or so until they reached a point just beyond the town of Drannom, which Andurad had mentioned. There Aradis and Girion dismounted, and Andurad and Belwin, bidding them a safe journey, turned back to Galwell. The lads sat for a few minutes discussing their journey's progress and then shouldered their packs and prepared for a long day's march.

And that it was. They walked on and on over mile after mile of gently undulating prairies, and in the course of the day, they passed only two villages: Gaddock about an hour before noon and Hamdall in the late afternoon. They stopped to rest only four times, and all of these halts were relatively brief. Then, as the sun was setting, they found themselves leaning against a stout tree in a little grove several hundred yards south of the road. A small, clear stream trickled along just south of the trees, and there they had gulped the cool water and washed their hair. Now they were simply waiting for their legs to stop aching with the soreness of the many long miles that now lay behind them.

"I don't think I've ever felt so utterly weary in my whole life," Aradis moaned.

"Nor I," Girion responded, sighing.

"I know we've still got so far to go to get to Tarwyn and so little time, but I simply can't walk another step," Aradis grumbled, as he rifled through his pack looking for food. When he came across a pouch of nuts, he pulled them out and began munching on them.

Meanwhile, as they sat there against the bole, Girion reached into his jerkin and pulled out a modest-sized notebook with a dark brown leather cover. A moment later, he pulled out a peculiar cylindrical instrument that was about five inches in length. It looked to be made of a very dull copper, and when Girion removed a small cover from one end, Aradis saw that there was a black stub of sorts underneath.

"What is that?" he asked, fascinated.

"A gift from my father right before I left," Girion replied. "Your father gave you a sword; mine gave me a notebook and tylon."

"A what?"

"This little metal thing here," Girion explained. "It's called a tylon. It was invented by the Field-Gnomes of central Estereth. My father saved for a long time to purchase this in Aragest. It works much like a quill, but you needn't sharpen it, and you needn't replenish the ink nearly so often. My father wanted me to make a record of our journey, so he gave me these things as a parting gift."

"Where is Estereth anyway?" Aradis inquired, only marginally interested in a reply to his query.

"Don't you remember your Neathmarda?" Girion asked patiently. "Orona, as you know, is divided into the Moieties of Huldion in the north and Aradath in the south. The five Greater Neathmarda are Murnia, Tassaru, Estereth, Quarana and Byram. The first three, of course, are in Huldion, and the latter two are in Aradath. And then there are the Lesser Neathmarda: Jassuna, the Eldritch Isles, which are also known as Lakarnia, and frozen Fenrost. Jassuna is north of the Bushbelt, and the other two are south of it. And the Bushbelt, that is, Xengula, sometimes erroneously called Sabakwani's Girdle, is also considered one of the Lesser Neathmarda. But more specifically, Estereth is—"

"Please, Girion, I really just wanted to know where the tygon was from," Aradis grumbled, exasperated. "You can draw me a map of Orona and show me later. I do better with pictures anyway."

"It's called a *tylon*, Aradis. And you really should learn to read. Then you could learn all of this stuff on your own."

"Don't start that again," Aradis sighed. "Why would I want to learn all that bunk anyway? You and your family and Tas the potter are the only ones in all of Siloa who know how to read, and you know what? Everybody else gets along just fine without it. Besides, unless there are books out there on the best way to go about defeating Witches, my time would probably be better spent elsewhere." Closing his eyes, he continued eating. A few seconds later, he cracked one eye open and looked over at Girion, who appeared to indeed be drawing a map of Orona. "You can show me in the morning," Aradis muttered and then closed his eye again.

Girion laughed quietly and then said, "Aradis, Aradis. You certainly don't fare well when you're tired."

"No I don't," the blacksmith's son agreed. Then he stowed the pouch of nuts back in his pack and said, "I truly think I shall fall asleep this very instant. You can go on having fun with your tygon as long as you want."

"*Tylon*," Girion returned shortly. "I'll get you up a few hours before sunrise," he added, and Aradis responded drearily, yawning, "Thank you, and I really do appreciate you, Girion. I just feel so beaten right now. Too many hard goodbyes in the last two days, you know. Goodbye Siloa, goodbye Father and Mother and Brother and Sister. Goodbye warm bed, goodbye peace of mind and goodbye sanity. But I know it's been hard for you too."

"Not as much," Girion replied softly.

Aradis rubbed his eyes, then sighed deeply, "Oh, Girion. What is going to become of us? I'm afraid all this adventuring business is rather beyond me."

"Well, if nothing else," Girion returned, "you're still alive, you've got decent clothes to wear and food to eat, and even though we've no shelter as such, the weather is lovely right now. There are many Barada in Orona who lack those things, you know. Poor Yeti children down in Fenrost who ..."

"Come on, Girion," Aradis moaned. "At least those poor Yeti children have homes and are with their families."

"Some of them aren't," Girion gently remarked.

Aradis grunted, "Oh, I suppose you're right." Then, opening his eyes, he wearily said, "I don't think I would be half so upset about everything that's happened if I didn't know the Danna was directly involved. That makes everything ever so much worse because it means that all this misfortune was brought about intentionally. You know, I didn't tell you this yet, Girion, but Nagello told me that his true purpose in coming to Siloa was to tell me that I had received the Call of the Danna, whatever that is. Sounds like a heap of mystical gibberish to me. Now I rather wish the Danna had given this blasted call to someone else."

Girion looked up at the sky thoughtfully, replying, "Well, whatever it is, it wasn't given to someone else; it was given to you. So I advise you to make the best of it. Now get some rest, Aradis," he said, as he went back to working in his notebook.

Aradis sighed once more, shut his eyes and nestled as comfortably as he could against the tree. It was not long before he was overtaken by slumber. Girion stayed up writing until it became too dark, and then he too lay down and fell asleep.

Girion roused his friend several hours before dawn, and they set out on another long march. That day they covered another eleven leagues and a bit more, passing the hamlets of Orrig, Calmen and Sturbick. And that night they lay on a grassy knoll not far from the road. Girion wrote in his notebook again, and Aradis once more passed into slumber even before sunset.

The following morning, Girion awakened Aradis especially early, for this was the day Nagello had warned them to arrive at Tarwyn before the Passing of Marda; that is, before twilight. They tried to push their pace the whole day and went through a number of villages: Herrin, Tabbis, Forwall and Dumark. Yet, as Marda drifted by overhead, both of the lads could feel their bodies simply worn out from exhaustion. Consequently, in the early afternoon, they lay down to rest when Tarwyn lay only twelve miles away, and they could practically smell the sea air from the Brines of Ferassi, thinking only to rest their legs for half an hour. But before they realized it, they both had fallen fast asleep.

Some time later, Aradis awoke, alarmed. He looked up at the sun and guessed they only had a few hours left before sunset. "Girion!" he exclaimed, as he shook his friend. "We've fallen asleep like a pair of stupid Neldon Broadbuckles on a lazy spring afternoon!"

"What?" Girion yawned, rubbing his eyes. When he was fully roused, he was every bit as dismayed as Aradis, and he blurted out, "Aradis, we've got to reach Tarwyn by sunset at all costs! Nagello told us not to fail in this, and we must not!"

They quickly gathered their accoutrements and ran off down the road. Several wayfarers on the highway gave them funny looks, for they certainly were a sight racing like mad down the road, but the Siloans cared not. They absolutely had to reach Tarwyn before Marda disappeared into the west. After a while, the sea appeared before them, for the land dipped downward to the east, and they could see the port of Tarwyn spread out along the coastline. Aradis had never seen the ocean before and had they not been in such a hurry, he would have lingered there and gazed long at it in amazement. But he knew there was no time to lose, for already the sun's light was beginning to fail.

Aradis and Girion reached the edge of town nearly at a full sprint and asked the first person they encountered, who was a young Plains-Elf lady, where they might find the port office. She gave them precise directions, for which they quickly thanked her, and then breathlessly raced down to the seashore, navigating through the crowded streets of Tarwyn as quickly as they could, wending their way through people pushing carts and carrying crates and barrels and nets and anything and everything else. Among the bustling folk of Tarwyn, there were Menfolk, Plains-Elves, Dwarves and Gnomes. Aradis, of course, had seen Plains-Elves before, but in his entire life, he had only seen a handful of Dwarves. Yet, this was the very first time he had ever laid eyes on a Gnome. The experience was almost overwhelming; it is not every day that one has his first sighting of the sea and a Gnome all within an hour or so. All Gnome-and-sea-sightings aside, after navigating a number of thronging streets, the two Siloans found the very building the young lady had told them about. At this moment, Marda was a fiery red. Sunset had come.

There was an open window in the front of the port office. They dashed up to it, panting, and Aradis asked the sour-faced Plains-Elf at the window, "Excuse me, is there a ship leaving for the Fontskals tonight?"

"I beg your pardon?" the Elf answered, in the most dilatory manner possible, obviously just to aggravate them since they were in such a hurry.

"Is there a boat leaving for the Fontskals this evening?" Girion repeated, out of breath.

"Well," the Elf drawled, "there *was* a ship going *through* the Fontskals, but it just left a short while ago. And there won't be another going that way for at least three months." When he had said this, he busied himself with stamping an official ledger, just as he had been when they ran up to the window.

Aradis and Girion looked at each other in despair. They had come all this way for nothing. Everything had been provided for them: escape from the Sardolia, transportation and supplies by Harlin, lodging and mounts by Andurad and a huge sum of money for the voyage by the Danna himself—and they had blown it all with a stupid little nap.

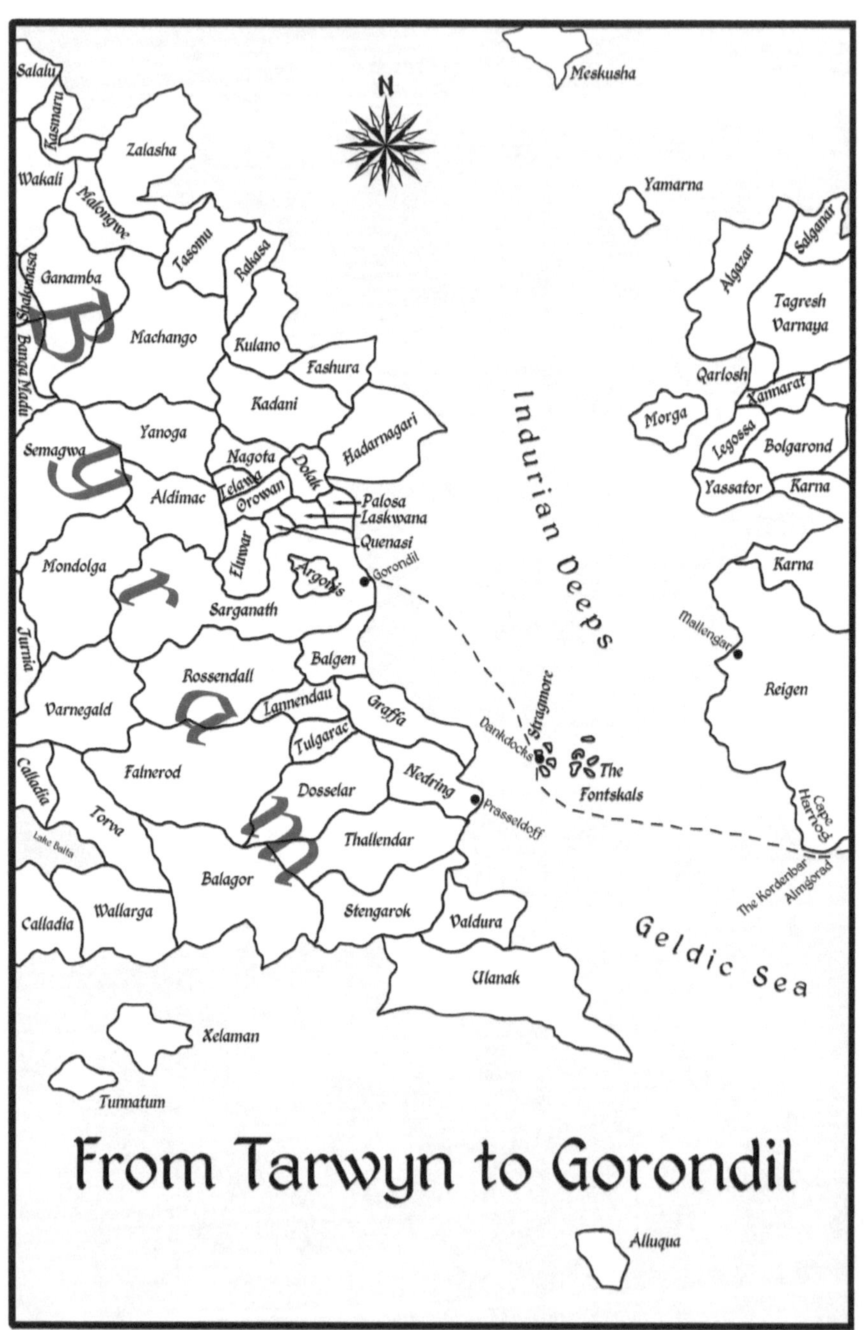

From Tarwyn to Gorondil

From Tarwyn to Gorondil

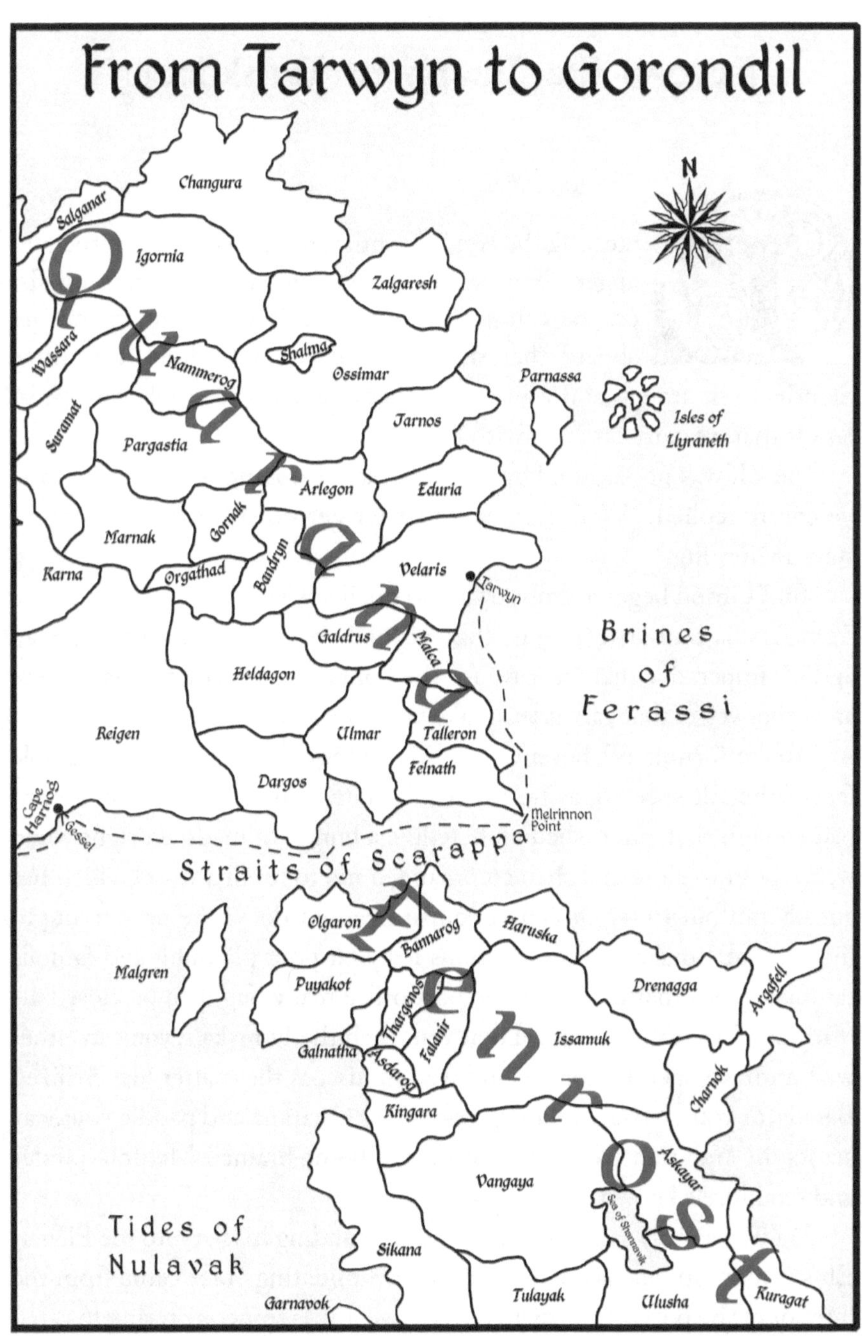

CHAPTER FIVE

Across the Deeps to Dankdocks

ike a flash, Aradis' sentiment turned from despair to anger. "Now see here!" he demanded, banging his fist on the counter. "We've come a very long way to get aboard that ship, and we certainly don't have three months to sit around and wait for another one! Now it simply can't be so far off that we can't catch up with it!"

The Elf was not amused by Aradis' tirade. Looking up from his work, he coldly replied, "Well then, you'd better get down to the Brines and start swimming."

"Sir," Girion began calmly, trying to quell any conflict that might arise from Aradis' outburst, "it's just that we really have come a very long way, and it's imperative that we leave for the Fontskals immediately. Isn't there any other vessel that can at least take us in the right direction?"

"You're fortunate I haven't shut this window right on your miserable faces," the Elf sneered, as he tossed his stamp down. "Now, if it weren't bad enough that you rushed up here like a bunch of madmen right when we're about to close and then commanded me to recall a vessel which has already put out to sea, which of course I cannot do, you're now trying to dictate that I make accommodations for your poor planning and fatuous tardiness. As a matter of fact, the port office really ought to be closed already, so if it's really so critical that you reach the Fontskals, you can either wait until we open tomorrow, and we can discuss the matter like civilized Barada, or you can start walking west across Quarana and paddle your way across the Indurian Deeps to that nest of blunt-brained Menfolk pirates and scoundrels known as the Fontskals."

Aradis was only a moment away from pounding his fist into the Plains-Elf's contemptuous face when a rather intimidating voice came from the interior of the port office, saying, "I say, Lacardi, is someone trying to catch the *Meridot* before it leaves for the Fontskals?"

Lacardi's face reddened, and he turned away from the Siloans, replying, "I'm quite certain it's left already, hasn't it, Orzoni?"

Another Plains-Elf came up to the window from behind him and sternly answered, "No, it hasn't, and you're well aware of that. Now give these men the passage they're seeking."

Orzoni turned to the Siloans now and asked, "Have you the fare for the voyage?"

"Indeed we do," Aradis replied curtly, tossing the coin pouch Nagello had given him upon the counter.

"Count it," Orzoni said brusquely to Lacardi. Lacardi dumped the coins out and began slowly sorting through them.

Orzoni was visibly irritated. "Enough of your games, Lacardi!" he fumed. "Sign their papers, and I'll count it!"

Lacardi dutifully did so, while Orzoni rapidly tallied the money. "It's all there," Orzoni affirmed, nodding to his subordinate. "Thirty-two skrannas; that makes four taldryns even."

Lacardi, thoroughly disgruntled, wordlessly handed the port documents to Aradis and Girion.

"Safe travels to you," Orzoni bade them. Then he said hastily, "Now the *Meridot* will be leaving momentarily, so I suggest you not delay in getting aboard. The ship will be departing precisely at the time of Marda's Passing this night." Then he pointed to a vessel some ways down the wharf. "That's your boat," he said. "Sorry about the trouble here at the office. Not all of us are as unreasonable as Lacardi," he finished, shooting his clerk a nasty glance.

Lacardi's face remained hard as ever. He knew full well that Orzoni could not terminate his employment without dire repercussions (especially in a place like Tarwyn) merely for giving grief to a few vagrant Menfolk. Severe antipathy and deeply-ingrained prejudice toward their kind was widespread in nearly all the coastal regions of Velaris, and routine mistreatment of them, though not officially sanctioned, was generally applauded by the populace.

"Thank you, sir," Aradis and Girion responded simultaneously, as they pounded off over the flagged stone pavement toward the *Meridot*, a ship bearing the name of the beautiful yellow flower that grew bountifully in the springtime in Agleri and was regarded as something of an emblem of that region.

"Pardon us! Excuse us!" the two called out over and over again, as they weaved recklessly among the stevedores, porters and passersby. The Tarwyn docks at sunset were a hub of bustle and activity; there were merchants, sailors and townspeople galore all rushing about their evening business. Presently, however, the Siloans reached their goal, the *Meridot*, stationed far down the pier. It was a rather large ship, a three-masted barque bedecked with a great many clean white sails, square-rigged except at the stern, which was fore-and-aft rigged. From stem to stern it stretched nearly ninety yards and from port to starboard it was a good forty feet. The hull was exceptionally sturdy, constructed with mortise and tenon joints. Atop the mainmast was an unfurled ensign of Velaris, a scythe crossed over an axe in the midst of a sapphire sea.

A Plains-Elf in naval uniform, trousers of dark green and a dark blue jacket, stood at the top of the gangplank. Aradis and Girion rushed up to him and handed him their papers.

"Well, well," he muttered wryly, going through the forms, "had you been a few minutes later, you would have been a sorry lot indeed, for tonight we expect no delay, and there isn't another craft headed to Pollona from Tarwyn for quite some time."

"We know," Aradis responded, exasperated. "They told us down at the port office. But we aren't going to . . . what is it? Pollona? We're going to the Fontskals."

It was now the seaman's turn to be exasperated. Rolling his eyes, he explained, "The Fonstskals are a port of call on the way to Pollona. They would never be an ultimate destination, for there's little of interest to a cargo ship like the *Meridot* in that rocky dungheap. You seem a bit confused; are you sure you've bought passage for the right ship? See, the *Meridot* is a trading ship. Well, it's primarily a trading ship, but we carry some passengers as well. On this particular voyage, we're taking grain of Agleri, fine merchandise from the artisans of Belestro and Aragest, tapestries from Vengoli, and pearls from Parnassa and exchanging them for spices, oils, animal hides, gold, ivory and crystals in southern Pollona, with stops in Gessel in Reigen and the Fontskals in the Indurian Deeps on the way there, as well as the Goblin colony of Morga, the Fontskals and Gessel on the way back to Velaris. Now if you're *wanting* to be left in the Fontskals, that's one thing, but I can't imagine why anyone would want to be left in a place like that. Perhaps you've made a mistake," he offered.

"There's no mistake," Girion corrected. "We do indeed wish to be left at Dankdocks in the Fontskals, and we were told that the *Meridot* is the only vessel that will be going that way for several months."

The officer was incredulous. "Why in the name of all that is sane and decent would you wish to be left in the Fontskals of all places?"

Aradis explained, "Actually, we hope to find a boat there that will take us to—what was that port's name?"

"Gorondil," Girion supplied.

"Yes, to the port of Gorondil in the Elder Forest. From there we will be going on to Anganor in the Kingdom of Argonis," Aradis finished.

Now the Elf laughed in outright disbelief. "Gorondil? Gorondil! Are you mad? Not even those devil-may-care privateers in the Fontskals would be foolhardy enough to take you there! I'll tell you what, lads; if you go back to the port office right now and request a refund for your passage, you'll save yourselves a tremendous sum of money that would otherwise be going to waste. I would hate for you to go all the way around the south bounds of Quarana and halfway across the Indurian Deeps, only to be denied your ultimate destination."

"Sir, we must go to Gorondil one way or the other," Aradis insisted, "and we were told there was a man in the Fontskals who would take us there."

"By whom?" the Elf pried. "What are you on about anyway? I've half a mind not to let you aboard this ship, papers or no papers. First, you want to disembark in the Fontskals, which is suspicious enough by itself, and then you seem to think you'll find a contact there who will take you to a place hardly anyone's been mad enough to approach in more than a decade."

"What's so terrible about Gorondil?" Girion inquired.

Now the Elf's expression darkened and a disquieting dread become apparent in his eyes as he said, "You haven't been abroad lately, have you? Probably a couple of backcountry yokels from Agleri, I'd say. You haven't heard then, eh? Those who value their lives keep well away from Gorondil and any place within a hundred miles of it. You see, Gorondil lies on the coast of a land that in former times was called Garwanna. When it was known by that name, it was perfectly safe; I went there many times throughout my years as a sailor, in fact. But a great shadow has fallen over that land, and it has of late been given a new name, Sarganath. The name means Ebonreach, though it is also referred to as Ravensrealm. People who go there disappear and are never heard from again. There's a great evil there, a Witch they say. And she takes all those who pass into her realm and carts them off into the dark and does who knows what with them. A Witch is not to be trifled with, and I say, as long as she remains deep in the Elder Forest, the rest of us would be wise to keep out. Of course, the whole region isn't under her control—not yet anyway—but if you're headed for Argonis, you'll be going directly through her territory. Some even say Argonis has already been vanquished by the Witch. I say, if it hasn't, it soon will be. Now take my advice and forget whatever delusional caper you've got planned and leave well enough alone."

"With all due respect, sir," Girion insisted, "may we be permitted to spend our money as we please?"

The Elf was visibly unsettled, and he looked back and forth intently between Aradis and his companion. "Very well then," he finally consented, handing their papers back to them. "But if ill should come upon you, as it most certainly will, it is no fault of mine."

Just then, another Plains-Elf in the raiment of a sea captain called from the forecastle, "Lindello, get those louts onshore to loose the *Meridot*, and then raise up the gangplank and let's be off!"

"Aye, Captain Turni!" the Plains-Elf with whom they had been conversing shouted in return. Then he addressed the Siloans once more, instructing, "Now, go over to that fellow on the quarterdeck in the green jacket and ask him about your accommodations and whatnot. That's Boatswain Colazzo; he can tell you about how we do things on the *Meridot*. Now, if you'll excuse me, I have several things to attend to in order for us to set sail." And with that, he went down onto the dock and began giving orders to dockworkers to untie the ship's ropes from a series of bollards.

Meanwhile, Aradis and Girion went up the steps to the quarterdeck and introduced themselves to Colazzo. He briefly explained to them where they would be sleeping below deck, where food and beverage supplies were and how much they would be allotted per day, general principles of behavior aboard a ship and a few regulations specific to the *Meridot*. By the time he had finished doing this, the ship was underway. A sailor had turned the windlass and hauled up the anchor; the ship had pulled away from the pier and was now sailing eastward into the gleaming Brines of Ferassi.

Before they went below decks, Aradis and Girion leaned on the starboard bulwark and looked back at Tarwyn, which was growing more distant all the time. The town was still abuzz with the business of port life, and the evening bells were ringing out over the swells of sea spray which pounded against the wharf. They looked back to the east and there the ocean stretched out like a great vat of sparkling red wine graced with the first beams of starlight. Once more, Aradis turned to gaze at Tarwyn and the eastern coast of Quarana, quietly lamenting, "Goodbye, Velaris—for now. Wait for me, Father, Mother, Teric, Mellora. May Telyon keep you until I return."

Girion put his hand on Aradis' shoulder and smiled. "It will be all right, Aradis. We'll come back. Let's go below decks and find our bunks." And so they went over to the main hatch and passed into the hold of the *Meridot*.

Now, in the days and weeks that followed, the two Siloans had a number of experiences that were utterly unlike anything they had gone through before. Aradis quickly learned that he had a moderate aversion to sea travel, and there were more than a few occasions when he could be found leaning on one of the bulwarks, attempting to keep nausea at bay. However, as the days passed, he grew more and more accustomed to the steady rolling of the ship. And although he cared little for seasickness, he loved looking at the sea. It was, in fact, almost more beautiful to him than the prairies of Agleri, which he so dearly missed. He even found it gorgeous, in a way, during tantrums of violent weather. The majesty of the high waves and the fierce lightning illuminating the dark waters of the deep were strongly captivating to him, though, of course, at those times he was sicker than ever. And whenever they came within sight of the coast, Aradis loved to scan the shoreline for fishing boats and seaside towns and villages, and he thoroughly enjoyed the sound of turbulent surf striking rocky outcrops and stony cliffs or washing up on gentle sandbars.

Girion, on the other hand, experienced little discomfort aboard the ship, but he renewed his love for the sights and sounds of the sea, for that was a world he had previously been acquainted with since he at one time had lived in Aragest. His mind ever hungry, he inquired much of the sailors about the workings of the *Meridot* and came to know many of the names of the ropes and sails and much terminology of seafaring.

One afternoon, he learned that the *Meridot* was propelled not only by the wind but also by a remarkable invention of the same Field-Gnomes of Estereth who had designed his tylon (which he used extensively while aboard the *Meridot*). This apparatus, the acrynon, was accommodated within a room in the hold of the ship, and it consisted of a set of metal cylinders, containers and rods that held water of varying heats. In one of the metal chambers, there were emplaced several rare crystals called jade-rites which interacted with each other (in some way which even Girion found incomprehensible) to heat the water into steam. This vapor, in turn, drove a set of machines called rhetharnas (entities which all possessed in-terior spinning components), which were housed in the same room and connected to another device called a pharnaela. Girion was unable to fully comprehend the operation of the pharnaela in the manner it was described to him, but he did discern that the end result of its activity was a peculiar force named holarnis, at once both subtle and rather potent. This holar-nis, whatever it may have been, was used to drive a set of curved paddles beneath the hull of the ship near the rudder. This paddling device was dubbed a grammalon, and it was the grammalon which ultimately drove the ship on with greater rapidity toward its destination.

All this utterly fascinated Girion, as this technology was quite rare, and he was told that not a great many ships in all the southern Moiety of Orona employed it, primarily because of the high cost and difficulty of obtaining jaderites. Girion tried several times to explain the acrynon to Aradis, who was even less enthusiastic about it than he was about Girion's tylon, and so the cooper's son had to content himself with drawing dia-grams and providing explanations of it in his notebook.

However, both Aradis and Girion enjoyed the company of the other two hundred and sixty-some occupants of the ship, of which about fifty were members of the *Meridot's* crew (nearly all of these were Plains-Elves, with a few Dwarves tossed in). The rest were a mixture of Elves, Dwarves, Gnomes and Menfolk. The Siloans spent many hours conversing with them about their backgrounds, their present business and their plans for the future, and they relished the rich repository of stories among their fellow passengers. As expected, whenever the Siloans discussed their in-tention to travel to Argonis, they were met with disbelief and disapproval (at least by those who were familiar with the name). When asked why they would ever dream of going to such a place, they responded by saying that if one were going to go have an adventure in some dangerous place, it is much better to do it when he is young rather than old (this idea had come to them from a comment made by Harlin). And that was their claim: that they were simply going on an adventure, for they deemed it unwise to say that the Danna himself had sent them to rescue that land from the Witch whom everyone feared so greatly, for then they should really be thought as daft as a drunken Dwarf dancing on a dappled donkey. But as a result of all this, they came to be regarded on the *Meridot* as something of an oddity and an object of definitive interest. Aradis and Girion didn't mind this too much though, as their perceived status as bona fide, old-fashioned seekers of fortune made other Barada more willing to converse with them. If nothing else, this frequent banter with other passengers seemed to make the voyage go by faster.

The first leg of their voyage consisted of sailing southward along the coast of Quarana for approximately eleven hundred miles, a distance which they covered in less than four full days due to the additional speed provided by the acrynon. This journey took them past the kingdoms of Malca and Talleron and then on to Felnath. The coastline of this region was much like that around Tarwyn; plains bordered the east coast almost all the way to the southeast corner of the Neathmarda. But as they drew nigh unto the southern bounds of Quarana, the landscape became significantly more undulating, and there were occasionally steep cliffs that plummeted directly down into the sea. At length, they came to Melrinnon Point, the land at the southeastern extremity of all Quarana, where a brigade of idyllic grassy hills clad in brilliant wildflowers marched down to broad, sandy shores. Gulls circled overhead and called out in reply to the soothing wash of sea foam on golden sand.

After rounding Melrinnon Point, they turned directly westward, leaving the Brines of Ferassi behind and entering the Straits of Scarappa, the wild waters which lay between southeastern Quarana and northwestern Fenrost. There the vagaries of the Sea-Realm, or Solansu, as the inhabitants of Orona call it, became much more pronounced. The weather grew noticeably antagonistic within a matter of hours and remained thus for several days. In addition, the motion of the *Meridot* became habitually more erratic, continuously assaulted by unruly waves and ill-favored winds.

From what the Siloans gathered from the deckhands, this region of the ocean was generally disliked among seafarers for several reasons: first, it was subject to strange currents from the Tides of Nulavak, the sea that lay west of Fenrost, which made navigation something of a nuisance, if not a hazard; secondly, it was generally more perilous due to the presence of shrewd and barbarous Yeti mariners from the cold shores of Fenrost who preyed upon merchant ships that strayed too far from the shores of Quarana.

Yet, for all its dangers, Scarappa too possessed a wild beauty. Indeed, its darker, more quarrelsome waters complemented the more rugged coastline of south Quarana quite well. The climate was certainly cooler this far south, and a great many pines, spruces and firs dotted the rocky shoreline, thriving in the perpetual mist. A grim fog often hid the land from their sight, but occasionally it would lift, and they would catch glimpses of steep valleys and stony crags blanketed in deep evergreen forests. But, as they progressed westward, having passed from Felnath to the Kingdom of Ulmar and then Dargos, they entered what was known as the Geldic Sea, named for a Dwarven people called the Gelds, who had much traffic there in days gone by. The previous terrain now gave way to a milder topography of hills and grasslands, though in the far southwest reaches of Quarana, coniferous forests again dominated the landscape, and in the north, low, frowning mountains could be seen keeping watch many miles inland.

Now on the twelfth full day of their voyage, the *Meridot* made berth overnight in a Dwarven port called Gessel, which lay about sixteen hundred miles west of Melrinnon Point near the southwestern edge of Quarana. Gessel was set in a rocky bay surrounded by Baudig Wood, a vast pine forest which lay in the even vaster Dwarven kingdom of Reigen that occupied that corner of the Neathmarda.

Many novelties awaited the lads in Gessel. Here they were confronted by a very rhythmic and extremely complex-sounding Dwarven language called Tazbek, which Girion found fascinating but Aradis disconcerting, since he had never heard anything but his native language of Daiga before. Fortunately for the Siloans, though, almost everyone they met spoke at least some Daiga.

And it was not only the linguistic landscape that was different; the architecture of the Dwarves was also unlike anything either Aradis or Girion had ever encountered before (this particular Dwarven style, they were informed, was called Morastic and dated from late in the Bridging of the Tides, the Fourth Age of Orona) and, of course, Girion made sure to record sketches and observations of it in his notebook. The harbor's structures employed a great many arches, and the whole city seemed to be one giant stone complex, as if it were not many buildings, but one. In fact, they were told by some locals that one could go from anywhere in the city to anywhere else without going outdoors, and this they were inclined to believe, for there were many tunnels, galleries, covered alleyways and skybridges that crisscrossed over each other in a vast, perplexing network. There were occasional open courtyards and even a few open streets, but the general sense of the city's layout was that of a multi-layered, magnificent labyrinth.

After exploring the old part of the city for a while, the Siloans spent a few hours at a local watering hole called The Raven's Crest where they sampled some local Dwarven cuisine, rhingast and maschi, rhingast being a variety of fish caught off the coast of Gessel, and maschi being dumplings made from the regional grain, minndalot. As they had no coinage to pay for their supper, they traded in several of Aradis' rations from the ship from meals he had not felt like eating. After it got dark, they walked around the torch-lit waterfront for a while and then went back aboard the *Meridot.*

They set sail from Gessel the following morning around sunrise, and the *Meridot* continued skirting along the southwestern coast of Quarana for another four hundred miles. Their course now took them around the head of Cape Harnog. Early on the day after they departed from Gessel, they passed the ancient fortress of Almgorad, a monumental feat of Dwarven engineering. The place was so well known that even Aradis, who had cared little for the wider world for much of his life, had heard of it. Almgorad was a towering pink marble citadel that lay a mile and a half offshore on an island that had been built by the Tharlogs of long ago (that is, the powerful rulers of the Dwarves) who, over the course of several centuries, had piled up a great many stones of immense size in the sea. The fortress's original structure, much of which remained, had been constructed some two and a half thousand years previously at the height of the age of Orona known as the Apex of Archaea. Aradis and Girion stood on deck staring at the place in amazement, as the ship skimmed along between it and the forested coastline. The mere sight of its splendid battlements and bold banners evoked the valor of days long ago when Almgorad was the most powerful fortress south of the Bushbelt, and great and heroic battles had been fought there between the Dwarves and Trolls of southwestern Quarana.

Later that same day, they sailed along a section of the coast known as the Kordenbar, which was renowned for its many beautiful waterfalls which plummeted down into the sea from the dark, timbered cliffs above. As the late afternoon sunshine passed through the spray of the misty cataracts, it produced a series of brilliant rainbows, thus weaving a tapestry of light, water and sound that was truly marvelous.

Around noon, on the third day out from Gessel, the *Meridot* left the coast of Quarana behind and headed west by northwest out into the Indurian Deeps, the sea between Quarana and Byram, for the remaining nine hundred miles to the Fontskals. The thought that they had at last come to the far side of the Neathmarda in which they had spent their entire lives excited Girion greatly but was somewhat unnerving to Aradis; it seemed to him that they were traveling off the edge of the world.

Girion had accrued a decent amount of knowledge about Byram from his studies in Aragest as a child, and he decided to share some of it with Aradis one day with rather mild weather when the sun was reflecting clearly off the face of the water, and they were resting against the starboard railing of the ship up on the quarterdeck.

"So in Byram there are five principal regions," Girion began eagerly.

Aradis was already succumbing to listlessness.

His friend went on, "The Elder Forest in the east, where we're going, a land characterized by temperate woods and wild meadows; Pollona in the northeast, where sprawling deserts and broad savannah reign supreme; Rannadalf in the southwest, covered with green hills, narrow, forested valleys and snowy mountains; Soyawat Piyani in the northwest toward the Bushbelt, a vast region of tropical forests and grasslands; and the Wide Lands in the southeast, where gray plains, broad marshes and rocky coasts predominate."

"And how is all this going to help us defeat Ravinia and restore peace to the Kingdom of Argonis?" Aradis inquired tiredly, as he was wont to do whenever Girion began explaining some point of history or geography or otherwise (as he saw it) worthless general knowledge to him.

"That's all you can think about, isn't it?" Girion sighed, disheartened.

"Listen, Girion. I didn't want to leave Siloa in the first place," Aradis grumbled dejectedly, "and if I've got to do these things for Telyon or Nagello or whomever, then I might as well go and do them and be done with them and not waste time learning about Byram according to Girion Ringmark."

"So, it's not that you don't care about the landscape of Byram," Girion said. "It's just that you're still angry about being rendered powerless to do aught about the situation back in Siloa."

"Perhaps," Aradis admitted glumly. "And I'm sorry for being such a grouse, Girion, but I just can't shake this horrible feeling, this feeling of betrayal, this feeling of being used. I'm really beginning to wonder if I'm not some sort of grand jest in Erdion."

"Whatever you may be, Aradis, you're not a jest in Erdion," Girion assured, as they leaned against the starboard rampart, looking off into the almost indigo expanse of the Indurian Deeps. "Have you already forgotten how much was provided for us on our way to Tarwyn?"

"It's not what *was* provided for us that concerns me now but what *will* or *will not* be provided," Aradis returned.

"Well," Girion mused, "I expect we shall be given just what we need. And I should say that the reason we can expect that everything *will* be provided for us is that it already has been."

Aradis looked over at his friend. "How do you figure that?" he asked, puzzled. "This journey is only just beginning. We've got a long way to go, and there are so many things that can yet go amiss. We don't even know how we're going to pay for food and drink once we reach the Fontskals! And how are we going to pay this Starwash fellow for our voyage to Gorondil anyway? What if Nagello made him up? What then? Did you ever think of that, Girion? You know as well as I do that the four taldryns we spent for passage on this ship only sufficed for a voyage to Byram. Where are we going to get the funds to sail back to Velaris?"

The Menfolk had, with no small amount of consternation, realized on the evening they departed from Tarwyn that the tickets they had purchased were for a one-way voyage to Pollona. Due to their haste at the port office and Lindello not making mention of the matter, they had only discovered this fact some hours later when Girion had looked through their papers in the hold.

Ignoring Aradis' last few inquiries, Girion clarified, "I'm not saying nothing will go amiss. I'm merely trying to point out that what we really need at the moment is assurance—assurance and trust. Above all else, we need an incorruptible certainty that all we shall be faced with has already been foreseen and is accounted for and that the one who commissioned us for this task will grant us what we need to complete it. And we've already been given that."

Aradis thought about this for a moment and then replied, "And what assurance have we been provided with? Why should I be persuaded to trust this Telyon, after all, other than you and my father are so keen about him?"

"You trust your father, don't you?" Girion asked.

"I've not been given any reason not to," Aradis replied.

"You trust me, don't you?"

"Yes."

"And you yourself said that Nagello showed you his true form, did you not?" Girion queried.

"Yes, I did."

"Well then, it was as if he were opening a window unto the Haedra for you. And, he told you things that none might know in natural circumstance, and your father also testified unto the veracity of Nagello's message, as did I. If it should be objected that one should only believe such things as he can know by sense—well, is that not how you came to know Nagello for what he truly was?"

"It is," Aradis admitted.

"In addition, Nagello was proved right in all the other matters of which he spoke, which we have so far been able to verify. He told us all our needs would be provided for, and so it came to be. And he warned us to arrive at Tarwyn before Marda's Passing had ended on the fourth day of our journey and, lo and behold, that is precisely when the *Meridot* departed for the Fontskals. Do you not see that our commissioner has knowledge that is undoubtedly of a superior nature and that his fidelity in provision is impeccable? That is why I say it is only reasonable to still your fears about what is to come. And, for the record, I count it an absolute certainty that when we arrive in Dankdocks in a few days, we shall most certainly encounter a man called Felding Starwash, just as Nagello said we would."

"But what of all these terrible things which people have been saying about Gorondil and Sarganath and the near impossibility of reaching Anganor in Argonis?" Aradis objected, running his hands through his windblown hair.

"They are most likely true," Girion answered shortly. "For even Nagello warned us that we would only come to complete our task by passing through great blackness and sorrow. Will not the powers of evil seek to destroy us? Of course! And will not grief poison our hearts? Undoubtedly! Is that not what darkness and shadow do to mortal flesh? Is that not how they behave? Are they not the enemies of the Barada? But if the Danna is really our advocate—and I think it is quite clear that he is—then let evil do its worst. For our part, we must simply focus on what we have been asked to do."

"That's what I was trying to do when this conversation began!" Aradis protested.

"No, you were trying to get out of learning about geography," Girion grinned, as he lightly elbowed Aradis in the side.

Aradis laughed a little, conceding, "You can draw me a map of Byram later. Let's go get some lunch."

And with that, the lads went off to the galley for some praschen (Dwarven noodles) and hobst (almond bread made specifically for seafaring expeditions), recent acquisitions from the *Meridot's* stop at Gessel.

Now, at last, the lads' journey from Tarwyn to the Fontskals was nearly complete. The trip from Gessel to Stragmore in the Fontskals took seven days in all, and on the seventh day, Aradis and Girion spoke about their departure to the seasoned Elven pilot of the *Meridot*, Captain Turni.

"I hate to see you abandoned in such a dismal place as Stragmore, but if that be your course, then so be it," Captain Turni drawled somberly.

"Thank you for accommodating us, Captain," Aradis said. "You can't imagine how glad we are that we made it aboard your ship just in time back in Tarwyn."

"Accommodating you?" the Plains-Elf chuckled. "We're passing through the Fontskals anyhow. I certainly wouldn't have made a special trip there to drop you off. It's just that they're directly on the way to pick up our shipments of tassagon, zimari, haskanesh and kadanu oil, among other things, in Pollona. Just be sure you don't leave anything aboard when you depart. Now I know you've got it in your head that you'll find someone who will take you on to Gorondil, but just in case you don't—" Then he muttered under his breath, "and you won't—" and finished, "if your desire is to return to Velaris, your best option is to wait for the *Meridot* to come-back through Dankdocks around the first of Ildurion. Hope you can make it until then. There will undoubtedly be another trading ship coming from Byram or Quarana between now and then, but I've no way of knowing when or where or anything like that. You'll just have to ask around."

"We'll be all right, sir," Girion assured. "I suppose we'll be putting into port in a few hours, then?"

"Aye," Turni answered. "We're already drawing nigh to the isle of Dunlim, and you can see the Fontskals Fog, as folk call it, hovering off in the north. We should reach Smag's Cove in Stragmore by nightfall, and there lies Dankdocks."

"Good then," Aradis pronounced. "We'll go and get our things together."

This didn't take them terribly long, especially since the packs Harlin had given them had unfortunately gone missing the night before they reached Gessel (the lads guessed they had been purloined by a petty thief). So they sat at a table down in the hold talking for a while, then made the rounds and said farewell to the friends they had made while aboard the *Meridot*. Finally, they collected all their belongings, went up on deck and watched Marda plunge westward toward Byram, as they approached the island of Stragmore in the Fontskals. About an hour after sunset, a gentle rain began, and they saw the isle's dark coastline looming out of the fog. A few minutes later, they noticed an assortment of fishermen's boats here and there among the shadowy waters, lit by lanterns. On the rocky shore, the firelight in windows of little stone cottages winked in and out of the growing gloom. The *Meridot* turned eastward into Smag's Cove and then the Siloans waited in anticipation, as the pale mist off the dark waters of the cove unveiled the dingy piers of Dankdocks, which were illuminated only by a few swinging lanterns. The rain was considerably heavier now, as the ship pulled up to the pier.

Aradis and Girion, in turn, shook Captain Turni's hand. Then he grimly said, "Be careful, lads. You might be safer here than an Elf, being Menfolk and all, but the Menfolk of Stragmore are not like those in Velaris. These are a right treacherous lot, cutthroats and mercenaries who would sell you to the dogs if it suited them. If you make it to the Elder Forest alive, may you find the fortune you seek, but don't go down in Dankdocks. Promise me that."

"We'll keep an eye out for trouble, Captain," Aradis responded, as they walked down the gangplank alongside some of the sailors who were going ashore to load up supplies needed for the remainder of the *Meridot's* voyage.

The port of Dankdocks was nothing like Tarwyn. This was not a jolly place. It was a morose, decrepit expression of the life of a somber mariner set adrift in a cold, dark sea. The docks were badly in need of repair and creaked in the wind. The rain was cold and angry, and all the ramshackle wooden buildings on the waterfront were obviously suffering from the frequent assault of squalls off the sea. Disgruntled sailors plodded about the wharf with their coats wrapped tightly about them, smoking stout pipes and muttering under their breath. Fog lay across the rocky coast like a shroud, and ominous thunder could be heard in the distance. And the whole place reeked of dead fish.

"Excuse me, but could you direct us to the Draughtfish Inn?" Aradis asked a passing Manfellow, a somewhat elderly chap who looked to be a Dankdocks regular.

"Up thataway," the sailor nodded toward a muddy lane that ran up from the shoreline. "On the left, look for the sign of the mug and fish." Girion caught a whiff of the herb in his pipe; smoking was common in Aragest, and Girion knew the smell of cheap smollerus (that is, the cherry brown smoking herb used by various Barada throughout Orona). This was cheaper than cheap.

"Thank you," Girion mumbled in reply, as the sailor pushed on through the wind and the rain, and the Siloans turned and trudged up the crooked lane.

Some ways up the street, the road turned to the south and then they saw, on the left-hand side of the lane, what must without a doubt be the Draughtfish Inn. Over the door, there was a crude sign swaying in the wind with a picture of a frothing mug and a sickly fish that might well have been painted by a half-drunk sailor, of which Aradis and Girion had seen several already, stumbling around the streets of Dankdocks singing poorly pitched shanties and only half-intelligible poetry about unrequited love. The building's windows were exceptionally dingy and only with great difficulty could one make out anything of the interior of the place.

So, taking a deep breath, Aradis sighed, "This is the place, then, the place Nagello spoke of. Well, we'll soon see if there's any such person as Felding Starwash." And with that, he opened the creaky wooden door of the Draughtfish Inn, and he and Girion went inside.

The place was a raucous, disheveled excuse for a tavern and certainly would be hard-pressed to qualify as an inn. The floor was filthy, the tables were filthy, the fire barely sputtered away in a hearth that badly needed to have its ashes removed, and half the chairs looked as if they would collapse if a grasshopper sat on them. A good portion of the clientele looked to be on the verge of passing out, and the rest looked like a bunch of no-good ruffians who'd stick a dagger in their own mothers without a second thought. Beer and stout and ale were splattered on nearly every surface: the flagged stone floor, the stained wooden walls, the rotting tables and even the sagging ceiling. Behind the counter stood a fellow who looked like he had quite a bit of sense about him, but there was also a dangerous glint in his eyes, as if it would be a very unwise thing to cross him.

"So Nagello intends for us to pick up a captain from this lot of beer-brains?" Aradis muttered to his companion.

"So it would seem," Girion replied, raising his eyebrows in alarm and near disbelief, as he scanned the miserable patrons of the Draughtfish Inn.

"Let's go ask the bartender about him, then," Aradis suggested, "collect him, and get out of here before we end up in a barrel of fish in downtown Dankdocks."

Aradis and Girion strode as naturally as they could in a place like this up to the counter and nodded at the bartender.

"What'll it be then, buckoes?" the greasy-haired, narrow-eyed Manfellow asked slyly, as he walked over to where they were leaning against the bar. "Would this be your first time in Dankdocks, good strangers? Maybe ye'd like to try a bit of our own Stragmore stout. It's not the best ye can get, but ye can't get it nowhere else."

"No drinks for us at the moment," Aradis replied. "We're looking for a particular man."

"Are ye then?" the barkeep squinted. "And who told ye Carrican Kedgewick could do aught 'bout that?"

"You're Carrican Kedgewick then, I take it?" Girion confirmed.

"Aye, that I be," the barkeep answered. "Now who is it ye be looking for?"

"A ship captain by the name of Felding Starwash," Aradis answered. "Do you know him?"

Now Carrican squinted even more, and his eyes glinted a little in the light of the rusty lantern that swung from the rafters above the counter. "Hmm, it seems ye've been given a bit of bad information," he slowly replied. "No such person has crossed my path of late or in days long gone by. Now who was it that told ye Starwash'd be found here?"

Aradis hesitated and then answered haltingly, "Someone who would, uh, know those kinds of things."

Carrican let out a sort of gurgly, gravelly laugh. "Well, looks like your source ain't so reliable as ye thought. Washed ye all the way up in Dankdocks left high and dry. Now if ye be needing a ship captain of sorts, I know a few, but Starwash ye must seek elsewhere, for sure as a dandy drink drowns out the Dullen damp, if I don't know him, he's not been e'er to Stragmore—of that I can assure you. And curse the thought, ye know, but it may be he's no real person at all, and ye've been had for a fish and a fool by whoever told ye such a yarn."

"Very well, then. Thank you, Mister Kedgewick," Girion said brusquely, as he put his arm around Aradis and pulled him away from the counter.

"Glad to be of service to ye!" Kedgewick laughed, as he went back to filling large steins from a barrel behind the counter.

"Now what?" Aradis grumbled, very irritated indeed from their dead-end conversation with Carrican. "Nagello said everyone around here would know Starwash. Not *everyone*, apparently. But I suppose you'll say we should ask every sailor in this whole place if he knows him."

"That's a start," Girion replied optimistically.

Aradis sighed and then impulsively sat down at a table around which five rough-looking sailors were sitting. He was obviously not welcome there; nonetheless, he quickly interrupted, "Pardon me, but do any of you know a man by the name of Felding Starwash?"

The barkeep had overheard this, and he was not at all pleased. He leaned over the counter and menacingly and quite deliberately said, "Now I already told ye we don't know any Starwash of any sort around here. Like I said—if I don't know the fellow, then no one does, and if ye think it a great lark to go around pestering me customers, then I've no choice but to show ye out the door so these poor sailors can down their grog in the way it's meant to be downed—in peace. Now drop this business right quick, lads, or you'll regret it."

"Have we not leave to simply speak with your patrons?" Girion inquired innocently.

Now Carrican was really mad. "Is this how ye always treat with strangers, bucko? First you take me word as swinefeed, as if I were lying to ye, then start sassing back at me when I'm only looking out for me customers' best interests!"

Girion, never one to escalate a conflict, hastily replied, "We meant no harm, really sir, we didn't, so we'll just be going now." And he moved to do exactly that, desperately hoping Aradis would do the same.

But Aradis had already arisen and walked over to the counter. Now he got right up in Carrican's face, growling, "Well, Mister Bilgemouth, you seem to have forgotten the fact that we also are your customers, and what you're doing right now is certainly not in our best interests."

Now, one of the bigger sailors at the table got up and laid his hand roughly on Aradis' shoulder. Without hesitation, Aradis turned and punched the sailor full-on in the face, shouting, "Don't touch me again, scum, or I'll knock you halfway to the Bushbelt!"

A mad melee ensued. Aradis was a veritable tiger when enraged, and Girion could handle himself quite well, but with an entire tavern full of angry sailors converging on them, they didn't stand much chance of making it out of the Draughtfish Inn in one piece. The first man whom Aradis had struck fell backwards into the table, knocking mugfuls of liquor everywhere and causing several more sailors to fall backwards out of their already unstable chairs. A second sailor went after Aradis, but the latter grabbed him and threw him over the counter so that he struck Carrican, who then fell back with tremendous force against a full cask of ale. The cask promptly ruptured, spurting brown liquid everywhere, and then it rolled and knocked another cask to the floor, which also ruptured, shooting fountains of the famous Stragmore stout all over the place.

Meanwhile, Girion had knocked several attackers aside with a series of swift strikes with his staff, and he quickly motioned to Aradis to make a run for the door. They both darted toward the exit, with Girion dodging an assailant's grasp, and Aradis leaping on the counter and then jumping from table to table as various opponents sought to lay hold of him. As the door was blocked by three enraged sailors, Aradis grabbed a barrel by the wall and threw it at the window. The glass shattered and Aradis dove through the opening. At the same time, Girion upended a table to delay those coming after them and then also lunged through the broken pane. An irate mariner just barely missed catching his right foot.

Neither Aradis nor Girion escaped wholly unscathed; they were both cut up some by the glass, though not badly, and they both had been hit by wild punches of their half-inebriated attackers. But they hadn't a moment to spare. Though they had jumped headlong into the mud, they arose immediately as the door to the inn burst open, and a half dozen angry sailors rushed out into the street.

"Come on!" Aradis shouted, as they raced back down the lane. His only thought was that they must reach the safety of the *Meridot*, Starwash or no Starwash, for even these ruffians, drunk as they were, would not dare come against a company of several hundred.

But the way to the ship was blocked now, for three more men came trudging up the lane, and the sailors pursuing them called, "Hey, Ronnigan! Murdock! Harko! Help us bag these two!" These three immediately began running toward them, so Aradis and Girion instinctively rushed into an alleyway on their right. This led into a dark, close maze of alleys and tumbledown buildings, which they navigated like panicked rabbits on the run from a band of hounds. Before long, they had lost even themselves, to say nothing of their pursuers, and they huddled under a ragged awning to take a little shelter from the rain. They were so confused by the chase that they were unsure which direction they had gone or how close they were to the docks or the inn or anything else, but they could no longer hear the shouts of those running after them, for the rain had intensified and the thunder rumbled violently over and over again.

Though nearly out of breath, Girion managed to scold his companion, "Now, I'm only going to say this once, Aradis, and then I'll drop the matter: perhaps it wasn't the most prudent course of action to wallop that fellow in the face."

Aradis was about to make a pert reply when, suddenly, a creaky, raspy voice came from the shadows farther down the alleyway. "So you're looking for Felding Starwash, are you?"

It seemed the chase had now come to an end; the lads had been discovered.

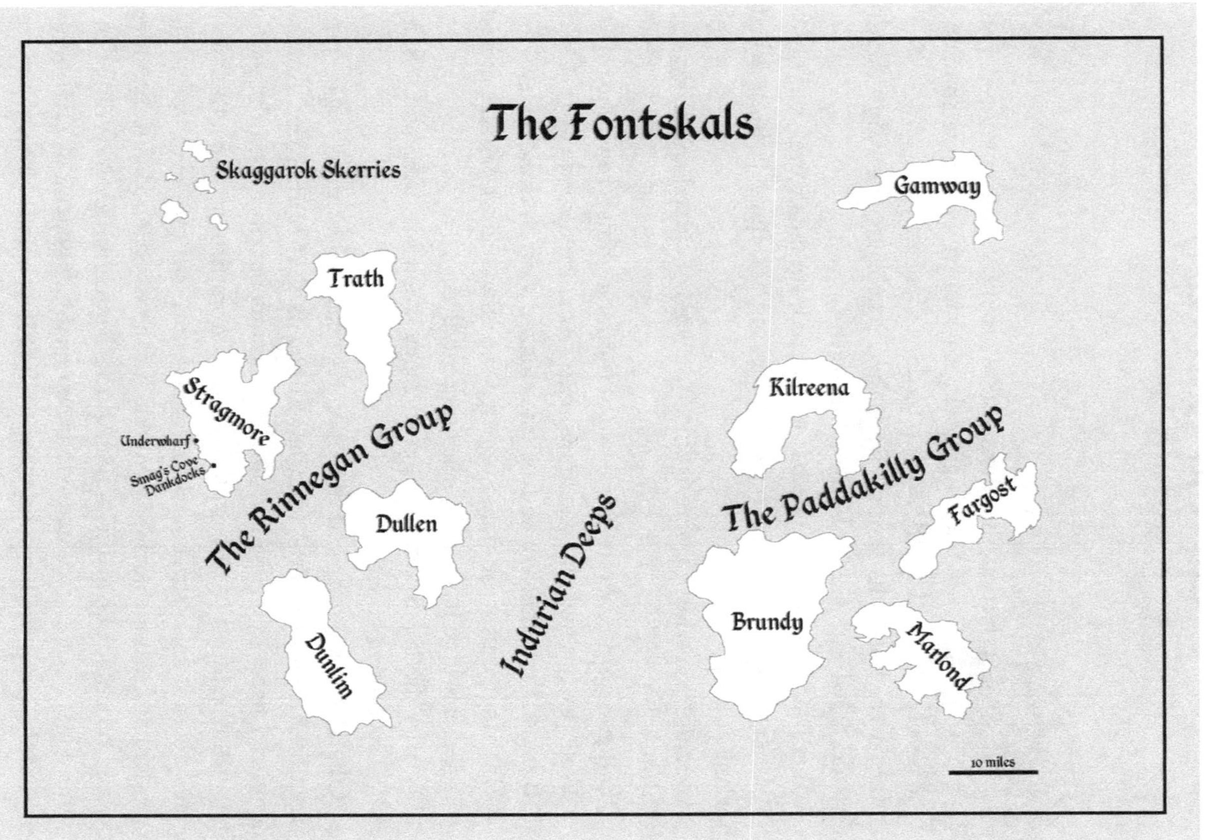

The Fontskals
Skaggarok Skerries
Gamway
Trath
Kilreena
Stragmore
The Rinnegan Group
The Paddakilly Group
Underwharf
Smag's Cove
Dankdocks
Dullen
Indurian Deeps
Fargost
Brundy
Dunlim
Marlond
10 miles

CHAPTER SIX

Captain Starwash

tartled, the Siloans spun around rapidly and saw a bent figure with a gray cloak wrapped around its shoulders and a dark hood pulled over its face.

They were both still panting from their harrowing flight, but Aradis stuttered, "D-d-did you say Felding Starwash?"

"That I did," the voice replied. It was an old woman's voice.

"What makes you presume we're looking for him?" Girion asked, shocked.

"Because you said you were, laddie," the woman chided amusedly.

"But . . . but . . ." Aradis stammered.

"Did you not ask about him down at the Draughtfish Inn?" she pried.

"Well, yes, but how did you know that?" Aradis returned.

"Because I was there, of course," the cloaked woman explained.

"Oh. Strange that you found us when the others didn't," Aradis mused.

"Age aids where haste fails," the crone riddled.

"So why did old Kedgewick get so cagey when we asked about Starwash?" Girion demanded.

"Oh, I'd wager a mug and the moon it's because he thinks you're some sort of fleet agents from the Indurian Rimlands Port Authorities. You see, the official fleets of all the surrounding nations haven't a great liking for Starwash due to his . . . ah, exploits, and so from time to time, they send agents down here to the Fontskals to root him out. However, due to the revenue that Felding's activities provide for these wretched, forsaken isles, it would very much be in any ol' Dankdocks Manfellow's—including Carrican Kedgewick's—best interests to keep Felding's general whereabouts a secret. But I know the look and the speech of fleet agents better than Carrican knows his own name, and I'd never mistake you two for fleet agents. You see, Carrican is much too clever for his own good. He imagines you to be cunning cosmopolitans posing as witless wanderers, while anyone with a decent amount of sense ought to be able to see you for what you really are—witless wanderers. Besides, no fleet agent would ever just walk up to the counter and inquire directly about the whereabouts of Felding Starwash, nor would he dare to incite a brawl among that lot of rabble down at the Draughtfish, as long as he was in his right mind. Indeed, there isn't a fleet agent in the whole of Orona who could play the simpleton half as well as you have."

"That could be taken as a compliment in this particular instance, I suppose," Girion replied, somewhat annoyed.

"Well, it's best if we don't stand here talking much longer, for Fedric and the boys will find you shortly if you don't get out of Dankdocks," the woman warned. "Follow me," she instructed, as she hobbled off down the alleyway.

"To where?" Aradis asked, perplexed.

"To Felding of course," the woman snapped. "Now shush or we'll be heard and caught, you ninnies!"

"You really know Felding Starwash?" Aradis asked, a bit boggled.

"O' course I do. So does everyone else in Dankdocks, for that matter," the woman muttered.

"But don't you want to know why we're looking for Felding before you take us to him?" Aradis inquired hurriedly.

The woman spun around to face him and hissed, "Now, what did I just say? This is no time for explanations! Even I won't be able to save your skins if the Draughtfish boys nab you! Besides, my mind is already made up to let Felding hear your business and decide what to do about it, for it's him you've come seeking, not me. Furthermore, if you've taken the trouble to sail all the way out to the Fontskals—from Velaris, I'd guess, since you came in off the *Meridot*—it must be a matter of some gravity that drove you. Now, far be it from me to hinder your errand with Felding if it warranted a journey of that magnitude." Once again, she began slinking off down the alleyway.

Girion, his curiosity whetted, audibly wondered, "How did you know we just got off the *Meridot* and how did—"

"How did you come to have so little sense?" the crone raged, as she wheeled about, glaring at Girion with unbridled aggravation. "I've already told you dolts to shut your fat mouths, and I meant it! Now do as I say, and do as I do. Keep out of sight and consider everyone we see a potential antagonist, at least until we're out of Dankdocks. Now, come on!" Having said this, she hastened to the end of the alleyway and irritably motioned for them to follow her.

Aradis and Girion looked at each other, dumbfounded, and then hastily followed, always keeping to the shadows.

Now the old lady led them through a bewildering maze of winding alleyways filled with rank mud and barrels of fish. Twice they had to duck back into hiding to keep from being spotted by their roaming pursuers, but, at last, they reached the northeast side of Dankdocks. There the woman led them up to a collapsing stone wall that marked the town's edge and through a rusted iron gate standing in it. Beyond the gate, there was a poorly maintained road that led off into the countryside. Now that they were out of town, the woman quickened her pace, scuttling hastily along the path like some wild animal in a hurry to return to its den. So swift was the old woman, in fact, that the Siloans were rather caught off guard by how speedily they had to move in order to keep up with her.

The road they were taking wound back and forth across the stony landscape and kept reasonably close to the coastline. There were occasional cottages along the way but, for the most part, just low stone walls acting as fences to contain a few sorry-looking animals, mostly sheep and a handful of horses. All the while, the rain poured down in an unforgiving torrent, and the lads shivered in the cold wind.

When they had gone on like this for a good hour or so, Aradis and Girion began to get a bit aggravated. Every time they had tried to inquire something of the old lady, she shushed them and hissed, "Not now. Just wait." But just when their patience had really reached its limit, she turned and said to them, "Be careful, now. The rocks are slippery, and the cliff is steep. We wouldn't want you to go plunging down into the sea, would we?"

Then she began wending her way down a tumbled, rocky slope that led to the edge of a jagged cliff, a hundred and fifty feet or more in height, and they heard the sound of the Indurian Deeps pounding heavily against the rocks below. Crouching down behind a large heap of stones, of which there were many in this area, she took a roundish rock and rapped a certain distinct and difficult rhythm upon a sizable stone. Then, to their amazement, a large slab of rock to her right began to shift out of its place. Soon it was revealed that beneath the rock there was a gaping hole with a rickety wooden ladder that led down into a flickering blackness. The woman beckoned to them to follow, as she quickly climbed down the ladder. Aradis and Girion hastily clambered down after her, and when they had reached the bottom of the ladder, some forty feet below, the rock above shifted again to cover the exit.

Now they stood in a cavern lit by torchlight. The lads looked around in mild apprehension, and their eyes came to rest upon a stone arch off to the left of the ladder, which led to a winding staircase.

Taking note of their gaze, the crone explained, "That goes up to Dugan Hardrake, the one who opened the door for us. Older than me he is; now he can't be out on the wave with the others anymore, so he gets to keep the books and pull the lever when people knock."

"The others?" Girion asked. "What is this place?"

"Underwharf," the old woman replied, as she removed her hood, revealing a weathered face with a largish nose, long, stringy, gray hair and darting blue eyes. "And don't you say a thing to any soul about this place or you'll be drowned in the Deeps quicker than lightning off the coast of Kilreena."

"Kilreena?" Aradis repeated.

"One of the Fontskals," the woman hastily explained. "Now this is a smuggler's den, sure enough, but I've brought you here because, like I said, there's no guile about you. You're straight as they come, and the fact that you're out in these forlorn, accursed parts of Orona looking for a dirty old salt like Felding tells me you really need him. Although I could have fetched him and brought him to you so as to avoid you finding out about this place, I couldn't live with myself if those scoundrels back in Dankdocks had gotten a hold of you. And I don't think you'd be the sort to blab about this place anyway. And well—I can't put my finger on it, but I'd say you two were—well, I'd say there's something about you that just makes me inclined to trust you, and that's as far as I can explain it. Now let's go down and see Felding. Let me do all the talking with the others, but you can speak freely to Captain Starwash. What are your names by the way?"

"I'm Aradis Kingblade," Aradis said.

"Girion Ringmark," Girion stated, nodding politely at the old woman.

"Decent names for decent folk, I'd say," the old lady remarked.

A broad tunnel led off to the north, and the woman went down this passage with Aradis and Girion behind her. The passage sloped down gently, then turned right, then left, always going down, with a great many passages and rooms running off of it. When they had walked for a good ten minutes, the passage leveled off and came to a great set of wooden doors. The old woman knocked on the door, again with a peculiar pattern (although this one was quite different from the one she had used before), then loudly called out, "I've struck the stone and passed your kin; now loosen the bolt that I may come in."

And with that, the doors were unbarred from the other side, and they swung open to reveal a truly remarkable sight. An immense cavern lay beyond the doors; it appeared to be a sea cave, for water filled much of the cavern's floor, but there seemed to be no exit to the sea. There was only a huge rock face where there ought to have been an opening. Quite in keeping with the name of Underwharf, there was a set of ramshackle docks along the water's edge, with an assemblage of small ships and dinghies all along them, although the Siloans could not help wondering how the vessels entered or left the cavern. Behind the docks sat a rock shelf upon which a number of wooden structures and buildings had been constructed, as if this place were a fully functional port. The grotto itself stretched a good six hundred feet from end to end and rose at least a hundred feet up into the blackness, where the light of the torches and lanterns failed to illuminate what lay above. A series of passages led from this cavern, some farther inland and some, on the far side, farther north down the coastline. A number of Menfolk, all dressed in sailors' garb, went to and fro along the docks and up and down ladders and through trapdoors and in and out of buildings and along swinging rope bridges and boardwalks that ran from building to building. The woman spoke briefly to the smugglers stationed at the doors through which they had just come and then motioned again for Aradis and Girion to follow her. They walked together down the docks, and the passing smugglers eyed them curiously, but not maliciously, since they were escorted by one known to them.

When they had come almost to the far end of the docks, they knocked on the door of a small house, and a no-nonsense, muscular man emerged. He was bald, but had a thick, round beard, and wore only a blue vest, two gold earrings, green breeches and tall black boots; he had an exceedingly hairy chest, and a curved sword rested at his side.

"Captain Torbett," the old woman addressed him, "I've got two fine young lads here. I just wanted to inform you that they are here with me, and I'll fully vouch for them."

Torbett smiled and replied, "You know, Risella, if just anyone marched two strangers into Underwharf, I'd surely have 'em keelhauled at the Skaggarok Skerries, but if *you're* vouching for them, I'll do them no harm. Now, how is it I may aid ye?"

"I'm looking for Felding," she replied.

"Oh, he's just around the corner helping himself to some ale he brought in from a raid last week," Torbett said, as he pointed his thumb toward the north side of his house.

As Torbett went back inside, Risella and the Siloans walked around the side of the house and were greeted with a rather preposterous sight. A sturdily built man with tousled, sandy-blond hair and a prominent belly lay sprawled on the ground underneath a barrel of ale, with the tap open so that the ale was shooting into his mouth. In his right hand, he was filling up a mug with ale from another barrel. He was dressed in an incorrectly buttoned white shirt and a stained sea vest, poorly patched breeches and knee-high brown sailor boots. A dirty brown rag was clumsily tied around his forehead as a bandana, and his left ear was pierced with a gold hoop. And he was singing softly to himself about the beauty of Lady Barrel.

"Felding!" the woman scolded. "What in the blazes are you doing?"

Both Aradis and Girion stared at the man in near disbelief. If this were indeed the fellow intended to convey them to the Elder Forest, it would seem they had much cause for concern.

The man sat up and closed the tap on the first barrel, hiccupping loudly as he did so. Then, in a drawling baritone, his voice slightly slurred, he said, "Mum, what else is a man to do when he lacks two in his crew? Reddo and Baggs have gone off to Marlond for a spell, and I can't well set sail with just Jiff, now can I?"

"Mum?" Aradis asked, bewildered. "Are you his mother?"

"Yes," Risella sighed. "That I am. Now, Felding, close off the other barrel. Don't be wasting good ale."

"Right. Right," Felding muttered, as he turned the other spigot shut. "Can't be wasting good ale. Now what are you on about, eh?" he asked, as he looked at her, squinting with one eye.

"These lads here—Aradis and Girion—they apparently need to see you about something. Pretty urgent, I would think, since they nearly got torn to bits by Carrican and Fedric and their lot over it." Now she turned to the Siloans. "What did you need from Felding, anyhow?" she asked.

"Well, we were going to ask him if he could take us to the port of Gorondil in Sarganath," Girion said, and Risella's face was instantly filled with a multitude of misgivings.

"Gorondil? Sarganath?" she exclaimed, alarmed. "Why, that's suicide! What in the name of all that is sane and decent would possess a pair of innocent bumpkins like you to enter that devilish domain?"

"Well, if it were up to us, we wouldn't be going there at all," Aradis assured her.

"Well, if it's up to me, you're not going to throw your lives away so thoughtlessly!" she countered.

"Mum, dear Mum," Felding mumbled lovingly, interjecting. "Will you just let me handle this?"

"You're drunk, Felding, and in no condition to make judgments about whether you have any business going off to Sarganath."

"I was there not four months ago, and it was, in fact, a quite profitable venture. Got loaded up with a fair amount of korgenosch, I did," Felding returned saucily.

Risella rolled her eyes. "Oh, and it's a right surety I know what's coming next. I can give your whole speech, Felding. Profitable venture—let's see, you got loaded up with your blasted korgenosch and then took the cargo of Goblin amulets and silver ingots from the four ships from Mallengar. Oh, and then you'll bring up your excursion to Prasseldoff in the Wide Lands to pick up all those ancient Gnomish artifacts. And, after that, you'll roll out all the old classic escapades: the incident with the Ogre cannibals in Tukarat up in the Bushbelt, the Yeti mercenary business with the Maktusuk and Pungalak tribes down in icy Garnavok, the ruse you pulled on those mad Shore-Elf merchants out in the Eldritch Isles and so on and so forth. The moral of the story is: Felding Starwash is invincible, and when he does something that's certain to lead to death, he ends up basking in gold and jewels instead of in a grave."

"Mum, it really is a lot better when I do it," Felding huffed, as he stood up, using the barrel to help raise himself. "Now what's one more little excursion in the grand scheme of things? If these lads want to go wander around in Sarganath, what business is that of yours? And, if I've no concern about taking them there, then what clout have you got to gainsay my good intent?"

"Do you know what you're getting yourselves into?" Risella asked the two Siloans, exasperated, her arms akimbo.

"With Felding?" Aradis inquired, as he motioned toward the cockeyed sailor.

"No, with going to Sarganath. No one ever knows what they're getting themselves into with Felding."

"We know that it's going to be extremely dangerous," Girion offered. "But we were told that your son would take us there anyhow."

"And that I will," Felding said, stumbling forward. Then he seemed to sober up all at once; he was in adventure mode now. Abruptly, he shouted out at the top of his lungs, his words now considerably more articulate, "Jiff! Get your miserable carcass over here!"

Moments later, a shortish, scruffy Manfellow with stubble on his chin and short, dark hair, who looked to be around thirty or thereabouts, jumped off of a rope bridge down the way a bit and came scurrying up to Felding. The man was nibbling on a little sausage.

"This is my first mate, Jiffaloo Timtale, or Jiff as we all know him, a fine man at sea and on land," Felding boasted.

Jiff extended his free hand to the lads and bubbled in a funny, rustic accent, "So good to meet you fellows! Care for a sausage?" He offered his half-eaten one to them. When they did not immediately reply, he prattled on, "It's biyelti, the most delicious animal on earth. Are you familiar with it? Probably not, I would guess, judging by your faces. Most people aren't, so that's not too surprising. Well, you've been missing out. The biyelti is really quite extraordinary. It comes from Pollona. It's somewhat like a deer but faster and a bit bigger, and it lives on the savannah and can jump quite high for its size. But the most important thing about it is how tasty it is. Come on, then! Would you like to try some?"

Aradis and Girion slowly looked at each other, not even really sure what to say at this point, as they had never been offered a sausage and a faunal description so abruptly upon meeting someone, but, at length, Aradis awkwardly said, "No thank you, not at the moment," as he slowly shook Jiff's hand.

"Well, my ship's already loaded up," Felding bellowed. "Why wait, eh? Let's be off this instant."

"Felding, this is ridiculous!" Risella protested. "You don't even know why these lads want to go to Sarganath. You yourself said you didn't fancy running the ship with just you and Jiff, and you haven't asked them about payment."

"Dear mother," Felding sighed exasperatedly, putting his hands on her shoulders. "All your objections are easily set to rest. First, I couldn't care less what they're going to do jaunting about in the Elder Forest. Secondly, I won't be running the ship just with Jiff; I'll have two more crewmates to replace Reddo and Baggs until they get back. And thirdly, they shall pay me in their service as maties aboard me ship. Besides, I shall be rewarded handsomely with korgenosch once we arrive on the mainland."

"You don't know the first thing about running a ship, do you?" Risella inquired of the Siloans.

"A little," Girion replied.

"Absolutely nothing," Aradis said flatly.

Felding was not remotely taken aback. "Well, there's nothing you don't know that I can't teach you in an hour or so. Now, to the *Blue Moon*!"

Felding then flung open the door to Torbett's house, walked in and grabbed a hefty pack near the front door, announcing, "I'll be seeing you around, Captain." He briskly saluted Torbett and then boldly marched off down the docks with Jiff trailing behind him. Aradis and Girion ran to catch up with him, as Risella shook her head in vexation and amazement.

"Your ship is called the *Blue Moon*?" Aradis asked, as he matched Felding's stride.

"That's right," Felding replied. "Jiff, give me some of that biyelti."

"My pleasure, Captain," Jiff said, as he handed him the remaining portion.

"How did it come by that name?" Girion inquired.

Felding grabbed a sack from atop a pile of crates, slung it over his shoulder and then turned onto one of the piers jutting out into the subterranean harbor. As he pointed at the ship they would be boarding, he said, "I liberated this beautiful vessel from her former owners, who badly mistreated her, primarily by forcing her to convey them on errands of great mischief. She's a single-masted cog that once belonged to a bloodthirsty band of Ice-Gnomes up near the Luminous Meridian on the island of Kelvikanursa. Well, as I was driven by need to depart from that place, in the dead of night I stole aboard by the light of a blue moon and steered her out of the harbor. The sky is strange up that way; there are weird lights up in Vyndar, the Sky-Realm. You'd have to see it to believe it, but Eoreth the moon was as blue as blue can be. Needless to say, the Gnomes were none too pleased to discover what I'd done, and I barely made it out of there alive. I had to lose them in the ice floes and nearly sank the ship. But she's served me well for many years now."

Now they were walking up the gangplank onto the vessel. "But the Luminous Meridian is as north as north can be, far up in Huldion," Girion protested. "How then did you manage to bring her down to Aradath? There's no watercourse that flows all the way through the Bushbelt!"

Felding turned and raised his eyebrows, as he tossed the sack and his pack onto the deck. "Is there not?" he asked quizzically, and then laughed to himself. "Well, the ship's here now, isn't she? And she did come from the far north. So there must be a way, mustn't there?"

"You can't argue with that," Jiff chided, as he flung a little pack of his own toward the forecastle.

"But . . . but . . ." Girion stammered.

Starwash silenced him, saying, "Now, now lad, you'll find that the longer you're around me, the more your notions of possibility will be expanded." Then he obnoxiously called, "Ain't that right, Mum?" Risella rolled her eyes once more and shook her head.

"Now let's hoist anchor, Jiff, and say 'Ta ta' to Underwharf!" Felding barked, and presently this was done.

"Farewell, me hearties!" Felding called ostentatiously from the helm, as he blew kisses to all the smugglers standing on the docks, who were only mildly interested in his departure, it seemed. Risella was now standing on the nearby pier, still shaking her head. "Felding Starwash, if you weren't my own son, I'd say you were the most harebrained buffoon this side of Sabakwani's Girdle!" she raved.

"No doubt I am! And the other side too!" Felding laughed in reply.

All of a sudden, Aradis and Girion noticed that the rock face which blocked their exit out into the sea was beginning to sink beneath the water. As it did so, there was a deep rumbling and a loud splashing. Then, in utter amazement, they perceived that the stone wall was really a sort of well-disguised gate, for the vast Indurian Deeps were now visible before them. Apparently, the entrance to Underwharf was in fact part of the cliff-lined coast of Stragmore, but it must have been undetectable from the outside, just as it was from the inside. They surmised that someone had been operating a mechanism somewhere in the cavern to open the gate once they saw that Felding was setting out on the *Blue Moon*.

Now the captain turned to look at them, grinning widely. "Are you ready for your adventure, boys?" he laughed loudly.

Just then, the *Blue Moon* bumped the walls of the grotto on its starboard side. "Whoops," Felding said, as he turned around to focus on his steering.

"May Erdion deliver us. What have we gotten ourselves into?" Aradis murmured to Girion, as the *Blue Moon* passed out into the turbulent sea.

When they were safely clear of the gate, the cliff wall slowly rose back up to conceal the subterranean harbor of Underwharf. Indeed, as they had suspected, it was impossible to tell from the outside that such a portal even existed. Felding set their course for due northwest, and, before long, the rain and the fog made the shores of Stragmore utterly indiscernible. Jiff and Felding barked instructions to them on what to do to aid in running the vessel, and so they spent their first night aboard the *Blue Moon* out in the cold, driving rain, running here and there, messing with lines and whatnot, while trying to keep seasickness at bay.

When dawn came, they were exhausted, miserable, freezing, tired and wet, but Felding and Jiff were just as chipper as ever, for the sun had come out, the rain had drifted away to the south, and they were sailing free on the beautiful Indurian Deeps. After a little while, Felding released the lads from their duties and encouraged them to go below decks and get some rest, a request with which they gladly complied.

They awoke a number of hours later, discussed their present situation for a short while, and then set about exploring the hold of the *Blue Moon*, which was not terribly extensive. It contained ten narrow bunks, five on the port and five on the starboard, and in the middle of the hold was a table with four chairs around it. There were crates, sacks, barrels, bags, chests, nets, lanterns, lengths of rope, hooks and various other implements lining the hull. And, not surprisingly, there was a fair amount of liquor stashed in various places about the compartment. As they were looking around the hold, they heard what sounded like hearty, vivacious singing commence on the deck above them; Felding and Jiff were apparently thoroughly enjoying themselves. Ignoring this for the moment, the lads continued poking around.

In the aft bulwark, they noticed a low, wooden door. Girion opened the hatch, held aloft a lantern and peered into the blackness of the small, dark chamber. To his astonishment, he saw what appeared to be a rather small, modified acrynon of some sort. "Aradis, Felding's got an acrynon!" he exclaimed. The machine was not running at the moment, however.

Aradis came over for a look. "Aren't those rather rare?" he queried, looking about the compartment.

"Exceedingly," Girion replied, setting the lantern on a hook hanging from the overhead and climbing up the ladder to the deck.

Just as the lads had guessed, Felding and Jiff were making merry in the bright sunshine and the cool spray of the sea. They were, in fact, standing on the forecastle singing a silly ditty, swinging their arms jovially, Felding with a mug in hand and Jiff with, unsurprisingly, a sausage.

"Were half of old Brundy now under the waves,
And the lads of lone Gamway all scoundrels and knaves,
And the whole of the dear isles turned heartless to me,
I'd cling to me flagon and cling to the sea!"

    "Oh hey-do! A ring-diddly-oh!
    Ba-diddle a riddle a derry yo ho!
    A hey-do! A ring-diddly-oh!
    Ba-diddle a riddle a derry yo ho!"

The captain and his mate finished boisterously, laughing and slapping each other on the back.

"Wonderful," Girion said in a most congratulatory manner when they had finished. "Absolutely delightful. And a 'derry yo ho' to you too. Now I must ask rather frankly—Captain Starwash, that acrynon you've got down in the hold; how did you come by it?"

"Oh, you found my acrynon, did you?" Felding asked, as he downed a gulp of whatever happened to be in his stein. "It's more than a bit surprising you knew it to be that or even that you're familiar with the term."

"The ship we took into the Fontskals had one," Girion explained.

"That'd be the *Meridot*, I'll wager," the captain replied.

"Yes, but how did you know that?"

"To begin with, there's but a few ships in this Moiety that have acrynons. Besides, a smuggler's got to know his ships, don't he? Us seafolk in Rinnegan's Rovers know the comings and goings of all sorts of vessels, especially the big ones."

Aradis had now emerged from the hold. "Rinnegan's Rovers? Is that your smuggling ring?" he queried.

"That it is," Felding nodded, taking another swig from his mug. "The four westward isles in the Fontskals: Stragmore, Dunlim, Dullen and Trath—together they make up the Rinnegan Group, and our people in Underwharf take a keen interest in anything that comes through them. And that's a fair amount of merchandise, mind you. Why, blazing barnacles and smoldering seaweed! In Dankdocks alone we see ships hailing from just about everywhere—from Fenrost to the Eldritch Isles and every place in between!"

Aradis now remarked, "I don't know much about the Eldritch Isles. What's out there, anyway?"

"People who stay in certain regions of that Neathmarda too long go mad," Jiff explained, hopping down the ladder to the main deck. "There's talk of a Sorcerer in those parts who cast a foul enchantment upon a certain isle, and the closer you get to his island, the worse it gets. But in my opinion, everyone out that way is a bit balmy."

"It seems like everywhere in Orona some evil power is rising," Aradis noted concernedly. "There are people going mad in the Eldritch Isles, Yetis running amuck in Fenrost and a Witch terrorizing the Elder Forest. The leader of our own land of Velaris is oppressing the Menfolk like never before, and from what I've heard, the Bushbelt is nothing but a breeding ground for monsters and murderous natives."

"You don't know the half of it," Felding muttered darkly.

As he untangled a length of rope lying on the deck, Jiff expounded, "Some say it's a coordinated effort. A plan by the Druids to destroy the Menfolk once and for all. For the Menfolk seem to be targeted more than anyone else in all this. You know, Felding knows quite a bit about happenings all over Orona, and he's nearly certain it's a plot like that."

Girion and Aradis both looked up at the captain, who was squinting now, looking north over the sea. "Sure as the Fontskals Fog, there's trouble brewing in Tassaru," he muttered ominously. "The Druids of old are coming back. Meddling with dark powers not fully roused since the Forgotten Days and the Years of Yore. They're not afraid to plumb the depths of Daegar and stir up the black abyss of evil in Massarat."

Now he turned to them and, his voice saturated with sinister memories, said, "I've seen the old city of the Druids, lads, out in the desert. The abandoned fortress city of Grath. And mind you, Felding Starwash don't get scared. But I was terrified there, and I barely made it out of the place alive. The Druids are returning out of the gathering gloom. Mark my words. And when they do, we Menfolk will have to make our last stand. For they won't rest until we're all dead or they're defeated, once and for all. Mark that, lads."

"What's in Massarat?" Aradis inquired.

"And what exactly is Daegar?" Girion added.

But both Felding and Jiff were unresponsive, stoically silent. When the Siloans had waited a rather awkward length of time for an answer, they concluded it would be proper to drop the matter, at least for now. So, eventually, when the silence had become quite oppressive, Aradis commenced, "Um, well then, what can you tell us about Sarganath or Ebonreach or Ravensrealm or whatever people call it these days?"

Felding, now somewhat withdrawn, vacantly responded, "Not a safe place at all. There's a Witch about. That's all I know."

"Yes, but the Witch isn't anywhere close to Gorondil, is she?" Girion asked.

"Goodness no!" Felding returned, laughing. "If she were, even I probably couldn't be talked into taking you there! That's if I were in my right mind, anyway, which is not always the case. You'd have to catch me on the right day."

"Is Gorondil really as perilous as people say then, since the Witch hasn't taken up lodging there?" Aradis inquired.

Felding replied, "Now about this Gorondil business, what's gotten you so fixated on getting into Sarganath through that port in particular? You know, there's more than one way to tame a seal."

"We were given instructions by the fellow that sent us on this journey to go to Gorondil and from there to the city of Anganor in the Kingdom of Argonis," Aradis explained.

"Argonis, eh?" Felding returned. "Sounds like you lads have a death wish. I already had a feeling we'd get along quite well, but now I'm certain of it!" the captain chuckled. "Now what sort of fellow was this who suggested you try to enter Sarganath by way of Gorondil?"

"He's the sort of fellow who ought to be trusted and held in very high regard," Girion replied. "After all, he was the one who told us that you would take us to the Elder Forest, even though no one else would, and in that matter, it seems he proved to be correct."

"Hm. What was the chap's name, eh?" Felding inquired, looking dolefully at the diminished contents of his mug.

"Nagello," Aradis answered. "Do you know him?"

"Nay, lad," Felding replied. "But that's not too surprising. There are a great many people to whom I am known who are not known to me. I've got rather a far-reaching reputation, I'm afraid." Then, idly drumming his fingers on the forecastle railing, he said, "I'm not entirely certain about this Nagello fellow, though. Why would he send you into Sarganath through Gorondil, of all places?"

"I'm certain he wouldn't have told us to go there unless there was a very good reason for it," Girion asserted.

"Well, if it were me," Felding mused, "I would have recommended entering via the port of Forellos, which lies some fifty miles north of Gorondil, but that's not really safe either. But if you've really got your minds set on Gorondil, well then—"

"Gorondil is exceedingly dangerous, then?" Aradis interrupted.

The captain replied, laughing, "Ha! Dangerous? Dangerous? Gorondil's a Dwarven deathtrap. Anyone who lands at the wharf, if they make it that far, who doesn't work for the Witch is either killed or kidnapped. It used to be quite a nice place, and I went there on a number of occasions in my youth, so I know the city quite well, in fact. Of course, it was run by Elves at the time. But the Dwarves of the Iron Highway—that's the main east-west road in the Elder Forest—came and slew the Elves and took a number of ports on the coast of the Elder Forest, all under the Witch's orders. And that was some years ago now. Since then, communication with the interior has all but ceased. The happenings in the Kingdom of Argonis in particular are a mystery. Seems the kingdom still survives, but it may collapse on its own before the Witch ever gets to it. I'm not sure exactly what the trouble is, though. All I've got to go off of are disconnected rumors."

The captain paused, then finished, "But like I said, going to Gorondil's little better than suicide. Actually, trying to get over to Argonis by landing at Gorondil is like trying to get into a monster's mouth by jumping off a cliff."

Utterly crestfallen, Aradis and Girion mourned the directive that Nagello had given them to go to such a perilous place.

Perhaps, Aradis thought, it wasn't so important that they enter via Gorondil after all, especially if the captain refused to take them. A few moments later, he asked quietly, with a very grim expression indeed, "You will not take us to Gorondil, then?" He rather hoped Felding would answer in the negative.

The captain pondered this a moment, then said, "I'd be a fool if I did. But if I told you that you'd have a better chance of reaching Argonis if you came in through Forellos, I'd be lying. There's no gettin' to Argonis these days. And there's no safe way into Sarganath. But Gorondil is the least safe way of all."

After he had said this, Felding cocked his head, scrunched up his right eye and muttered to himself, "Then again, there's far more korgenosch in Gorondil than there is in Forellos. Maybe it wouldn't be such a bad idea to go there after all."

"Korgenosch?" Aradis said. "And what is that?"

Felding instantly perked up at the word. "Korgenosch? Oh, it's a sumptuous liquor, which is only produced by the Dwarves of Hammergast, a great fortress that lies some distance down the Iron Highway. Ever since the lands now known as Sarganath became inaccessible, that murderous bunch in Gorondil has been selling it abroad for a ghastly amount. People will pay the Dwarven merchants' prices too, since they can't get it elsewhere. On occasion, I make runs to Forellos or one of the ports farther north and help myself to a shipment of korgenosch, which I then release for a fair price—certainly lower than that of those deplorable Dwarves— to trade ships passing through the Fontskals. In fact, I'll wager korgenosch is one of the main reasons your Captain Turni of the *Meridot* stopped off in Stragmore. That rogue has undoubtedly purchased several crates of it from one of our agents, and he'll sell it off in Pollona and split the money with the crew."

"Surely old Turni wouldn't be the sort of fellow who would consort with smugglers!" Girion exclaimed.

"If the price is right, he most certainly would," Jiff chimed gleefully.

"And if the price is right, I'll take you to Gorondil," Felding remarked.

"We are willing to pay whatever you require," Girion assured. "For as I said, the one who told us to go to Gorondil would not have done so out of ignorance, and I think it is very important that we follow his instructions. The only problem is that we haven't a single coin, I'm afraid. We spent it all on our voyage to Dankdocks."

Felding kindly replied, "I've no need for your money. You're paying me with your assistance in running the *Blue Moon*." Then he added knavishly, "But, of course, even I wouldn't be crazy enough to take you to Sarganath, especially to Gorondil, unless there was something of considerable value that I could get out of it, and I can tell you that the *Blue Moon* ain't pulling back into Underwharf if she ain't laden with precious cargo." The captain abruptly took a swig from his mug and then winked roguishly at the lads.

The Siloans mulled this statement over for a few moments. Then Aradis, having caught the drift of Felding's riddling, probed with undisguised annoyance, "So the only reason you decided to take us to the Elder Forest to begin with is that you're going to make out well with a batch of Dwarven spirits?"

"That's it exactly, my lad!" Felding chuckled. "Listen to this boy, Jiff! A sharp one he is."

"Well, seeing as no one else would take us there," Girion noted, "I'm glad you agreed to it, even if it is only for money."

"Money . . . and an adventure!" Felding added excitedly. "The two often go together, I say."

"So it's settled then," the captain announced dramatically, clapping his hands together loudly. "We shall go to Gorondil, and I'll come up with the best scheme I can to get you through the port and to the Kingdom of Argonis safely. But it will take me a few days to figure all that out. And once the two of you are ashore, free of the Dwarves and on your way westward, Jiff and I will return to Stragmore with a jolly load of korgenosch."

Now Felding climbed down the ladder to the main deck and went over to a brass bell, which was affixed to the mast. He struck it with a metal hammer, which was hanging by a cord also attached to the mast and boomed, "Now what are we doing standing around here wagging our beaks like a bunch of starving seagulls? Let's hop to it! You gentlemen have a great deal of seafaring to learn under the skillful tutelage of Mister Timtale."

"One more question, Captain," Girion ventured. "Aren't you the least bit curious to know why we're going to Argonis?"

Felding looked at the lad with a rather confused expression. Then clarity seemed to come to him, and he replied, "Oh, well that would spoil the fun, I think, if you told me what you were up to so soon. I do enjoy mind games, lad, and right now I can't think of a single reason why anyone would have any reasonable business in Argonis in these dreadful days. Therefore, you must be conducting unreasonable business. Give me a few days; I want to see if I can guess the nature of your errand, and if I cannot, then I shall perhaps ask you to divulge it."

Felding now went over to his cabin door, flung it open and went inside. A moment later, his blond head reappeared, and he remarked, "By the way, me cabin's off limits to you, boys. If you ain't Jiffaloo or Felding, keep out, see?" Then he popped back inside.

After the captain had said this, Aradis and Girion spent the remainder of the day receiving instructions on how to run the cog and repeatedly refusing biyelti sausages, although, eventually, both of them did break down and try some. To Jiff's considerable disappointment, they found their first biyelti consumption experience to be remarkably mundane, although this did not quell his determination to have them give it another go.

Five more days passed after this, and the *Blue Moon* made rather good time. Occasionally, Felding turned on the acrynon, which hastened their journey, and much of the time they were aided by a friendly easterly wind. The weather wasn't terrible like it had been the first night but neither was it spectacular.

Sailing with Felding was a unique experience, to be sure; he was an endless supply of curious and silly idioms and colorful accounts of his many adventures, though no more could be pried from either him or Jiff about the matters of Massarat and Daegar, for the captain said it was bad luck to speak of such things, especially for sailors. And every time they asked him about his plan for helping them pass safely through Gorondil and on to Argonis, he said that he was still in the process of what he called "plotcraft."

As the days passed, the lads learned several Fontskals ditties, as Felding called them: songs mostly about booze and women, typical sailor fare. One clear evening, the four of them sang raucously for an hour or more about such things as the bonnie dame of Trath, the lusty lads of the Fargost fish market and the boisterous barrel of the Briny Baywatch.

Now, in the late afternoon of the seventh day out from Stragmore, Jiff was down in the hold doing who knows what (probably something sausage-related), Girion was sitting on a bench on the main deck, writing in his notebook, Felding was casually leaning against the railing of the poop deck and Aradis was peering over the port gunwale into the water. He was feeling seasick again and wanted to be in the right place to dispose of his lunch if the need arose to do so.

Just then, he noticed an extremely large, dark shape down in the water, appearing almost as if it were the shadow of a cloud drifting by overhead. It was a good fifty feet in length, nearly as long as the *Blue Moon*. The shadow seemed to drop down, diminish and move, as it were, underneath the vessel. Then it disappeared utterly from sight.

Aradis was set to wondering about this, when all of a sudden, the ship swayed violently to the port side, and he was nearly knocked overboard. Then there was an extremely loud splashing off the starboard side of the *Blue Moon*, as if some massive being were thrashing wildly in the water. Girion immediately stowed his notebook in his tunic and stood up in alarm. It was only a moment later that Captain Felding boomed from the helm in the most voluminous voice they had yet heard him employ, "Akwursa!"

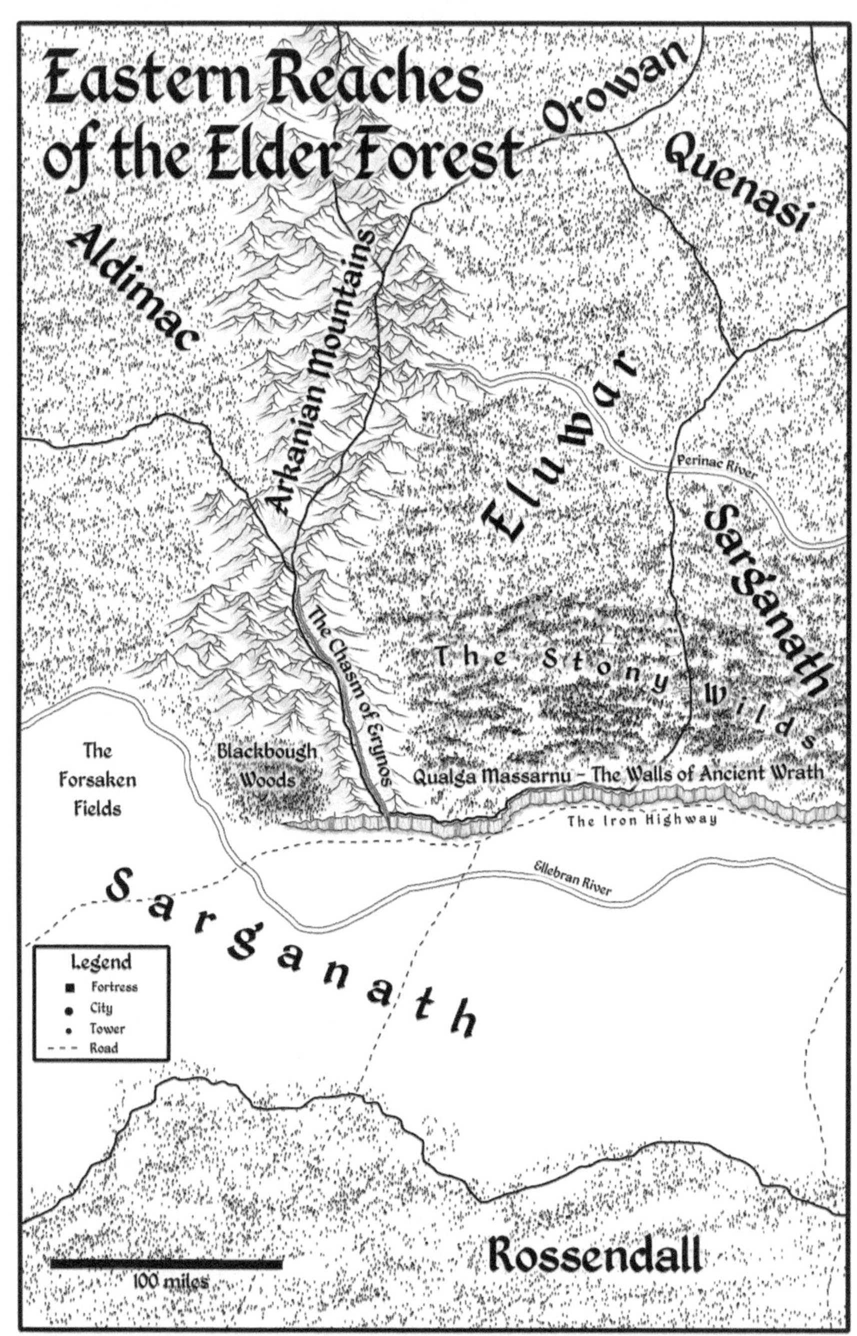

Eastern Reaches of the Elder Forest
Orowan
Quenasi
Aldimac
Arkanian Mountains
Eluwar
Perinac River
Sarganath
The Stony Wilds
The Chasim of Erynos
Blackbough Woods
The Forsaken Fields
Qualga Massarnu – The Walls of Ancient Wrath
The Iron Highway
Ellebran River
Sarganath
Legend
Fortress
City
Tower
Road
Rossendall
100 miles

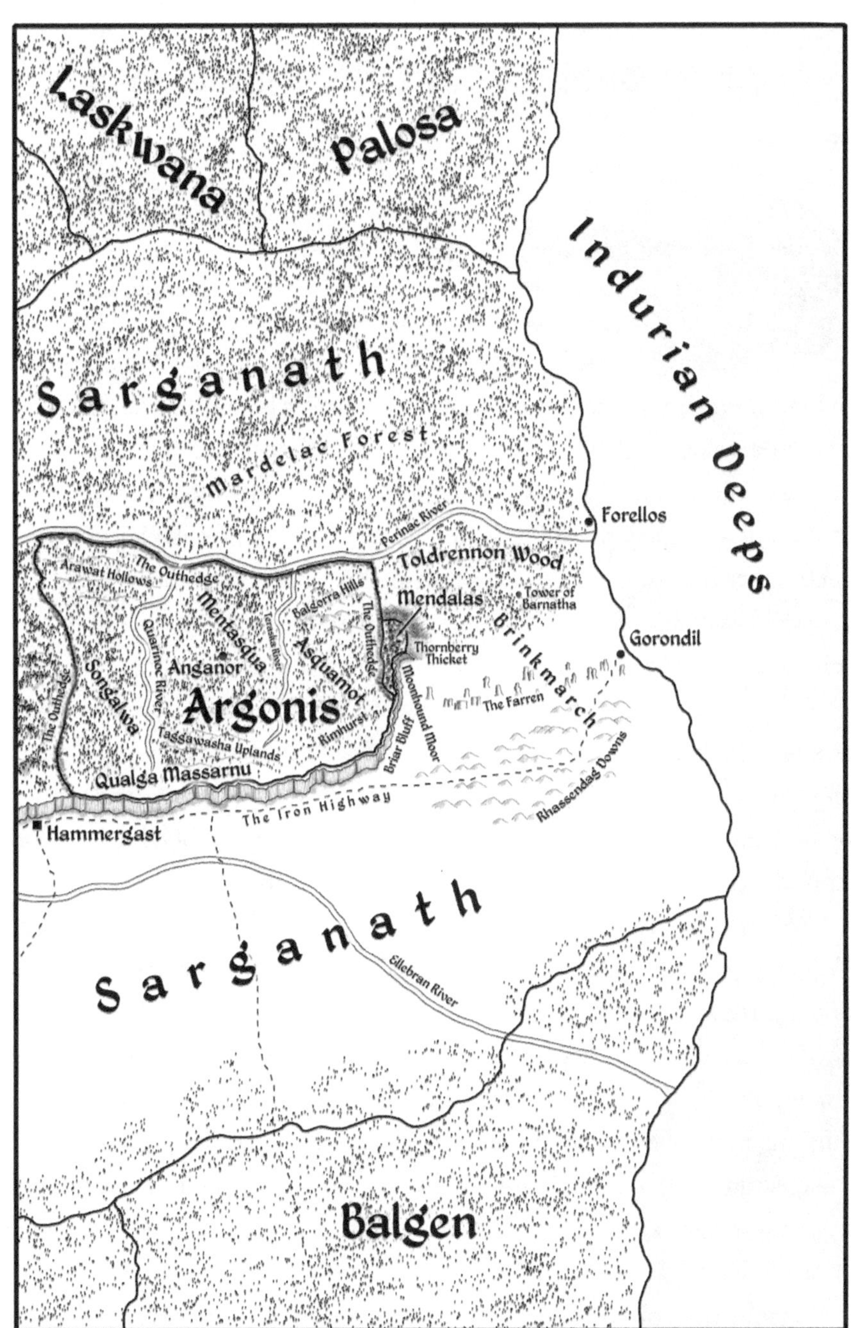

Laskwana
Palosa
Indurian Deeps
Sarganath
Mardelac Forest
Perinac River
Forellos
Toldrennon Wood
Arawat Hollows
The Outhedge
Baldorra Hills
Mendalas
Tower of Barnatha
Mentasqua
The Outhedge
Brinkmarch
Gorondil
Quarinac River
Terenlac River
Asquamot
Thornberry Thicket
Anganor
Argonis
The Outhedge
Songaluva
Moonhound Moor
The Farren
Tassawasha Uplands
Rimhurst
Briar Bluff
Rhassendas Downs
Qualga Massarnu
The Iron Highway
Hammergast
Sarganath
Ellebran River
Balgen

CHAPTER SEVEN

Of Monsters and Machinations

here was no need to ask what the word signified for, a moment later, the ocean churned violently, and there rose from the roiling blue of the Indurian Deeps a truly monstrous creature. Its body was a hulking mass of brown fur above blending into shiny blue scales below, and its head rose up like a colossus above the ship. Indeed, its head alone was enormous, and its mouth could have swallowed a man whole. Its hideous face could best be described as that of a demented bear, with teeth like long, jagged spikes, eyes of a glossy black and fur dripping with briny wash. Its gigantic forearms were raised above the water; they were covered in scales but terminated in vicious, tearing claws that gleamed in the sunlight.

Only a moment more after the akwursa had appeared above the waves and Felding had shouted his warning, the hatch to the hold popped open, and Jiff sprang up onto the deck. He did not look terribly dismayed; rather, he was prepared for action. In fact, he immediately grabbed a harpoon from the deck and tossed it up to Felding on the poop deck.

"Well, what are you doing standing there, lads?" the captain shouted. "Waiting for it to shake hands? Get ye some harpoons and stick that foul beast in the eye!"

Aradis and Girion hastily sought out harpoons, a few of which were strewn about the deck, as the akwursa let out an unearthly, screaming, gurgling roar. Felding ran to the starboard rampart and flung a harpoon at the creature's left eye, but it turned away from him at the last second and was instead struck in the side of its head; this, of course, enraged it. Felding abruptly shouted to Girion, "Get away from the gunwale!"

Girion sprang back from the starboard railing just in time, for the akwursa had swiped at him with its murderous claws.

"Jiff, there'll be no vanquishing the beast with harpoons alone!" Felding yelled, hurling yet another at the beast as it dove down into the water, causing the ship to intensely roll back and forth once more. "Let's give this Scion of Sharga a Starwash Special! Number Five, I think."

"Righto, Captain!" Jiff shouted in reply, as he ducked into the cabin beneath the poop deck.

Meanwhile, both Aradis and Girion had grabbed harpoons and were looking frantically about for where the akwursa would strike next. They did not have to wait long, for the monster rose up near the port bow now, and its eyes fixed angrily upon them. In vain, they instinctively threw their harpoons at the hulking head before them, but their projectiles bounced harmlessly off the thick fur and fell shamefully into the waves below.

Felding had managed to procure the end of a hanging line affixed to the top of the mast, and now, harpoon in hand, he swung from the poop deck, passing right in-between the two Siloans. The rope stopped dangerously close to the akwursa's face, and there Felding hurled his weapon at the creature's right eye. It did not strike its intended mark but pierced its hide just above it, and the akwursa again howled in rage and made another swipe, just barely missing the daring captain, as he swung back and then jumped onto the deck.

"Now don't you be trying that, lads!" Felding laughed, as he grabbed a harpoon with each hand and threw both of them at the akwursa as it disappeared into the brine again. He really seemed to be enjoying himself, despite their grave peril. Perhaps too much Stragmore stout had gotten to him, Aradis thought.

"Where's it gone now?" Girion cried out.

"I'll wager the devil will pop up off the starboard again," Felding conjectured, and he was correct in this estimation. The captain now leapt up on the rampart with a single harpoon, as he balanced himself by holding on to the rigging.

"Come here, you briny bastard!" the seaman taunted. "See if you can make a meal out of Felding Starwash! Or, if you haven't got the nerve for it, have a bite of Dwarven iron!" Accompanying this gibe was yet another harpoon. This time it landed smack in the akwursa's gums; it bit down ferociously and the metal shaft was sundered. Once more the beast hastily submerged.

Then, without warning, the massive, scaly tail of the beast shot up out of the water, thrashing wildly, and one of its flukes smacked the *Blue Moon* on its hull, rocking the vessel dangerously and knocking Aradis and Girion off their feet.

The akwursa darted back beneath the waves, and as soon as the ship grew somewhat stable, Felding barked, "Quickly lads, go stand by the port gunwale! Akwursas will only take so much abuse before they attack ships directly. We haven't got much time before that happens. I need you to shout at the top of your lungs at it and throw whatever you can at its face. We've got to coax it in for my final throw."

"Are we really to be bait for a sea monster?" Aradis shouted angrily.

"Just trust me, will ya?" Felding yelled back. "I swear an oath on the sand of the Farthest Shore that no harm will come to you!"

Neither Aradis nor Girion had any idea where or what the Farthest Shore was, but the captain's oath sounded quite serious. And so, terrified as they were, they did as the captain said.

When the akwursa emerged again, the Siloans shouted all sorts of nasty things at the monster and flung buckets and bottles and other assorted miscellany at its face. It had not yet moved to attack them, but its face was growing flush with rage, and crimson blood poured from its threefold wounds. It was getting ready to strike violently, to destroy and devour at any instant.

Just then, Jiff raced out of the cabin holding a bottle with a flaming rag extending from it.

"Ah, yes! The Starwash Special!" Felding exulted.

"Just like you ordered, Captain," Jiff said, as he tossed the bottle to Felding, who deftly caught it.

The Captain now scrunched up one eye and looked straight in the akwursa's terrifying maw. "You've tangled with the wrong sailor, you foul devil!" Felding spat, as he hurled the burning device directly into the creature's mouth.

The blazing bottle whizzed just past Aradis' ear, struck the akwursa's sharp teeth and shattered; instantly, its face was enveloped in violent flames. Writhing in pain, it plunged frantically beneath the surface of the sea but not before Jiff had quickly hurled another object into its open mouth. Neither Aradis nor Girion had seen clearly what it was, but it appeared to be a metal canister of some sort.

Moments later, a shocked Aradis and Girion observed a ferocious explosion underwater, and a geyser of blood and brine shot up high into the air above where the akwursa's head had burst into oblivion. The *Blue Moon* pitched and rolled in the upheaval, and the Siloans fell to the deck in dismay, as blood and water showered them.

"What was that?" Aradis inquired, as he picked himself up from the deck, attempting to wipe the akwursa's blood from his hair.

"That, my friends, was a Starwash Special," Jiff responded, quite amused with himself.

Meanwhile, Felding whooped and hollered in delight. The giddy captain needlessly hurled a harpoon at the spot where the akwursa had been, then shouted, "Did you see that boys? Hoo hoo! Ha ha! Bammo! Open your mouth, you sea-filth, and no more akwursa!"

"Whoo! Whooie!" he shouted with great elation. Then he unexpectedly leapt up on the starboard rampart, let out one more, "Whoo! Whooie!" and excitedly jumped overboard. Aradis and Girion were dumbfounded.

"I beg your pardon," Girion hesitantly said to Jiff, "but what is he doing?"

Jiff pulled out a biyelti sausage from his vest, took a substantial bite of it and casually replied, "Oh, he almost always does that sort of thing when one of his plans works, which happens about, oh, I'd say half the time." Then he strolled over to the gunwale and tossed a rope down to the captain, who swam around whooping and hollering in joyous merriment for a minute or so and then climbed back up onto the *Blue Moon*.

"You'd think by now that akwursas would have learned not to get anywhere near the *Blue Moon*," Felding chuckled.

"Have you fought those things before, then?" Aradis inquired, as the captain climbed back up to the ship's wheel.

"That was my fifth," Felding replied. "I didn't do too well with the first one; nearly lost my life you know, but as you can see, I've improved since then. They're highly territorial, you see, and will fight with each other if one enters another's area. And they don't much care for ships passing through their range. They're fairly predictable as far as sea monsters go though, and they'll always check your ship out first before they attack. And they go from one side to the other if you attack 'em, just like you witnessed, but eventually, if they get mad enough, they'll outright attack the ship instead of those aboard it. They're smart enough to recognize that the ship ain't no creature, but that it's got people on it, so they go after the people to begin with, and if that doesn't work, they come after the ship."

"Will we run into any more, you think?" Aradis asked uneasily.

"Nah," Felding replied, as he uncorked a bottle and downed a swig of stout. "There ain't many akwursas left these days—far fewer than in my grandfather's day anyway, and there's only a narrow strip that runs north to south in the Indurian Deeps where you'll run across 'em."

"What was that thing Jiff threw, anyway?" Girion inquired, as he sat back down upon the bench he had been using before all the chaos erupted.

"The Starwash Special is a two-course meal, you see, and that was the second course," Felding replied, winking.

"Yes, but how does it work?" Girion pressed.

"Well, the Starwash Special is also the Starwash Secret, and Jiff's the only other one in Orona that knows how to prepare it," the captain explained. "Ain't that right, Jiff?"

Jiff was messing with some lines on the rigging, but he turned and nodded to Felding, briefly replying, "Yep."

Aradis now sat down next to Girion, exhausted, and quietly muttered to him, "I'm certainly glad we have Felding taking us across this wild sea; any other man would have been at a loss to save us. But I'll tell you one thing—he's as crazy as they come."

Felding chuckled to himself at the helm, "Mum will love hearing about that one. That was a good piece of work, Felding Starwash. Yes it was."

And so the *Blue Moon* sailed on westward. The rest of the day passed without incident—certainly nothing as exciting as the battle with the akwursa. When night came, they sang and danced to celebrate their victory and had a supper of salted mutton, seabiscuits, laver, and, of course, biyelti (at Jiff's insistence).

The next three days were kind to them in that no further denizens of the deep assailed them, and the weather was reasonably cooperative. A serendipitous easterly sped them along toward the hither shores of Byram, and the waves were as docile as one might hope for in this region of the Indurian Deeps. However, the Siloans noticed that the captain and his first mate seemed to be growing increasingly alert as they drew closer to the Elder Forest; anxious they were not, but somehow more attentive. There were fewer ditties, fewer tales and less consumption of biyelti and Stragmore stout, but there was a great deal more scanning of the horizon and pensive mumbling. Eventually, Aradis and Girion inquired of the captain when they would arrive in Byram and what they were to do when they arrived there. He replied that only a few days more would bring them to Gorondil and that he was presently putting the finishing touches on a scheme to discreetly enter that treacherous anchorage. He said he would notify them as soon as his machinations were fully laid out.

Now on the tenth day since their embarkment from the Fontskals, twilight had come and gone and Jiff was manning the wheel while Felding had retired to his cabin, which lay aft, directly beneath the poop deck. Aradis and Girion, meanwhile, had just finished a series of menial tasks assigned to them and were getting ready to clamber down to the hold for a short respite. In fact, they had already opened the hatch and were partway down the ladder.

Just then, Felding stuck his head out the cabin door and snapped, "And just where do you laddies think you're off to? Nodaway Island, is it? Not now, you dozy landlubbers!" Then he laughed good-naturedly. "He he! Aye, that'll come in a trifle, mind you, but now we must do a bit of cooking! Come into me kitchen," he invited, as he motioned amiably to them.

"But we've already eaten, Felding," Aradis countered.

The captain chuckled again. "No, no, you silly grandywhack! It's not stew that's needing brewing, but a plan. We'll be pulling into Gorondil in the morning, and you two have got to be privy to everything I've concocted to dupe those diabolical Dwarves."

Aradis did not especially appreciate being identified as the rather unsightly fish they had often consumed on their voyage, but he knew that it was vitally important for them to be debriefed on whatever harebrained stratagems the captain had devised. Additionally, he was intrigued to see what lay inside Felding's cabin, for they had respectfully followed his directive to stay out of it. So, after Felding had imparted a few brief instructions to Jiff, Aradis and Girion slowly stepped down into the lantern-lit cabin of Captain Starwash.

The cabin contained, as expected, Felding's bunk and a wooden table with a number of maps, charts and navigational devices on it. But the room was crammed full of all sorts of odd items. Some were recognizable, such as bottles and jugs of various substances (most of them liquors, no doubt), but there was also a myriad of mysterious little metallic devices and a scattering of crystals of different shapes and sizes here and there. In addition to these, there was a wide array of beakers, tubing, flasks, vials, funnels and cylinders. On the floor, there were wicks and wires of varying lengths and materials, and throughout the cabin lay an assortment of orbs, exotic artifacts, little metal tools and the more conventional smugglers' plunder of gold, silver coins and jewels. And, wherever there was room, there were piled capacious chests, crates and boxes. It was anyone's guess as to what these might contain.

"Well, laddies, have a seat," Felding began congenially, waving his hand at two chests that served as benches by his table. They heeded this invitation, and then Felding stationed himself on a crate opposite them.

"Now, me hearties," the wily captain commenced, "we've quite a bit to go over, seeing as you'll soon be passing into great peril, and I want to give you the best shot I can on staying alive. So I've got to make sure you understand every angle of my plan in case we have to modify it midstream. So now, it's time for a pointed lesson on the successful navigation of the cutthroat quays of Gorondil."

"Ha. I'd say such a lesson is long overdue," Aradis remarked, moderately perturbed. "We've been waiting for over a week now to hear what we need to do when we arrive there. Please continue," he requested, as he leaned back a little.

Now it was Felding's turn to be annoyed. "Well, you can't rush a Starwash masterpiece, now can you? Besides, I didn't finish formulating my plan until just now."

"And your plan is . . .?" Girion said expectantly, raising his eyebrows.

"Oh, yes—me plan!" Felding said excitedly. "Here's how it goes, laddies. Tonight we raise a Forellosian flag—that's a flag from the port of Forellos, which is currently occupied by Dwarves in league with Ravinia—and that will keep the blasted Dwarven blockade from hindering us before we reach the coast."

"You mean there are patrol ships running up and down the coast, and we're just going to sail right through them?" Aradis asked, baffled.

"That is the intention, anyway," Felding smugly retorted.

"How did you come by a Forellosian flag?" Girion pressed.

"That would take quite some time to explain," the captain remarked, "so suffice it to say that I have one, and I'm going to use it to bluff our way past the patrols."

"Very well, then," Aradis returned. "But will our ruse not be discovered when we arrive at the port?"

"Nooo," Felding slyly rejoined, "because we will be attired as Druids, and, as everyone knows, the Druids of the Elder Forest are in league with Ravinia, and thus we shall be treated to immunity. Besides, there are a decent number of Druids in Gorondil—though most of 'em are in the southeastern part of town in a district called Potters' Wharf—so it won't raise a great deal of suspicion if a few Druids pull into port. Furthermore, we shall be posing as emissaries of the Druid Allaroc," he said proudly, as he adjusted his jacket.

"Who is Allaroc?" Girion queried.

"I am," Felding prosaically replied.

"You're a Druid?" Aradis asked, astounded.

"No, you barrelbrain! I'm going to be pretend to be a Druid!" the captain returned.

"But I thought you said you were going to pretend to be an *emissary* of Allaroc," Girion objected.

"I am," Felding confirmed.

"So you're going to pretend to be a Druid and his emissary all at the same time?" Aradis inquired, thoroughly perplexed. "Felding, are you drunk?"

"Not at the moment," the captain replied matter-of-factly. "See, it's like this. I've been up to Forellos a number of times and established a persona as Allaroc the Druid, who, as far as all them Dwarves know, works as a special agent for Ravinia."

"So there is no real Allaroc," Girion said.

"Correct. I made him up to get me safely in and out of Forellos on multiple occasions. But in any event, I am quite certain the folk in Gorondil have heard of Allaroc via regular communication with Forellos, so if we pose as messengers sent by him, the guards down at the wharf will be less likely to pry into our business. Additionally, I will claim that we have an artifact of some importance to send to Ravinia. The line I'll feed them is that we are to meet a certain Druid, a personal messenger of Ravinia, at the Gorondil stables, which are on the far side of town. It is there that you shall purloin two horses and make your escape, and I shall make my getaway back to the *Blue Moon*."

"Captain, I hate to dampen your enthusiasm about all this, as I know you've spent a great deal of time on it, but in all honesty, this whole scheme sounds pretty precarious," Girion said concernedly. "How likely is it that the Dwarves will believe you?"

"My dear lad," Felding blustered, "you are speaking to a man who has hoodwinked some of the cleverest individuals in all Orona with his disguises, pretenses and brilliant maneuvers. My plan is foolproof."

"No sense arguing about it then. If Felding Starwash says nothing can go amiss, then nothing can go amiss," Aradis declared facetiously.

Felding, apparently missing the sarcasm, beamed. "Aye, nary a thing."

"So what exactly is our part to be in all this?" Girion inquired.

"You, my lads," Felding explained, "will have the following primary task: keep your mouths shut and don't speak unless directly spoken to. I'll do all the palavering, for I know all the right phrases to employ, all the right names to bring up and all the right protocol to observe. The both of you will be dressed up in Druid cowls, and as far as I'm concerned, you needn't do anything more than look sour and dour, as you walk along behind me. But, if the worst should happen, and it's unavoidable for you to converse with the Dwarves, here's all you need to remember: Aradis, your name is to be Curronath; Girion, you are to be Hadarion. You work for Allaroc just like I do, and my name is to be Galbarra. We have been charged with the custody of an artifact which is of great significance to Ravinia, and our instructions are to meet a Druid from Blackbough Woods at the Gorondil stables, who will then transport it directly to the Witch herself. His name is to be—oh let's see—Drannic. Yes, Drannic the Druid. The artifact is to be carried ashore in a crate and left at a warehouse down by the wharf. We will entrust it to the Dwarves' keeping there, while we sally down to the livery to see if the envoy from Blackbough has arrived. For any knowledge which falls outside of what I have just told you, you must defer to me. Whatever you do, don't try to come up with the information on your own. Is all that quite clear?"

Aradis and Girion looked at each other anxiously, wondering if the captain was truly out of his mind or if he really was as much of a genius as he seemed to imagine himself to be.

"Well, have you got all that down, Curronath? Tucked away for the morning, Hadarion?" Felding inquired insistently.

"Yes, I think we've got all we need to know," Aradis affirmed. "I'm Curronath, Girion's Hadarion, and you're—uh, Galbarra. And we're to say nothing at all unless it's absolutely necessary. But supposing the Dwarves buy your whole story and we make it all the way through Gorondil without incident—how are we going to steal the horses and escape without the Dwarves noticing?"

Felding gave them a decidedly odd look, then moaned, "You do ask the silliest questions, Curronath. Why, haven't you ever stolen a horse before?"

Girion now chimed in, "I'm afraid not. It's considered a crime where we come from."

"It's considered a crime here, too, but that doesn't—" Felding began, then checked himself. "Well, you ain't really the horse-stealing type, I reckon. But you'll have to be tomorrow—if you want to have any chance of making it to the Kingdom of Argonis alive, that is."

"Yes, but are we to simply jump on the horses' backs and ride off, or has your plan a little more sophistication at that point?" Aradis pressed.

Felding took a sizable gulp from a flagon of Stragmore stout, which he had setting out on the table, and then eagerly explained, "The key to all first-rate larceny is first-rate diversions. The reason I designated the stables as our meeting point with the imaginary Drannic is that I can distract the guards there by making inquiries about him and explaining our fictitious scenario in a needlessly complex manner. So, while they're engaged with me, you two can sneak in, select the most robust mounts and saddle up. As soon as you've managed that, you've got to ride like mad straight west across the plains. If the guards don't notice your departure, that will be fantastic. But even if they do, I've got another layer to my plan." The captain grinned deviously.

"And what would that be?" asked Girion.

"Another Starwash Special," Felding replied gleefully. "Suffice it to say that by the time I've finished serving it up—if I end up needing to do so— the stables will be fully ablaze. The guards will, of course, try to save their animals, and that will give you more time to flee. But even if they do get them out, I'm hopeful I can cause a stampede, so they'll have no mounts left to chase you with. And I'm confident I can pull all that off discreetly enough that the guards don't realize I'm responsible for it. Then, whilst all the mayhem I just described is transpiring, I'll be free to race back to me ship and leave Gorondil in my wake."

The Siloans looked at each other and then at the captain incredulously.

"You really think you can make all that happen and not be caught?" Aradis asked.

"I'm absolutely sure of it," Felding replied brightly. "Just leave the details to me."

"But what about your korgenosch?" Girion inquired. "How will you—"

"Oh, don't you worry about that," Felding chortled. "You can be sure I've got that taken care of. As I said, all you boys have to worry about is keeping your mouths shut tight, and, when we get to the stables, choosing your steeds well."

"How then will you and Jiff manage the return voyage to Dankdocks after we have gone?" Girion wondered.

The captain replied, "It's possible to run the *Blue Moon* with only two sailors, especially with the acrynon at work, but, of course, it's a lot easier with four. Jiff and I will be all right. Right now I want to make sure you lads can handle yourselves once you've escaped Gorondil."

"Yes, where do we go once we leave the port?" Aradis asked. "What landmarks can we look for on the way to Argonis?"

"Hmm," Felding said, scratching his head. He reached over to a stack of charts sitting on a nearby crate, thumbed through them and pulled out a decently detailed map of Argonis and its neighboring lands, which he set on the table in front of him. While explaining the lads' prospective route for fleeing from Gorondil, he pointed to each location on the map, as he mentioned its name. "You'll need to ride due west and just a little south across Brinkmarch, which is this region here between the Indurian Deeps and the Kingdom of Argonis. It's about a hundred miles or so across, I'd say. Don't stray too far south, though, or you'll come to the Iron Highway and the Rhassendag Downs, which you need to avoid at all costs, for that whole region is teeming with Dwarves who are in the service of Ravinia. And don't go too far north either, mind you, for then you'll draw nigh to Toldrennon Wood, which is also thoroughly Dwarf-infested. Your route must keep to the area between the Downs and the Wood, a coastal plain known as the Farren; it's littered with strange boulders and weird rock formations that will provide you with cover should you run into any roving Dwarven patrols. That's the reason why I advised you to ride a bit south, even though you'll have to come back north a few miles once you've reached the western side of Brinkmarch. So, as I've said, you need to head due west across Brinkmarch, veering slightly to the south, and, at length, you'll come to a place called Moonhound Moor. And let me tell you, lads—you don't want to be anywhere near that moor when night falls."

"Why is that?" Girion asked, intrigued.

Now the captain looked up from the map and straight at Girion. A shadow fell over his expression in the flickering light of the lantern, and he said darkly, "Let it be put this way: if night should come and you find yourselves in Moonhound Moor, you'd be better off in Gorondil carrying a banner that says 'Down with Ravinia!' in broad daylight. You see, Moonhound Moor takes its name from the monsters that dwell there in great burrows under the ground—the moonhounds. You won't see 'em in the daytime, for they only come out when evening commences, at the Dawn of Eoreth. They roam to and fro across the moor all night, stalking their prey. Then they slink back to their holes at the Call of Marda, just before the sun comes up. They're horrifying, massive devils, seven feet or more in length and about that high at the shoulder. They run about hunting in the dark, giving off a sickly silver sheen. Their distant baying means certain death to all who hear it, for the foul beasts can run as fast as the wind in a Gamway gale. And should they fall upon you, they'll tear your miserable body limb from limb and devour it piece by piece. So, as I was saying, if I were you, I'd pass through the moor as quickly as possible and only while Marda is smiling upon you."

"Of course we couldn't pass through a *decent* moor," Aradis grumbled under his breath. "It has to be a moor with monsters."

Girion, ignoring Aradis' comment, inquired, "Is there no other way to the Kingdom of Argonis except through the Farren and then Moonhound Moor?"

"I'm afraid not." Captain Felding mournfully shook his head. Then, returning to indicating various locations on the map, he said, "Argonis is fenced on its eastern, northern and western boundaries by a great wall of thorns known as the Outhedge. It's a protective barrier that was planted long ago, back in the Bridging of the Tides, perhaps some nine hundred years ago, and it has grown to an immense breadth and height in that time. And Argonis' southern boundary is guarded by the Walls of Ancient Wrath, a sheer rock face of three thousand feet or more which runs for more than four hundred miles from east to west along the southern border of both Argonis and the Stony Wilds, the region which lies to the west of there. In former times, folk would go down the Perinac River—that's this river here—which has its mouths by Forellos, and enter Argonis by one of the three northern gates. All three of the gates lie directly on the Perinac, in fact. But these days, all territory between the Deeps and Argonis has been swallowed up by Sarganath. So, unless you fancy clambering up the Walls of Ancient Wrath or jaunting through Toldrennon Wood and on into Mardelac Forest, there isn't any other way in besides the Moor. But if you take the path through the Wood, you may count it an absolute certainty you'll be picked up by the Dwarves, for both Toldrennon and Mardelac are crawling with 'em. And even if, by some strange chance, the Dwarves don't get you, the Blackwings will, at least in Mardelac Forest, anyway."

"And what exactly are Blackwings?" asked Aradis, who was rather dismayed to learn of yet another set of foes between them and their destination.

Girion looked at his friend and said, "Aradis, you and I have talked about this before, remember? I told you about them that day we were hiking up by Sarmallen Hill in Rimwold Forest. It was the time we saw all those huge birds, and you asked if the stories you'd heard about winged

Barada were true. Blackwings, also known as Farga, are one of the Kindreds. They're a Narthaya of Barada, just like Dwarves, Elves, Menfolk or what have you."

"Oh, they're the ones you described as being somewhat Mannish, yet having huge black wings like those of a bat," Aradis recollected.

"I suppose you could put it that way," Felding said, as he finished taking a quick sip from his mug. "The Blackwings were originally from the steamy jungles of Soyawat up in northwest Byram, from the four great kingdoms of Telucca, Elukatai, Salalu and Shakunasa. But in the last few hundred years, there have been a number of them that have migrated farther south in Byram, to more temperate climes. A while back, you see, some Blackwings settled in the land where Ravinia now holds sway. In the last ten years or so, they have assisted the Witch in her conquests in exchange for her repeated assurances that she would help them build a great empire. That's why there are so many of them to be found in Mardelac Forest."

"I thought you said you didn't know all that much about Argonis," Aradis remarked, somewhat peeved.

"Well, there's quite a lot to know," Felding replied unabashedly, "and I know only a very small amount of it—comparatively, that is."

Girion sighed resignedly, then said, "I suppose Moonhound Moor is our only option. Where do we go from the moor, then?"

"North," Felding replied, pointing to a particularly dark spot on the map, "to Thornberry Thicket, a dense boscage of trees and brambles rife with vicious thorns. It lies just on the northern edge of the moor. Not to put a damper on your resolve, but, as far as I know, no one's ever found his way through it, apart from the aid of the Elves who live just beyond it. But there's a first time for everything, eh? And if you should come to their land, you'll be close indeed to the Kingdom of Argonis, for its sole eastern gate lies in the wood of the Elves, there atop Briar Bluff, a huge cliff, probably two thousand feet or so in height. From the outside of Argonis, that gate can only be reached from the dominion of the Elves. You see, Moonhound Moor is bounded on the west by the bluff, but the cliffs become lower as they march northward; then they turn eastward, and the last of their broken stones fall at the edge of Thornberry Thicket. The thicket spreads a number of miles to the north, and there's no going around it to reach the

Elves, for their land is utterly hemmed in. On its northern and northeastern marches is Thornberry Thicket, and, beyond that, Toldrennon Wood. Its more southerly eastern flank is guarded by the unscalable Briar Bluff. And on the south and west, the Elves' land is bordered by the Outhedge."

"Why is everything around here so hard to get to?" Aradis muttered peevishly.

"Argonis and the lands surrounding it have suffered much at the hands of their enemies over the centuries," Felding replied, "and the people have learned that they must take great measures to protect themselves."

Girion was still puzzling over their route to Argonis, which posed such a great number of obstacles and difficulties. "These Elves—" he asked, "they're not in the employ of Ravinia are they? How will they regard us? As foes? Friends? Spies? Curiosities?"

"That's hard to say," Felding returned, as he set the map of Argonis back on the crate where he had gotten it. "They're sworn enemies of both the Witch and the Dwarves, due to the fact that it was Ravinia herself who instigated the attacks on their ports, and it was the Dwarves who carried them out. But the Elves may well view all strangers with strong suspicion. I wouldn't count on them aiding you, but, at the very least, they may grant you access to the Kingdom of Argonis, for it is said that they are the wardens of its eastern gate."

"At least we may hope they show us that kindness," Aradis sighed.

The captain folded his arms, then abruptly announced, "I give up."

"What?" Aradis and Girion said simultaneously. They weren't entirely sure they had heard Felding correctly, for his statement made no sense whatsoever in the context of their conversation.

"I give up!" he repeated adamantly.

"You give up on what?" Girion queried.

"I can't figure it out," Starwash lamented. "I've been trying for days, and I can't come up with anything, reasonable or unreasonable."

"What in the world are you talking about?" Aradis asked, wondering if the captain even knew what he was saying.

"The reason you two are going to Argonis," Felding returned. "I've been running through all the possibilities I can think of and haven't hit upon a single one that makes any sense whatsoever. So I give up. I've lost the game. Now, why is it that you're so keen on going to the Kingdom of Argonis? What is your business there?"

At this time, Aradis figured they may as well tell the captain what they were up to, for a man who has laughed in the face of an akwursa shouldn't have much latitude for mocking anyone else's foolhardy ventures. In addition, Felding obviously was exceedingly frustrated that he had been unable to divine the cause of their journey, and it would simply be indecent to leave such a matter undisclosed at this point.

"Well," Aradis began awkwardly, "I don't really know how to explain this without just saying what happened, but Girion and I were visited by one of the Hadathi, an emissary of the Danna. This Hadathi commanded us to go to the Kingdom of Argonis and unify its people, and then go west into Blackbough Woods and destroy the Witch Ravinia." Having said this, he awaited Felding's reaction, which (knowing the captain) could very well range anywhere from exuberant gusto to phlegmatic unflappability.

Felding said nothing at first; he only took another drink and swallowed it. After that, he looked back and forth thoughtfully between the two lads, then began very quietly chuckling. "You know, you're lads after my own heart," he said at length. "If you're going to do something, do something big, I always say. And it's a good thing the Danna's the one that suggested you take out Ravinia, for it's certain as a Skaggarok squall you couldn't destroy the Witch with any aid less than that of Telyon himself. Yes, I've had my fair share of interaction with Hadathi in my day, and I can tell you this right now: you're in for a grand adventure indeed if they come a-knockin' at your door."

Aradis was quite taken aback at the captain's revelation. "You too have encountered the Hadathi?"

"Aye," Felding confirmed somberly. "My travels have taken me to places and situations where encounters with creatures of the Haedra were nearly unavoidable. If a man tampers with such things as I have, he's bound to have a brush with a Hadathi or two. But I'll tell you this: a man is instantly out of his depth the moment Telyon and the Hadathi come into the matter."

The captain continued gravely, "But if the Danna's ordered you to slay the Witch, slain she will be and by your hand. Yet who can say what will become of the both of you in the end? Of course, Telyon himself is always in the right; none of his aims e'er go amiss. But he isn't obligated to tell you the end of your own story. The end of all stories is known only to Telyon, but the tale of each Barada is not known to the Barada himself until after the pages of his life are unsealed. And the thing which unseals them is time, the relentless passing of the hours and the days. So we all must wait to know the end of our own tales. And I do hope yours is a happy end."

Their conversation had taken a very serious turn indeed, and the lads now fully perceived that Felding was a man of many masks. When they first met him, he had seemed to be little more than a soused, scatterbrained screwball. As their voyage on the *Blue Moon* progressed, they came to think of him as an itinerant seeker of fortune, certainly experienced and widely traveled, but also somewhat delusional. And after the battle with the akwursa, they looked upon him as a first-rate strategist and a daring, but reckless warrior. But now they saw that there was much greater depth to him than they might have guessed; for his past, whatever it may have been, had not been untouched by the Haedra.

Girion now addressed the seaman quizzically, "Captain Felding, from your statements I gather that you have plumbed deeply such things as mortals ought not to meddle with. What is your story? How did you come to be the man you are, a smuggler on the run from many nations, a man of many disguises, an adventurer who seems all at once terribly clever and decidedly foolish?"

The captain gazed pensively at the tremulous flame in the lantern resting on the table, then looked up at Girion. After a few moments, he replied distantly, "My tale is long and sullied, filled with great adventure and daring exploits but touched also by great sorrow. Perhaps someday you shall hear it in full, but now, I must see to the raising of our Forellosian flag, and the both of you must get off to bed in order to be ready for our performance in the morning and for your long flight across the Farren."

Both of the lads remained seated a moment more, pondering Felding's words, and then Aradis arose. As he did so, he reached out to shake the captain's hand, and said, "Thank you, Captain, for everything you've done for us. If it hadn't been for you, we'd never have made it all this way toward the Elder Forest, we wouldn't have learned a number of delightful Fontskals ditties, we wouldn't have known how to vanquish an akwursa and we wouldn't have been privileged to meet one of the craziest swashbuckling men Orona has ever known."

Felding now grasped Aradis' hand and smiled, as he responded, "You lads have been a great pleasure to have aboard the *Blue Moon*, and if the Danna should keep you and you manage to bring the reign of Ravinia to an end, you will have the gratitude of many. And, to be sure, you will have mine as well. Of course, korgenosch won't fetch as high of a price anymore, but if Ravinia's empire falls, it certainly will be a lot easier for me to come over to the Elder Forest for my smuggling runs. And if you come back through the Fontskals and I happen to be around, you'll always have a mate there ready for an adventure."

Now Girion also stood up, and the young Siloans opened the cabin door and stepped out onto the deck of the *Blue Moon*. The ship was cloaked by the night, cutting through the water with little resistance on its westward journey. A gentle ocean breeze stirred the sails, and a thousand stars gleamed overhead in the spangled firmament. Among them was Tyracus, the great blue South Star, which had guided many a journey of the people of Aradath, the Southern Moiety of Orona. To the Siloans, it was a cherished token of their home, a living link to their little village in the Plains of Agleri, which now lay so very far away. For Tyracus' light shone brightly each night there, just as it did here over the expanse of the great sea.

Felding now joined the lads on the deck and sighed, "Beautiful, ain't it? The Indurian Deeps are a marvelous place, at night especially. Truth be told, I feel more at home out here than anywhere else."

Then the captain looked at them once more and said, "Well, get on down to your berths, then. We'll be sailing into Gorondil shortly after dawn, and you've got to change into your Druid garb before we arrive."

Aradis and Girion now wished a pleasant evening to Jiff, who was still at the helm. Then they thanked the captain once again and climbed down into the hold. There, within a few minutes, they were lying upon their bunks, and they both soon fell into an anxious slumber, lulled to sleep by the gentle rolling of the ship.

They were roused by the voice of Jiffaloo Timtale and the distinct odor of biyelti about an hour before dawn. Ushered into Felding's cabin, they received some brief instructions on Druidic customs and mannerisms from the captain and then donned the Druid robes which he gave them.

"Do Druids really appear exactly as Menfolk except for their garments?" Aradis asked, for he had never actually seen a Druid.

"For our purposes, they do," Felding replied nonchalantly, as he fiddled with Aradis' dun brown robe. Then he stood back and examined his handiwork. "Good, that'll do," he chuckled, then added, "Now both of you need to remember to look somber and disgruntled at all times. There's no such thing as a merry Druid, you know."

Girion made a ridiculously glum expression in response to this directive, and Aradis snickered when he glimpsed it.

"Now listen here, you scallywag! No laughing!" Felding chided, as he removed his earring and then artfully adjusted his own Druidic apparel.

When all this primping of their wardrobe was accomplished, the three of them went out onto the deck. Sunrise had begun. The coastline of Byram was now in sight, and the port of Gorondil lay directly before them, its numerous waterfront structures bathed in morning sunshine.

"There's your first sight of Byram and the Elder Forest, lads," Felding announced, motioning along the length of the land which lay before them. "And now Gorondil awaits us."

Aradis and Girion went over and stood up near the bow for a while, watching apprehensively as the *Blue Moon* drew nearer and nearer to the wharfs of Gorondil. Meanwhile, Felding disappeared down into the hold, and not long after, they heard a quiet hum coming from the stern of the ship.

"It sounds like Felding's doing something with the acrynon," Girion remarked.

"I wonder what he's up to," Aradis brooded uneasily.

A few moments later, Felding came back up to the deck, whistling cheerily.

"Any particular reason you just turned on the acrynon?" Girion inquired casually.

"You'll see," Felding glibly replied, as he clambered up to the poop deck.

The Siloans looked back at Gorondil again and noted that several Dwarven ships were running back and forth near the shore. A little nervous to see whether the ships would try to intercept them, Aradis asked over his shoulder, "Captain Felding, did you have any run-ins with the Dwarven patrol ships last night?"

Felding, who was now talking in hushed tones with Jiff, called back, "We sighted two ships a few hours ago, but they didn't harass us, I expect, because they saw the friendly banner we were flying."

Relieved that Felding's stratagems had not been exposed thus far, they waited, standing vigil at the bow until they were sailing among the very Dwarven vessels they had seen from a distance. "Hoods on now, lads," Felding instructed, and the Siloans placed the cowls over their heads and peered out from underneath them.

"If there's anything you need from down in the hold, go and get it now," Felding advised, as he carefully steered the ship midway between two passing patrol boats.

"Hey, Felding!" Jiff called from the main deck. "Can you toss me some comestibles?"

"Absolutely, matie!" the captain replied, as he grabbed a link of biyelti sausage from a little box up by the wheel and chucked it down to Jiff's waiting hands.

Jiff bit off a hefty chunk of it and, his mouth full of the prized Pollonan mammal, said, "Make it two!"

Felding immediately threw another one down to his companion. Right after Jiff caught it, he ducked into Felding's cabin.

Aradis and Girion went down to the hold for the last time; the only thing Girion had to grab was his staff, and Aradis needed only to gird Brightbeam and his dagger about his waist. He did this under his Druid robe, of course, since he did not know entirely what to expect from Dwarven security officers, and he imagined it would be better to keep the fact that he was carrying weapons a secret, if at all possible.

Some two minutes later, after having taken care of their business in the hold, the lads emerged back onto the deck.

Now the *Blue Moon* had very nearly reached the piers of Gorondil, and Felding began to do something very bizarre indeed. As the Siloans were climbing out of the hold, he spun the wheel hard so that the ship turned sideways. Now the lads realized that, apparently, the maneuver that Felding was about to conduct would only be possible with the acrynon's assistance, which was the reason he had engaged it. By the time they were only a matter of yards from the jetties of the Dwarven port, the *Blue Moon* was facing completely backwards and was awkwardly zigzagging back and forth into the docks. Aradis was on the verge of covering his eyes when their ship scraped some of the wooden pilings that held the piers above the water. Unfortunately, Felding's careless navigation knocked a crate from the wharf off into the water below.

Gorondil was crowded with Dwarves in black and red military uniforms or in civilian garb, ambling about the docks, some lugging cargo and some simply tramping on their way from one place to another. But as soon as Felding had commenced his queer antics, it seemed every Dwarf in sight began staring in disbelief at the *Blue Moon*, as it haphazardly backed into the harbor. Their eyes narrowed, and upon seeing the crate tumble off the docks, they all began walking slowly over toward the ship. Felding continued to let the vessel drift, and then he bounded down to the hold, presumably to turn off the acrynon.

Girion was highly disconcerted. "What in the world has gotten into that loon?" he whispered to Aradis. "We might have actually gotten into the harbor fairly unnoticed if he hadn't pulled a ridiculous stunt like that!"

A great many Dwarven guards and dockworkers were now gathered at the wharf where the *Blue Moon* was drifting to a halt. Much to the Siloans' relief, they were not left alone to greet them, for Felding popped up from the hold once more and called out in a significantly modified voice, "Gar mendas holdrag um trok!"

"Do these Dwarves not speak Daiga?" Aradis whispered to Girion. "Will we not be able to understand anything they're saying?" Daiga, the Siloans' native language, was the tongue spoken by the vast majority of the Barada in Orona. Originally the language of the Pine-Elves in Murnia, in the last five hundred years or so, it had come to be used in every single Neathmarda in some capacity.

"Tagurel!" a burly Dwarf with a thick, red beard called back. He looked to be someone of considerable importance, as he was dressed in an opulent crimson tunic, costly brown breeches and a short burgundy cape. A steel sword hung at his side, and the insignia of a jet-black raven rested on his chest. A little over four feet in height, he was quite muscular and looked as if he could handle himself exceptionally well in a fight.

"Tagurel um trok badri!" Felding responded, as he tossed a rope to the Dwarves on the jetty. This they tied to a bollard, and then Felding set about lowering the gangplank. When he had done this, he walked down in the midst of the Dwarves and spoke to their leader, the Dwarf who had called out to him.

"Tagurel Raviniak!" he said, saluting the Dwarf.

"You're from Forellos, I see," the Dwarf replied, nodding at the *Blue Moon's* proudly waving hunter-green banner, which was dominated by the symbol of a slender gray tower with blue waves crashing at its base.

Aradis and Girion now breathed a tremendous sigh of relief. Not only did these Dwarves speak Daiga, they also apparently had been fooled by Felding's flag.

Felding handed a wrinkled piece of parchment to the Dwarf and stated, "Galbarra's my name. I was sent by the Druid Allaroc."

"Was it Allaroc who told you to bring your ship in backwards and knock our cargo into the drink?" the Dwarf replied sharply.

"No, that was my own doing, sir," the captain replied courteously, his voice still greatly altered so that it was lower and much smoother than his normal manner of speaking. "You see, my vessel was damaged in a storm some days ago, and the rudder hasn't been working quite right since then."

"I see," the Dwarf nodded, obviously not fully satisfied. After a few moments of eyeing Felding, he turned to dismiss the crowd which was pressing around him. "Get back to your work, all of you! There's nothing of interest here," he shouted, as he returned the parchment to Felding.

"I'm Captain Fordrak of the Gorondil Garrison. Now what is it that brings you to our port?" the Dwarf asked.

"Well, Captain," Felding said, "you are familiar with Allaroc, I assume."

"Indeed, I know the name well," Fordrak answered.

"Good then. Allaroc has acquired an artifact which is of great importance to Ravinia's war with Argonis, and he thought it best to send it via an escort down the Iron Highway all the way to Blackbough Woods. A Druid named Drannic is to meet my comrades and me at the stables on the west end of town sometime this morning in order to pick it up and ensure its safe transference to the Witch herself."

"What do you need from me, then?" Fordrak inquired, as his dark brown eyes scanned the *Blue Moon*.

"We're going to carry the artifact ashore," Felding relayed, "and store it in one of the warehouses, and from there, we're going to go check on arrangements at the stables."

"I'll have a guard posted at the warehouse, then," Fordrak assured. "You may as well carry it to the old Splinter Men warehouse, as it's the closest."

"No guard will be necessary," Felding stated authoritatively. Then he leaned in close to the Dwarf and said in a hushed voice, "In fact, Allaroc said the only Dwarf in Gorondil he would trust with knowledge of what was going on was you, Captain Fordrak."

The Dwarven captain looked quite surprised, but pleased, by this, and he said, "Only me? Why, that's a high recommendation coming from Allaroc! Well, if he wants to keep this whole thing a secret, then just carry the artifact ashore and set it in a back corner of the warehouse where no one's likely to mess with it, and I myself will keep watch over it."

"Excellent," Felding returned, as he marched back onto the *Blue Moon*. "Curronath! Hadarion!" he called. "Give me a hand with the crate in the cabin!" Aradis and Girion dutifully followed Captain Starwash into his quarters, while Fordrak looked on.

Once they were inside, Felding said, "All right, lads, this is the one we've got to carry into the warehouse." He motioned to a rather large crate set right next to the door, and after Girion had set his staff on top of it, they lifted it up.

"My, this is heavy!" Girion grunted. "What have you got packed in it?"

"A present for the Dwarves," Felding responded, winking. "You don't think I'd just cart off a load of their korgenosch without giving them something in return, do you?"

They brought the crate out onto the deck and then down the gangplank onto the wharf. Aradis and Girion wondered all the while what sort of gift Felding might be leaving for the Dwarves.

"Right this way," Fordrak directed them, as he led the way down the docks toward a large warehouse which had obviously not been kept in the best repair. In front of it was a large pole to which had been tied a rather foreboding flag; it had a lurid burgundy field with the charge of a monstrous black raven with yellow eyes. It was the same hideous symbol which garnished Fordrak's uniform, the symbol of the dreaded Witch Ravinia and the Fell Alliance.

The three Menfolk carrying the crate followed the Dwarf through the passing porters, all the while trying to keep their expressions as grim as possible. As they drew closer to the warehouse, they noticed that its front façade was expertly carved with a large and rather complex image, that of a long, sharp dagger, its point downwards, and a twisted tree branch with lots of twisted twigs. Fordrak led them through a creaky side door into the building.

There were several Dwarves meandering about in the warehouse, and each of them saluted Fordrak as he passed by them. Fordrak led the Menfolk through several rooms in the warehouse and then pointed to a relatively secluded area between large stacks of crates and sacks that reached up toward the ceiling.

"Lay it down here," the Dwarf instructed, "and I'll see that no one disturbs it."

"Thank you, Captain," Felding said, as they set the crate down and Girion grabbed his staff. Now Felding came over to Fordrak and said, "We'll be down at the stables if anything should come up. And we'll be sure to send word to you as soon as Drannic arrives or else come back here ourselves. Just make certain no one disturbs this crate in the meantime."

"Gladly," Fordrak conceded. "It sounds like this artifact, whatever it may be, is of no small significance. I want to make sure we do everything we can to get it safely to Ravinia."

"Tagurel Raviniak!" Felding enthused once more, saluting the captain. Then he strode off toward the warehouse's exit. But before he left the room, he stopped abruptly and shouted, "Magrun dassa!" in a burst of aggravation. Clearly distraught about something, he turned to face Fordrak and said, "Captain, may I speak to you about one final matter?"

Fordrak emerged from between the piles of crates and responded, "Aye, what is it?"

Felding held up a little scroll and waved it at the captain. Fordrak now came over to where Felding was standing. Felding then fumbled in his cloak for a good half-minute or so, muttering to himself; this was a very awkward half-minute indeed, and Fordrak nervously cleared his throat several times. Finally, Felding exclaimed, "Aha!" and then produced another small scroll with delight.

Handing the scrolls to the Dwarf, he explained, "Both of these are for you, sir. The first is a personal letter from Allaroc to you. I know not what it says, only that it is to be for your eyes only. The second parchment is, according to Allaroc, needed to decode the first. Read them at your leisure," he stated and then turned and left the room, with Aradis and Girion right at his heels.

Much to their amazement, it really seemed as if Felding's plan (despite his blundering when pulling into the dock) was going to work beautifully.

CHAPTER EIGHT

The Perils of Brinkmarch

nce they were safely out of the warehouse, Felding turned right and began going up a winding street that led inland. There were a great many shops on the street, and more Dwarves than Aradis had seen in his entire life were rushing to and fro about their morning business. The Dwarves were speaking primarily in Daiga, although the lads heard snatches of a language that sounded very much like the one Felding had spoken to Fordrak.

"What just happened in there?" Girion asked quietly, as he kept as close as he could manage to Felding. "What did that letter say?"

"This is neither the appropriate time nor place for questions, Hadarion," Felding offhandedly replied. "But if you must know, the letter, when he decodes it, will say 'My most profuse apologies, good sir, but you have just been thoroughly bamboozled. My companions and I have successfully hijacked Allaroc's vessel, done away with his emissaries and absconded with Ravinia's artifact. I have escaped to the high seas, and my companions, if you are wondering, have ridden off to Toldrennon Wood, though it is doubtful whether you will be clever enough to find them. We are special operatives in the employ of the Kingdom of Argonis and intend to convey the previously mentioned artifact to King Thornoak unless you can make us a better offer than the good monarch. If you are interested in making such an offer, come to the abandoned Tower of Barnatha in Toldrennon Wood during Eoreth's Tale, an hour before midnight, on the 17th of Tannaril, three days from now. Come alone and without guile, or my companions will not reveal themselves. Consider your options carefully. Merry Marda to you!"

Aradis and Girion had been concentrating very hard on maintaining perpetually surly expressions, so as to appear more authentically Druidic, but now they were barely able to keep from laughing outright.

"However did you manage to come up with such an extraordinarily brilliant scheme?" Girion asked, still marveling at Felding's acumen. "After he translates that note, Fordrak will be stewing day and night about an artifact that doesn't even exist, and then he'll send troops to scour the whole of Toldrennon Wood, while his real quarry will be somewhere else entirely! Such cunning devices really must have entailed some serious contemplation on your part."

"Well, what do you think I've been doing for the past ten days?" Felding asked jovially.

"Singing sea shanties and filling your gut with Stragmore stout," Aradis replied quite honestly.

At this comment, the captain laughed roguishly.

"Say, what's Jiff up to?" Aradis asked, as they pressed on through the masses of Dwarves on their way up the street.

"Probably stowing korgenosch aboard by now," Felding discreetly replied.

"But how?" Girion queried.

"That warehouse we just went into was filled with more korgenosch than you can imagine," Felding muttered. "All he has to do is sneak out of there with as much as he can manage."

"But how will he get in without being noticed?" Aradis wondered.

"You helped carry him in yourself, lad," the captain blithely replied.

Then it dawned on them—Jiff had been the gift inside the crate! Of course, for he had gone into the cabin the last time they saw him, and he must have climbed into the crate. And Felding's whole purpose for the business with the letter was to give Jiff time to climb out of the crate and scramble out of sight. The Siloans looked at each other, once more completely stupefied by the seemingly limitless inventiveness of Felding Starwash.

Felding tried, but failed, to stifle his laughter, as the lads had their realization. "Now how's that for a plan?" he chortled. "'Magrun dassa' was the code phrase for Jiff to climb out, you see," he explained. "It means 'rotten fish' in Rokklag—Dwarven Pidgin, that is." The Captain couldn't help but chuckle at his own cleverness.

"Well, you sly dog," Girion said in a most congratulatory manner, "this plan of yours really is one of the most multilayered, audacious concoctions imaginable. Yet surely Jiff can't just march out of the building with an armful of korgenosch without being caught!"

"I wouldn't underestimate Jiffaloo Timtale," Felding recommended. "His background in thespian antics and the art of fast fingers leaves one wondering if he couldn't walk out of just about anywhere with just about anything. Most of the time, I'm not even sure how he does it. I usually just tell him what needs doing, and next thing I know, it's already done."

As they continued to make their way down the relatively narrow street, Girion politely remarked to the captain, "Barring the fact that you're essentially expecting Jiff to take care of himself, it seems you've got this whole thing planned down to the last detail. I was just wondering—is there any particular reason you pulled the ship in backwards?"

"Course there is," Felding returned casually. "First, Jiff and I will undoubtedly need to make a fast escape; it's better to be facing forward for that sort of thing, you know. Secondly, I wanted to go right to the top of the chain of authority here in Gorondil, and I've learned the best way to get such a person to come to you is to make a great nuisance of yourself."

Aradis and Girion were beyond mind-boggled by Felding's comprehension of Baradic psychology.

Just then, the captain came to an abrupt halt. "You lads don't have any supplies to get you across Brinkmarch, do you?" he asked.

"Well, no," Girion answered, "but I think it's more important right now for us to get safely out of Gorondil than anything else."

"Nonsense," Felding returned. "You can't be riding a hundred miles or more with nothing to eat or drink! How could I be such a poor guide to ye? Let's stop in this shop here, and I'll purchase you a few things to get you through at least until you come to Argonis. Also, I'll be able get both meself and you some rixenmaller. They're Dwarven honey cookies with different kinds of nuts in them, and, if I do say so myself, there are few things tastier than a jolly rixenmall." Felding now turned aside into a store on the right-hand side of the road with a large sign depicting what appeared to be some sort of liquor over it.

"They sell korgenosch here, evidently," Aradis whispered to Girion. "That's the real reason we're stopping, I'll wager."

Once they were inside the store, they looked around and saw that it did contain a good many travelers' amenities and provisions, although it prominently featured a sizable stock of various types of liquor. Felding walked up to the middle-aged, black-haired Dwarf at the counter and began asking him about his inventory.

"Well then," the captain said, after he had heard the Dwarf run through the litany of his current merchandise, "we shall be purchasing two sacks of nutmeal, two waterskins and two tins of rixenmaller."

"All right then," the Dwarf replied, as he mentally calculated what was due him. "That will be sixteen tolgas. The rixenmaller are up here behind the counter, the waterskins are over there by old Jandrick and the sacks of nutmeal are right next to them." The clerk pointed over to an area in which an aged Dwarf with a long white beard sat on a rickety-looking rocking chair.

"Go ahead and grab the waterskins, Hadarion, and if you would, Curronath, get the sacks of nutmeal and bring them over here," Felding requested, as he opened his money pouch to scrounge up sixteen tolgas.

Girion went over and procured the waterskins, while Aradis simultaneously bent over to pick up the bags of nutmeal. As he did so, Brightbeam's sheath stuck out a little from the bottom hem of his robe. Old Jandrick loudly babbled, "Oy, what's this? Is that a sword I see? I've never known a Druid of the Elder Forest to carry any weapon save a staff. That's very strange. Yes, very strange indeed."

Aradis was aghast. He put the sacks back on the floor and immediately straightened up.

"What's that, Jandrick?" the Dwarf at the counter called, looking over at the wizened Dwarf in the corner.

"Why, Mosgar, this Druid's got a sword. Isn't that peculiar? Not in all my years have I seen a Druid carry a sword."

Girion was also severely flustered, and his face showed it, but Felding remained uncannily calm and balanced.

"You're right, Jandrick," Mosgar replied loudly, in an incriminating tone. "Druids of the Elder Forest don't carry swords. Let's have a look then, fellow."

Aradis stepped farther back into the corner, and Felding quickly spoke up, "Of course Druids around here don't carry swords. And my associate isn't carrying one either. I'm afraid old Jandrick may be seeing things. Go ahead, Curronath, show him you haven't got any sword. We've nothing to hide here."

Felding did not realize that Aradis had hidden Brightbeam under his robe, so as far as he was concerned, there was nothing to hide. Aradis racked his racing thoughts to find a way to tell Felding that they really were in trouble and that he couldn't show them what was under his robe without endangering the entire plan. After a few tense moments, he could think of nothing prudent to say, so he said the first thing that popped into his head. "I haven't got anything to hide, but I don't have to prove that to you or anyone else," he defiantly told the clerk.

"Well then, what's all this about?" Mosgar said. "We'll just see whether you have anything to hide or not!" He came out from behind the counter and walked over to the front door of the shop. Felding gave Aradis an exceedingly irate look, and Aradis pointed furiously at his left hip where the sword lay. Felding now grasped what was going on, rolled his eyes and began looking frantically about the shop, probably for items that he would use if this debacle turned into a full-on fight, a possibility which seemed increasingly likely.

"Hey, Horenz!" Mosgar shouted out the door. A few moments later, an ill-tempered Dwarven soldier with a broadsword buckled to his waist stepped in with a few cohorts.

"We've got a customer who's acting real funny," the clerk explained. "Edgy as can be. Old Jandrick said he saw a sword hidden under his cloak, and as we all know, no self-respecting Druid of the Elder Forest would ever carry such a thing. But seems this fellow doesn't want to show us what he's got under his cloak."

"Is that so?" Horenz asked, as he began marching over toward Aradis. "Let's see if I can't change his mind."

"Go for it, lad," Felding said in his unmodified adventure-mode voice, motioning as if he were swinging with a blade. He had already dropped his pretense. "Show 'em what you've got. And I really mean that."

Aradis knew the captain was ready to fight, and he would have to trust that the daring Starwash could help them take out these soldiers and escape Gorondil alive.

"You want to see what's under my cloak?" Aradis erupted. "I'll show you then!" Flinging his cloak aside, he drew Brightbeam and rushed at Horenz.

The Dwarf was rather caught off guard by this sudden aggression, but he was prepared enough to draw his own blade and ward off Aradis' attack. Meanwhile, both Girion and Felding had cast off their Druidic garments and sprung into action. Mosgar and a soldier both ran toward Felding, but he leapt into the air and kicked hard against a shelf full of bottles, which fell directly toward them. Girion grabbed a bag of flour and hurled it as hard as he could against another soldier. All this while, Jandrick was attempting to keep from getting injured in the furious melee, abandoning his rocking chair and hunkering off toward the door. Felding continuously grabbed bottles of korgenosch off the counter and flung them with deadly aim at their opponents, all the while shouting out a barrage of insulting names at the Dwarves.

In the midst of this mayhem, Aradis was viciously dueling Horenz, mustering every last one of the skills his father had taught him and holding his own rather well. At an opportune moment, he leapt behind a bench and then fiercely kicked it at Horenz, who was coming at him in a rage. The Dwarf faltered, and Girion, who happened to be nearby, held up a bag of flour, which Aradis cut open so that the white powder dumped all over Horenz's head.

"Now, lads!" Felding shouted. "Run for it!" he yelled, as he shoved over another large shelf. After he had grabbed a bottle of korgenosch from the counter and tucked it in his vest, he raced out the door. Aradis and Girion dodged the remaining soldiers who were not immobilized and joined Felding in the street.

As soon as they rushed out, they turned right and immediately heard soldiers shouting some distance in front of them. Then they saw Jandrick pointing frantically, directing a group of guards right toward them.

"Back this way!" Felding instinctively cried out, and they turned and ran back to the east. On their left, just past the shop, Felding darted into an alleyway, and the Siloans followed him.

There were high stacks of chests and crates there, from which one could reach the roof of the shop, which was flat, as it was used for storage. Felding deftly clambered up these boxes and gained the rooftop; Aradis and Girion followed suit.

"New plan!" Felding panted, as they reached him. "Follow me back toward the ship. I'll draw them after me, and when we reach a suitable spot, I'll direct you on how to get to the stables without me. Quickly now, lads!" He began to climb up a ladder to a higher roof to the north, and as he did so, he called, "Now I hope you've learned your lesson, Aradis! Next time you're disguised as a Druid from these parts, don't carry a sword!"

"How was I to know something like that?" Aradis griped, as he climbed up after the captain.

"Ah, let driftwood be driftwood," Felding replied. "What's done is done. Now do exactly as I do!" Felding looked back and saw that a few Dwarven soldiers were dragging themselves over the edge of the rooftop they had just come from, and he shouted, "And hurry up about it!" He hastily directed the lads to jump to the rooftop just to the west of them, which was shingled and had a bit of a slope to it.

Meanwhile, their pursuers were swiftly scaling the ladder from the shop's roof, and Felding was more than ready for them. With a stout shove, he knocked the ladder off the upper roof's edge and sent all the Dwarves sprawling to the rooftop below. "Safety first, gentlemen! Unsecured ladders are notoriously unstable!" he called back to the soldiers, as he leapt to the building where Aradis and Girion were waiting for him.

A great deal of ruckus could now be heard in the streets below. They could distinguish Horenz's bearish voice shouting out an array of instructions and the pounding of many Dwarven feet racing off to the north, west and east. The Dwarves who had been flung off the ladder by Felding had set it up again, and had now gained the rooftop that lay two buildings behind them.

A trapdoor suddenly opened up just in front of the three Menfolk, and several Dwarves climbed out of the opening, fiercely brandishing various weapons.

"This way!" Felding shouted, as he grabbed a wooden plank from a nearby pile of building supplies and then turned and sprang to a rooftop just to the north. The Siloans leapt right after him, following him onto the top of a stone arch that crossed over a rather large street that ran down to the harbor.

"Keep going, lads!" Felding roared, as he turned to face the Dwarves right behind them. Aradis and Girion obeyed, as the captain charged furiously at his attackers. He swung at them mightily with the plank, and, despite their best efforts to deflect the blows, two of them were knocked off the arch and tumbled to the street below. A third met the same fate, as he was punched full-on in the face by Felding's brawny fist. With a victorious laugh, the delighted captain hurled the plank at the remaining Dwarves and then turned and bolted away from them.

Now the three Menfolk continued to leap from rooftop to rooftop, making their way back to the docks, for the buildings were all rather close together; however, this endeavor proved to be rather tricky, as many of the roofs had somewhat of an angle to them. Nonetheless, as difficult as this may have been for the Menfolk, it was even more so for the Dwarves who were still pursuing them. Indeed, their physique was not exactly conducive to running, and some of the jumps were a bit long for them. However, not long after the fugitives left the arch, a bell tower down by the shore began pealing out loud, frantic tolls. The alarm had been raised, and all of Gorondil was crawling with angry Dwarves. Now it was a race against time, and Aradis and Girion were going in the opposite direction of their ultimate destination. It seemed exceedingly doubtful whether this venture would end well for the fleeing Menfolk.

Felding stopped on an especially high, slanted rooftop, one just to the south of the red-shingled bell tower, in fact, and scanned the harbor to see how things were at the *Blue Moon*. Once he saw that it was as of yet unmolested, he panted, "All right now, I'm going to get these Dwarves really hopping mad and hope that as many of them as possible come after me. Do you see that building off on the west edge of town with the red banner with the black raven on top of it? That's Ravinia's emblem flying over the stables; make for it as fast as you can, for if my plan does the trick, the majority of the Dwarves will be down this way near the wharf chasing after me. Grab a saddle if you can, but if not, ride bareback, and don't stop until after nightfall unless your horses just can't go any farther, for all the Barada of Gorondil will still be able to hunt you down mounted on horses or ponies, since I obviously can't aid you now by setting the stables ablaze and stampeding the animals."

"Will do, sir," Girion assured him.

"It's been a pleasure, lads," the captain said, as he shook their hands in turn. "Best of luck to ye, and may the Danna smile upon you."

"Goodbye, Captain," Aradis said, as he saluted the inimitable mariner.

After Aradis had said this, Felding raced over to the edge of the roof and, with a magnificent leap, landed on a rooftop some distance away. With one more jump, he reached a lower roof that stood adjacent to one of the larger streets of Gorondil, where there was presently the most hubbub.

"Ahoy, you daft, dilly-dallying dumbheads!" the captain shouted to the Dwarves below, all of whom looked up to see from whence the voice had come.

"That's right, I'm talking to you, you sour-breath landlubbers! Go ahead and grovel at the feet of a half-baked joke of a Witch and see where that gets you! Someday you'll all get what's coming to ya, you traitorous, short-legged, fat-bellied ding-a-lings! Why, you're nothing more than a crew of biddy-daddy-widdy-duddy, muddle-headed, lazy-lolly oafs in the service of a crotchety kook of a crone!"

After Felding had finished this series of exceedingly demeaning taunts, there was a shower of all kinds of objects hurled up at him. Some were legitimate weapons, harpoons and spears and the like, and others were nothing of the sort (Aradis and Girion were fairly certain they saw several fish flying through the air). But Felding had already backed away from the edge of the roof and was now racing like mad to the east via whatever route was available.

As soon as the captain had achieved his objective of capturing all the Dwarves' attention, Aradis and Girion dashed back westward and, much to their chagrin, they saw that there were several companies of Dwarves on various rooftops making their way toward them. The lads bounded onto a roof just to their left, trying to first head southward before then turning west toward the stables. Upon reaching a largish thoroughfare (the one with the arch farther down), they saw that the distance from one side to the other was too far to jump. Fortunately, there was a single long wooden beam that protruded from a roof on the hither side and joined the top of a gable on the far side; a series of iron lanterns, ostensibly used as street-lights, dangled from it.

Aradis and Girion stepped gingerly upon the crosspiece, doing their best to keep their balance with such narrow footing. Below them, tumul-tuous masses of Dwarves pushed eastward down the street, evidently in an effort to apprehend Captain Felding. However, a few of them did spot the two Siloans traversing the beam above them and began shouting to their comrades and pointing up at the two Menfolk.

Just then, the Dwarves who had been chasing them across the rooftops reached the beam's end behind them. One of them took out his axe and swung furiously to sunder the crosspiece. The beam shook violently, but did not break, although both the lads were nearly knocked off of it. As soon as they regained their balance, they raced to the roof on the far side. And none too soon, for but a moment after Girion's feet left the beam, the Dwarf's second axe stroke split it in twain, and it creaked as its weight pulled it out of the bracket on the south side, falling onto the roaring crowd below.

Meanwhile, Felding was crossing the same street, although, true to form, his method of getting across was considerably more outrageous. He had reached a spot rather close to the harbor's edge (just behind the warehouses, in fact) where there was a windlass wound with a strong rope that ran down at a rather steep angle to a second story balcony on the far side of the street, where it passed around a heavy-duty pulley and then ran back up to the roof where the windlass was. The rope had a massive hook on it for attaching cargo, which was to be carried up to the top level of the building, upon which Felding was currently standing; it so happened that the hook was now positioned up by him.

The captain noticed that a flag bearing Ravinia's blazon was flying next to him. Gleefully, he drew a long dagger from the sheath at his side, sliced the eyes of the raven and cut the cords which bound the banner to the short pole to which it was affixed. Then he called out triumphantly, "Down with the crusty hag of Blackbough!"

Having once more fanned the flames of the Dwarves' wrath, he flung the mutilated flag upon the mob below, released the winch on the windlass that the rope was run around, grabbed the hook with both hands and sailed down the line to the far side of the street, whooping raucously and having the time of his life the whole way.

Reaching the balcony on the south side of the street, he raced inside the building, plowed through two Dwarves who tried to stop him and flung open a window on the east side of the room. Hastily, he jumped to the ground some fifteen feet below and lunged into an alleyway, just barely escaping the grasp of the Dwarves who were thronging behind him. After making two sharp turns through the narrow streets behind the warehouses, he scurried up a ladder onto the roof of the Splinter Men warehouse. Within a minute or so, he had gotten to the very top of the building, where he nimbly walked out onto an exceedingly long wooden projection to which was attached a pulley and a rope with an immense hook used for lifting heavy objects off of incoming vessels. From this projection, he leapt with all of his might toward a ship that was pulled up right next to the dock and just managed to catch the rigging. Dexterously, he clambered around to its back side, sprang off of it, caught a rope and swung to the rigging on the far side of the vessel. Then, with the skill of an acrobat, he jumped to a line dangling from a spur on the ship and swung to the jetty just to the south, where he landed artfully on the pier that led directly out to the *Blue Moon*. Five Dwarves (none of them soldiers) barred his way, but he charged them like an enraged bull, all the while shouting like a madman. Three of the five ended up in the water next to the pier. At last, Felding came to the *Blue Moon* with a huge, angry mob hot on his tail. As soon as the captain was aboard, he kicked the gangplank and the *Blue Moon* sped eastward at an almost unbelievable rate, a speed that could only be reached with the aid of an acrynon.

When the ship was a little ways out from the wharves, leaving the fist-shaking throng of nettled Dwarves behind, another figure appeared on the deck of the *Blue Moon*. It was none other than Jiffaloo Timtale! Felding now gleefully produced the prized bottle of korgenosch from his vest. Jiff held a bottle aloft as well; in his other hand there was a partially consumed sausage. As the *Blue Moon* sped eastward across the Indurian Deeps, Felding and Jiff triumphantly clinked their bottles together and waved farewell to the thronging, cursing Dwarves on the wharves of Gorondil.

"Farewell, me hearties!" Felding called happily to the Dwarves.

"Would you care for some biyelti, sir?" Jiff inquired courteously.

"Don't mind if I do," the captain replied.

And thus the daring duo escaped from the Dwarves of Gorondil.

All this while, Aradis and Girion had been dashing across the rooftops, jumping more often than not, taking whatever path was necessary to reach the stables. They had crossed the street with Mosgar's shop by leaping from a high building to a much lower one on the far side. Several Dwarves had taken note of this and raised the alarm anew. Yet, at least for the time being, they were safe from Dwarves scampering about on the rooftops.

The lads crossed the same street once more farther to the west a few minutes later. Then, not long after that, they came upon a wide avenue that ran north and south (and thus stood in-between them and their destination), which would be impossible for them to cross without going down to the ground. And so down they went. Lowering themselves from a series of balconies, the lads soon reached the main street of Gorondil.

Now every single Barada in Gorondil knew that something was afoot, due to the unceasing racket from the bell tower and the commotion down at the harbor. But word had not yet spread of exactly what that commotion was all about. Nonetheless, two Menfolk dropping into the street from a second story balcony would seem mighty suspicious under any circumstances, much less these. Aradis and Girion knew that guards would be after them any moment now, so they wasted no time in weaving in and out of the civilians who shouted after them things such as, "Hey, you there!" and "Someone stop those two!"

Once the Siloans reached the western side of the avenue, they entered a series of alleys and backstreets of Gorondil. Although the lads had now successfully passed through the most populous districts of the city, they did not flag in their haste, for they still encountered occasional Barada, most of whom cried out in alarm when they saw them tearing down the narrow streets. In addition, there were several waves of angry shouts behind them and in nearby alleys. It seemed the guards were now privy to which direction they had gone.

After only a few minutes of this mad racing through the maze of one of Gorondil's least prestigious residential districts, they reached the street which ran along the western edge of town. There they looked up and saw Ravinia's banner just to the south of them, perched atop the stables. They raced up to the building and heard voices inquiring about the "uproar down by the port" just around the corner. Immediately, they rushed inside.

To their amazement, no one was inside watching the animals, which consisted of an array of horses and ponies. Evidently, the stable hands were the ones outside asking what was going on. Taking full advantage of this good fortune, the lads quickly selected their mounts, led them out of the stalls and threw saddles on their backs.

Just as Aradis and Girion had gotten settled on their horses, three Dwarves entered the stables from the south side.

"Oy, get those two!" one of the Dwarves called out. But before this order could be carried out, the Siloans vigorously dug their heels into their mounts and charged out the west door.

The Menfolk nearly ran down a few Dwarves in an alleyway that led out to the very western edge of town, but after they had gotten past this last obstacle, the lads were free of Gorondil. Now they sped westward unhindered, and their pace did not slacken until the port was left several miles behind. Indeed, they rode as if a fire had been lit behind them, for, in a sense, it had.

When they were about six miles out from the city, Aradis remarked, "I certainly hope Felding made it out of there all right. He really did a great deal for us, and it would be just terrible if those Dwarves got their hands on him."

"Oh, I've no doubt he escaped totally unharmed, probably laughing the whole way," Girion replied, smiling. And he really believed the daring captain had done exactly that.

"Well, I do hope we find out for certain someday, one way or another," Aradis returned.

That morning they traveled for ten miles or so across rolling grassland until they reached the Farren, where the landscape began to be punctuated by huge, queer, tower-like rocks. The sight of these set them at a little more ease, for they could provide a place to hide from anyone who might be following them. Once they had gone a few miles into the Farren, they came across a shallow brook, and Girion suggested that they ride south a bit in the water, so that anyone trying to track them would have more difficulty picking up their trail. They rode for nearly a mile southward in the brook and then continued westward.

All that day, they rode as fast and as far as their mounts would allow them, stopping at cool streams occasionally to allow themselves and their horses to drink. However, heeding Felding's advice, they did not altogether cease their journey until nightfall. They had crossed many miles of open plains dotted with fantastic assemblages of oddly-shaped rocks, and, just after sundown, they rode into an area that was surrounded by particularly large formations of this sort. Before they dismounted, they debated what to do about the horses, as they had nothing with which they might tie them up. Aradis' proposal was that one of them watch the horses while the other slept and that they take turns in this manner throughout the night. Girion, on the other hand, insisted that they both badly needed slumber, and the horses might potentially give them away if the Dwarves were still looking for them. In the end, it was Aradis who won the argument, as usual, for he possessed greater tenacity than Girion in getting his own way, but as a compromise, it was agreed that Aradis would take the first watch.

So they spent the night there among the strange rocks in the moonlight, and, to their relief, the horses did not attempt to run off. Rather, they contentedly munched on grass and even lay down for a while. The Menfolk secretly envied them, for they had consumed no food for nearly a full day, and their prospects of finding food any time soon were not good.

The following day they rode westward again, now heading a little to the south as well, just as Felding had told them. The terrain was much the same as it had been in the area they traversed the day before. Once, around midafternoon, they were exceedingly grateful for the numerous rock formations that provided cover, for they encountered a roaming Dwarven patrol mounted on ponies. Aradis and Girion did not imagine they were from Gorondil, still hunting them down. Rather, they supposed they were Dwarves of the Rhassendag Downs to the south, or of Toldrennon Wood to the north, simply going about the Witch's business. Nevertheless, after that incident, they grew increasingly paranoid that attempts might still be made to track them down, so they rode in confusing patterns for a few hours to try and obscure their trail.

Again, they brought their journey to a halt when twilight came, but they had not traveled as far this second day and guessed they had at least another thirty miles to go before they reached Thornberry Thicket. This night they stayed in a little cave which was in the side of a rather large monolith. Using the same arrangement as the previous night, Aradis remained awake until after midnight, when he awakened Girion to take over the watch. Again, the horses did not flee from them, for they ate their fill of grass and lay down for a while once they were satiated. Meanwhile, the lads' stomachs nagged at them incessantly, for they still had gotten nothing to eat.

When Marda appeared on the horizon, Girion went and sat just outside the cave and began chronicling in his notebook all that had befallen them since they had left the *Blue Moon*. He worked for quite some time, drawing maps and diagrams and filling several pages with his commentary about their adventures. Then he became impatient that Aradis had not yet awakened, so he went and roused his companion, and, a short while later, they resumed their westward journey.

On the third day of their toiling across Brinkmarch, they found it difficult to keep up a decent pace, for their hunger preoccupied their thoughts, and thus they wasted a considerable amount of time poking around in the grasses of the Farren looking for some plant they might be able to eat. But they found nothing they recognized, so for their labor they received naught in return.

Now, as the day drew on, the sporadic groupings of rocks became more and more infrequent, and the companions deduced they were drawing nigh to Moonhound Moor. As they traveled westward through this region, a cold, gray mist descended upon the land, and the farther they went, the thicker the mist seemed to get. It was not long before the lads grew greatly unsettled.

"Night will be upon us in only a little while," Aradis remarked concernedly. "We'd better turn northwest soon to try and strike Thornberry Thicket."

"Agreed," Girion concurred. "We must make it to the northern edge of the moor before dark at all costs!"

Suddenly, the lads heard a horse whinny off to the east, and they immediately turned to scan the landscape behind them. The mist was quite heavy now, and they could not espy the animal that had produced the sound. A few moments later, a lonesome whinny came from the deep mist yet again and Aradis worriedly said, "Perhaps that's someone from Gorondil that's finally caught up with us."

"Perhaps," Girion returned, "but whoever it is, we can almost be certain he will be no friend to us, for we have now journeyed quite far into Sarganath."

For a moment, the mist unveiled four riders about a half-mile away on a hill. They were all clad in brown robes and had dark hoods over their heads. The figures remained stationary on the hilltop but seemed to be facing directly toward them.

"Druids!" Girion breathed. "From Gorondil, no doubt."

"Let's be off immediately," Aradis said, and so they pressed in a north-westerly direction into the mist. The riders remained motionless.

"Do you think they're hesitant to enter the moor?" Aradis asked.

"Aren't you?" Girion asked darkly.

Aradis did not reply to this. He really didn't want to contemplate what might become of them if they were still on the moor when the sun fell. And so he rode swiftly onward into the gathering mist. The lads were now truly hard-pressed by the perils of Brinkmarch; there were wicked Druids behind them and unspeakable monsters ahead. Their only chance of survival was to reach Thornberry Thicket before nightfall. Yet the thicket itself was another peril, a peril which might prove to be deadlier than any of the others.

The newfound urgency wrought by their current predicament drove the Siloans to a significantly faster pace. Now their ears were ever alert for both the dreaded baying of the moonhounds and the sounds of pursuit by the Druids. But even with their increased haste, the miles went on before them. Afternoon came and went, and they had not yet come to the thicket. And the mist grew thicker all the while.

Around sunset, they had practically given up hope of escaping the moor before the surfacing of the terrible moonhounds. But still they rode northward; they did not know exactly how far away the thicket was and could only hope that it was closer than they imagined.

Just as twilight fell, Girion shouted out exuberantly, "Look, there's the thicket up ahead. We've made it, Aradis!" Sure enough, the black edge of the thicket could just be seen through the passing mist.

But Girion's enthusiasm was short-lived, for just then, there came from behind them, off to the south, the most ghastly, repulsive howling they had ever heard. It was the cry of a solitary moonhound, echoing across the moor like a nightmare incarnate in auditory form, seeping through all the vapors of the dark, crawling mist. The lone howl was soon joined by a chorus of cacophonous, eerie yelping as other moonhounds emerged from their burrows to begin the hunt for the night.

"May the Danna save us from these monsters!" Aradis mouthed in terror, and both he and Girion clung desperately to their horses' backs, as their mounts took off across the moor at breakneck speed.

The moonhounds now let out a new sort of howling, one of blood-thirsty instincts utterly unchecked. Looking over their shoulders, Aradis and Girion saw nothing but mist. But a moment later, there appeared a number of distant glimmers of pallid silver darting across the moor. These were, without a doubt, the dreaded moonhounds, closing in at an almost unbelievable rate.

"If we can just reach the thicket," Girion shouted, "everything will be all right!"

But could they reach the thicket in time? They both felt certain they were outmatched here. The distance was too far and the moonhounds' speed too great. Yet, as they came closer to the black wall of trees and brambles before them, their hope was again kindled, although the race would be desperately close. They turned again to look at their pursuers and saw the flickering of their vile silver luminescence, as they bounded after their quarry.

"We'll have to leave the horses behind!" Aradis yelled. "The thorns are too close. They won't fit!"

"I'd hate to be responsible for them being devoured by those terrible creatures!" Girion shouted back.

"We haven't any choice in the matter!" Aradis returned, as they came to the very edge of Thornberry Thicket.

The moonhounds were nearly upon them, their devilish cries almost unbearable. They had emerged fully from the ghastly mist and were now bounding toward them with hellish ferocity.

"Fly! Fly into the thicket!" Aradis called out, as he and Girion dismounted and rushed headlong into the mass of cruel thorns and briers.

The horses they had abandoned now fled eastward in a panic, and the moonhounds turned to follow them, their massive paws pounding the ground with a horrible, swift thudding. Meanwhile, Aradis and Girion struggled through the unforgiving, tangled boughs of Thornberry Thicket, and, having gone no farther than ten yards into the place, they were already badly cut and bleeding from the monstrous spines for which the thicket was so renowned.

To their great dismay and sheer terror, a single moonhound had come up to the very edge of the thicket, to the very spot where they had entered, and was snarling viciously at them. The lads were both shocked by how huge the moonhound actually was, for at this distance, they could see its massive body heaving and rippling in the pale moonlight. It pawed the earth furiously, yellow eyes burning with rage, as it stared at them through the web of the thicket's contorted branches and vines.

Panting heavily and frightened nearly to death, Aradis and Girion strove to fight back their terror. They were nearly frozen in horror for several moments until Aradis breathed, "Surely he can't come in here after us! If we can barely make it through this mess, there's no chance he can get in here!"

"Right," Girion concurred. "There's only one thing to do. We have to go in deeper."

And so, they turned their backs to the monster and pressed farther into the thicket. But the moonhound did not cease its ominous growling, nor did it immediately abandon them, but remained for several minutes ruing the loss of its quarry, before it trotted off back onto the moor.

Now the lads made their way more carefully, laboring to avoid as many of the thorns as they could, although this proved exceedingly difficult, and they suffered grievously from being jabbed and poked and snagged by the innumerable black daggers. It was a troublesome business to constantly extricate themselves from the spines, and it seemed almost as if the vines and branches would tense up or even move to ensnare them further when they tried to pull away.

They sought to maintain a generally northerly bearing at first, thinking the ascent to Briar Bluff would be less arduous if they approached the slope to the west some distance into the thicket. So they went on, ducking as needed, wending their way through the spiky labyrinth in the pale moonlight and the encompassing mist. Yet this task soon became impossible, for everywhere they attempted to persevere in that course, there were masses of brambles and thorny vines blocking their way. Once they were perhaps three furlongs into the thicket, they despaired of going farther northward and began to make their way westward with the aim of gaining the top of Briar Bluff. It was rather a simple matter to discern which bearing was west, for the land rose at a considerable slope in that direction, but the going was much more perilous now, for the ground was littered with jagged rocks that sliced their hands open, as they clawed their way up the incline.

As they labored on their hands and knees up the slope, Aradis and Girion soon began to feel overwhelmingly exhausted. Their skin was shredded and their clothing tattered. They hadn't eaten in days, and it seemed the way before them grew more tangled and treacherous with every step they took. Still, the lads went on in tormented desperation, navigating the sinister network of murderous briers, while simultaneously attempting to retain their footing among the knifelike stones.

But their injuries from the thorns were numerous and deep, and as the slope leveled off slightly, they both began to feel themselves drifting toward delirium. Perhaps it was the ghoulish howling of the moonhounds off in the distance that was driving them to it. Or, perhaps it was the sheer bewilderment of being hemmed in by the labyrinth of thornbushes and brambles. But whatever it was, they began to see lights—strange, pale lights—appear before them. They were distant and cut in and out like orangish will-of-the-wisps darting from tree to tree. Even the moonlight seemed to be slightly changing colors now, and the lads begin to feel rather dizzy and markedly unsure on their feet.

All of a sudden, Girion cried out in dismay. He had become enmeshed in a particularly nasty mess of thorny vines. Aradis quickly drew Brightbeam and hewed asunder the larger tendrils which held his companion. It was then that Aradis really began to wonder if he had lost his mind already, for he saw the vines unmistakably move to snag Girion again. Aradis pulled him away, exclaiming in horror, "Girion, those things are alive!"

"No, Aradis," Girion gasped. "You're imagining things. I am too. We're both over the brink. You know what I mean? We can't go any farther," he panted, as he dropped to the ground.

"We have to!" Aradis returned insistently. "We've got to get out of this place or we'll both go mad! There must be some foul enchantment here, and we've got to be rid of it." Aradis looked at the ground and thought he saw it surge beneath him, moving up and down and swaying left and right. As he continued to stare downward, his vision grew blurry and then clear again. Aradis then peered at the tenebrous entanglement before him and saw the phantom lights flitting amongst the shadows. There were other strange things now too: spectral forms that floated just above the ground like grim vapors. They were nebulous, cold, gray, shrouded things and seemed to emit a low moaning. Aradis rubbed his eyes in hopes of dismissing the apparitions, but to no avail. The things were still there, and the moaning had not ceased, but was now joined by a high, fell wailing from overhead.

"Come on, we haven't a moment to lose!" Aradis exclaimed. Then he continuously shook Girion until he arose, and they stumbled forward once more through the terrors of Thornberry Thicket.

But it was not long before they really could go no farther. Their bodies were vanquished by absolute exhaustion, and their minds were plunged into a bestial frenzy. The far-off howling of the moonhounds, the acute pain of a thousand thorn pricks, the mesmerizing meshing of shadows and moonlight, the phantasmagorical wailing and moaning and the weird, ephemeral lights that haunted the path before them all merged into a maelstrom of overwhelming intensity. The lads were broken in nearly every sense of the word, and they succumbed to a madness that was only too eager to envelop them.

Screaming in anguish and despair at the lunacy they were so desperately trying to keep at bay, they both collapsed to the ground amidst an especially dense spread of dark brambles and twisted trees. They lay there for a minute or so moaning in their misery, and then Aradis began to cry out.

"Please! Someone! Anyone!" he shouted. "Get us out of this place!"

"It's no use, Aradis," Girion groaned, as he pressed his bloodied face to the earth. "No one will hear you. We're just not going to make it."

"Don't say that, Girion," Aradis gasped in reply. "We can keep going. We just need a little rest. We've come so far already. I know there's so much more, but we can't just . . ."

But he could say no more. His body was shutting down, and there was nothing he could do about it. Girion seemed already to have fallen unconscious, and Aradis would be close behind. He resignedly supposed that neither of them would wake again. Their journey had come to an end.

But just as Aradis' eyes were closing, perhaps for the last time, he looked up and saw a light. It was a curious red light, like that of a fire passing through red glass. There were soft footfalls as the bearer of the flame stepped up to where the two lads lay. Aradis blinked and saw the face of a man by the flickering light. It was familiar to him—very familiar. It was his father! Could it be that, against all hope, help had come? Aradis tried desperately to call to him but had not the strength to utter even a single word, only managing a dry gasp. A moment later, he blacked out.

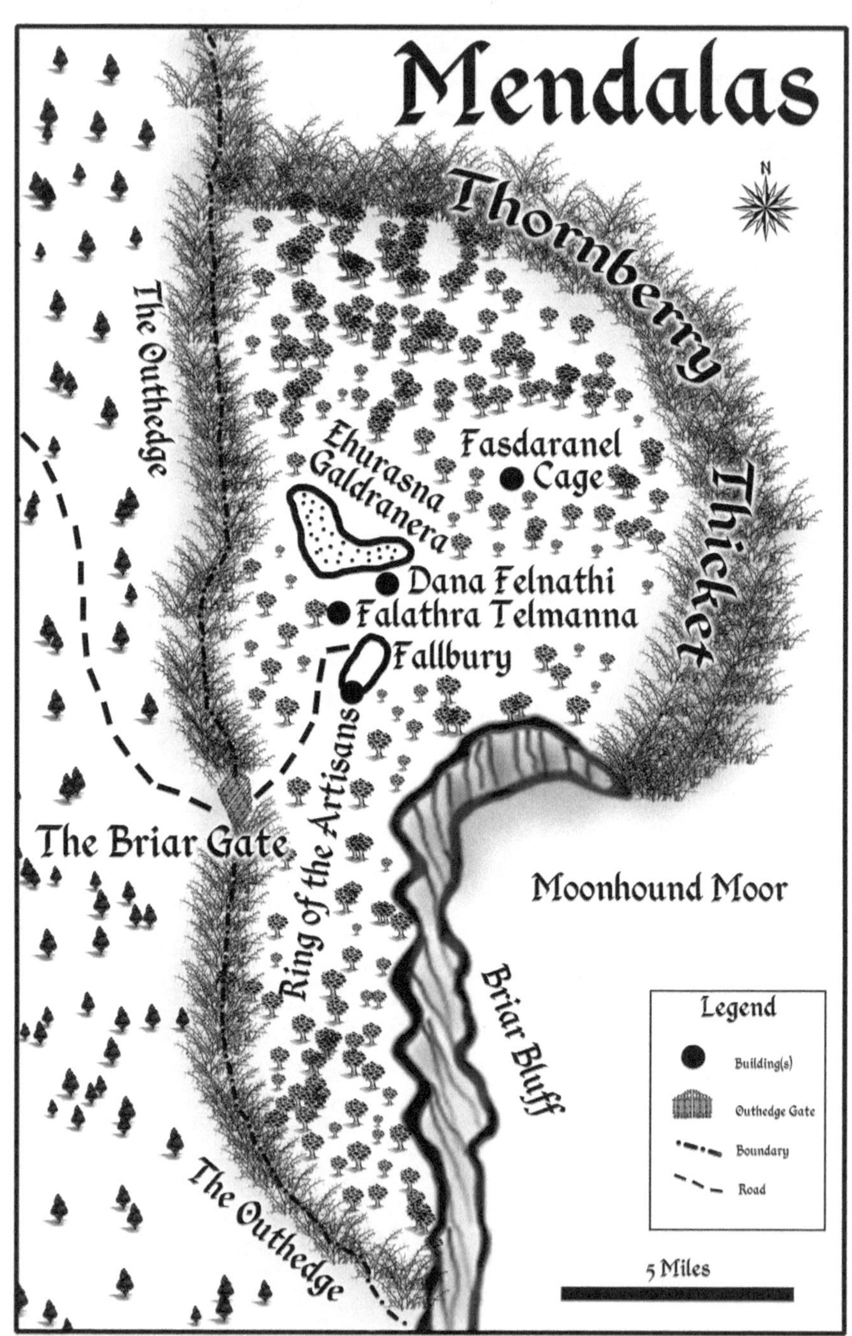

Mendalas
N
Thornberry Thicket
The Outhedge
Ehurasna Galdranera
Fasdaranel Cage
Dana Felnathi
Falathra Telmanna
Fallbury
The Briar Gate
Ring of the Artisans
Moonhound Moor
Briar Bluff
The Outhedge
Legend
Building(s)
Outhedge Gate
Boundary
Road
5 Miles

CHAPTER NINE

Candarron's Tale

It was morning now, Aradis guessed, for a vague semblance of light presented itself even to his unopened eyes, and a scattering of birds sang tunes that, although strange to his ears, sounded decidedly well-suited for the bright hours before noon. He heard the rustling of leaves by a crisp breeze and felt almost as if he were swaying back and forth a little. As to what had preceded his current state, Aradis could recall general sensations of terror, blackness, pain and madness, but that was all. Trying desperately to remember where he had last been and what had become of him, Aradis slowly opened his eyes, hoping that whatever he saw now would trigger his memory. But such efforts were suddenly and fully overwhelmed by sheer wonder and bewilderment as he saw what lay around him.

Aradis was suspended some forty feet above the ground in a cage skillfully woven from sturdy vines. The cage was affixed to a number of robust woody creepers, which were twisted together to form cables. These extended up to a massive bough, which hung out over the glade in which the cage was stationed. The glade itself was magnificent, filled with huge, old trees some hundred and fifty feet in height, and all the trees were clothed in beautiful autumn foliage: vibrant orange, gold, purple and luscious red. The forest floor below was spread with fallen leaves of these many marvelous hues, and the golden morning sunshine shone in clear rays through openings in the forest canopy above to illuminate this glorious autumnal cathedral.

Now Aradis looked about in the cage and saw that the only means of escape was a door also wrought from vines and having a lock that was carved into the wood. He saw also that his friend Girion was lying next to him, still unconscious it seemed. For a few moments, the lad looked quizzically at him, realizing how very odd it was that they were where they were. Then his wandering recollections all came rushing back.

He and Girion had been fleeing from the moonhounds into Thornberry Thicket. They had had an absolutely miserable time getting ripped open by the huge black spines in the moonlight, and on their way up the slope to the top of Briar Bluff, they had begun to feel more and more delirious. They had seen queer things; there had been spooks and lights and bizarre screams. And then their strength had simply failed them; they were overcome and fell to the ground and night had closed their eyes and their rabid minds. Yet, just before Aradis passed out he had seen—what was it? It was his father! His father had come to rescue him. But how was that possible? Had he too come to Byram? Or was it only in his mental aberrance that he had conjured up an image of his father?

In any event, they were no longer in Thornberry Thicket. Now they were, by all appearances, captive in a strange forest where summer had already come and gone. But how could that be? They had left Siloa in late spring, and their journey had only taken them a month and some days more; it certainly had not been three or four months! "Perhaps this is a dream," Aradis thought to himself. "Well, if it is, I should probably ask dream-Girion if that is the case, and maybe he'll set me straight."

And so Aradis took Girion by the shoulders and gently shook him. "Girion! Girion Ringmark!" he quietly urged him to escape his troubled slumber. As he did so, he noticed how many gruesome wounds his companion had upon his arms and hands from the cruel grasp of countless thorns and how badly his clothes were torn. Dismayed, Aradis then realized that he was in the same condition as his friend in both regards.

A few moments later, Girion's eyes creaked open, and he said groggily, "It's not time yet, Aradis. The harvest can wait; it's not as if the wheat is going anywhere. And just tell Corim that Neldon and Tallis will talk to what's-her-face some time tomorrow night."

"Come on! Get up, Girion! I'm not going to be telling Corim anything any time soon. We're not in Siloa or anywhere close. We're in . . . well, frankly, I don't know where we are," Aradis trailed off, as he looked about the glade again, still every bit as mystified by it as he had been when he first came to.

At length, Girion rubbed his eyes and began to stare, wide-eyed, at the forest that surrounded them.

"Great Sea and Sky, Aradis!" Girion exclaimed. "Where is this place? What has become of us? Do you remember what happened before … well, before we were here?"

"Yes, unless this is all a dream," Aradis replied.

Girion temperately slapped Aradis in the face, and together they concluded, "It's no dream."

"Thornberry Thicket, Girion," Aradis exclaimed. "Don't you remember? We were running from the moonhounds across the moor, and we entered the thicket, and then—"

"Yes, I recall it now," Girion interrupted. "But where have the months gone? It cannot already be autumn! And why are we contained in this strange prison?"

"Well, what day did we come to the thicket?" Aradis inquired, straining to recall the sequence of events that had preceded that night.

"Hm, let's see," Girion said, calculating. "The evening on which we both encountered Nagello was the 10th of Elaya. And it took us four days to reach Tarwyn; that would make it the 14th. And we were at sea on the *Meridot* for … what was it? Twelve days. And thus we reached Gessel on the 26th. And then it was seven days to the Fontskals. That would take us into the month of Tannaril. So that would have been the 3rd of Tannaril. And we left that same night with those kooks, Felding and Jiff. And then it was at dawn on the eleventh day that we came to Gorondil. So that whole debacle occurred on the 14th of Tannaril. And then we spent three days crossing the Farren, so we came to the thicket on the 16th."

"Then it wasn't yet midsummer!" Aradis cried. "Where then went Harasa, Ildurion, Bellin and the better part of Serona, that we should already be deep in the throes of autumn?"

"Perhaps we've been asleep for months due to some spell from the thicket," Girion pondered.

"There's no doubt that thicket had some dark spell laid upon it," Aradis remarked. "Right before we were overcome by exhaustion, I could not discern the real from the imagined."

"Nor I," Girion said.

Aradis looked about the glade once more and then softly declared, "Girion, just before I fell unconscious, I saw—well, I saw my father."

Girion looked at Aradis, searching his face, and replied, "I do not doubt that you did, but do not hope too strongly that what you saw was really your father and not some trick of the thicket, or I am afraid you might be disappointed."

"You're probably right," Aradis sighed. "But anyway, what are we doing in this cage?"

Just then, an incisive utterance came from among the trees just outside of the glade. "Eduri diyelgo nahathara!" the voice called.

Within moments, an assemblage of what looked to be Elves appeared at the edge of the clearing. Their woodland habiliment was remarkably well camouflaged, for it was made of varying shades of red, orange and yellow cloth.

"Elves, eh?" Aradis remarked quietly. "They must be the ones Felding told us about, wouldn't you think?"

"Oy!" Aradis shouted out at them. "Who are you? Let us down from this contraption!"

"Why must you always be so impulsive, Aradis?" Girion muttered agitatedly. "It's usually best to let others speak first in situations like this."

"They *did* speak first," Aradis returned hotly, "and besides, what do you mean by 'situations like this?' When's the last time you were locked up in a cage hanging from a treetop?"

Girion would have countered Aradis' snippy polemic, but the same Elf who had spoken before now said loudly to his comrades, "Teranara uo laye massa eduri diyelgo nahathara, teri garala somda adi nar Malaraneth, bago? Quesdara-ona mero adi roselda, fanara uo!"

There was light laughter and snickering among the Elves, and this infuriated Aradis, as he was certain they were the subject of their mirth.

"Hey, do you louts speak Daiga?" he shouted brashly. "Let us out of here this instant!"

"Aradis, don't be such a churl!" Girion scolded. "We're not at an ideal point right now to be making demands like that."

Now the lead Elf, the one who had been speaking thus far, a tall fellow with longish, light-brown hair dressed in a gray cloak, hunter-green breeches and high brown boots, looked up at them and stated rather disdainfully, "You know, your friend is right. You would be well-advised to refrain from making such boorish biddings in your present predicament, Manfellow." The last word came out with some definite derision.

"So you do speak Daiga," Aradis said contemptuously. "Well, let's not have any more Elven babble then. Now, how long are you all going to stand there and leave us locked up in this cage?"

In response to this, the Elf put his hands on his hips and looked up at them with a cold and threatening expression. "You're quite fortunate to be alive in a cage rather than dead in Surgana Amdara, the Thornberry Thicket. It is never prudent to insult those who have spared your life, and this is especially so, considering that it is our full prerogative to let you rot up there, if we so choose. And presently, I am rather inclined to exercise that prerogative."

Aradis was but a moment away from releasing a load of invective when Girion quickly laid his hand on his back and whispered, "Please, just this once, hold your tongue and let me speak with him."

Aradis bristled, but capitulated to Girion's request nonetheless.

"Please, sir," Girion commenced. "Heed not my friend's outbursts, for he is ever on the verge of fury, and his tongue is often lacking in wisdom for that reason. But know that we are exceedingly grateful to you for removing us from Thornberry Thicket, however you managed it, for we would certainly have perished there apart from your aid. We have been several days now without food, and little have we rested. Please, tell us—where are we, who are you and what day is it? For when we came to the thicket, summer was not yet fully ripe, and yet here we are in the midst of fall's dominion."

The Elf turned to the company behind him, made a remark to them in his own tongue, then looked back up at the prisoners and replied, "You possess considerably greater tact than your companion, but do not think that for this alone we shall be disposed to show you great kindness. Yes, you shall be released now, as was our original intention, but only so that you may be taken bound to our leader, that he may decide what to do with you. Once you are down here and your hands are firmly tied, we shall begin our journey, and I shall answer such queries of yours as I deem worthy."

Aradis desperately wanted to call out some first-rate aspersions that had been simmering in his mind, but, heeding his better sense, kept his mouth shut.

"Yelasari tano gwendar!" the Elf ordered his subordinates, several of whom went over behind a thick clump of bushes which was adorned with bright red foliage.

All of a sudden, Aradis and Girion felt their prison jerk and jostle back and forth, as it began its descent to the forest floor. They looked up and saw that the vine cable, which was slung over the bough above them, ran down to the collection of bushes where the Elves had gone, and they surmised that there was some sort of crank and pulley mechanism there that enabled the slow release of the cable.

In short order, the cage came to rest on the piles of fallen autumn leaves, and the lead Elf stepped up to the door. He had an ornate wooden key in his hand, and this he inserted into the lock that had been carved into the vines that made up the door. The wooden bolt holding it shut now slid aside, and the door swung open. Aradis and Girion slowly stepped out into the glade and were immediately surrounded by a number of Elves, who roughly pulled the Siloans' hands behind their backs and lashed their wrists together with thin, strong ropes.

It was then that Aradis noticed Brightbeam's absence, which led him to the realization that his dagger and half-leaf medallion were gone as well. "Say, where have you put our effects?" he demanded of the Elf leader.

"It is customary to remove weapons from prisoners' possession, Aradis," Girion answered in lieu of the Elf. "It wouldn't be very shrewd to place suspected enemies in a cage made of vines and leave them with something they could use to cut their way out, now would it?"

"Well said, Manfellow," the Elf remarked, "although even a sword could not easily cut through those particular vines. The fasdaranel vine is remarkably tough."

Now the Elves had completely finished binding the lads' hands, and they nudged them to march behind the lead Elf amidst the company. About ten Elves were behind them, and ten were in front. Aradis and Girion were walking next to each other, but one Elf stood to Aradis' right and another to Girion's left, to guard any move they might make to the side of the pack.

Passing over a thick carpet of fresh-fallen leaves, the company exited the glade and went off into the forest in a southwesterly direction.

As soon as they were out of the clearing, the Elves' leader, who was walking along right in front of them, remarked, "Now, as to your questions, Manfellow, I tell you these things not because I am particularly disposed to being informative at the moment, but rather because I am an Elf who honors the virtue of a generally courteous demeanor. Do not press me, however, or you shall find that I am not so courteous after all."

"Very well," Girion said. "We shall take with gratitude whatever explanations you are willing to grant us."

"Hm," the Elf sniffed. "My name is Tandarron," he stated proudly, "or Keeneye in your tongue. I am the Master Warden of the Bounds, the head watchman of the security of this dominion. My people are the Fall-Elves, the Mentalara, so named for the perpetual season of our land. This is the five hundred and thirty-fourth year of perennial autumn in this domain, which is called Autumn Dreamscape; its name is Mendalas in our own fair speech."

"So it is fall here year-round, then?" Girion inquired.

"Aye," the Elf confirmed.

"Yet, it was summer on the last night we could remember," Girion stated, puzzled. "Please, sir, can you tell us what day it is?"

"Nardis, the 17th of Tannaril," the Elf replied.

"You discovered us in the thicket last night then," Aradis noted, "for that was the 16th."

"Yes, we came upon you yesterday evening while we were checking our traps," Tandarron drily related. "There is a creature called the quenaddoril, a medium-sized, long-tailed, furry rodent, which lives in the midst of the thicket and feeds on the thornberries for which the thicket is named. The majority of our quenaddoril snares are set deep in Surgana Amdara, for the equenaddoril do not live near its boundaries. Some time after sunset, we heard those accursed moonhounds all worked up in a dither about something and perceived that they had come very near to the edge of the thicket. As their frenzy was unusually raucous, we came downslope to investigate and heard you two crying out like tormented madmen, for so you were. Then, after you fell unconscious, we carried you up here to our own domain."

"Is the thicket enchanted?" Girion asked. "For surely such horrors of mind and body as bore down upon us last night came not from mere exhaustion!"

"Enchanted? Bah, no!" Tandarron scoffed. "The thorns of Surgana Amdara are, if you will, animate in a sense, but so are other plants in Orona, in that they may possess limited abilities of motion. However, you came through the thicket after nightfall, the time when they are least alert. During the day, they are downright malicious, and even the Fall-Elves will not pass among them while Marda is out. They contain a particular poison called vallonin, which has a number of pernicious effects including insanity, hallucinations, extreme sleepiness and rampant delirium. Every prick injects more vallonin into your blood, and, if left untreated, it can lead to death within a matter of hours."

"You really did save our lives, then," Aradis realized, as he bit his lip, regretting his earlier impertinence.

"Yes, and sagacious would you be if you did not forget it," Tandarron remarked loftily.

"Was there another man there?" Aradis asked expectantly. "Did you see my father?"

Tandarron gave the lad an odd look and replied, "No, you two were the only ones we found. Was your father separated from you in the thicket?"

"No, he did not come with us," Aradis glumly replied. "He's far, far away. But I saw him carrying a lantern just before I passed out."

"That was me carrying the lantern," Tandarron stated. "More than likely you saw some figment due to the vallonin."

"So I had supposed," Aradis muttered morosely.

"Might I ask, sir," Girion inquired, returning the conversation to its main trajectory, "how your people navigate the thorns without being pricked?"

The Elf explained, "There are winding paths through the thicket known only to us, made long ago by a people known as the Thorn-Gnomes; these paths have been maintained by my own people, the Mentalara. In addition, we always carry the antidote to vallonin with us into Surgana Amdara, that same antidote which we administered to you to spare your lives. And we wear thick clothing to protect us from having our skins pierced as well."

As they were talking, they had gone some distance through an area strewn with boulders of considerable size that rested beneath the looming trees. Now the ground alternately rose and fell before them, as they began making their way through a sequence of little hollows.

"What manner of spell is laid on this place, that it should always remain autumn?" Girion asked after a few minutes, as Tandarron had grown silent.

The Elf returned, "That is a long tale indeed, the account of this enchantment, which we call Tarandelas Adrasanel, the Mercy of Adrasanel. Nonetheless, I will tell you the story of how our land came to be a bastion of the glorious season of autumn, though not in full, for that would take many days."

After they had walked a few steps more, Tandarron launched into a substantial narrative. Using such a voice as is fitting for the relating of venerable legends and in a tone which only skilled storytellers possess, he wistfully commenced, "The ancestors of the Mentalara came from the now vanquished kingdom of Sendarrim, which lay along the central eastern shores of Tassaru. They departed from that land seeking freedom from the terrible oppression they suffered at the hands of the surrounding peoples. As it was not far into the Latter Epoch at that time, the way to Aradath had just been made known by that great explorer, Vastia the Pathfinder. They were a brave and adventurous people and came south through the Bushbelt into Aradath through great peril and hardship. At last, they came to the eastern coast of Byram, and there they developed a healthy trade with the Dwarves of the Wide Lands to the south and also with the remarkable Thorn-Gnomes who dwelt farther inland, on the edge of the Kingdom of Argonis—in this very land, in fact. The first leader of our people, Daseldo by name, grew very close indeed to the chieftain of the Thorn-Gnomes, who was called Bannagrik. When hostile Troll invaders from western Quarana began to attack our ports some time after the year 100 of the Latter Epoch, Bannagrik offered sanctuary to our people in this land and led them on secret paths through Thornberry Thicket. Some Elves stubbornly remained behind to defend our harbors, but they were all eventually captured or killed. Those who had fled to the safety of this dominion, which was then called Baku Sondag, or the Surrounded Land in the Gnomes' tongue, learned much in skill and craft from the Thorn-

Gnomes. They were also instructed how to harvest thornberries from the thicket and how to pass through it unharmed."

"However," Tandarron went on, "a young, contentious Gnome named Golgastor murdered Bannagrik out of jealousy and then turned his people against the Elves through disseminating cunning deceptions and venomous untruths. After Golgastor's foul work had borne its noxious fruit, he demanded that the Elves leave their land immediately or else be slain. Daseldo refused this mandate, and thus there came bloody strife between the Thorn-Gnomes and the Elves. This led to the death of nearly all the Thorn-Gnomes, and all but a few of the Elves. Golgastor himself escaped to the south, but Daseldo was slain, and leadership passed to his nephew Adrasanel, who sought to rebuild what the Elves had lost."

"Golgastor wandered about in the Wide Lands for some time, but finally he came across a tribe of Goblins who were led by a wicked Goblin Warlock named Ugrusa. He enlisted the aid of these fiends, and with promises that they were to conquer a people of great wealth, he convinced them to march northward in an attempt to slay our forebears and so gain his revenge."

"When they arrived here, he guided them through Surgana Amdara by night, for it was their intent to fall upon the Elves while they were sleeping. However, Adrasanel was awakened earlier that same night by a terrible dream that warned him of Golgastor's imminent attack. He, in turn, warned all the other Elves that they must flee; they hearkened to him and thus went into hiding before Golgastor and the Goblins arrived. When the Goblins came and found the Elven village abandoned, they searched through every dwelling seeking the riches Golgastor had promised them. Finding none, for the Elves had not yet reestablished profitable trading, they become enraged. The Goblin Warlock laid a curse upon Golgastor, saying, 'You have deceived us, wretched Gnome, leading us on a far journey in hopes that we might gain mounds of treasure. But you have brought us to a forsaken hamlet of indigent peasants! Where is our gold, our silver, our abundant produce? We are denied even the pleasure of wanton slaughter, for your reputedly fierce enemies are nowhere to be found. Yes, you have won back your land by all appearances, but it shall become a thing of abhorrence to you, for from this day forward until the ruin of this age, this land shall be forever enthralled by but one season—that of hard, bitter, cold, merciless winter! So stay and reign here if you will, but you shall rule only over snow and ice, even while the land around you rejoices in summer. Now get out of our sight before we slay you in place of the Elves you have so despised!'"

"And no sooner had the Warlock spoken these words, then snow began to fall from the heavens and the trees and flowers began to wither away. So Golgastor fled from his presence, and the Goblins returned to the Wide Lands, greatly disgruntled. Now it came to pass that Golgastor encountered the Elves as he was fleeing, and he was captured by them. Adrasanel questioned him about all his doings, and most especially about the cause of the sudden advent of winter, for it was early summer then, as it is now. Golgastor told him all, and Adrasanel thought Golgastor to be one of the most pitiful, wretched and miserable creatures on earth. That contemptible Gnome had butchered a just and kind leader in cold blood, utterly destroyed a bond of friendship between two peoples and sparked a terrible feud between them. He had connived with cruel Goblins to continue his murderous deeds; yet, for all this, he received only their malice and a dreadful curse upon his homeland. Now he had fallen into the hands of his foes. Adrasanel, though he loathed Golgastor, said to him, 'Vile Gnome, it would not be unjust for me to end your life here and now, but I will not have the blood of such a sorry creature upon my hands. I will let you go whithersoever you wish in Orona, but rest assured that the powers of Erdion will bring your deeds back upon you wherever you find yourself in the days to come, for none of the Barada can forever conceal themselves from justice. But come not back to this land, for if we should meet again, you will surely die.'"

"And so Golgastor went out from them, and, so far as anyone knows, was never heard from again. But precisely when he stepped beyond the bounds of Baku Sondag, something truly remarkable came to pass. Though snow was mounded up in great heaps and cruel wind howled, and every green thing had been shorn of its foliage, at the departure of Golgastor, the snow and ice melted away, the bitter wintry gale became a crisp autumn breeze, and all the trees sprouted unparalleled fall foliage. Thus has it been ever since. The Elves were enamored with this new beauty of Baku

Sondag, and they decided to remain. From that time on, this land has been known as Mendalas, Autumn Dreamscape."

"As to why this turn of events came about," Tandarron explained, "some believe that the curse of winter only held as such while Golgastor remained within the bounds of the land, yet the Warlock's malediction of this place remaining ever in one season was so strong that it could not be utterly broken. So Mendalas now lies in perpetual autumn. But, it is the belief of my people that the grace of Adrasanel played a part in altering the curse even more than the removal of Golgastor, and thus we call the enchantment, as I said earlier, Tarandelas Adrasanel."

The two Siloans filed along amongst the Elves, marveling at Tandarron's story, still gazing about in amazement at the enchanted forest through which they were traveling.

"That is a strange tale indeed," Aradis remarked after a while, "and I am almost certain I would not believe it, except that I now see the reality of the Warlock's spell before my eyes. I am grateful to whatever it was that altered the curse, however, so that we were spared the misery of coming upon a land that was locked in winter."

"Yes, that would have been a curse indeed, but autumn is a blessing," Tandarron replied. "We are ever in a condition of harvest, and it is but a few months for us from sowing to reaping. Also, we may enjoy the hues of the fall leaves month after month, and yet they never accumulate too thickly upon the ground. It is our belief that the enchantment causes new leaves to quickly replace those which have fallen, and it carries a great number of leaves away at night so that we are not troubled by an excess of them. And at moonrise, you see, all the tree trunks bear a marvelous silver sheen; it is quite beautiful to behold. And the temperature is never terribly hot, nor terribly cold, but always pleasant."

"For my part," Aradis commented, "I prefer the changing of the seasons. But I suppose if autumn is all you've ever known, you wouldn't mind so much."

Tandarron didn't seem to take this last statement too well. Apparently his affinity for autumn was rather deep-seated, and he did not speak for some time after that. Girion shot a perturbed glance at Aradis after his comment, but the latter simply shrugged and mouthed, "It's true, you know."

When they had been walking for perhaps an hour and a half through this rolling autumn woodland, the forest faded away and a huge open field spread before them. It was covered with running vines and large, orange, roundish vegetation of some sort.

"What are those things?" Girion asked, as they began to march around the edge of the field.

"What, the crop?" Tandarron said. "They are called pumpkins in your tongue. We call them galdranera: that is, orange harvest. They grow here in Byram, but also in Murnia and Estereth. They ripen only in the fall elsewhere, but here we have them year-round. They provide us with a bountiful crop and can be used to flavor a good many dishes. It is primarily for that purpose that we employ them, but their stems also furnish us with hafts for our daggers, and their rinds, when thoroughly cleaned, make excellent lamps. In our language, Menrelda, this place is called Ehurasna Galdranera, the Gardens of the Orange Harvest."

They continued around the border of the field and were struck by how immense it was. The pumpkins just seemed to go on and on, consuming acre after acre of farmland. A number of Fall-Elves, all dressed in colors that matched their environs, were laboring in the fields, pulling the pumpkins from the vines and hauling them over to small pyramids of the peculiar orange produce.

After twenty minutes or so, they reached the far side of the pumpkin tract and entered the forest once more. Just a short distance inside the trees, there were pumpkins of enormous size, large enough to serve as dwellings for the Elves. In fact, many of them fulfilled this very purpose, for doors and windows had been cut out of them, and there were Elves passing in and out of their pumpkin habitations.

"How do these pumpkins grow so massive?" Girion wondered aloud.

"They are a different, much rarer variety," Tandarron replied offhandedly. "Long has this village of Dana Felnathi used them as dwellings."

Girion had by no means exhausted his inquiries, but he judiciously refrained from asking further questions now, for he could sense that Tandarron was somewhat put out by having to spend the majority of his morning escorting them such a great distance and being obliged to appease so much of their curiosity.

Once they had passed the pumpkin village of Dana Felnathi, they went through an increasingly dense portion of the forest. However, although the forest seemed closer here, the topography was tamer. Indeed, the landscape became decidedly smoother as they went farther to the southwest. They trod on for the better part of an hour through several miles of this woodland, and, all of a sudden, as they came over a little hill, they came upon a sizable hollow in which rested a splendid village unlike anything either Aradis or Girion had seen before.

The trees tapered off at the edge of the village and there began a pleasant lawn blanketed by autumn leaves that was bordered by a series of long wooden houses, each perhaps forty feet in length. These houses were built of hewn timbers and had a generally arching shape. They were all windowless, but had holes in their roofs to allow trails of smoke to pass upward into the sky. These curious habitations ran a half-mile or more along the lawn, and at the end of this delightful avenue, a modest hill rose up, and atop the hill stood a grove of magnificent trees that appeared to have been converted into dwellings of some sort.

"This is Yaldana, or Fallbury, as you would name it," Tandarron remarked, as the company passed into the town.

There were a great many Fall-Elves here, entering and leaving their dwelling places, carrying various materials and supplies, having brisk conversations with each other and looking generally industrious. There were several cauldrons and kettles set outside these dwellings, and there were comely Fall-Elf women stirring whatever was contained in them. Luscious aromas came from the large kettles, those of fresh, hot cider and savory stews of wild game. Fall-Elf children played merrily upon the lawn and stared with great interest at Aradis and Girion, as they were led toward the far end of Fallbury.

When they reached the other side of town, the lads passed a huge lodge on their right and another rather like it on their left and saw that the grove of trees they had noted earlier was arranged in a sort of semicircle around a large, flat area on the hilltop. Each of the trees (there were nine of them) was extremely large, possessing both a massive diameter and height. Structures quite similar to the houses they had seen in the village below had been built around their bases, although these buildings were much larger and were connected to great halls at their back ends. Also, there were additional structures farther up the tree trunks at various intervals, which appeared to be private quarters of sorts. They were bedecked with wide balconies and numerous windows; each possessed unique adornment and was carved with a variety of scenes and symbols. These upper buildings were not directly stacked on top of the buildings beneath them; rather, they were supported by scaffolding that projected out from the tree trunks.

Each treehouse was fronted by a single large wooden door, and above every door was a brightly colored banner with symbols sewn upon it. The four trees to the left of the center had, in turn from the outside to the center, an orange flag with an elaborately painted clay vase, a blue flag with a coil of rope and an open hand, a silver flag with a pile of gems of various hues, and a white flag bearing a loom. The four trees to the right of the central tree depicted, also in order from the outside to the center, a dark yellow ensign with a closed, brawny fist and a bolt of blue lightning, a green banner with a sharp dagger and a twiggy tree branch (Aradis and Girion recognized this emblem from the warehouse in Gorondil), a brownish flag with a large stone and a chisel, and a crimson banner with a brilliant blue flame and a diamond. The treehouse in the middle had several more floors than the others; the banner that hung above its door was striped from left to right with orange, white, red and yellow, and it had no symbol upon it.

"What are all these buildings?" Aradis inquired, as they strode across the lawn toward the central treehouse.

Tandarron promptly explained, "They are the ehasurdana, the lodge-dwellings of the Fall-Elf guilds. This is Galetha Esarnathi, the Ring of the Artisans." Now Tandarron seemed to be almost eager to explain this prized aspect of his society, as he expounded, "Those guilds closest to the middle are the most prestigious. On the left are the guilds for the women. First is the Earth Moulds, the pottery guild headed by Guildmaster Stammi. Next to that is the Wild Watchers, the guild of snares and traps for wild game, run by Elwina. Farther in is the Stone Charmers, the jewel-cutting guild led by Kamarra, and then there's the Woven Souls, the cloth guild run by her twin sister, Kelmora. The guilds for the men are on the right. Farthest to your right is the Thunder Dukes, the smiths' guild under Guildmaster Volando. Next to them is the Splinter Men, the guild responsible for making all our bows and arrows and doing all our decorative woodcarving; those folk are led by Yortallin. The one with the brown banner is the Mineral Mortals' hasurdana, where you'll find all those who make our stone weapons and our masters of the chisel under the leadership of Guildmaster Gillamar. And then comes the most enviable guild, that for which we are known throughout this region of Orona—the Diamond Flames. They're the glass blowers, renowned for their remarkable red glass sculptures. They're headed up by Enrion. The lodge behind you on the left is the central meeting hall for the women artisans; the one on the right is for the men."

By the time Tandarron had finished this explanation, they had come to the door of the central hasurdana, and Tandarron ordered the company to a halt. Then he went and knocked on the large door of the building and called out "Esso! Uo Tandarron, heth teri lasdora uo mello Malaraneth!"

It was not long before the door swung open, and a well-dressed Fall-Elf steward appeared, beckoning for them to enter. The rest of the company now parted from Aradis and Girion, save Tandarron and one Elf to guard each of them. They stepped into the hasurdana, which was well-lit by morning sunshine passing through its many windows. A scattering of Elves were hard at work in this spacious room; many of them were fastidiously polishing, cleaning or brushing the many ornate works of Elven skill on display throughout the chamber. Others were busy preparing an assortment of foods on counters over against the left wall.

As the lads looked about the chamber, their eyes came to rest upon a large oaken table directly before them that was bedecked with various fruits and vegetables, including an especially large cluster of fall grapes. Aradis and Girion were both painfully hungry, as they had not eaten in a number of days, but they knew it would not do to simply help themselves to the Fall-Elves' food. Besides, their hands were tied.

On the right hand side of the room was a large fireplace in which a cheerful fire was crackling away. On the far end of the chamber was the tree trunk around which the lodge had been built; on either side of the massive bole lay sturdy oaken doors. The steward led them over to the one on the right, and once they had passed through it, they went down a hallway with a number of doors on both sides. At the end of this corridor, they came to a magnificently carved oaken door, indubitably the work of the Splinter Men. The portal was decorated with various scenes of Autumn Dreamscape; there was a depiction of the pumpkin fields they had passed earlier that morning, another of a feast in Fallbury, and a remarkably detailed representation of the Ring of the Artisans.

"You are to see the Lodgemaster now," Tandarron informed his captives curtly. "Mind your manners, Menfolk, or you may regret it," he warned, as he turned toward the portal before them.

The steward slowly opened the door and motioned for Tandarron, the soldiers and their captives to enter. This they did, and the door was shut behind them.

CHAPTER TEN

The Gateway to Garlenwood

ow they stood in a medium-sized room at the back end of the hasurdana. Its only occupants were the five who had just entered, an Elven courier who was just getting ready to depart and another Elf with long pearly-white hair pulled back in a ponytail, who was seated at a desk, scribbling furiously with a quill on parchment. The courier nodded respectfully to Tandarron, then marched past him out of the room.

"Lodgemaster Goldquiver, sir," Tandarron commenced, as he addressed the Elf at the desk. "I have brought the Menfolk we found lost deep in Thornberry Thicket last night."

The Elf who had been writing intently now ceased, looked up slowly and disdainfully, then tossed his quill upon the parchment and leaned back in his chair. His sharp, statuesque features were lined with an only partially concealed condescension, as his orangish brown eyes glared at them. "So, children," he drawled superciliously in a smooth, measured voice, "you're the half-wits who think yourselves capable of reuniting the Kingdom of Argonis and destroying Ravinia the Heartless."

"I beg your pardon!" Aradis replied, more shocked than angry. "Just what exactly gave you that idea?"

Goldquiver reached into a drawer of his desk and took out Girion's notebook, which he contemptuously tossed onto the parchment before him. "Is this not your notebook?" he asked drily.

"It's mine, actually," Girion said.

"All the way from Velaris. Tut tut," Goldquiver sighed. "And nearly killed by some nasty thorns. That would have been a very sad way to end your adventure, wouldn't it?"

Aradis, livid at Goldquiver's mocking of them, spat, "Listen, Elf, what are you on about anyway? Just what have you got against us that before we've even had a chance to be introduced, you start making sport of us?"

"Oh, I've had all the introduction I care for," Goldquiver haughtily replied. "You are Aradis Kingblade, I take it, by your poor control of your temper. And your companion is Girion Ringmark—it's all in the journal. You come from a village of no significance whatsoever in the Kingdom of Velaris over in Quarana, and, apparently, you encountered one of the Hadathi, who told you that the Danna himself had appointed you to come save the Kingdom of Argonis and put an end to the power of the Witch Ravinia over in Blackbough Woods. Am I not correct?"

"Just who do you think you are, going through Girion's notebook like that?" Aradis raged, as he struggled against the guard who was restraining him.

"I am Malaraneth, or Goldquiver in your miserable Daiga drivel, the Lodgemaster of the Fall-Elves. And as you have trespassed into my dominion, I have every right to do as I please with both you and your things," Goldquiver enunciated, as he leaned forward menacingly. "And I must say it is rather a shame, Manfellow, that my folk spared you from the poison of Surgana Amdara."

"Well, if you think so little of us, why did you have us brought here to tarnish your glorious presence?" Aradis angrily retorted.

"It is no fault of mine that some of my people were inclined to show you mercy," the Elf airily replied, mindlessly brushing his finely embroidered, gray tunic. "But when Tandarron, who found you by lantern light deep in the thicket, discovered this notebook and examined its contents, he enlisted the aid of those with him to have you brought out of the thicket and held captive that I might have the opportunity to question you about your business, for he assumed it might interest me. And in truth, it does, but only marginally so."

"How is that?" Girion asked calmly.

"Hm," the Elf snorted. "No one attempts to pass through Thornberry Thicket on a whim, for it is well-known that none but the Fall-Elves can survive its terrors. And yet you spurned your very lives in an attempt to pass through the fence of our land. Strictly as a matter of curiosity, I want to know what drove you to it. That is, I only care to speak with you to learn the real reason you have come to Argonis. Who sent you, and what are you trying to accomplish?"

"You already read the answers to all those questions when you were snooping through Girion's journal!" Aradis hotly replied.

Now Goldquiver looked back and forth between them, and, for a second, his contempt was almost replaced with puzzlement. "You mean to tell me you really believe that Telyon—the very same Telyon who is known as the Danna of the Menfolk, the reputed ruler of the Haedran realm of Erdion—sent you across the sea to save a kingdom singlehandedly?" he laughed incredulously.

"Nobody said anything about doing it singlehandedly," Girion meekly corrected.

"No, that's not the point," Goldquiver said dismissively. "I'm asking if you really believe you have received your mission from no less a personage than Telyon of Erdion."

"Yes, of course," Aradis said. "What else do you think would cause us to do all those crazy things you read about in the journal?"

"Stupidity," the Elf flatly replied.

"Stupidity will only get you so far before it gets you into trouble," Girion noted.

"Well, if even half the nonsense in your journal isn't made up," Goldquiver remarked, "then you've been in trouble many times already."

"What I meant was that you can't simply come through trials like we've been through merely by luck," Girion clarified.

"Can't you?" Goldquiver rejoined. "It seems to me that most of the time you were rescued by the cleverness or good will of another, not by the intervention of Telyon, as you seem to imagine." The Elf uttered the name of Telyon with unveiled disregard.

"Who is to say it wasn't Telyon who guided such folk to our aid?" Girion responded. "You may dismiss our quest all you like, but you were not present on the night when both Aradis and I encountered the Hadathi and he revealed himself to us."

"You mentioned in your scribblings that you were down at the tavern right before you met him. Perhaps there was a little too much tilting of the tankard going on," Goldquiver mocked, making a motion as if he were imbibing out of an imaginary stein.

"If all you're going to do is sit around and accuse us of being a pair of woolgathering drunkards, you're just wasting all of our time," Aradis muttered irritably. "Haven't you got more parchments to draw on?"

"Of course I do," the Elf snapped. "Unfortunately, I have to decide what to do with you two nitwits first."

"I have a suggestion," Aradis remarked pertly. "You could provide us with a nice luncheon, gather provisions for our journey, give us back the items that belong to us and send us on our way. Then you can go back to your ciphers or whatever jolly nonsense it was you were playing around with."

Goldquiver's face turned cold as ice. He rose from his chair, livid, and strode slowly over to Aradis, stopping inches from his face.

"Listen to me, you impertinent cur," he uttered slowly and dangerously, as he shook his finger at Aradis, looking down at him with a perilous expression. "I will not be told off by a hot-tempered boor of a Manfellow, who is operating under the delusion that he has been summoned by the powers of Erdion to do something the boldest and most intelligent of the Barada would fail to accomplish. You're nothing but a straw-headed transient, who just happens to have been saved out of every disaster you've gotten yourself into by the good graces of circumstance and timely aid from others. And don't you ever think yourself superior to me, you churlish dullard! You had barely entered Surgana Amdara when you succumbed to its poison, and if my people hadn't rescued you, you would be lying there right now: stone-cold dead, having gasped away your last breaths in brutish madness. No, you are no match for Thornberry Thicket. But I, on the other hand—I eat that place daily for breakfast!" he finished, as he grabbed a tart filled with purple berries from his desk and took a large bite out of it.

"Is that a thornberry tart?" Girion asked quietly, hoping to diffuse Goldquiver's rage.

"What do you think?" Goldquiver snapped. "Better make a note of that, boy. Day 38: learned from Goldquiver that the Fall-Elves make thornberries into pastries called thornberry tarts. Thornberries are small, round, purple and delicious. Goldquiver didn't give us any to try, though."

It took every last ounce of Aradis' willpower not to lunge forward and bowl Goldquiver right into the wall, but he was able to rein his anger in long enough to clear his head, as the Lodgemaster walked back over and sat down at his desk.

"Let's see," the Elf said, "Now where were we before that unpleasant outburst? Oh yes—what to do with you."

Aradis spoke up again, this time not seeking to provoke Goldquiver, only to remain firm in his conviction. "Sir, why is it a matter of such great concern to you that we are committed so strongly to this quest? If you are certain we will fail, what is our conviction to you but the ill-spent fervor of madmen? It would seem strange, then, for you to be so vexed by the matter. Is it perhaps that you are afraid we might succeed? And would it be such a terrible thing if we did?"

"What did I just tell you, boy?" Goldquiver returned angrily. Then he looked hard at Aradis' face, not in fury this time, but in perplexity.

"You really won't let this go, will you?" he sighed, after a few moments. "I've met a good many fellows before who share your temperament, as stubborn as an ass and as cantankerous as an old bull. Most of them were Dwarves. But as much as I am loath to say it, you are not merely a hot-tempered fool. You really, really believe this rot about Telyon and your quest, don't you? And no amount of good sense will wrest that from you, I'm afraid. Very well, then. I can be reasoned with."

Just then, the steward reentered the chamber and politely said, "Malaraneth, danno, san mura talgenas mayath haldasora."

Goldquiver nodded, then turned to the Siloans and said, "It appears that we shall be finishing this conversation over my lunch."

He arose and motioned for the guards and Tandarron to follow him, as he exited through the door and into the hallway after the steward. Goldquiver then turned into a room on the right side of the hall, and there they came upon the back side of the tree trunk around which the hasurdana was built. A sizable archway had been cut into the trunk itself, and inside the trunk, there was a wooden spiral staircase with a beautifully carved bannister. They took this staircase up past three landings and stopped at the fourth, though the stairs went up one floor higher. There was a doorway there, which Goldquiver opened into an airy room containing a large bed, several shelves filled with books and a table with a number of tidy stacks of paper on it.

Goldquiver now opened a set of highly decorated, double wooden doors onto a balcony that overlooked all of Fallbury. The view was nothing short of magnificent. The enchanting lawn of Galetha Esarnathi lay below them, and the quaint dwellings of Fallbury lay beyond that. And where the village ended, the autumn landscape stretched away before them to the northeast, punctuated only by the distant pumpkin fields.

On the balcony on which they stood, there was a table with a veritable feast piled upon it. There were various cuts of meat on a platter, a pot filled to the brim with piping hot quail stew, crisp grapes and apples and an assortment of pastries and cakes, all emanating the odor of the sweet, plump, purple thornberries. And, to complement all of this, there was a large jug of spiced ale. Goldquiver sat down at the table and began to partake of this repast, and, as he did so, he gave some orders to Tandarron and the other guards, who began to untie Aradis' and Girion's bonds.

"You're quite harmless, I have decided," Goldquiver said, as the two guards departed, although Tandarron remained standing by the double doors. "Sit," he said to them, motioning to two chairs, which were positioned at the table. "But don't eat, mind you. This is *my* lunch."

"Why the sudden change in mood?" Aradis inquired. "A minute ago you wanted nothing to do with us, and now you've invited us up into your private quarters."

"Got to keep my schedule." Goldquiver smiled coldly. "If I must work during meals, so be it. Better than falling behind in what needs to be done for the day."

Both Aradis and Girion felt their stomachs gurgle at the sight of this plethora of scrumptious victuals.

"Sir," Girion tactfully began, "we certainly wouldn't take any of your food, but is there any other food you wouldn't mind giving us? We haven't eaten for several days now, you see."

"Well, that's a shame," Goldquiver moped, with the utmost sarcasm. "No doubt about it. But, my apologies, you shan't be receiving any food from me. The Danna is taking care of your needs in that regard, remember?"

Girion did not reply to this jab, and he was grateful that Aradis didn't either.

"Now," Goldquiver mused aloud, "by the laws of my people, as you have been shown mercy, I cannot simply kill you, nor would I, had I the choice.

If the truth must be told, I am not the bloodthirsty sort, but I do not take trespassing on my lands lightly. I must release you, one way or the other, so now it only remains to be decided whether I have you escorted back to Moonhound Moor or on into Argonis. But, if I let you on into Argonis, who knows what folly you will engage in! Yet, if I bring you back to the moor, you will likely as not be devoured by the moonhounds or snatched by the Dwarves and hauled off to Blackbough Woods or maybe simply be killed then and there. But, on the other hand, how could I sleep at night having unleashed such a pair of bunglers upon the unsuspecting folk of Garlenwood?"

"Garlenwood?" Aradis asked, annoyed.

Goldquiver brusquely replied, "Argonis, you ignoramus. Garlenwood and Argonis are one and the same. Garlenwood is just a rough translation of what the word Argonis actually means in the local Ingan language, Asla'gu. Argonis literally means 'land of the garlen grove.' And since you don't seem to know much of anything, I'll probably have to explain what a garlen is as well. The garlen is a variety of tree that grows in the eastern regions of the Elder Forest."

"Well, if I'm such an ignoramus," Aradis irritably returned, "then why don't you tell me—"

"Sir, I have been wondering about something for some time," Girion cut in, trying to avert an altercation. "Why is it that the Dwarves have joined up with Ravinia? Was it not a great risk to treat with someone so vile and treacherous? What profit did they gain by swearing allegiance to her?"

Goldquiver popped a grape into his mouth, chewed it, then spat out the seeds. "Hm, it is apparent that you really know nothing about this whole situation. This is even worse than I thought!" he laughed derisively. "Are you not conversant with the formation of the Fell Alliance? Do you even know what a Witch is? Do you know anything at all about Argonis or Sarganath?"

"A few things," Aradis calmly returned. "But certainly not a great deal."

"Well," Goldquiver said patronizingly, "allow me to educate you, then."

Ceasing for a time from his luncheon, he took a swig of spiced ale and then expounded, "Ravinia is a Witch, as you know, but I perceive that you don't know Witches for what they really are. You imagine them, I would guess, to be evil women with substantial magical powers. That is not incorrect, but that isn't the half of it. Witches are beyond the Barada in more ways than one. Speculation is rife as to how this is so, with some saying they are mighty, malevolent spirits merely guised in flesh and others claiming they are Barada who have been transformed into beings of greater potency through entering a pact with wicked spirits of the Haedra. Regardless, it is clear they have great skill in Daegar—dark magic, that is. They have unparalleled powers of persuasion, powers to pervade the minds of the Barada and infect them with an inexplicable willingness to carry out great evil, powers to make them despair beyond all hope."

Goldquiver now leaned across the table, his eyes filled with ominous foreboding, "You mean to destroy Ravinia, but you are, I gather, completely unaware that Witches are, for all practical purposes, invincible. Even a very mighty mortal could hardly hope to slay a Witch; he'd be lucky if he could drive her off to another land. In the few cases in which legends do speak of a Witch being destroyed, it is almost always through the direct intervention of some Haedran power, which, I suppose, is what you're depending on. But as for Ravinia, she would be formidable even if she weren't essentially invincible. She is a Druidess, not one of the Menfolk, and can take the form of a huge black raven with glowing yellow eyes. And if that weren't terrifying enough, she has the power to summon a truly awful and devastating enchantment known as the Deathwash."

"The Deathwash?" Aradis repeated the term with trepidation, biting his lip.

"Indeed. The Deathwash," Goldquiver returned. "It is a foul curse, a heinous sorcery summoned by the weeping of Ravinia. I do not pretend to know a great deal about the magic of Orona, but I do know this: for dark power there is a dark price. And in exchange for the Deathwash, Ravinia must pay in tears—terrible, black tears. Some say tiny fragments of the Witch's soul pass out of her into each droplet, but I will not venture to speculate on the matter, though I do not doubt that a grievous payment is being exacted from Ravinia for that which she has acquired. In any event, when Ravinia weeps, these enchanted black tears stream down her face, and when they strike the ground, they hiss and steam like the fires in the heart of Orona, instantly killing anything they touch. But the tears from her accursed eyes are not that which is so greatly feared by the Barada, for one would have to very close to her to be in danger of being touched by them. Rather, it is the tears of the heavens that are summoned by her weeping that cause such great dismay. It is these tears that are usually being referred to when people speak of the Deathwash, though the Witch's own tears are called the Deathwash as well."

Goldquiver took a heavy breath and went on, "When those black tears trickle down the Witch's cheeks, the sinister spirits of the air are aroused and empowered, and dark storm clouds appear in the heavens, mounting up like great black mountains. Then it begins to rain, gently at first and then in torrents. But each droplet is a deadly scourge, for the rain has the very same effect as the tears of Ravinia. All the ground which is touched by it remains cursed thenceforth. And if one of the Barada should be touched by even one black drop, he will scream in wretched agony, his heart will fail him, he will convulse and then pass into blackness and death moments later. In battle, Ravinia has on several occasions brought forth this great evil and many valiant Barada have perished from it."

"If what you say is true," Aradis gulped, "Ravinia really would be practically unassailable."

"Yes! Haven't you been listening to anything I've been saying? And of course it's true," Goldquiver returned snappily. "I've seen it with my own eyes! Indeed, some of my own people were lost in battle to the Deathwash."

"For that I am truly sorry," Girion sighed, shaking his head dejectedly. "I must confess that you have shed much light on the severity of our task. I did not realize Ravinia was such a great foe as you have revealed her to be. But where did she come from, and what brought her to the Elder Forest?" he asked.

"Thirteen years ago," the Elf recommenced, "in the year 704 of this age, late in the deep autumn of Serona, Ravinia came out of the wild woods to the west. From whither she came, the Barada know not, nor, if they had any wit about them, would they care to discover it. Many believe the Druids of Knobstaff Village over in Blackbough Woods played a role in summoning her. Those particular Druids, led by the Archdruid Malatar, are known to have dabbled deep in Daegar. Indeed, with such evil magic they overcame the good Menfolk of Blackbough who once lived not far from the Druids' village. And thus many of the Menfolk were driven into hiding in the deep forests of a region known as Rebel's Wake, which lies to the west of their former domain. As far as anyone knows, those poor

Menfolk still dwell there in secret to this day or else they have fled to fairer lands, lands that have not fallen under the Witch's shadow. In my opinion, the latter is more likely to be the case. However, their castle, the Burg of Ilderath, was taken over by the Druids, and its ruins are now used as a meeting place by those foul Barada. In any event, Ravinia formed a pact with the Druids of Blackbough; they would serve her, and she would help them enlarge their territory."

"Together, Ravinia and the Druids approached the Blackwings of Shardclaw Caverns, a great system of grottoes just to the northeast of the Druids' lands. A few years before all this, the Blackwings of Shardclaw had tried—unsuccessfully—to expand their colony to the south and east. With the arrival of the Witch, they saw an opportunity to employ her magical powers against their opponents, who were a number of hardy Ingan natives living in scattered villages throughout the forests of Black-bough, some of whom had already been expelled by the Druids. Ingans are Barada who look rather like trees, by the way. Everyone knows that, of course, but you're exceptionally ignorant, so I figured I'd help you out." The Fall-Elf smirked.

"That must be the group of Blackwings that Felding mentioned, eh?" Aradis remarked to Girion, while forcing himself to ignore Goldquiver's last comment, though it stung considerably.

"Most likely," Girion replied. Then, turning to Goldquiver, he asked, "Did Ravinia then succeed in enticing them into forging a league with her and the Druids?"

Goldquiver nodded, then said, "The Blackwings were only too happy to gain Ravinia's assistance in fulfilling their lust for conquest. At that time, the amalgamation of Ravinia, the Druids and the Blackwings came to be known as the Fell Alliance. Though the Blackwings and the Druids did—and still do—retain a degree of autonomy under their respective leaders, for all practical purposes they sacrificed their freedom on the altar of military expansion. And so they became the vassals of Ravinia. To this day, they ultimately serve her ends, not their own, though many of them may not see it that way."

Goldquiver paused, took a drink of spiced ale, then continued, "Thus, the Witch, having secured the allegiance of two formidable groups, took up residence deep in Shardclaw Caverns in a place called Witch's Grotto. And there she plunged deep into Daegar, for fearful rumors came to us out of the west of Ravinia imposing some foul enchantment upon herself. The full terror of that enchantment is, from what I gather, known to no one. Regardless, it was not long after such sinister stirrings that the attacks began."

"The first to fall to the Witch's armies were the remaining Ingans to the south and east, whom the Blackwings had previously sought to conquer. They all soon fled or were slain, and their villages were burned to the ground. Then Ravinia began to press her advantage to the east, into a vast region known as the Stony Wilds that lies in-between the Kingdom of Argonis and Blackbough Woods. That is a rugged, wild land inhabited primarily by bands of nomadic Trolls. Now the Trolls owe no allegiance but to themselves, so they did not explicitly ally themselves with Ravinia, but neither did they hinder raiding parties of Blackwings that crossed the Stony Wilds to harass the western borders of Argonis."

"During that same period, two more groups joined the Fell Alliance: the Yetis of Mornasok and the Dwarves of Hammergast, Toldrennon Wood and the Rhassendag Downs. You see, over in Blackbough Woods, there is a steep canyon called Jaggenfall Gorge, and the northeastern end of it is riddled with a great many caves and crags. A number of vagrant Yetis settled in that place some decades ago, and their habitation is now called by the name of Mornasok. Well, these Yetis succumbed to the same allure as the Druids and the Blackwings when Ravinia approached them, and so they joined forces with her."

"Meanwhile, the Tharlog, the ruler of all the Dwarves in this region of the Elder Forest, a fellow by the name of Nolgar, began to consider all that Ravinia had accomplished in such a short time. Hoping to share in the benefits of her great power, he sent her a proposal stating that the Dwarves under his dominion would gladly swell her ranks, if only she would help them gain control of a few prominent ports on the coast of the Indurian Deeps. Nolgar knew that, by seizing them, the Dwarves would amass much wealth. Yet this proposal was sent in secret, and it was only some time later that this dark agreement became known to the Dwarves' former allies, which included the Kingdom of Argonis. As it turned out, Ravinia was delighted with Nolgar's offer, but she counseled him and the Dwarves to continue feigning friendship with those they would soon betray, at least until she was able to concoct a plan to overthrow the garrisons of Gorondil and Forellos in one fell swoop. And it was not terribly long before she did exactly that. It was then that the trouble really began for the Fall-Elves."

"What sort of trouble?" Girion asked, noticing that Goldquiver seemed to be showing, for the first time since they had met him, a hint of sorrow and pain.

"A great number of my people used to dwell in the ports of Gorondil and Forellos, but thanks to Ravinia and the Dwarves, today there is not one single Fall-Elf left there," Goldquiver replied bitterly. "In a matter of hours, Ravinia and the Dwarves brought such woe upon my kin that words do not suffice to tell of it. That rueful day was on the 15th of Galrim in 706, a day I shall not soon forget. Dwarves from Hammergast and the Rhassendag Downs came in full force down the Iron Highway, and, at sunset, they entered the city and slew as many of my kin as they could. Ravinia was with them, flying about in the form of a great, uncouth raven, grabbing my people with her vicious claws and then dropping them from a great height. I was fortunately not in Gorondil at the time, although I often was in those days. But on that occasion, I was riding on horseback not far from the city. I saw the chaos in the harbor and rode northward to get reinforcements. That same evening, the Dwarves of Toldrennon Wood fell upon Forellos to the north, and there the slaughter was grim as well. Many Elves perished that day—many dear Elves. And so those terrible losses in Gorondil and Forellos became known as the Bloody Gloaming of Galrim."

Goldquiver paused for a few solemn moments before continuing, "When I returned to Autumn Dreamscape, I rallied all of our best warriors to at least attempt to retake Gorondil. But our soldiers were too few for the task, so I at once sent a message to King Thornoak of Argonis requesting aid."

"Is Thornoak your ally then?" Girion asked.

"He is my sovereign, Goldquiver replied. "Yea, though Mendalas lies outside the bounds of Argonis proper, for at least five centuries the leader of the Fall-Elves has been a member of the Verdinnion, bearing both the burdens and benefits of fealty to the monarch of Argonis."

"What is the Verdinnion?" Aradis inquired.

Goldquiver sighed in aggravation, "You were supposedly sent by the Danna to restore peace to Argonis, and he didn't tell you about the Verdinnion?"

Aradis shook his head and Goldquiver explained, "The Verdinnion is the council of all the regional leaders of the Kingdom of Argonis that meets in Tallequana Hall in Strongbranch Citadel, the great tree fortress of Anganor, the capital of Argonis. Well, it used to meet there, anyway. Now it doesn't meet at all."

"Why? Is that why there is so much strife?" Girion asked. "Or did the Verdinnion cease to meet because unrest had already come about?"

"Most of the members of the Verdinnion are a pack of fools," Goldquiver scornfully remarked, "but I can tell you why I stopped attending their silly meetings. When I asked Thornoak for aid to reclaim Gorondil and drive out the Dwarves, he refused, insisting that the bands of Blackwings roaming around Argonis' western borders were a greater threat. After I received his thoughtless reply, I never returned to the Verdinnion again. And shortly thereafter, petty strife tore the rest of its already frail associations apart. And, following the Sundering of the Erynos, Thornoak himself decreed that it would be best if the Verdinnion no longer met."

"What is the—" Aradis began.

"Let me guess," Goldquiver cut in haughtily. "You don't know what that is either. Well, eventually Ravinia did mount a massive attack from the west, but Thornoak got wind of it and sent out all his forces to meet her at the western edge of the Stony Wilds. There they clashed atop a huge ridge known as the Erynos Divide. And the Witch was prevailing, for none could stand against the power of the Deathwash which she had summoned. Thornoak's ranks were just dropping dead, and those foul opportunists, the Trolls, decided to help Ravinia in that conflict, though they had no official ties to her. But when it looked like Ravinia had decisively gained the Erynos, Thornoak did something which no one to this day quite understands. It seems he knew some pretty deep magic, for he spoke a single word, and his voice was heard for miles around. When the echoes of it had died away, Ravinia had withdrawn her Deathwash, and the Erynos collapsed into the earth, forming a great chasm and sending many of both Thornoak's and Ravinia's forces to their deaths. And from the bottom of the chasm, there shot up a wall of magical green energy—sparkling, scintillating and radiant. It ran for ten leagues to the south and nearly thirty to the north, and it remains there to this day. The barrier is called the Greenwall; it runs from the bottom of the gorge to more than a thousand feet above its brink. And it, along with the chasm in which it stands, the Chasm of Erynos, is practically the only thing that is keeping Ravinia and the Fell Alliance from bringing the Kingdom of Argonis to utter ruin. Fortunately, Ravinia can't simply bring her troops around it, or she certainly would. For its northern terminus coincides with an especially perilous region of the Arkanian Mountains, a cruel range of jagged peaks inhabited by giant winged monstrosities known as malaquassa. And going south will do her no good either, for neither the Stony Wilds nor Argonis can be reached from that direction, since the Greenwall ends at a huge precipice, several thousand feet in height, known as the Walls of Ancient Wrath. But if things continue as they are, Ravinia won't need to do a thing to bring the land to its knees, for it is nearly already there. This has been especially so since Prince Makwaru disappeared."

"That's Thornoak's son, I take it," Girion surmised.

"Yes," Goldquiver nodded. "The Sundering of the Erynos took place in the month of Bellin of 707, and after Thornoak performed whatever magic it was that made the Greenwall, his strength all but left him. It seemed he aged many years from accomplishing that one deed, and he became utterly disengaged from the affairs of the kingdom. His son, Makwaru, was convinced that Ravinia would find a way to dismantle the Greenwall and that it was only a matter of time before she would strike. As he could not urge his father to take any action whatsoever, Makwaru snuck off toward Blackbough Woods in early Ferenos of 710 and has not been heard from since. It is generally believed that Blackwing patrols roaming the Stony Wilds picked him up and that he was brought to Ravinia, who slew him. But no one really knows."

Now Goldquiver took another drink of his ale, shoved another grape in his mouth and said, "And no one really cares. Argonis is nothing but a lost cause now, and there's nothing that can be done about it, not by you or anybody else. Ravinia is, quite frankly, unstoppable. The most sensible thing we can do at this point is live our lives and carry on business as best we can within the walls of Thornberry Thicket and the Outhedge until the Witch's black night falls upon us. And fall it will. Now I've spent enough time explaining all this rot about Argonis' sorry past to you. I've let my stew get cold, and I've gotten behind on my work."

"Tandarron," the Lodgemaster suddenly said, and the master warden perked up.

"Escort these lads to the Briar Gate and let them go on into Argonis." Having said this, Goldquiver produced a large metal key from inside his tunic and handed it to Tandarron.

Aradis and Girion were both shocked and almost speechless.

"B-b-but I thought you . . ." Aradis sputtered.

"Oh, don't think for a moment that I'm giving you a vote of confidence," Goldquiver snarled. "My reasoning is this: say I send you on your way into Argonis and you fail. No harm done; it will simply be shown that I was right all along. Now say you go on and succeed; well, you can't have even entered Argonis without my permission, so I can take partial credit for your victory. But I simply couldn't send you back to the moor. I couldn't bear the guilt of sending such blundering dunces to such gruesome deaths. But, if you continue on your doomed journey, you will perish, one way or the other. It is only a matter of time. Now, get out of my sight so that I may finish my lunch and get back to work." Goldquiver then set about swiftly, but tidily, devouring his meal.

"Gladly," Aradis remarked, as he turned to follow Tandarron back into the interior of the hasurdana.

"Sir, might you tell us how to reach the city of Anganor?" Girion asked hopefully, before he also turned to go. "That is our ultimate destination, you see, and—"

"Most certainly not!" Goldquiver snapped. "After all, is not Erdion to be your guide? Thus, you shan't be needing any direction from me. No, I'm afraid you must find Anganor on your own; that's what you get for being a brace of overconfident clodpolls. Although, I will tell you that once you get into Argonis, you'll soon come to the territory of those fatuous Leprechauns and their even more fatuous leader, that hog-faced twit, Shillelagh McDasher. You might get along well with that half-wit git and his folk, come to think of it. Perhaps he'll even fan the flame of your ill-founded, asinine optimism. Wouldn't that be nice?" Goldquiver obviously didn't want to leave the slightest amount of ambiguity regarding how he really felt about the Menfolk and their mission.

Then, after taking a sizable gulp of some of the stew before him, the Lodgemaster added vehemently, "Now get out of here before I change my mind and have you taken back the way you came!"

The lads now really and truly moved to depart, for they had no more desire of Goldquiver's company than he had of theirs.

Abruptly, before they went any farther, Goldquiver called out, "Oh, and Tandarron, give them back their precious possessions or they won't be able to fight all the fierce monsters they're going to encounter and keep a careful record of them." Aradis and Girion both did their best to ignore this parting shot.

Wordlessly, Tandarron led them down the spiral staircase, back into the hallway, through the front room and then out onto the greensward of the Ring of the Artisans. There he said to them, "The Briar Gate, the eastern gate of the Kingdom of Argonis, stands two leagues from here. I must gather your possessions and also a few provisions for my own journey. I will return shortly. In the meantime, wait here."

Then Tandarron went back into the hasurdana, and it was less than five minutes before he emerged with a hefty pack slung over his shoulder, as well as Brightbeam, Aradis' dagger and medallion, and Girion's staff and notebook, all of which he returned to them, although he retained the pack and did not then divulge its contents. "Come on, then," he said, then led the Siloans back northeast toward the middle of Fallbury. There they embarked upon a road that led nearly straight west out of the town. This road wound up into hillier country, and, after a mile or so, it bent away to the southwest and jogged through a pleasant area with many streams and mossy boulders.

Tandarron resisted all efforts to strike up conversation, and as Aradis and Girion felt it would be awkward for them to converse with each other in his presence, they simply attempted to enjoy the walk as much as their stomachs would allow them. However, they kept mulling over how much they resented Goldquiver for knowing they had not eaten and yet purposely gorging himself in front of them.

As the day drew on, the sky grew increasingly gloomy and gray, and the path continued gradually sloping upward into a thicker part of the woods. At last, two and a half hours or so after they had left Fallbury, the road led directly up to a huge, black wall of thorns; it was the Outhedge, which surrounded much of the Kingdom of Argonis. And in the midst of the wall was a massive set of spectacularly wrought metal portals. This was the Briar Gate.

The gates were perhaps twenty feet high, although the Outhedge was over double that in height. The width of the hedge was cleared away where the gates were, so that the three Barada walked into the midst of the hedge and looked up at its tyrannous whorls arching over them. The lads could see through the gate to the other side and saw that autumn ended abruptly at the spiny barrier of the Outhedge, for beyond it, inside Argonis, the woods looked as they ought to in the midst of Tannaril in early summer.

Now Tandarron turned to them and said, "Menfolk from across the sea, I know not whether to believe your tale or to think you as foolish as Goldquiver does. But despite what that fellow's opinion may be of you, I wish you the best of luck, and I do hope you succeed in your quest, even if it is well-nigh impossible. And, for the record, I do not think it would be right for you to have visited this fair realm of Mendalas and not have tasted one of our luscious thornberry tarts."

"Here," he said, as he handed them the pack he had brought. "Take this, and may these provisions suffice until you come to a more hospitable place than the hasurdana of Malaraneth."

"Thank you very much, sir," Girion said awkwardly, as he took the bag. Tandarron's unexpected kindness had rather caught both him and Aradis off guard.

A few moments later, Girion hesitantly said, "We wouldn't want you to undermine your superior, sir, but if it's not too much trouble, could you direct us to the road to Anganor?"

"You're on it," Tandarron replied succinctly. "This very road will take you all the way there—all the way to the magnificent capital of Argonis. If you keep on this road, you will soon enter the Balgorra Hills. The road will split after—oh, I don't know—about twenty miles, and if you take the side road, you will come to the mouth of a huge cave which is the entrance to the Emerald Run, the home of the Leprechauns. They will, I think, give you lodging and food if you ask them. Their ruler, one Shillelagh Mc-Dasher, the one of whom Goldquiver spoke, is generally well-disposed toward strangers, though he is a master of mischief, so be wary of him. But, if you would rather not have dealings with him and his folk, keep on the main road, and you'll eventually come to Anganor. Be wary on your way, though, for there are merciless thieves and wild animals all along the road, especially once you get west of the hills. But I will not give you false hope that you will be able to see King Thornoak once you reach Anganor, for he has been sequestered in a place just south of there for years now and hasn't granted an audience to anyone but his daughter in all that time. But I suppose you are determined to go to Anganor regardless of all that, eh? Well, I hope this Telyon to whom you're so devoted will honor your loyalty to the quest he has given you." The Elf said this last bit with the utmost sincerity.

As Tandarron was speaking, it had begun to rain. For a few moments, it was merely a gentle sprinkling, but this was rapidly succeeded by a heavy downpour. The Siloans greatly desired clarification from the Elf on some things he had just said, but they ascertained that he was now eager to depart.

"Let's get you on through the gate," Tandarron said. He drew the key Goldquiver had given him out of his cloak and fitted it into the massive lock of the Briar Gate. Then he turned the key and pushed the huge gate so that it swung open.

Aradis and Girion walked through to the other side, and the Elf pulled the portal shut behind them and locked it. The lads then turned to face him.

"Well," Tandarron said, as he pulled his gray hood over his head, "farewell, lads, and may we meet again in better circumstances." And, with that, he turned and strode off down the path back to Fallbury.

"Goodbye and thank you again!" they called after him.

For a minute or so, the lads simply stood there in the rain, watching him go. Then Girion reached inside the pack and rummaged around to see what it contained. To his delight, he discovered that Tandarron had put two gray hooded Elven cloaks in it. "So that's why this thing was so bulky!" he exclaimed, as he handed one of the cloaks to Aradis.

"We shall be very glad to have these in the rain, I'm sure," Aradis said, as he and Girion donned the garments, pulling on their hoods.

"Let's see what else Tandarron's given us," Girion said, as he dug around in the pack a bit more. After a few moments, he pulled out two thornberry tarts, which had been wrapped in a piece of brown cloth. He kept one for himself and handed the other to Aradis, after which they both took a tentative bite.

"This is delicious," Aradis stated between mouthfuls, pleasantly surprised by the rich, exuberant flavor of the berries, whose source had nearly sent them to their graves.

"Exquisite," Girion agreed. "I must say that most of what's happened to us today hasn't been all that encouraging, but this thornberry tart is a huge step in the right direction."

Aradis laughed, then said, "Too bad there's only one for each of us. Come on, Girion."

And so the lads set off down the road, which led on through the vast, wild forests of eastern Argonis.

After they had been walking for a few moments under the spreading trees, Aradis remarked, "You know, Girion, for most of this journey, I've resented the Call of the Danna that I told you about. Nagello said that this mission was *a* call of the Danna, but not *the Call*. So I can't rightly say that I know what the Call is. But I can say for the first time that I actually want to find out what it is. For the first time, I don't feel like the Danna is my enemy. For the first time, I almost feel like he's on our side, you might say."

Looking up at the clouded, gray heavens, he went on, "Even now, I'm struggling to fully trust the Danna because we still have so far to go, and the road ahead of us is going to be much darker than the road behind us. But in all honesty, I didn't believe we'd even make it to Argonis, and yet here we are."

"Yes, it's truly remarkable that we've come to this place that so many swore could not be reached," Girion concurred. "Nearly everyone on the *Meridot* told us it would be impossible to enter Argonis alive. But it seems all those folk didn't know what was within the realm of possibility as well as they thought they did," he chuckled.

The lads continued down the road a few moments more. Then Aradis glanced over at his friend and said, "I just had an odd thought, Girion."

"Did you? What was it?" Girion asked.

Aradis replied, "If the Danna offered to transport me to Siloa this very instant, just like that—if he gave me the choice of handing this quest over to someone else—do you know what I'd do?"

Girion gave Aradis a curious look, then asked, "What? What would you do?"

"I think I'd turn the offer down," Aradis softly answered.

"Really?" Girion said, his eyebrows raised. Then, looking forward again, he smiled and remarked, "That's funny. So would I."

In the midst of the pouring rain, the Siloans walked down the winding road that led on westward into the Kingdom of Argonis, on to Anganor. Somber clouds had all but consumed the sky to the west, but they knew that a bright afternoon sun lay beyond the thunderheads, though it might be some time before they would see it again. Regardless, they were now fully determined to heed the call of the Danna, for they had come at last to the edge of the kingdom they had been sent to deliver. That fact alone had kindled such a great resolve in them that no rain, however dismal, could dampen it.

THE END

Author's Note on the Appendices

As was stated regarding the appendices of this saga's previous volume, Call of the Danna, the following appendices are included for the sake of the reader who is interested in the sorts of information they contain, information which some readers may, I fear, find dull and boring. However, readers should note that Appendix 4, which contains the Legend of Falderon, is a story in its own right, and the majority of persons will likely find it far more stimulating than, say, Appendix 2, which is an exposition of Oronic timekeeping. In fact, some may even consider the narrative there to be as engaging as the main text of the book. But that judgment I leave to the readers themselves.

As before, I have been obliged to write these appendices, but no one is obliged to read them. They contain linguistic, cultural, geographical, historical and chronological information and the like—things which are of great interest to Oronic loremasters and persons of that ilk. However, it must be made very clear that one may ignore the appendices altogether and still find the main story rich and satisfying.

Sincerely Yours,
Jarrett J. Skaddisson

Glossary of Useful Terms

The following glossary, which is by no means comprehensive, has been included for two purposes:

- To act as a quick reference guide for terms which are either used frequently in the story or are of great importance to it.
- To provide additional information about certain entities which the reader may find to be of interest.

The reader may note that several items which are presented in the main text are left unexplained here in the glossary; this is intentional on the author's part, especially as regards things pertaining to the Deep Lore of Orona, as it would be imprudent to reveal elements critical to the unfolding of the Kingblade Chronicles prematurely. Hence, for the time being, the reader must be left as perplexed about some things as are Aradis and Girion. Please note that items pertaining to timekeeping in Orona (such as the names of ages, months, days of the week and times of day) are not included in this glossary, as they are dealt with in Appendix 2. This is also the case with foods of the Emerald Run, which are addressed in Appendix 3.

Agleri – A region in central Velaris which encompasses nine barolli, one of which is Feldryn, wherein lies Siloa. The primary geographical feature of the area is the Plains of Agleri. The regional capital is the city of Temerrin.

Anganor – The capital of the Kingdom of Argonis.

Aradath – The Southern Moiety of Orona; all those regions of Orona, which lie south of the Bushbelt. It contains the Neathmarda of Byram, Quarana, Fenrost and the Eldritch Isles.

Aragest – The capital city of the Kingdom of Velaris and a port of international significance. It lies on the northeastern shore of Cape Loresso.

Arbor of the Sancalli, The – The palace of the Ruphani in Aragest, a lavish complex of mansions near the west end of the city. The compound is heavily guarded and has a number of outer defenses, including a deep moat and two separate, high stone walls surrounding the entire area. The interior is decorated with gold, silver, jewels, marble, costly woods and intricate carvings, as well as numerous murals, paintings, mounted animal heads, elaborate rugs and tapestries. However, it is most renowned for its use of exotic flora to grace its many balconies, corridors and indoor and outdoor gardens.

Argonis, Kingdom of – A relatively small Ingan kingdom in the eastern region of the Elder Forest. Argonis is also known as Garlenwood, which is a rough translation of its name from Asla'gu, a tongue of the Ingans of the eastern Elder Forest.

Barada (sing. Barada; adj. Baradic) – The intelligent inhabitants of Orona, as opposed to the Telnari, the animals. When preceded by the definite article, the word can refer to all Barada as a whole, a group of Barada or an individual; the meaning must be determined by context.

Barolla (pl. Barolli) – One of 27 counties, or districts, of the Kingdom of Velaris.

Belestro – A sizable port on the southeastern shores of Cape Loresso in the Kingdom of Velaris.

Biyelti – An ungulate native to the savannahs of Pollona. It is somewhat like a large antelope.

Blackwings – See 'Farga.'

Bornad – A Dwarven kingdom which predated the founding of Velaris and contained the regions which are now known as Rimwold and Parlaedia.

Brundy – An island in the Fontskals.

Bushbelt, The – One of the Neathmarda. It separates Huldion and Aradath, circumscribing the entire world of Orona, lying roughly along its equator, which is called Sabakwani's Girdle. It is covered by dense jungle, steep mountains and regions of active volcanism and is several hundred miles wide at all points. The Bushbelt is occupied by savage, aggressive Barada and strange, terrifying beasts; thus, it presents a formidable barrier to movement between the Moieties of Orona. Consequently, almost all travel through the Bushbelt occurs along established routes, which are protected by cooperative garrisons of Barada from various kingdoms in both Huldion and Aradath. This cooperation occurs primarily for the advancement of trade interests.

Byram – One of the Neathmarda. It lies in Aradath, to the west of Quarana. The Kingdom of Argonis lies near the eastern coast of Byram.

Cape Loresso – See Loresso, Cape.

Daiga (adj. Daigan) – Historically, the language of the Pine-Elves of Murnia. However, due to the wide geographical and cultural interaction of the Pine-Elves with other Barada, Daiga was used increasingly as a lingua franca throughout Orona in the 2nd-7th centuries of the Latter Epoch. By the opening of the 8th century of the Latter Epoch, it was widely spoken in every Neathmarda, though not by culturally-resistant or isolated populations. Daiga is the daily language used in both Velaris and Argonis.

Deep Lore – Lore of Orona which pertains to either matters of the Haedra or to those matters of the Haedra which affect Kazamar. The term is also used to refer to events of great significance in the former ages of Orona, some of which have been largely forgotten by the Barada.

Druids (adj. Druidic) – One of the Narthanna. Druids are extremely human-like Barada, possessing height within the normal human range of variance and having an average life-span of around 400 years. Notably, Druids retain a high level of fitness into their fourth century of life.

Dullen – An island in the Fontskals.

Dunlim – An island in the Fontskals.

Dwarves – One of the Narthanna. Dwarves are short, human-like Barada, between 4 and 4 ½ feet tall, with an average lifespan of 130 years. They have thick skin and round noses, and their bodies are stout and muscular.

Ebonreach – A literal translation of the Druidic name Sarganath.

Elder Forest, The – One of the Five Fabled Lands. The Elder Forest lies in eastern Byram and is characterized by various types of woodlands. In the north, semitropical forests prevail; the central regions are dominated by deciduous forests; the southern regions contain primarily coniferous forests. The Kingdom of Argonis lies in the eastern region of the Elder Forest.

Eldritch Isles, The – One of the Neathmarda, an archipelago of large islands that lies in Aradath, far to the west of Byram and far to the east of Quarana.

Elves – One of the Narthanna. Elves are extremely human-like Barada, although they are slightly taller than humans as a general rule, possess an average lifespan of 300 years and have pointed ears.

Eoreth – The moon of Orona.

Equenaddoril – The plural form of quenaddoril. The quenaddoril is a medium-sized rodent which thrives in Thornberry Thicket, which lies on the eastern edge of the Kingdom of Argonis.

Erdion – One of the realms of the Haedra.

Falzari – A barolla in the Cape Loresso region of Velaris.

Far Forest, The – A dense forest in the far western reaches of Velaris. The Far Forest lies up in the Parlaedian Mountains and is almost exclusively inhabited by wild beasts and bandits.

Farga (sing. Farga; adj. Fargese) – One of the Narthanna. Farga are human-like Barada with many bat-like characteristics, possessing height within the normal human range of variance and having a lifespan of around 60 years. They are distinguished from all other Barada by large, leathery wings that protrude from their shoulders. Their ears are like those of a bat, and their noses are a hybrid between bat and human noses. Many parts of their bodies are covered with hair.

Fargost – An island in the Fontskals.

Feldryn – A barolla in the Agleri region of Velaris. The village of Siloa is on the western edge of Feldryn.

Fenrost – One of the Neathmarda. It lies in Aradath, to the south of Quarana.

Five Fabled Lands, The – The five regions of the Neathmarda of Byram. These are the Elder Forest in the east, Pollona in the northeast, Rannadalf in the southwest, Soyawat Piyani in the northwest and the Wide Lands in the southeast.

Fontskals, The – A group of rocky islands in the southern Indurian Deeps, which is inhabited primarily by Menfolk. The term is also commonly used to refer to the nine largest islands in the group.

Gamway – An island in the Fontskals.

Garlenwood, Kingdom of – See 'Argonis, Kingdom of'.

Gnomes (adj. Gnomish) – One of the Narthanna. Gnomes are short, human-like Barada, between 3½ and 4 feet tall, with an average lifespan of 150 years. Gnomish morphology varies considerably; Gnomes can have faces ranging from squarish to triangular, and their body frames can either be skinny and nimble or broad and muscular. Their ears can be, variously, indistinguishable from Mannish ears, slightly pointed or shaped almost like a conch shell.

Goblins (adj. Goblin) – One of the Narthanna. Goblins are shortish, human-like Barada, between 4 ½ and 5 feet tall, with an average lifespan of 90 years. They generally have rather gangly, slender frames and possess large, triangular ears. Their noses can be a range of shapes or sizes, and their skin color can vary considerably.

Greater Neathmarda – Those Neathmarda which are considered to be generally more civilized and climatically benevolent than the others. The five Greater Neathmarda are Tassaru, Estereth, Murnia, Byram and Quarana.

Hadathi (sing. Hadathi) – Powerful beings of the Haedra.

Haedra, The (adj. Haedran) – The immaterial realm in the universe of Orona.

Hammergast – A huge Dwarven fortress built at the very foot of the Walls of Ancient Wrath. In fact, the fortress itself is connected to a system of tunnels delved into the face of the cliff. Hammergast lies some distance east from the halfway point of the eastern and western extent of the Walls of Ancient Wrath. The Dwarves of Hammergast have allied themselves with Ravinia, and their Tharlog, Nolgar, functions as the sovereign of all the Dwarves of Sarganath.

Haskanesh – A spice made from a red flower, also called haskanesh, which grows in the montane regions of Pollona. It tastes somewhat similar to saffron.

Huldion – The Northern Moiety of Orona, all those regions of Orona, which lie north of the Bushbelt. It contains the Neathmarda of Tassaru, Estereth, Murnia and Jassuna.

Indurian Deeps – The ocean which lies between the Neathmarda of Byram and Quarana.

Indurian Rimlands, The – The lands surrounding the Indurian Deeps—i.e. the eastern coast of Byram and the western coast of Quarana.

Ingans (sing. Ingan; adj. Ingan) – One of the Narthanna. Ingans are tree-like Barada, generally between 7 and 7 ½ feet tall, with an average lifespan of 250 years. Their morphology is essentially that of a tree with human-like features: eyes, ears, nose and a mouth, along with jointed, bark-covered legs and arms.

Kadanu Oil – A flavorful oil extracted from the kadanu tree which grows on the savannahs of Pollona. The oil is used in cooking and also for medicinal purposes.

Kazamar – The material realm in the universe of Orona.

Kilreena – An island in the Fontskals.

Kindreds, The (sing. Kindred) – See 'Narthanna.'

Korgenosch – A highly-prized Dwarven liquor which is distilled only at the Dwarven fortress of Hammergast in the Elder Forest.

Lakarnia – The proper name of the Eldritch Isles.

Leprechauns (adj. Leprechaun) – One of the Narthanna. Leprechauns are short, human-like Barada, between 3 and 3½ feet tall, with an average lifespan of 200 years. They have a generally slender build, and their faces are characterized by slightly pointed ears and sharp chins.

Lesser Neathmarda – Those Neathmarda which are considered to be generally less civilized and more climatically adverse than the others. The four Lesser Neathmarda are Jassuna, the Eldritch Isles, Fenrost and the Bushbelt.

Loresso, Cape – A prominent cape on the northeastern coast of Velaris. The term also refers to a region of Velaris which encompasses six barolli on the cape.

Luminous Meridian, The – The most northerly point in all Orona.

Maena (pl. Maenas) – A term designating a female individual who is one of the Menfolk.

Manfellow (pl. Manfellows) – A term designating a male individual who is one of the Menfolk.

Mannagron – A Gnomish kingdom which predated the founding of Velaris and contained the regions which are currently known as Cape Loresso, the Marlassi Coast and Agleri.

Marda – The sun of Orona.

Marlassi Coast, The – A region in southeast Velaris which encompasses four barolli. The Marlassi Coast, which stretches from the southern end of Cape Loresso to the southern border of the Kingdom of Velaris, is the primary geographical feature of the area.

Marlond – An island in the Fontskals.

Menfolk (masc. sing. Manfellow; masc. pl. Manfellows; fem. sing. Maena; fem. pl. Maenas; adj. Mannish) – One of the Narthanna. Menfolk are human Barada, possessing height within the normal range of human variance and having an average lifespan of 70 years.

Moieties of Orona, The – The northern and southern hemispheres of Orona: Huldion and Aradath.

Narthanna (sing. Narthaya) – In the singular, the term for one of the distinct varieties of Barada, such as Menfolk, Druids, Elves, Dwarves, Gnomes, Ingans, etc. The plural refers to several or all of the varieties of Barada.

Neathmarda (pl. Neathmarda) – A translation of the Daigan term 'dhar-marda', which literally means 'situated under Marda'. The Neathmarda are the nine most populated land-masses of Orona. Technically, one of them is actually a collection of landmasses rather than a single landmass, as it is a group of islands. The nine Neathmarda are Tassaru, Murnia, Estereth, Byram, Quarana, Jassuna, the Eldritch Isles, Fenrost and the Bushbelt.

Nolgar – The Tharlog of Hammergast. Although ultimately subject to Ravinia's authority, Nolgar is effectively the ruler of all the Dwarves of Sarganath.

Northern Moiety of Orona, The – The northern hemisphere of Orona, another name for Huldion.

Nutmeal – A mixture of various dried berries, nuts and roots. Nutmeal is a staple in the diet of the Druids of the Elder Forest. Sometimes it is ground into a powder and mixed with water or milk to make a porridge of sorts.

Ogres (adj. Ogric) – One of the Narthanna. Ogres are large, human-like Barada, between 8 and 9 feet tall, with an average lifespan of 60 years. They have thick skin, big ears, broad noses and are extremely muscular.

Orona (adj. Oronic) – The world of the Kingblade Chronicles.

Parlaedia – A region in far western Velaris, which encompasses two large barolli. The Par-laedian Mountains are the primary geographical feature of the area.

Parlaedian Mountains – A mountain range, rich in mineral deposits, in the far western reaches of the Kingdom of Velaris.

Parnassa – An island nation in the Brines of Ferassi off the eastern shores of Quarana with a mixed population of Elves and Gnomes. Parnassa is renowned throughout Orona for its high-quality pearls.

Passera – A barolla in the Cape Loresso region of Velaris.

Pollona (adj. Pollonan) – One of the Five Fabled Lands. Pollona lies in northeastern Byram. Its terrain consists of deserts, savannah, mountains and tropical forests.

Quarana – One of the Neathmarda. It lies in Aradath, to the east of Byram and to the north of Fenrost. The Kingdom of Velaris lies on the eastern shores of Quarana.

Ravensrealm – Another name for the land of Sarganath.

Rayalta – The Star-Realm—i.e. the region of Kazamar, which lies beyond the sky of Orona.

Regent – The official title of the governor over one of Velaris' five regions: Cape Loresso, the Marlassi Coast, Agleri, Rimwold and Parlaedia.

Rendanna (sing. Rendaya) – In the singular, a subdivision of one of the Narthanna; that is, a particular variety of a particular Narthaya. E.g., Plains-Elves are a Rendaya of Elves.

Rimwold – A region in western Velaris, which encompasses six barolli. The primary geographical feature of the area is Rimwold Forest.

Rokklag – A Dwarven pidgin language used in the Indurian Rimlands in the 5th-8th centuries of the Latter Epoch.

Ruphani, The – The official title of the ruler of the Kingdom of Velaris. The Ruphani lives in the city of Aragest.

Sabakwani's Girdle – The equator of Orona.

Sancalla (pl. Sancalli) – A species of large seabird, in appearance very much like a seagull, only somewhat larger, that frequents the shores of eastern Quarana, especially regions farther to the north. Sancalli have glossy white plumage and a six-foot wingspan. Feeding primarily on fish, they are quite amiable toward Barada. In fact, they can be domesticated and are sometimes used to deliver objects or messages along coastal routes.

Sardolia, The – A government organization of the Kingdom of Velaris. The agents of the Sardolia act as tax collectors, constables and a standing army. The Sardolia has barracks in the capital of every barolla in Velaris.

Sarganath – The name for all the lands under the sway of Ravinia. Sarganath completely surrounds the Kingdom of Argonis.

Siradel – A colorful songbird with plumage of various shades of red and orange. Siradels can be found in the coniferous and temperate forests of central and southeastern Quarana in the summer. In the autumn, siradels migrate to the tropical forests of northern Quarana, and they do not migrate southward again until the late spring.

Skaggarok Skerries – A cluster of extremely small, rocky islands in the northern reaches of the Fontskals. The Skerries are a rendezvous point for smuggling operations of the Menfolk in the area and are also frequented by large colonies of migratory seabirds.

Southern Moiety of Orona, The – The southern hemisphere of Orona; another name for Aradath.

Stragmore – An island in the Fontskals.

Tassagon – A spice made from crushed seeds of the tassagon plant, which grows along the coasts of Pollona. Its taste is somewhat similar to cardamom.

Tellig – The provincial capital of the barolla of Feldryn.

Telnari (sing. Telnara; adj. Telnaric) – Refers to the animals of Orona, as opposed to the Barada, the intelligent beings of Orona. The word applies specifically to animals with blood and bones and thus includes mammals, birds, reptiles, amphibians and fish.

Tharlog – The official title of the ruler of a Dwarven kingdom.

Tolga – A bronze coin used by the Dwarves of the Wide Lands and the Elder Forest in Byram.

Trath – An island in the Fontskals.

Treefolk (masc. sing. Treefellow; masc. pl. Treefellows; fem. sing. Treemaena; fem. pl. Treemaenas; adj. Treeish) – See 'Ingans.'

Trolls (adj. Trollish) – One of the Narthanna. Trolls are large, human-like Barada, between 8 ½ and 9 ½ feet tall, with an average lifespan of 50 years. Some aspects of Trollish morphology vary considerably; they can have faces ranging from oblong to triangular, their ears and noses can either be round or pointed and the skin colors of different Trollish Rendanna can be quite diverse. However, Trolls' body frames are generally more slender than stocky, and they are consistently muscular.

Vastia the Pathfinder – The renowned Elven explorer who pioneered a route through the Bushbelt from Huldion to Aradath. The Latter Epoch is considered to have begun the year after he returned from his expedition. In fact, his opening of the way through the Bushbelt is the event which launched the present age of Orona.

Velaris, Kingdom of (adj. Velarisian) – An Elven kingdom in eastern Quarana, having substantial populations of Elves and Menfolk, as well as pockets of Gnomes, Dwarves and Druids. Velaris is divided into five regions: Cape Loresso, the Marlassi Coast, Agleri, Rimwold and Parlaedia.

Vengoli – The chief city of the Maldinian Isles, which lie some miles offshore from Aragest and are under the political jurisdiction of the Kingdom of Velaris. Vengoli is home to a number of highly prosperous Elven merchants and boasts a community of widely-renowned artisans.

Yetis – One of the Narthanna. Yetis are large, ape-like Barada, between 6 ½ and 7 feet tall, with an average lifespan of 60 years. They are covered in thick hair, usually white in color, and are extremely muscular.

Zimari – A spice cultivated in northern Pollona. Its flavor is rather like cinnamon, but it has a distinct, sweet aftertaste.

Timekeeping in Orona–
The Manus-Romelliad Calendar

A Brief Note on the Manus-Romelliad Empire

Early in the Third Age of Orona, which is known as the Apex of Archaea, two great Elven empires arose in the Neathmarda of Tassaru. These were known as the Manusian and Romelliad Empires. Through a series of national upheavals, political intrigues and great battles, they were unified into what was undoubtedly the most powerful political construct of the Apex of Archaea: the Empire of Manus-Romella. Manus-Romella held sway over much of Tassaru and many lands beyond for a great many centuries, disseminating its cultural, philosophical, political, artistic, architectural and societal institutions, models and values throughout Huldion. For this reason, it is regarded by many Oronic historians as the single most important political entity in the history of Orona. In fact, so significant was the Manus-Romelliad Empire that its sundering and subsequent transformation marked the close of the Third Age of Orona.

One of the entities which was inherited by the Barada from the Empire of Manus-Romella is the Manus-Romelliad (M-R) Calendar. This is used to mark the five ages of Orona, the twelve months of the year, the seven days of the week and the various times of day. This appendix details the divisions of the M-R timekeeping system, which is used to describe the transpiring of events throughout the Kingblade Chronicles.

The Five Ages of Orona

In the standard M-R reckoning, there are five ages of Orona, which are as follows:

The First Age of Orona: The Mists of Old (MO or simply 'The Mists') has no specified commencement point, and its length is much disputed by the learned Barada of Orona. Dates are only occasionally attached to events which are believed to have transpired in the Mists of Old. When they are, they are cited as having occurred a certain number of years before the termination of the age. Thus, the notation MO 130 would signify the year 130 years prior to the commencement of the Second Age of Orona. [NB: those Barada who accord credence to the Mannish volume known as the Elyrion refer to the First Age of Orona as The Forgotten Days (FD) and assign it a specific duration. Dates for the Forgotten Days are listed forward in time from FD 1, the first year of that age, to FD 2312, its final year.]

The Second Age of Orona: The Years of Yore (YY or simply 'Yore') are reckoned as having begun in the year after the founding of the great Druidic fortress city of Grath. The end of the Years of Yore is marked by the destruction of the ancient Mannish capital city, Yaruzadar, by the Druids of Grath, which occurred in YY 1895. This particular date was chosen by Oronic loremasters because of the extent and significance of the Druid kingdom and its successors, which rose to prominence as a result of the defeat of the Menfolk. [NB: adherents of the Elyrion mark the start of the Years of Yore as having occurred 209 years before the date used in the M-R calendar. Consequently, in that system, the date assigned to the Fall of Yaruzadar is YY 2104. In cases where clarification between the two systems is needed, the Mannish system is prefaced by the indication EYY, with the E standing for Elyriac, the adjectival form of Elyrion.]

The Third Age of Orona: The Apex of Archaea (AA or simply 'Archaea') began the year after the Fall of Yaruzadar and ended with the sundering of the Empire of Manus-Romella, which occurred in AA 1087. The term 'Archaea' refers to the southern and central regions of Tassaru, which is where the great empires of this age flourished.

The Fourth Age of Orona: The Bridging of the Tides (BT or simply 'The Bridging') is determined to have commenced in the year after the sundering of the Manus-Romelliad Empire; it was concluded in BT 1290 by the return of the great Elven explorer Vastia the Pathfinder from his expedition to find a viable route through the Bushbelt. The name of the age comes from the expression coined by the renowned Manus-Romelliad statesman Salarna, who famously said, "Time is a tide; someday our children will reach the latter days, and what stands between us and them will be a bridge across the tides."

The Fifth Age of Orona: The Latter Epoch (LE or simply 'The Latter') began the year after the Elven explorer Vastia the Pathfinder returned to Huldion from his fabled expedition into Aradath. Aradis and Girion's departure from Siloa for the Kingdom of Argonis occurred on the 10th of Elaya in the year LE 717.

A Note on the Commencement of Ages in the Manus-Romelliad Calendar

Even though the events which triggered the onset of a new age occurred during the middle of each of the respective final years of the age in which they occurred, the following age, primarily for the ease of scribes' and loremasters' calculations, is determined as beginning on the first of Bellin which most closely follows the event which heralded the new age. Thus, even though Vastia the Pathfinder returned from his expedition some time during the year BT 1290, it was not until the first of Bellin, the beginning of the next year, that the Latter Epoch began.

The Ages of the Manus-Romelliad Calendar in Brief

1—The Mists of Old

2—The Years of Yore 1-1895

3—The Apex of Archaea 1-1087

4—The Bridging of the Tides 1-1290

5—The Latter Epoch 1-the present (717)

The Months of the Manus-Romelliad Calendar

The Manus-Romelliad calendar is both lunar and solar, using twelve months consisting of 30 days each and a special set of five days called the Middings (also called Pelarond), which are placed in-between the first two months of Huldion's summer (Aradath's winter) in order to complete a 365-day solar year. The Middings is celebrated all over Orona as a five-day holiday with festivities, parades and joyous feasting. The Manus-Romelliad year begins in the springtime, and the first month is roughly equivalent to our month of March. Though to be entirely precise, it begins in the last few days of our February—February 21st to be exact. Very minor adjustments have been made to the calendar periodically throughout the centuries in order to maintain astronomical integrity, much like the case of our own calendar, but in Oronic reckoning, the extra days have always been added to the Middings. Customarily, every eight years, two days are added to the Middings for a total of seven days for Pelarond on the eighth year. Such years are called Years of the Middings. The names of the generally correspondent months are as follows:

Bellin (March)—30 days

Serona (April)—30 days

Alareth (May)—30 days

Landrenna (June)—30 days

Pelarond [also known as 'The Middings'] (end of June)—5 days

Ularos (July)—30 days

Galrim (August)—30 days

Ferenos (September)—30 days

Derrig (October)—30 days

Elaya (November)—30 days

Tannaril (December)—30 days

Harasa (January)—30 days

Ildurion (February)—30 days

The Days of the Week in the Manus-Romelliad Calendar

The Manus-Romelliad calendar uses a seven-day week. These seven days are as follows:

Vardis—Sunday

Jurdis—Monday

Cordis—Tuesday

Nardis—Wednesday

Ragdis—Thursday

Maldis—Friday

Yawandis—Saturday

NB: the particle 'dis' does not actually mean 'day' but comes from the Vasornic (adjectival form of Vasorna, the language of the Manusians) word 'dissa,' meaning 'charge, entity placed under the protection of someone or something.'

The Times of Day in the Manus-Romelliad Calendar

The names for different times of day come from corresponding Vasornic expressions, which have been loosely translated into Daiga. According to the common parlance throughout Orona, the times of day may be arranged sequentially as follows:

Call of Marda—the first hint of Marda's impending arrival

Song of Marda—the first appearance of Marda's rays over the horizon

Marda's Glory—early morning

Marda's Feast—late morning

Crown of Marda—noon

Dance of Marda—early afternoon

Journey of Marda—late afternoon

Marda's Farewell—sunset

Marda's Passing—twilight

Dawn of Eoreth—early evening

Eoreth's Tale—late evening

Scepter of Eoreth—midnight

Hour of Rayalta—another name for midnight

Palace of Eoreth—the hours right after midnight

Eoreth's Lament—the hours just before dawn

NB: Marda is the sun of Orona, Eoreth is the moon and Rayalta is the Star-Realm.

NB: the M-R Calendar reckons days as beginning at the Call of Marda and thus does not correspond to our own commencement of days at midnight.

A Brief History of the Kingdom of Velaris

The land now known as Velaris was once actually two separate kingdoms; the first was a Gnomish kingdom called Mannagron, which endured for around 700 years, from the early 9th Century BT until LE 251. Mannagron contained the regions which are today called Cape Loresso, the Marlassi Coast and Agleri. The second kingdom was a Dwarven kingdom known as Bornad, which contained the Rimwold and Parlaedia regions and a small amount of territory farther to the west. Bornad was somewhat shorter-lived than Mannagron, lasting only from BT 1010 to LE 259, a period of around five and a half centuries.

The history of Velaris as an Elven dominion is reckoned to have begun early in the 2nd Century of the Latter Epoch, when Plains-Elves from Central Estereth came down the eastern coast of Quarana seeking a land where they might find much profit. On the 18th of Bellin, LE 118, nine Elven ships landed on the northern shore of Cape Loresso in what is now known as the barolla of Passera at the Jenolli Dunes, not far from the present-day port of Saldassi. The Elves established a fishing and trading colony there, and, over the next century or so, they gradually claimed land which had once belonged to a people group known as the Harvest-Gnomes.

At first, the relations between the two groups were quite congenial, but, eventually, another wave of Plains-Elves from Huldion came to join their kin in LE 229. This second wave was eager to partake of the lucrative ventures which had sprung up on Cape Loresso, but they saw the presence of the Gnomes as an impediment to their goals. Consequently, one of the freshly-arrived Elven leaders, Tarnolli by name, antagonized the Gnomes to the point that they struck back with acts of violence. Tarnolli used this opportunity to retaliate and thus incite a larger-scale conflict. In LE 239, full war broke out between the Elves under Tarnolli and the Gnomes under the leadership of Randabar, a Gnomish chieftain in the Cape Loresso region in the northern part of what is today known as the barolla of Corlanno. Loresso was much more forested then than it is today, and many skirmishes were fought in the woodlands there. This was much in the Harvest-Gnomes' favor, for they knew the land quite well. This initial conflict became known as the Wrath of Randabar, for things went rather badly for the Elves, and even those who were not directly involved with Tarnolli's actions suffered heavy losses from Randabar's raids.

Tarnolli, enraged by the successes of Randabar and his guerilla fighters, collected all the money from his people that he could persuade them to contribute and sent it with a young courier named Segardi to enlist the aid of Agrinov, a Dwarven ruler who dwelt in the eastern reaches of Rimwold Forest. At the time, Bornad, the land where Agrinov lived, was a sort of federation, rather than a kingdom. Thus, Agrinov, acting quite independently of other rulers in Bornad, agreed to send some Dwarves to swell Tarnolli's forces, for he thought he might use this opportunity to gain territory in Agleri, as he considered the Gnomes to be weak in the art of war.

When Randabar learned that a Dwarven army from Bornad was marching across Agleri, he immediately sent messages throughout Mannagron urging all the Harvest-Gnomes to rise to the defense of their homeland. Within days, war had erupted throughout the kingdom, and huge numbers of Harvest-Gnomes aggressively attacked Dwarven settlements on the edge of Rimwold and then poured up to Cape Loresso to strike against Agrinov's and Tarnolli's troops.

A bloody conflict followed, which became known as the Branding of Agleri. This war lasted for twelve long years and resulted in the deaths of thousands upon thousands of Gnomes, Dwarves and Elves. Tarnolli was killed during the war, as was Randabar.

Even though Agrinov had initially agreed to fight under the banner of the Elves, the Gnomish attacks on Dwarven communities in Rimwold caused him to declare war anew under the auspices of Bornad. And despite the fact that Agrinov still agreed to regard the Plains-Elves as allies in the war against the Gnomes, his actions greatly angered them, for they rightly feared that he would claim many of the spoils of war for himself. Nonetheless, the Elves knew they could not fight both the Gnomes and the Dwarves at once, so they largely overlooked what they saw as Agrinov's underhanded political maneuvers.

Finally, in LE 251, the Branding of Agleri was ended by the surrender of Fandarralon, the commander of the Harvest-Gnomes, at Skurridan Rock in the present-day barolla of Armallin along the banks of the River Algo. The Elves, though soundly defeated on many occasions, were ultimately victorious over the Harvest-Gnomes, as the brutal battle tactics of the Dwarves of Rimwold Forest had brought Mannagron to its knees. Agrinov, taking advantage of the crippled condition of the Elves, claimed all but Cape Loresso for the Kingdom of Bornad, just as they had expected he would.

After the war, many Elven settlers migrated down into the Marlassi Coast and a few Dwarven colonists moved into various regions of Agleri. A small number of Gnomes chose to remain in their historic communities on the prairies of Agleri, although they were kept in total subjection to Dwarven rule. Many Gnomes, however, were deported and sent to work as slaves in the Dwarven mines of Parlaedia. Others, shortly before the surrender at Skurridan Rock, had fled northward in droves across the plains of eastern Quarana up to the well-established Gnomish kingdom of Ossimar. Thus, Agleri was largely emptied of its formerly vast population of Barada.

Several years after the Branding of Agleri, a shrewd Elven warrior by the name of Segardi rose to prominence in the Elven community in Cape Loresso. This was the same Segardi who, at one time, had functioned as Tarnolli's personal aide and courier and had delivered the sum of money to Agrinov to secure his assistance in the conflict with the Gnomes. He had never forgotten what he viewed as the treachery of the Dwarves. In addition, he sought to fulfill Tarnolli's dream of establishing a vast and prosperous Elven colony in the Agleri region. So, in the spring of LE 256, after procuring the support of a number of influential Elves of Loresso, he sent a proposal to the Elven colony of Jarnos, which lay some hundreds of miles to the north of Cape Loresso along the eastern coast of Quarana.

This proposal invited Neranno, the leader of that land, to attack the Dwarves of Bornad while they were still recovering from war, and, with the help of the Elves of Loresso and Marlassi, to seize their kingdom and establish it as a colony of Jarnos. The agreement also stated that Loresso would become a colony of Jarnos. Segardi was nearly certain Neranno would agree to his plan, for he knew of his great contempt for Dwarves in general, for they ceaselessly harried the southwestern borders of Jarnos.

Neranno, just as Segardi had designed, gladly accepted the proposal and immediately sent a large force of Elven cavalry southward through the woodlands that lay several hundred miles inland from the coast of Quarana. Meanwhile, Segardi made his plans openly known to all the Elves, and all those who were akin to him in their desire for revenge on the Dwarves immediately mustered for battle. Within a matter of days, they swept across the Plains of Agleri, sacking and burning Dwarven communities as they went. Segardi urged the Gnomes who had stayed in Agleri to join his troops, promising them freedom from Dwarven rule if they fought for the Elves' cause. Some of them took him at his word, and others, still stinging from their defeat in the Branding of Agleri, did not.

The Dwarves of Rimwold were completely caught off guard by the sudden attacks by the Elves from both the north and the east, and Agrinov was furious when he discovered that the Elves of Jarnos, Loresso and Marlassi had united against him. He called for the aid of the chieftains of Parlaedia, who sent a formidable army of Dwarves down to strike at the Elven forces from the west. However, the Elves had already gained several strategic locations in Rimwold, and in addition, many Dwarven villages had already been massacred by the cavalry from Jarnos.

As the conflict unfolded, most of the Dwarves were forced to retreat into the Parlaedian Mountains, although bands of them remained scattered throughout Rimwold, hiding deep in its tall forests. These bands would conduct nightly raids on the Elven camps, a strategy which proved to be extremely effective for quite some time. Nonetheless, the sheer numbers of the Elven forces were overwhelming to such an extent that even these remaining groups of Dwarves were eventually forced to flee.

For the next two and a half years, the Elves of Loresso, Marlassi and Jarnos pressed hard against the Dwarves of Parlaedia until they finally surrendered in LE 259 at the mountain fortress of Hagrum in the present-day barolla of Talgryn. Agrinov, one of the last remaining chieftains of Bornad, and certainly the most pugnacious, was executed by the Elves at the close of the war, which came to be known as the Hammering of Bornad.

After the Hammering of Bornad, most of the Dwarves left in Rimwold and Parlaedia simply consented to Elven rule, having no other choice before them. Neranno dubbed Jarnos' new colony as Velaris, which means 'Southern Treasure' in Mancari, the Elven language spoken in Jarnos at the time. At that time, Velaris was divided into a number of barolli, not all of which were identical to the present-day barolli. The Gnomes of Agleri who had fought for the Elves were given freedom, just as promised, and the Gnomes of Parlaedia were released from their bondage in the Dwarven mines. Finally, Segardi was installed as governor of Velaris under the rule of Neranno.

In the decades following the Hammering of Bornad, the Elves of Velaris multiplied greatly and begin to construct settlements in the Plains of Agleri, which, at that time, were predominantly occupied by Gnomes once more. Rimwold then had a mixed population of Elves and Dwarves, but the Dwarves were ever restless, and Segardi feared that they might secure an alliance with Dwarves to the west and south of Parlaedia and then rebel against him. So he sought for a means to extinguish what he called the "Dwarven fire."

Such a means came to him in LE 268 when a great fleet of Mannish ships stopped for supplies at the port of Aragest, which was then only a modest town with several thousand Elves. The Menfolk who were aboard had recently come from Zalgaresh, a kingdom in northeast Quarana, where they had suffered much persecution at the hands of the Ogres who dwelt there. They were searching for a land where they might settle in peace, and it was their intent to continue sailing southward until they found such a place. Segardi offered the Menfolk free tracts of land in Agleri and Rimwold under the condition that they would, of course, submit to Elven rule. The Menfolk happily agreed, sold their fleet to the Elves of Loresso and promptly moved into the western regions of Agleri and the eastern regions of Rimwold.

Segardi had surmised that the presence of more Barada who were loyal to Elven rule would dampen the Dwarves' fervor for dissension, but, in this estimation, he proved to be only partially correct. The Dwarves knew that the Menfolk would side with the Elves in any conflict which arose, but they, like most other Barada, had no great love for Menfolk and were thus greatly aggravated by Segardi's actions.

Nonetheless, the population of Menfolk grew and prospered, spreading throughout Agleri and Rimwold and even into Parlaedia, living alongside the Gnomes of the plains and the Elves and Dwarves of the forests and mountains. Oftentimes, as the Menfolk moved into a particular area, the other Barada would move farther away, even outright abandoning their villages and towns on occasion. Consequently, there came to be rather clear geographic divisions between the Narthanna, the distinct varieties of Barada. However, the Menfolk who lived among the Gnomes learned the tongue of the Gnomes, which was called Argammon, and the Menfolk who lived among the Dwarves learned their language, which was called Sarnadog. And in this manner, many of the old Argammon and Sarnadog place-names were preserved. Yet all the Barada of Velaris spoke Meldanari, the language of the Plains-Elves of Loresso and Marlassi, as its usage was strongly encouraged by the Velarisian government for the sake of political unity.

As the 4th Century of the Latter Epoch drew to a close, Segardi, who had never let go of his vision of ruling an independent Elven kingdom, decided to cut ties with Jarnos. His opportunity for revolt came when Neranno died of a mysterious disease and was replaced by a young Elf named Talnaro. Neranno had no heir, and Talnaro was his most successful general; thus, he was the natural choice for the successor to the throne. Segardi began to spread malicious propaganda throughout Velaris about Talnaro, most of which was untrue. Nonetheless, so effective was Segardi's smearing of the young ruler that many of the Barada of Velaris despised him without entirely knowing why.

In Alareth of LE 378, Segardi secretly sent a document to Talnaro wherein he had forged the signatures of various governors of the Velarisian barolli. This document asserted

Velaris' full right to independence and stated that Jarnos would be receiving no further monies or resources as tribute from Velaris. Talnaro was flabbergasted when he read Segardi's declaration, for he was already in the midst of two wars: one with the Dwarven kingdom of Arlegon to the southwest and another with the Gnomish kingdom of Ossimar to the north. He was fully aware that he could not fight three wars at once, so he said nothing of Segardi's message to his counselors. Instead, he decided to pretend that he had never received it, and he sent tax collectors, as was customary in the month of Alareth, to receive tribute from Velaris.

When the tax collectors arrived late in Alareth, Segardi guessed that Talnaro had ignored his declaration, for his messenger informed him that it had indeed been delivered, so he decided to press the issue by imprisoning the tax collectors. Some days later, Talnaro learned of this seizure of his officials, and he knew that he had no choice but to send soldiers to deal with the situation in Velaris.

As soon as Talnaro's soldiers, which numbered several thousand, arrived in Aragest on the 15th of Landrenna, LE 378, Segardi prompted the people of Velaris to view Talnaro's actions as ratifying all the unpleasant things they had heard about him. Consequently, the soldiers stood no chance against the frenzied Barada of Velaris. In fact, all the officials, representatives and soldiers from Jarnos either fled from Velaris or were captured or killed by the 29th of Landrenna, LE 378, which is celebrated as the independence day of Velaris. For on that day, when the last ship from Jarnos sailed north out of the port of Rahalbo in the barolla of Falzari, Segardi read an official proclamation of independence and proclaimed himself the Ruphani of Velaris. This term, Ruphani, means 'protector' in Meldanari; Segardi used the term to refer to his swift reaction against the forces of Jarnos to preserve the people of Velaris.

Meanwhile, Talnaro had been captured by the Dwarves of Arlegon and had been sent to a prison in the Grellian Mountains in the northwest corner of that kingdom. He was left without a clear successor, for he was quite young and had not yet married. Consequently, Jarnos was thrown into a state of turmoil and was nearly overrun. However, although the kingdom was ultimately preserved by the actions of several bold commanders, the leaders of Jarnos simply considered Velaris a lost cause, as they had much more pressing matters to worry about. And thus Velaris received independence with a very small struggle indeed.

After Segardi had established himself as the Ruphani of Velaris, he set about fortifying all the borders of his land and founded an organization known as the Sardolia to maintain peace and order in the kingdom. Once these tasks had been accomplished, he began to focus on expanding the ports of Aragest, Belestro and Tarwyn. Before he died in LE 420 from choking on a fish bone, Segardi completed the construction of a huge palace complex in Aragest known as the Arbor of the Sancalli. To this day, the Arbor of the Sancalli functions as the palace of the Ruphani.

The intervening centuries between the founding of Velaris and the time of Aradis and Girion are not detailed here, except regarding the matters which involve the supplanting of Argammon, Sarnadog and Meldanari by Daiga and the advent of the Druids to Velaris' western regions.

By the beginning of the 6th Century LE, Velaris had long been established as an Elven kingdom, with numerous cultural ties to the Northern Moiety of Orona. As more and more colonists of all varieties poured into Aradath from Huldion, Velaris began encouraging its citizens to learn Daiga in order to more effectively trade with other Barada, especially those farther north along the coast of Quarana. Thus, in the final decades of the 6th Century LE, nearly all Velarisians used Daiga as their daily language, and by the opening of the 7th Century LE, Argammon, Sarnadog and Meldanari came only to be preserved, for the most part, in the names of places and people.

In the year LE 604, a substantial population of Druids began immigrating to Velaris. They had come from the northwestern regions of Quarana, specifically the Kingdom of Algazar and the island of Yamarna. These Druids settled primarily in Parlaedia and Rimwold, though some dwelt in the great cities of Cape Loresso. Within the span of a few years, great strife arose between the Druids and the Menfolk. At that time, the Dwarves of Velaris were confined almost exclusively to Rimwold, Parlaedia and large ports such as Aragest and Tarwyn. Gnomes could only be found in the deep south and far north of Agleri and in the larger ports. Elves were, by and large, residing in large numbers only in the Marlassi Coast and Cape Loresso. The Druids had no particular disdain for the Gnomes, Dwarves or Elves, and, for the most part, they lived far away from them anyhow. But they greatly detested the Menfolk, as do nearly all Druids, having never forgotten the great wars in the Years of Yore between the two Kindreds. As a result of this deep-seated hatred, the Druids committed many acts of violence and injustice against the Menfolk of western Velaris.

Later in the 7th Century LE, this ongoing turmoil led to the formation of an organization known as the Blades of Erdion, a vigilante group of Menfolk outcasts who would attack and burn Druid homesteads and villages and sometimes slaughter communities wholesale. Though this group remained elusive for some time, the Ruphani of those days, Malvardo by name, who is still reigning in Velaris in the present day (LE 717), finally found and killed the members of the Blades of Erdion at the Druidic village of Trommendall in the barolla of Osgaria. But the full tale of that encounter shall be told elsewhere.

Velaris, as it stands at the opening of the 8th Century of the Latter Epoch, is a wealthy Elven kingdom ruled by the Ruphani Malvardo. It is a land of high mountains, deep forests, vast plains and magnificent coastlines. Its citizens are a mixture of Elves, Dwarves, Gnomes, Menfolk and Druids. The land is divided into five regions: Cape Loresso, the Marlassi Coast, Agleri, Rimwold and Parlaedia. Each of these is governed by a Regent. The smaller political subdivisions of the nation are its 27 barolli. There are murmurs of unrest among the Menfolk, upon whom oppression by the government and other Narthanna has fallen rather hard.

In short, Velaris is a kingdom like many others, with a bold and fiery past and a future which remains unknown. It is a land where beauty and tragedy mingle freely, a land where heroism and cowardice both abound. Velaris is a kingdom of tears and triumph, and it is a land which many call their home, regardless of what ills it may hold.

What follows is a very brief timeline of important events in Velarisian history:

LE 118, 18th of Bellin—Landing of the Nine Ships at the Jenolli Dunes

LE 229—The Second Elven Wave

    LE 239—The Wrath of Randabar

    LE 239-LE 251—The Branding of Agleri

    LE 256-LE 259—The Hammering of Bornad

    LE 268—The Coming of the Mannish Fleet

    LE 378, 29th of Landrenna—The Freedom of Velaris

    LE 420—The Death of Segardi

    LE 604—Arrival of the Druids

The Velarisian Monetary System

The Historical Development of the Velarisian Monetary System

The present monetary system of Velaris, with its units of tarions, gerrins, grandigs, byrnas, skrannas, taldryns and orgellas, was introduced during the rule of Segardi, the first Ruphani. The original monetary system of the Gnomes of Mannagron used only gerrins, grandigs and tarions. When Mannagron was conquered by the Dwarves of Bornad under Agrinov in LE 251 (see Appendix 3 for details of this situation), this system was combined with the silver-based economy of the Dwarves of Rimwold and Parlaedia, which employed byrnas, skrannas and taldryns. This new system remained in place until after Velaris achieved full independence from Jarnos in LE 378. In the next few years, Segardi accrued sizable quantities of gold in trade with the Dwarven kingdom of Talleron, at which point he issued a proclamation authorizing the minting of gold orgellas in LE 385.

A Description of Velarisian Monetary Units

Tarion—The smallest monetary unit of the Kingdom of Velaris. It is a small bronze coin stamped with the image of a sheaf of grain, which represents the resources of the Agleri region of Velaris.

Gerrin—The second smallest monetary unit of the Kingdom of Velaris, generally considered the basic unit of the system. It is a small copper coin stamped with the image of a scythe, which represents the people of the Agleri region of Velaris. For reference, a mug of ale, along with two refills, costs one gerrin in most Velarisian taverns, although prices are slightly higher in the coastal barolli.

Grandig—The third smallest monetary unit of the Kingdom of Velaris. It is a large copper coin stamped with the image of a mountain and a pickaxe, which represents both the people and the resources of the Parlaedia region of Velaris.

Byrna—The fourth largest monetary unit of the Kingdom of Velaris. It is a small silver coin stamped with the image of a pine tree, which represents the resources of the Rimwold region of Velaris.

Skranna—The third largest monetary unit of the Kingdom of Velaris. It is a medium-sized silver coin stamped with the image of an axe, which represents the people of the Rimwold region of Velaris.

Taldryn—The second largest monetary unit of the Kingdom of Velaris. It is a large silver coin stamped with the image of a trading ship, which represents the resources of the Brines of Ferassi and the people of the Marlassi Coast region of Velaris.

Orgella—The largest monetary unit of the Kingdom of Velaris. It is a medium-sized gold coin stamped with the image of the Ruphani's face, which represents both the people and the resources of the Cape Loresso region of Velaris.

A Velarisian Monetary Conversion Table

4 Tarions = 1 Gerrin

4 Gerrins = 1 Grandig

2 Grandigs = 1 Byrna

8 Byrnas = 1 Skranna

8 Skrannas = 1 Taldryn

8 Taldryns = 1 Orgella

APPENDIX 5

Pronunciation Guide and Index

This final appendix is included for those readers who would like to delve deeper into the lore of Orona, especially its linguistic landscape. Accordingly, it contains an alphabetical listing of all the Oronic entities, along with their proper pronunciations, which appear in the text of this book in the main story and in the appendices. Each entry includes a page number reference, set within square brackets, which marks either the location of the term's first appearance in the text or the instance in which it is most clearly explained.

Due to its conciseness and suitability for accurately representing various phonemes, the IPA (International Phonetic Alphabet) system of phonetic transcription has been chosen to represent the pronunciation of persons, places, things and events used throughout this volume. Several tables of correspondence between IPA symbols and phonemes in the English language precede the listing of Oronic entities mentioned in this book. There is also a small list identifying grammatical abbreviations that are used in this appendix. Please note that items are generally listed with the singular form as the primary entry unless the plural form is more prevalent in the text, with the exception of the various Narthanna and a few miscellaneous items, which are all listed in the plural. If the plural is irregular, it will often have its own entry, as in the case of the Menreldan word 'ehasurdana.'

NB: Words which are of English origin are not generally provided with IPA representation, as their pronunciation can be readily deduced without it.

NB: A few terms which may seem to be rather mundane are included in this index because they are used in this book in a technical Oronic sense.

Consonants

b – <u>b</u>ook, mo<u>b</u>

c – hear<u>ts</u>, va<u>ts</u>

d – <u>d</u>og, ma<u>d</u>

f – <u>f</u>ire, lau<u>gh</u>

g – <u>g</u>old, fla<u>g</u>

h – <u>h</u>ill, <u>h</u>and

j – <u>y</u>ard, <u>y</u>ore

k – <u>c</u>astle, la<u>ke</u>

l – <u>l</u>oss, ca<u>ll</u>

m – <u>m</u>ark, ra<u>m</u>

n – <u>n</u>ail, bar<u>n</u>

p – <u>p</u>ond, ta<u>p</u>

r – <u>r</u>ow, ba<u>r</u>

s – <u>s</u>oft, pa<u>ss</u>

t – <u>t</u>ale, ra<u>t</u>

v – <u>v</u>ale, ha<u>ve</u>

w – <u>w</u>orld, al<u>w</u>ays

x – as in Scottish lo<u>ch</u> or German Ba<u>ch</u>

z – ma<u>ze</u>, tray<u>s</u>,

θ – <u>th</u>row, ba<u>th</u>

ð – al<u>th</u>ough, fa<u>th</u>er

ţ – be<u>tt</u>er, li<u>tt</u>le

ʃ – <u>sh</u>ore, a<u>sh</u>

ŋ – ri<u>ng</u>, a<u>n</u>ger

t͡ʃ – <u>ch</u>imney, la<u>tch</u>

d͡ʒ – <u>j</u>ar, a<u>ge</u>

ʒ – trea<u>s</u>ure, barra<u>ge</u>

ʔ – glottal stop as in uh(ʔ)oh

Vowels

ɑ: – f<u>a</u>ther, c<u>o</u>t

ɛ – l<u>e</u>t, h<u>ea</u>d

i: – f<u>ee</u>d, l<u>ea</u>f

oʊ – sh<u>ow</u>, m<u>o</u>le

u: – r<u>u</u>de, t<u>oo</u>

æ – s<u>a</u>t, sh<u>a</u>ck

ə – <u>a</u>gree, s<u>u</u>ppose

ɪ – l<u>i</u>d, p<u>i</u>n

ɔ: – f<u>a</u>ll, l<u>aw</u>

ʊ – sh<u>ou</u>ld, g<u>oo</u>d

ʌ – d<u>u</u>ck, s<u>u</u>n

aɪ – h<u>i</u>ve, p<u>i</u>le

eɪ – p<u>ay</u>, r<u>a</u>ce

aʊ – n<u>ow</u>, l<u>ou</u>d

ɔɪ – t<u>oy</u>, c<u>oi</u>n

ᵊ – mutt<u>on</u>, sudd<u>en</u>

Vowels Followed by 'R' Sounds

ɑr – f<u>ar</u>, c<u>ar</u>pet

ɛər – b<u>ear</u>, wh<u>ere</u>

ɪər – f<u>ear</u>, ch<u>eer</u>

ɔər – b<u>ore</u>, <u>oar</u>

ɝ – b<u>ur</u>n, w<u>or</u>k

' – This symbol precedes the syllable which is most strongly stressed. (e.g., delectable: dɪˈlɛktəbəl)

Abbreviations

Sing. – singular
Pl. – plural
Adj. – adjective
Masc. – masculine
Fem. – feminine
Disamb. – disambiguation

Acrynon [88] – 'ækrɪnɑːn

Adrasanel [182] – ə'drɑːsənɛl

Agleri [212] – ə'glɛəriː

Agleri, Plains of [3] – ə'glɛəriː

Agrinov [224] – 'ægrɪnɑːv

Akwursa [126] – ə'kwɝsə

Alareth [221] – 'ælərɛθ

Algazar [229] – 'ɔːlgəzar

Algo River [225] – 'ɔːlgoʊ

Allaroc [133] – 'ælərɑːk

Almgorad [91] – 'ɔːlmgəræd

Andurad Torfield [62] – 'ændɝɑːd 'tɔərfiːld

Anella Ringmark [37] – ə'nɛlə

Anganor [25] – 'æŋgənɔər

Apex of Archaea, The [220] – ar'keɪə

Aradath [212] – 'ɛərədɑːθ

Aradis Kingblade [3] – 'ɛərədɪs

Aragest [212] – 'ɛərəgɛst

Arbor of the Sancalli, The [228] – sæn'kɔːliː

Archaea [220] – ar'keɪə

Archdruid [198]

Argammon [227] – ar'gæmən

Argonis [212] – ar'gɑːnɪs

Arkanian Mountains [203] – ar'keɪniːən

Arlegon [228] – 'arlɛgɑːn

Armallin [225] – ar'mɔːlɪn

Asla'gu [196] – ɑːs'lɑːʔguː

Autumn Dreamscape [179]

Azaru, Mount [23] – ə'zɑruː

Baggs [109] – 'bægz

Baku Sondag [181] – 'bɑːkuː 'soʊndɔːg

Balgorra Hills [206] – bɔːl'gɔərə

Ballinod [62] – 'bælɪnɑːd

Bannagrik [181] – 'bænəgrɪk

Barada (pl. Barada; adj. Baradic) [212] – bə'rɑːdə (bə'rɑːdɪk)

Barnatha, Tower of [151] – bar'næθə

Barolla (pl. Barolli) [212] – bə'roʊlə (bə'roʊliː)

Baudig Wood [90] – 'baʊdɪg

Belestro [212] – bɛ'lɛstroʊ

Bellin [221] – 'bɛlɪn

Belwin Reinstay [73] – 'bɛlwɪn

Bernalla Elmensill [60] – bɝ'nɔːlə 'ɛlmᵊnsɪl

Biyelti [111] – bɪ'jɛltiː

Blackbough Woods [26]

Blackwings (sing. Blackwing; adj. Blackwing) [138]

Blades of Erdion, The [229] – 'ɛərdiːɑːn

Bloody Gloaming of Galrim, The [201] – 'gɔːlrɪm

Blue Moon, The [112]

Bornad [224] – 'bɔərnæd

Branding of Agleri, The [225] – ə'glɛəriː

Brandorgill [61] – 'brændɝgɪl

Briar Bluff [139]

Briar Gate, The [205]

Bridging of the Tides, The [220]

Brightbeam [32]

Bright Marda [60] – ˈmɑrdə

Brines of Ferassi [42] – fɛˈrɑːsiː

Brinkmarch [137]

Briny Baywatch, The [122]

Brundy [212] – ˈbrʌndiː

Burg of Ilderath [199] – ˈɪldɚæθ

Bushbelt, The [212]

Byram [213] – ˈbaɪrəm

Byrna [231] – ˈbɝnə

Caldric Torfield [70] – ˈkɔːldrɪk ˈtɔərfiːld

Call of Marda [223] – ˈmɑrdə

Call of the Danna, The [26] – ˈdænə

Calmen [76] – ˈkɔːlmɛn

Cape Harnog [91] – ˈhɑrnɔːg

Cape Loresso (disamb. geographical feature) [215] – lɔərˈɛsoʊ

Cape Loresso (disamb. region) [215] – lɔərˈɛsoʊ

Carello [44] – kəˈrɛloʊ

Carrican Kedgewick [98] – ˈkɛərəkᵊn

Chasm of Erynos, The [203] – ˈɛərɪnɑːs

Colazzo, Boatswain [86] – koʊˈlɑːcoʊ

Cordis [222] – ˈkɔərdɪs

Corim Timberfall [14] – ˈkɔərɪm

Corlanno [224] – cɔərˈlɑːnoʊ

Crown of Marda [223] – ˈmɑrdə

Cullet [72] – ˈkʊlᵊt

Cullet Stew [72] – ˈkʊlᵊt

Curronath [134] – ˈkɝənæθ

Daegar [197] – ˈdeɪgɑr

Daiga (adj. Daigan) [146] – ˈdaɪgə

Dallyn [41] – ˈdælɪn

Dana Felnathi [185] – ˈdɑːnə fɛlˈnɑːθiː

Dance of Marda [223] – ˈmɑrdə

Dankdocks [25]

Danna, The [37] – ˈdænə

Dargos [90] – ˈdɑrgɑːs

Darion Kingblade [10] – ˈdɛəriːᵊn

Darmon Barnwain [15] – ˈdarmᵊn

Dasari [45] – dəˈsɑriː

Daseldo [181] – dɑːˈsɛldoʊ

Dawn of Eoreth [223] – ˈeɪərɛθ

Death's Blade [1]

Deathwash, The [197]

Deep Lore [213]

Derrig [221] – ˈdɛərɪg

Dhar-Marda [216] – ðar ˈmɑrdə

Diamond Flames, The [188]

Doors of the Hours, The [24]

Dorman's Down [40] – ˈdɔərmᵊnz

Drannic [134] – ˈdrænɪk

Drannom [72] – ˈdrænəm

Draughtfish Inn, The [25]

Druids (fem. Druidess; adj. Druidic) [213]

Dugamar Ringmark [37] – ˈduːgəmɑr

Dugan Hardrake [107] – ˈduːgən ˈhardreɪk

Dullen [116] – ˈdʊlᵊn

Dumark [76] – ˈduːmɑrk

Dunlim [116] – ˈdʌnlɪm

Dwarves [213]

Earth Moulds, The [187]

Ebonreach [86] – ˈɛbᵊnriːtʃ

Ehasurdana (sing. Hasurdana) [187] – eɪhɑːsɝˈdɑːnə (hɑːsɝˈdɑːnə)

Ehurasna Galdranera [185] – eɪhʊˈrɑːsnə gɔːldrəˈnɛərə

Eladar [22] – ˈɛlədɑr

Elwina [187] – ɛlˈwiːnə

Elaya [221] – ɛˈlɑːjə

Elder Forest, The [213]

Eldritch Isles, The [213]

Elukatai [139] – ɛˈluːkətaɪ

Elves [213]

Elyrion, The (adj. Elyriac) [22] – ɛˈlɪəriːɑːn (ɛˈlɪəriːæk)

Emerald Run, The [206]

Empire of Manus-Romella (adj. Manus-Romelliad) [219] – ˈmɑːnuːs roʊˈmɛlə (ˈmɑːnuːs roʊˈmɛliːæd)

Enrion [188] – ˈɛnriːɑːn

Eoreth [213] – ˈeɪərɛθ

Eoreth's Lament [223] – ˈeɪərɛθs

Eoreth's Tale [223] – ˈeɪərɛθs

Equenaddoril (sing. Quenad-doril) [213] – eɪkwɛnˈɑːdɔəriːl (kwɛnˈɑːdɔəriːl)

Erdion [213] – ˈɛərdiːɑːn

Eribeth Kingblade [27] – ˈɛərɪbɛθ

Erynos Divide, The [202] – ˈɛərɪnɑːs

Estereth [74] – ˈɛstərɛθ

Everhold [23]

Faenard [7] – ˈfeɪnɝd

Faldora [62] – fɔːlˈdɔərə

Fallbury [186] – ˈfɔːlbɝiː

Fall-Elves [179]

Fall of Yaruzadar [220] – jəˈruːzədar

Falzari [213] – fɔːlˈzɑriː

Fandarralon [225] – fænˈdarəlɑːnFar Forest, The [214]

Farga (sing. Farga; adj. Fargese) [214] – ˈfɑrgə (farˈgiːz)

Fargost [214] – ˈfɑrgɑːst

Farren, The [137] – ˈfarᵊn

Farthest Shore, The [128]

Fasdaranel Vine [178] – fɑːsˈdarənɛl

Fayna Torfield [70] – ˈfeɪnə ˈtɔərfiːld

Fedric [105] – ˈfɛdrɪk

Felding Starwash [25] – ˈfɛldɪŋ

Feldryn [214] – ˈfɛldrɪn

Felduras [73] – fɛlˈdʊrəs

Fell Alliance, The [26]

Felnath [89] – ˈfɛlnæθ

Fenrost [214] – ˈfɛnrɑːst

Ferassi, Brines of [42] – fɛˈrɑːsiː

Ferenod [61] – ˈfɛərɛnɑːd

Ferenos [221] – ˈfɛərɛnɑːs

Field-Gnomes [74]

Fire-Realm, The [25]

Five Fabled Lands, The [214]

Fontskals Fog, The [96] – ˈfɑːntskɔːlz

Fontskals, The [214] – ˈfɑːntskɔːlz

Fordrak, Captain [147] – ˈfɔərdræk

Forellos (adj. Forellosian) [119] – fɔəˈrɛloʊs (fɔərɛˈloʊsiːən)

Forgotten Days, The [219]

Forwall [76] – ˈfɔərwɔːl

Fragezi, Captain [15] – frəˈgɛziː

Gaddock [73] – ˈgædᵊk

Galbarra [134] – gɔːlˈbarə

Malca [89] – 'mɔːlkə

Maldinian Isles [218] – mɔːldɪniːən

Maldis [222] – 'mɔːldɪs

Mallengar [110] – 'mælɛngɑr

Malvardo [229] – mɔːl'vardoʊ

Mancari [226] – mæn'kɑriː

Manfellow (pl. Manfellows) [215] –
see 'Menfolk'

Mannagron [224] – 'mænəgrɑːn

Mannish [216] – see 'Menfolk'

Manusian Empire, The [219] –
mə'nuːʒən

Manus-Romella, The Empire of (adj.
Manus-Romelliad) [219] – 'maːnuːs
roʊ'mɛlə ('maːnuːs roʊ'mɛliːæd)

Manus-Romelliad Calendar [219] –
'maːnuːs roʊ'mɛliːæd

Marda [216] – 'mardə

Marda's Farewell [223] – 'mardəz

Marda's Feast [223] – 'mardəz

Marda's Glory [223] – 'mardəz

Marda's Passing [223] – 'mardəz

Mardelac Forest [138] – 'mardᵊlæk

Marlassi Coast, The [216] – mar'læsiː

Marlond [216] – 'marlaːnd

Marnis Applecot [60] –
'marnɪs 'æpᵊlkaːt

Maschi [91] – 'mæʃiː

Massarat [117] – 'mæsəraːt

Master Warden of the Bounds [179]

Material, The [23]

Meldanari [227] – mɛldə'nariː

Mellora Kingblade [12] – mɛ'lɔərə

Melrinnon Point [89] – 'mɛlrɪnᵊn

Men [43]

Mendalas [179] – mɛn'dɔːləs

Menfolk (masc. sing. Manfellow; masc.
pl. Manfellows; fem. sing. Maena;

fem. pl. Maenas; adj. Mannish) [216] –
('meɪnə; 'meɪnəz)

Menrelda (adj. Menreldan) [185] –
mɛn'reɪldə (mɛn'reɪldən)

Mentalara [179] – mɛntə'larə

Mercy of Adrasanel, The [181] –
ə'draːsənɛl

Meridot [83] – 'mɛərɪdaːt

Meridot, The [83] – 'mɛərɪdaːt

Messengers, The [20]

Middings, The [221] – 'mɪdɪŋs

Midsummer Meadow [19]

Mineral Mortals, The [188]

Minndalot [91] – 'mɪndəlaːt

Mists of Old, The [219]

Moieties of Orona, The [216] – 'mɔɪətiːz

Moonhound [137]

Moonhound Moor [137]

Morastic [91] – mɔər'æstɪk

Morga [84] – 'mɔərgə

Mornasok [200] – 'mɔərnəsaːk

Mosgar [154] – 'maːsgar

Murdock [101] – 'mɝdaːk

Murnia [74] – 'mɝniːə

Nagello [20] – nə'gɛloʊ

Nardis [222] – 'nardɪs

Narthanna (sing. Narthaya) [216] –
nar'θaːnə (nar'θaːjə)

Narthaya (pl. Narthanna) [216] –
nar'θaːjə (nar'θaːnə)

Neathmarda (pl. Neathmarda) [216] – 'niːθmɑrdə

Neldon Broadbuckle [15] – 'nɛldᵊnNeranno [226] – nɛəˈrɑːnoʊ

Nodaway Island [131]

Nolgar [216] – 'noʊlgɑr

Northern Moiety of Orona, The [216] – 'mɔɪətiː əv ɔəˈroʊnə

Nulavak, Tides of [90] – 'nuːləvæk

Nutmeal [216]

Ogres (adj. Ogric) [216] – ('oʊgrɪk)

Orgella [232] – ɔərˈgɛlə

Orinn Berthaway [14] – 'ɔərɪn

Orona (adj. Oronic) [216] – ɔəˈroʊnə (ɔəˈroʊnɪk)

Orrig [76] – 'ɔərɪg

Orzoni [83] – ɔərˈzoʊniː

Osgaria [229] – ɑːsˈgɑriːə

Osora [24] – oʊˈsɔərə

Ossimar [225] – 'ɑːsɪmar

Outhedge, The [138]

Palace of Eoreth [223] – 'eɪərɛθ

Palrimmon [62] – pɔːlˈrɪmᵊn

Parlaedia [216] – pɑrˈleɪdiːə

Parlaedian Mountains [216] – pɑrˈleɪdiːən

Parnassa [216] – pɑrˈnæsə

Passera [216] – pəˈsɛərə

Passing of Marda, The [76] – 'mɑrdə

Pelarond [221] – 'pɛlərɑːnd

Perinac River [138] – 'pɛərɪnæk

Pharnaela [88] – fɑrˈneɪlə

Pine-Elves [213]

Plains-Elves [42]

Plains of Agleri [3] – əˈglɛəriː

Plotcraft [122]

Ploughman's Shanty, The [3]

Pollona (adj. Pollonan) [217] – pəˈloʊnə (pəˈloʊnən)

Pordis Steedback [48] – 'pɔərdɪs

Potters' Wharf [133]

Praschen [95] – 'præʃɛn

Prasseldoff [110] – 'præsᵊldɑːf

Pungalak [110] – 'puːŋgəlɑːk

Quarana [217] – kwɑrˈɑːnə

Quenaddoril (pl. Equenaddoril) [179] – kwɛnˈɑːdɔəriːl (eɪkwɛnˈɑːdɔəriːl)

Ragdis [222] – 'rægdɪs

Raglaniff [62] – 'ræglᵊnɪf

Rahalbo [228] – rɑːˈhɔːlboʊ

Rannadalf [92] – 'rænədɔːlf

Randabar [224] – 'rændəbar

Rastobeth [23] – 'rɑːstoʊbɛθ

Raven's Crest, The [91]

Ravensrealm [86]

Ravinia the Heartless [26] – rəˈvɪniːə

Rayalta [217] – raɪˈjɔːltə

Rayela [8] – rɑːˈjɛlə

Realm of the Sea-Lords [24]

Rebel's Wake [198]

Reddo [109] – 'rɛdoʊ

Redhouse, The [65]

Redic Twineweft [65] – 'rɛdɪk

Regent [217]

Reigen [90] – 'raɪgᵊn

Rendanna (sing. Rendaya) [217] – rɛnˈdɑːnə (rɛnˈdɑːjə)

Rendaya (pl. Rendanna) [217] – rɛnˈdɑːjə (rɛnˈdɑːnə)

Rhassendag Downs, The [137] – ˈrɑːsɛndɔːg

Rhetharna (pl. Rhetharnas) [88] – rɛˈθɑrnə (rɛˈθɑrnəz)

Rhingast [91] – ˈrɪngæst

Rimura [24] – rɪˈmɝə

Rimwold [217] – ˈrɪmwoʊld

Rimwold Forest [3] – ˈrɪmwoʊld

Ring of the Artisans, The [187]

Rinnegan Group, The [116] – ˈrɪnəgᵊn

Rinnegan's Rovers [116] – ˈrɪnəgᵊnz

Risella Starwash [109] – rɪˈzɛlə

Rixenmall (pl. Rixenmaller) [153] – ˈrɪksɛnmɔːl (ˈrɪksɛnmɔːlɝ)

Rokklag [217] – ˈroʊklɔːg

Romelliad Empire, The [219] – roʊˈmɛliːæd

Ronnigan [101] – ˈrɑːnɪgᵊn

Ruphani, The [217] – ruːˈfɑːniː

Sabakwani's Girdle [217] – ˈsɑːbəkwɑːniːz

Sadric [68] – ˈsædrɪk

Salalu [139] – səˈlɔːluː

Salarna [220] – səˈlɑrnə

Saldassi [224] – sɔːlˈdɑːsiː

Sandesso [43] – sænˈdɛsoʊ

Sancalla (pl. Sancalli) [217] – sænˈkɔːlə (sænˈkɔːliː)

Sardolia, The [217] – sɑrˈdoʊliːə

Sarganath [217] – ˈsɑrgənæθ

Sarmallen Hill [138] – sɑrˈmɔːlɛn

Sarnadog [227] – ˈsɑrnədɔːg

Scarappa, Straits of [89] – skʌˈræpə

Scepter of Eoreth [223] – ˈeɪərɛθ

Scion of Sharga [127] – ˈʃɑrgə

Sea of the Heavens, The [24]

Sea-Realm, The [89]

Segardi [225] – sɛˈgɑrdiː

Sendarrim [181] – sɛnˈdɑrɪm

Serona [221] – sɛəˈroʊnə

Shardclaw Caverns [199]

Sharga [127] – ˈʃɑrgə

Shakunasa [139] – ʃɑːkuːˈnɑːsə

Shillelagh McDasher [206] – ʃɪˈleɪliː mᵊkˈdæʃɝ

Shore-Elves [111]

Siloa [3] – saɪˈloʊə

Siradel [217] – ˈsɪərədɛl

Skaggarok Skerries, The [217] – ˈskægərɑːk ˈskɛəriːz

Skranna [231] – ˈskrɑːnə

Skurridan Rock [225] – ˈskɝɪdᵊn

Sky-Realm, The [113]

Smag's Cove [96] – ˈsmægz

Smollerus [97] – ˈsmɔːlɝəs

Solansu [89] – soʊˈlɑːnsuː

Song of Marda, The [223] – ˈmɑrdə

Sorcerer [117]

Southern Moiety of Orona, The [217] – ˈmɔɪətiː əv ɔəˈroʊnə

Southern Treasure [226]

South Star, The [143]

Soyawat [139] – ˈsoʊjəwɑːt

Soyawat Piyani [92] – ˈsoʊjəwɑːt piːˈjɑːniː

Splinter Men, The [187]

Staffborn, The [26]

Stammi [187] – ˈstæmiː

Star-Realm, The [217]

Starwash Special [130]

Stone Charmers, The [187]

Stragmore [116] – ˈstrægmɔər

Stragmore Stout [98] – ˈstrægmɔər

Straits of Scarappa [89] – skʌˈræpə

Strongbranch Citadel [202]

Stony Wilds, The [200]

Sturbick [76] – ˈstɚbɪk

Sundering of the Erynos, The [202] – ˈɛrɪnɑːs

Surgana Amdara [177] – sɚˈgɑːnə æmˈdɑrə

Surrounded Land, The [181]

Tabbis [76] – ˈtæbɪs

Taldryn [231] – ˈtɔːldrɪn

Talgryn [226] – ˈtɔːlgrɪn

Tallis Pestleman [15] – ˈtælɪs

Tallequana Hall [202] – ˈtɔːlɛkwɑːnə

Talleron [89] – ˈtælərɑːn

Talnaro [227] – tɔːlˈnɑrou

Tandarron [179] – tænˈdarən

Tannaril [221] – ˈtænərɪl

Tarandelas Adrasanel [181] – tarɑːnˈdeɪləs əˈdrɑːsənɛl

Tarion [231] – ˈtɛəriːən

Tarnadin [1] – ˈtarnədɪn

Tarnolli [224] – tarˈnouliː

Tarwyn [25] – ˈtarwɪn

Tassagon [218] – ˈtæsəgɑːn

Tassagon Plant [218] – ˈtæsəgɑːn

Tassaru [74] – təˈsɑruː

Tas [75] – ˈtæs

Tazbek [90] – ˈtæzbɛk

Tellig [218] – ˈtɛlɪg

Telnara (pl. Telnari; adj. Telnaric) [218] – tɛlˈnɑrə (tɛlˈnariː; tɛlˈnarɪk)

Telucca [139] – tɛˈlʌkə

Telyon [23] – ˈtɛljɑːn

Temerrin [212] – tɛˈmɛərɪn

Teric Kingblade [7] – ˈtɛərɪk

Tharlog [218] – ˈθarlɔːg

Thayah [70] – ˈθɑːjə

Thornberries [193]

Thornberry Tart [193]

Thornberry Thicket [139]

Thorn-Gnomes [180]

Thornoak, King [25]

Thunder Dukes, The [187]

Tides of Nulavak [90] – ˈnuːləvæk

Timeless Vaults, The [24]

Toldrennon Wood [137] – ˈtouldrɛnᵊn

Tolga [218] – ˈtoulgə

Tollard [68] – ˈtɔːlɚd

Torbett, Captain [109] – ˈtɔərbᵊt

Tower of Barnatha, The [151] – barˈnæθə

Trath [116] – ˈtræθ

Treefellow [218] – see 'Treefolk'

Treefolk (masc. sing. Treefellow; fem. sing. Treemaena; adj. Treeish) [25] – (ˈtriːmeɪnə)

Trolls (adj. Trollish) [218]

Trommendall [229] – ˈtrɑːmɛndɔːl

True King, The [23]

Tukarat [110] – 'tuːkəraːt

Tuldrak [32] – 'tʊldraːk

Turni, Captain [95] – 'tɜ˞niː

Tylon [74] – 'taɪlaːn

Tynaegryn [24] – tɪ'neɪgrɪn

Tyracus [143] – 'tɪərəkəs

Ugrusa [182] – uː'gruːsə

Ularos [221] – 'uːləraːs

Ulmar [90] – 'ʊlmar

Underwharf [107]

Vallonin [180] – 'væloʊnɪn

Vardis [222] – 'vardɪs

Vasorna (adj. Vasornic) [222] – və'sɔərnə (və'sɔərnɪk)

Vastia the Pathfinder [218] – 'vaːstiːə

Velaris (adj. Velarisian) [218] – vɛ'larɪs (vɛlar'ɪʒən)

Vengoli [218] – 'vɛngoʊliː

Verdinnion, The [202] – vɜ˞'dɪniːən

Volando [187] – voʊ'laːndoʊ

Vyndar [113] – 'vɪndar

Walls of Ancient Wrath, The [138]

Warlock [182]

Waybread of Erdion, The [39] – 'ɛərdiːaːn

Way of the Tarnadin, The [1] – 'tarnədɪn

Wide Lands, The [92]

Wild Watchers, The [187]

Witch [196]

Witch's Grotto [199]

Woven Souls, The [187]

Wrath of Randabar, The [224] – 'rændəbar

Xengula [74] – ksɛn'guːlə

Yaldana [186] – jɔːl'daːnə

Yamarna [229] – jə'marnə

Yaruzadar [220] – jə'ruːzədar

Yawandis [222] – jə'waːndɪs

Years of the Middings [221] – 'mɪdɪŋs

Years of Yore, The [219]

Yerrig Clayspin [48] – 'jɛərɪg

Yetis (sing. Yeti; adj. Yeti) [218]

Yortallin [187] – jɔər'tɔːlɪn

Zaladro [49] – zə'laːdroʊ

Zalgaresh [227] – 'zɔːlgərɛʃ

Zimari [218] – zɪ'mariː

Jarrett Skaddisson

Jarrett Skaddisson is a native of the Midwestern US, an accomplished musician and composer and an avid linguist, philosopher, author, researcher, mountain climber, spelunker and tea enthusiast. He lived in the Orient for several years as a child and has traveled to more than 30 countries for mission work, performance tours and good, old-fashioned adventures. His favorite pastimes are reading, writing, making music, learning languages, eating exotic foods, doing improv comedy, impressions and engaging in a wide variety of shenanigans. He lives with his wife, Michelle, and their son, Fritz, who is an exceedingly happy, curious and energetic toddler. Jarrett can be contacted via email at *jarrettskaddisson@gmail.com* or through his Facebook page, http://facebook.com/TheKingblade Chronicles. He also has a website, *thekingbladechronicles.com*, which features concept art for the series, along with other material not found in the books. You can follow him on Twitter at *@AradisKingblade* and on Instagram at *@thekingbladechronicles*.

www.ingramcontent.com/pod-product-compliance
Lightning Source LLC
Chambersburg PA
CBHW021006120726
47905CB00009B/2886